"You!" she exclaimed involuntarily.

He put down the thin black cigar he was smoking and stood up. He didn't acknowledge the exclamation or smile or make any kind of attempt at a formal greeting. He looked just as intimidating as he had in the elevator, and just as cold.

"You didn't need to bring your secretary to take notes," he told Bob Malcolm. "If you want to plea bargain, I'll stick to what I tell you after I hear the facts. Sit down."

"It's the Cullen case."

"The juvenile." Kilpatrick nodded. "The boys he's running with are scum. The younger Harris boy walked in and out of juvenile hall, but he's of age now. If I catch him again, I'll send him up."

Becky had been sitting stock-still. "And the Cullen boy?" she asked in a husky whisper.

Kilpatrick gave her a cold glare. "I'm talking to Malcolm, not to you."

"You don't understand," she said heavily, "Clay Cullen is my brother."

DIANA PALMER

Night Fever

*M&B™ and M&B™ with the Rose Device
are trademarks of the publisher.*

*Harlequin Mills & Boon Limited, Eton House,
18-24 Paradise Road,
Richmond, Surrey TW9 1SR*

© Susan Kyle 1990

ISBN-13: 978 0 263 85548 7
ISBN-10: 0 263 85548 1

136-0107

*Printed and bound in Spain
by Litografía Rosés S.A., Barcelona*

Also by *Diana Palmer*

ONE NIGHT IN NEW YORK
BEFORE SUNRISE

Coming soon
THE OUTSIDER

International Bestselling author **Diana Palmer** got her start in writing as a newspaper reporter and columnist, where she acquired many of her writing skills during her 16-year tenure. Once she wrote her first novel in 1982, however, she never looked back. Diana has a gift for telling the most sensual tales with charm and humour. With over 40 million copies of her books in print, she is one of North America's most beloved authors and considered one of the top ten romance writers in America. Diana's hobbies include gardening, archaeology, anthropology, iguanas, astronomy and music. She has been married to James Kyle since 1972, and they have one son, Blayne Edward.

For Linda

1990. The elevator was crowded. Rebecca Cullen was trying to balance three cups in a box without spilling coffee all over the floor. Maybe if she learned to do this really well, she thought, she could join a circus and go on stage with her performance. The lids on the Styrofoam cups weren't secure—as usual. The man who worked the counter at the small drugstore downstairs didn't look twice at women like Rebecca, and who cared if coffee spilled all over a thin, nondescript woman in an out-of-style gray suit?

He probably figured her for Ms. Businesswoman, she thought—some rabid man-hater with a string of degrees after her name and a career in place of a husband and kids. Wouldn't he be shocked to see her at home on Granddad's farm, in cutoff jeans and a tank top in supper, which this wasn't, with her mass of gold-streaked light brown hair down to her waist, and barefoot? This suit was pure camouflage.

Becky was a country girl, and the sole support of her retired grandfather and her two younger brothers. Their mother had died when she was sixteen and their father only stopped in to visit when he was broke and needed money. He'd moved to Alabama a couple of years back and none of them had heard from him since. Becky didn't care if she never did again. She had a good job. In fact, the law firm's recent relocation to Curry Station worked to her favor because her office in the industrial complex right outside Atlanta was now only a short drive from Granddad's farm where they all lived. It was just like coming home, because her people had lived in Curry County for more than a hundred years.

She didn't have a complaint about her job, except that she wished her bosses would remember to buy a new coffee urn before much longer. This several-times-daily trip down to the drugstore snack counter was getting to be a grind. There were three other secretaries, a receptionist, and two paralegals in the office, but they had seniority. Becky got to do the mule work. She grimaced as she headed for the elevator, hoping she wouldn't run into her nemesis on the way up to the sixth floor.

Her hazel eyes scanned the area quickly. She relaxed as soon as she was able to conclude that the towering figure was not waiting around the elevators. It wasn't bad enough that he had a stare like black ice, or that he seemed to hate women in general and her in particular. But he also smoked those god-awful thin black cigars. In an elevator, they were pure hell. She wished somebody would tell him that there was a city ordinance against smoking in crowded public places. She meant to, but there always seemed to be a crowd around, and for all Becky's toughness of spirit, she was shy in crowds. But one day it would be just her and that man, and she'd tell him how she felt about his extremely smelly cigars.

Her mind drifted as she waited for the slow-moving elevator to descend. She had worse problems than the cigar man, she reminded herself. Granddad was still recovering from the heart attack two months ago that had brought his career as a farmer to an abrupt halt. Now Becky was feeling the increased burden keenly. Unless she could learn to run the tractor and grow crops, in addition to working as a legal secretary six days a week, Granddad's truck farm was destined to be a total loss. Her oldest brother, Clay, was a senior in high school, constantly in trouble these days, and no help at all around the house. Mack was in the fifth grade and failing math. He was a willing helper, but too small to do much. Becky herself was twenty-four, and she'd never had a social life at all. She'd just barely finished school when her mom had died and her father had taken off for parts unknown.

Becky allowed her thoughts to drift for a moment, wondering what her life could have been like. There might have been parties and nice clothes and men to take her on dates. She smiled at the thought of not having people depend on her.

"Excuse me," a woman with an attaché case muttered, almost upending the coffee all over Becky.

She came out of her daydream in time to pile aboard the elevator, already crowded from its trip to the garage in the basement. She managed to wedge in between a woman who reeked of perfume and two men who were arguing, loudly, the benefits of two rival computers. It was a blinding relief when they, and almost everyone else, including the abundantly fragrant lady, got off on the third and fourth floors.

"Oh, God, I hate computers," Becky sighed out loud as the elevator slowly began climbing to the sixth floor.

"So do I," came a gruff, disgruntled voice from behind her.

She almost upset the coffee as she turned to see who had spoken. She had thought she was alone in the elevator. How she could have missed the man was the real question. She was only slightly above average height, but he had to be at least six foot two. It wasn't just the height, though—it was the man's build. He was muscular, with a physique that would have done a professional athlete proud. He had lean, beautiful, dark hands and big feet, and when he didn't smell of cigar smoke, he wore the sexiest cologne Becky had ever smelled. But his masculine beauty ended at his face. She couldn't remember ever having seen such a rough-looking man.

His face was all sharp angles and fierceness. He had thick black eyebrows and deep-set, narrow black eyes with a peculiar piercing quality. His nose was straight and elegant. He had a cleft chin—not terribly cleft, but noticeable. His face was kind of long and lean, with high cheekbones, and he had the kind of dark complexion that was natural and didn't come from sitting in the sun. His mouth was wide and well-formed. She'd never seen it smile. He was in his midthirties, but there were some hard lines in that dark face, and he had a coldness of manner that chilled her. His very best quality was his voice. It was deep and clear and very resonant—the kind of voice that could caress or cut, depending on his mood—and it projected easily.

He was well-dressed, in an obviously expensive dark gray pin-striped suit, with a white cotton shirt and silk paisley tie beneath it. And she thought she had avoided him, for once. Maybe it was her karma.

"Oh. It's you again," she said with resignation. She pushed the jolted Styrofoam coffee cups back into place. "Do you by any chance own the elevator?" she asked. "I mean, every time I get on it, here you are, scowling and muttering. Don't you ever smile?"

"When I find something to smile about, you'll be the first to see it," he said, bending his dark head to light a pungent cigar. He had the thickest, blackest, straightest hair she'd ever seen. He looked rather Italian, except for his high cheekbones, and the shape of his face.

"I hate cigar smoke," she said, to break the silence.

"Then stop breathing until the doors open," he replied carelessly.

"You are the rudest man I've ever met!" she exclaimed, turning back, infuriated, to watch the floors light up on the elevator panel.

"You haven't met me," he pointed out.

"Oh, lucky, lucky me," she said.

There was a muffled sound from behind her. "Do you work in this building?"

"I don't really work for a living." She glanced at him over her shoulder with a venomous smile. "I'm the kept woman of one of the attorneys at Malcolm, Randers, Tyler, and Hague."

His dark eyes slid down her trim figure, in its extremely conventional suit, to her small-heeled shoes, then back up again to her face, which had not a trace of makeup on it today. She had nice hazel eyes that matched her tawny hair, high cheekbones, a full mouth, and a straight nose, but her face was rather quiet. He guessed that she could look more attractive when she made the effort.

"He must have failing vision," he said finally.

Becky's eyes sparkled and narrowed as she got a firm grip on the cup holder and her own temper. Oh, the joy of dousing him with steaming black coffee, even if she had asked for it. But that might have unfortunate consequences. She needed her job, and he might know her bosses.

"He is not blind," she made a half turn toward him and replied haughtily. "I make up for my lack of looks with a fantastic bedroom technique. First I smother him in honey," she whispered conspiratorially, leaning forward, "and then I bring in specially trained ants…"

He lifted the cigar to his mouth and took a draw from it, blowing out a thick cloud of smoke. "I hope you take his clothes off first," he said. "Honey is hard to get out of fabric. This is my floor."

She stepped back to let him off, glaring at him. This wasn't their first encounter. He'd been making terrible remarks and scoring off her since the first day she'd been in the building, and she was heartily sick of him—whoever he was.

"Have a nice day," she drawled sweetly.

He didn't even turn. "I was, until you came along."

"Why don't you take your cigar and stick it up your…?!"

After the doors closed off her last word, the car carried

her unwillingly up to the fourteenth floor, where a man and woman were waiting to go down.

She noticed the floor number with a sigh. He was ruining her life. Why did he have to work in this building, when there was all of Atlanta for him to get lost in?

The elevator descended, and this time it opened on the sixth floor. Still fuming, she went into her bosses' lavish office, glancing as she walked at Maggie and Jessica, the other two secretaries, hard at work on opposite sides of the office. Becky had a cubbyhole adjacent to Bob Malcolm's. He was the junior partner, and her main boss.

Without knocking, she entered the big office to find Bob and two of his junior colleagues, Harley and Jarard, impatiently waiting for their coffee while Bob talked irritably on the phone.

"Just put it down anywhere, Becky, and thank you," he said brusquely, with his hand over the receiver. He glanced at one of his colleagues. "Kilpatrick just walked in the door. How's that for timing?"

Becky passed the cups of coffee quietly and received mumbled thank-yous from Harley and Jarard. Bob began to speak into the telephone again.

"Listen, Kilpatrick, all I want is a conference. I've got some new evidence I want you to see." Her boss banged his fist on the desk and his swarthy face reddened. "Dammit, man, do you have to be so inflexible?!" He sighed angrily, "All right, all right. I'll be up in five minutes." He slammed the receiver down. "My God, I'm praying he won't run for reelection," he said heavily. "This is only the second week I've had to deal with him, and I'm already sweating blood! Give me Dan Wade any day!"

Dan Wade was the Atlanta judicial circuit's D.A. Becky knew he was a nice man. But here in Curry County, the district attorney was Rourke Kilpatrick. Perhaps, she thought optimistically, her employer had just gotten off on the wrong foot with Kilpatrick. He was probably every bit as nice as Dan Wade when you got to know him.

She started to point this out to Mr. Malcolm when Harley broke in. "Can you blame him?" Harley asked. "He's had more death threats in the past month over this drug war than any president. He's a hard man, and he won't back down. I've had a couple of cases down here before, and I know Kilpatrick's reputation. He can't be bought. He's a law-and-order man from the feet up."

Bob sat back in his plush leather chair. "I get cold chills remembering how Kilpatrick once eviscerated a witness of mine on the stand. She actually had to be tranquilized after she testified."

"Is Mr. Kilpatrick really that bad?" Becky asked with soft curiosity.

"Yes," her boss replied. "You've never met him, have you? He's working here in this building now, temporarily, while his office is being redecorated. It's part of that courthouse renovation the county commission voted in. It's pretty convenient for us to go up a floor rather than over to the courthouse. Of course, Kilpatrick hates it."

"Kilpatrick hates most everything, including people." Hague grinned. "They say that mean temperament comes from his heritage. He's part Indian—Cherokee, to be exact. His mother came here to live with his father's people when Kilpatrick's father died. She died pretty soon afterward, so

Kilpatrick became the ward of his uncle. The uncle was the head of one of the founding families of Curry Station and he literally forced Kilpatrick down local society's throats. He was a federal judge," he added, smiling. "I guess that's where Kilpatrick learned his love of the law. Uncle Kilpatrick, you see, couldn't be bought."

"Well, I'll go up anyway and offer him my soul on behalf of our shady client," Bob Malcolm said. "Harley, get the brief ready for the Bronson trial, if you don't mind. And Jarard, Tyler's down at the clerk's office working on that estate suit you're researching."

"Okay. I'll get busy," Harley said with a smile. "You might send Becky up to work on Kilpatrick. She might soften him up."

Malcolm laughed gently. "He'd eat her for breakfast," he told the other man. He turned to Becky. "You can help Maggie while I'm away, if you don't mind. There's some filing to catch up."

"Okay," she said, smiling, "Good luck."

He whistled, smiling back. "I'll need it."

She watched him go with a wistful sigh. He was a caring kind of person, even if he did have the temper of a barracuda.

Maggie showed her the filing that needed doing with an indulgent smile. The petite, thin black woman had been with the firm for twenty years, and she knew where all the bodies were buried. Becky had wondered sometimes if that was why Maggie had job security, because she had a sharp tongue—she could be hard on clients and new secretaries alike. But fortunately, she and Becky got along very well—

they even had lunch together from time to time. Maggie was the only person she could talk to except Granddad.

Jessica, the elegant blond secretary on the other side of the office, was Mr. Hague and Mr. Randers's secretary. She enjoyed her status as Mr. Hague's after-hours escort—he wasn't married or likely to be anytime soon—and she primped a lot. Tess Coleman was one of the paralegals—a just-married young blonde with a friendly smile. Nettie Hayes, a black law student, was the other paralegal. The receptionist was Connie Blair, a vivacious brunette who was unmarried and in no hurry to change her status. Becky got along well with the rest of the office staff, but Maggie was still her favorite.

"They're going to buy a new coffee urn, by the way," Maggie mentioned while Becky filed. "I can go shopping for it tomorrow."

"I could go," Becky offered.

"No, dear, I'll do it," Maggie said with a smile. "I want to pick up a present for my sister-in-law while I'm out. She's expecting."

Becky smiled back, but halfheartedly. Life was passing her by. She'd never even had a real date, except to go to a VFW Club dance with the grandson of a friend of her grandfather, and that had been a real bust. The boy smoked pot and liked to party, and he didn't understand why Becky didn't.

The word around the office was that Becky was an old-fashioned girl. In such a confined society, eligible bachelors were pretty rare anyway, and the few who were left weren't looking for instant matrimony. Becky had hoped that when the law firm moved to Curry Station, she might have a little more opportunity for a social life. For a suburban area, it did at least have a small-town atmosphere. But even if she found someone to date, how could she afford to get serious about anybody? She couldn't leave her grandfather alone, and who'd look after Clay and Mack? *Daydreams,* she thought miserably. She was being sacrificed to look after her family, and there just wasn't any way out. Her father knew that, but he didn't care. That was hard to take, too—that he could see how overworked she was and it didn't even matter to him. That he could go away for two years and not even call or write to see how his kids were.

"You missed two files, Becky," Maggie said, interrupting her thoughts. "Don't be careless, dear," she added with an affectionate smile.

"Yes, Maggie," Becky said quietly, and put her mind to the job.

She drove home late that afternoon in her white Thunderbird. It was one of the older models with bucket seats and a small, squarish body with a Landau roof. But it was still the most elegant thing she'd ever driven, with its burgundy velour seats and power windows, and she loved it, car payments and all.

She'd had to go downtown to pick up some files from one of the attorneys who'd left before the firm moved. She hated midtown Atlanta, and was glad not to be working there anymore, but today it seemed even more hectic than usual. She found a spot in a car park, got the files, and hurried back out—just in time to get in the thick of rush hour.

The traffic going past the Tenth Street exit was terrible, and it got worse past the Omni. But down around Grady

Hospital, it began to thin out, and by the time she passed the stadium and the exit to the Hartsfield International Airport, she was able to relax again.

Twenty minutes down the road, she crossed into Curry County, and five minutes later, she rounded the square in Curry Station, still several minutes away from the massive suburban office complex where her bosses had their new offices.

Curry Station looked pretty much the way it had since the Civil War. The obligatory Confederate soldier guarded the town square with his musket, surrounded by benches where old men could sit on a sunny Saturday afternoon and pass the time of day. There was a drugstore, a dry goods store, a grocery, and a newly remodeled theater.

Curry Station still had its magnificent old red-brick courthouse with the huge clock, and it was here that superior court and state court were convened during its sessions. It was also here that the district attorney had his office, which they said was being remodeled. She was curious about Mr. Kilpatrick. She knew of the Kilpatricks, of course—everyone did. The first Kilpatrick had made a fortune in shipping in Savannah before he had moved to Atlanta. Over the years, the wealth had diminished, but she understood that Kilpatrick drove a Mercedes-Benz and lived in a mansion. He couldn't do *that* on a district attorney's salary. Curious, some said, that he'd chosen to run for that particular office when, with his University of Georgia law degree, he could have gone into private practice and made millions.

Rourke Kilpatrick had been appointed by the governor to fill the unexpired term of the previous D.A., who'd died in office. When his term ended a year later, Kilpatrick had surprised everyone by winning the election. It wasn't the usual thing in Curry County for appointees to garner popular support at the polls.

Even so, Becky hadn't been interested enough to pay much attention to the district attorney before. Her duties didn't involve courtroom drama, and she stayed much too busy at home to watch the news, so Kilpatrick was only a name to her.

Her mind drifted as she stared out her windshield at the residential area she was passing through. There were a number of stately homes on the main street of town, ringed by big oak and pine trees, and dogwoods that spread their petals wide in the spring in white and pink splendor. On the back roads to town were several old farms whose tumbledown barns and houses gave silent testimony to the stubborn pride of the Georgians who had held on to them for generations, no matter what the sacrifice.

One of those old farms belonged to Granger Cullen, the third Cullen to inherit it in a genealogy that dated to the Civil War in Georgia. The Cullens had always managed somehow to hold on to their hundred-acre possession. The farm was ramshackle these days, with a white clapboard house that needed everything done to it. There was television, but no cable because it was too expensive. There was a telephone, but on a party line with three neighbors who never got off the phone. There was city water and city sewerage, for which Becky thanked her lucky stars, but the plumbing tended to freeze up in winter and there never seemed to be enough gas in the tank to heat the house until money was saved to buy more.

Becky parked the car in the leaning shed that served as a garage, and then just sat and looked around. The fences were half down, rusted, and held up with posts that had all but decayed. The trees were bare, because it was winter, and the field had grown up with broom sage and beggar lice. It needed turning over before spring planting, but Becky couldn't operate the tractor and Clay was too wild to trust with it. There was plenty of hay in the loft of the old barn to feed the two cows they kept for milking, plenty of mash to feed the hens, and corn to add to the bulk of food the animals ate. Thanks to Becky's tireless efforts last summer, the big freezer was full of vegetables and the pantry had canned things in it. But that would all be gone by summer, and more would have to be put up. In the meanwhile, Becky had to work. Her whole life was one long, endless sequence of work. She'd never been to a party, or to a fancy dance. She'd never worn silk against her skin, or expensive perfume. She'd never had her long hair professionally cut or her nails manicured, and probably she never would. She'd grow old taking care of her family and wishing for a way out.

She felt guilty at her own horrible self-pity. She loved her grandfather and her brothers, and she shouldn't blame them for her lack of freedom. After all, she'd been raised in a way that would prevent her from enjoying any kind of modern lifestyle. She couldn't sleep around because it was against her nature to be that casual about something so profound. She couldn't do drugs or guzzle booze because she had no head for alcohol and even small amounts put her to sleep. She opened the car door and got out. She couldn't even smoke, because it choked her. As a social animal, she was a dead loss, she mused.

"I was never meant for jet planes and computers," she told the chickens staring at her from the barnyard. "I was meant for calico and buckskin."

"Granddad! Becky's talking to the chickens again!" Mack yelled from the barn.

Granddad was sitting on the sunny side of the porch in a cane-bottomed chair, grinning at his granddaughter. He was wearing a white shirt and sweater with his overalls, and he looked healthier than he had in weeks. It was warm for a February afternoon, almost springlike.

"As long as they don't answer her back, it'll be okay, Mack," he called back to the grinning, towheaded youngster.

"Have you done your homework?" Becky asked her youngest brother.

"Aw, Becky, I just got home! I have to feed my frog!"

"Excuses, excuses," she murmured. "Where's Clay?"

Mack didn't answer. He disappeared quickly into the barn. Becky saw Granddad avert his eyes to toy with his stick and pocketknife as she climbed the steps, purse in hand.

"What's wrong?" she asked the old man, placing an affectionate hand on his shoulder.

He shrugged, his balding silvery head bent. He was a tall man, very thin and stooped since his heart attack, and brown from years of outside work. He had age marks on the backs of his long-fingered hands and wrinkles in his face that looked like road ruts in the rain. He was sixty-six now, but he looked much older. His life had been a hard one. He and Becky's grandmother had lost two children in a flood and one to pneumonia. Only Becky's father, Scott, of all their four children, had survived to adulthood, and Scott had been a source of constant trouble to everybody. Including his wife. It said on the death certificate that Becky, Mack, and Clay's mother, Henrietta, had died of pneumonia. But Becky was sure that she had simply given up. The responsibility for three children and a sick father, added to her own poor health and Scott's ceaseless gambling and womanizing, had broken her spirit.

"Clay's gone off with those Harris kids," her grandfather said finally.

"Son and Bubba?" she sighed. They had given names, but like many Southern boys, they had nicknames that had little to do with their Christian appelations. The name Bubba was common, like Son and Buster and Billy-Bob and Tub. Becky didn't even know their given names, because nobody used them. The Harris boys were in their late teens and they both had drivers' licenses. In their case, it was more like a license to kill. Both brothers were drug users and she'd heard rumors that Son was a pusher. He drove a big blue Corvette and always had money. He'd quit school at sixteen. Becky didn't like either one of the boys and she'd told Clay as much. But apparently he wasn't taking any advice from his big sister if he was out with the scalawags.

"I don't know what to do," Granger Cullen said quietly. "I tried to talk to him, but he wouldn't listen. He told me he was old enough to make his own decisions, and that you and I had no rights over him. He cussed me. Imagine that, a seventeen-year-old boy cussing his own grandfather?"

"That doesn't sound like Clay," she replied. "It's only since Christmas that he's been so unruly. Since he started hanging around with the Harris boys, really."

"He didn't go to school today," her grandfather added.

"He hasn't gone for two days. The school called and wanted to know where he was. His teacher called, too. She says his grades are low enough to fail him. He won't graduate if he can't pull them up. Then where'll he be? Just like Scott," he said heavily. "Another Cullen gone bad."

"Oh, my goodness." Rebecca sat down heavily on the porch steps, letting the wind brush her cheeks. She closed her eyes. From bad to worse, didn't the saying go?

Clay had always been a good boy, trying to help with the chores and look out for Mack, his younger brother. But in the past few months, he'd begun to change. His grades had dropped. He had become moody and withdrawn. He stayed out late and sometimes couldn't get up to go to school at all. His eyes were bloodshot and he'd come in once giggling like a little girl over nothing at all—symptoms, Becky was to learn, of cocaine use. She'd never seen Clay actually use drugs, but she was certain that he was smoking pot, because she'd smelled it on his clothes and in his room. He'd denied it and she could never find any evidence. He was too careful.

Lately, he'd begun to resent her interference in his life more and more. She was only his sister, he'd said just two nights ago. She had no real authority over him, and she wasn't going to tell him what to do anymore. He was tired of living like a poor kid and never having money to spend, like the Harris boys. He was going to make himself a place in the world, and she could go to hell.

Becky hadn't told Granddad. It was hard enough trying to excuse Clay's bad behavior and frequent absences. She could only hope that he wasn't headed toward addiction. There were places that treated that kind of thing, but they were for rich people. The best she could hope for, for her brother, would be some sort of state-supported rehabilitation center, and Granddad wouldn't agree to that even if Clay would. Granddad wanted nothing that even looked like charity. He was too proud.

So here they were, Becky thought, staring out over the land that had been in her family for over a hundred years, hopelessly in debt, and with Clay headed for trouble. They said that even an alcoholic couldn't be helped unless he realized he had a problem. Clay didn't. It was not the best ending to what had started off as a perfectly terrible day anyway.

CHAPTER TWO

Becky changed into jeans and a red pullover sweater and gathered her long hair into a ponytail to cook supper. While she fried chicken to go with the mashed potatoes and home-canned green beans, she baked biscuits in the old oven. Maybe she could straighten Clay out, but she didn't have a clue as to how. Talking wasn't going to do the job. She'd tried that herself. Clay either walked away and refused to listen, or flew off the handle and started cursing. And to make matters worse, lately she'd noticed bills missing from the jar containing her egg money. She was almost certain that Clay was taking them, but how could she ask her own brother if he was stealing from her?

In the end, she'd taken the remaining money out of the jar and put it in the bank. She hadn't left anything around that could be sold or pawned for easy cash. Becky felt like a criminal, which added to her guilt about resenting her responsibility for her family.

There was no one she could talk to about her problems except Maggie, and she hated to bother the older woman with her woes. All her longtime girlfriends were married or out on their own in other cities. It would have helped if she'd only had that. She couldn't talk to Granddad. His health was precarious enough already, without taking on Clay. So she'd told Granddad that she'd handle it. Maybe she could talk to Mr. Malcolm at work and have him advise her. He was the only person outside her family who might do that.

She put the food on the table and called Mack and her grandfather. He said grace and they ate as they listened to Mack's complaints about math and teachers and school in general.

"I won't learn math," Mack promised her, staring at her with hazel eyes just a shade lighter than her own. His hair was much lighter, almost blond. He was tall for a ten-year-old, and getting taller by the day.

"Yes, you will," Becky told him. "You'll have to help keep the books one of these days. I won't last forever."

"Here, you stop talking like that," Granddad said sharply. "You're too young to talk that way. Although," he sighed, staring down at his mashed potatoes, "I reckon you feel like running away from time to time. What with all of us to look after..."

"You stop that," Becky muttered, glaring at him. "I love you or I wouldn't stay. Eat your mashed potatoes. I made a cherry pie for dessert."

"Wow! My favorite!" Mack grinned.

"And you can have all you want. *After* you do your math and I check it," she added with an equally wide grin.

Mack made a terrible face and propped his chin in his hands. "I shoulda gone with Clay. He said I could."

"If you ever go with Clay, I'll take away your basketball and hoop," she threatened, using the only weapon she had.

He actually paled. Basketball was his life. "Come on, Becky, I was just kidding!"

"I hope so," she said. "Clay is keeping bad company. I have enough trouble without adding you to it."

"That's right," Granddad seconded.

Mack picked up his fork. "Okay. I'll keep away from Bill and Dick. Just don't bother my B-ball."

"That's a deal," Becky promised, and tried not to look too relieved.

She'd done the dishes and cleaned up the living room and washed two loads of clothes while Granddad and Mack watched television. Then she supervised Mack's homework, got him to bed, settled Granddad, took a bath, and started to go to bed herself. Before she could, however, Clay staggered into the living room, giggling and reeking of beer.

The overpowering maltish smell made her sick. Nothing in her experience had prepared her to deal with this. She stared at him with helpless fury, hating the home life that had led him into such a trap. He was at the age where he needed a man to guide him, a man's example to follow. He was looking for a measuring stick, and instead of using Granddad, he'd found the Harris brothers.

"Oh, Clay," she said miserably. He looked so much like her, with his brown hair and slender build, but his eyes were pure green, not hazel like hers and Mack's and his face had a ruddy look.

He grinned at her. "I won't be sick, you know. I smoked a joint before I tanked up on beer." He blinked. "I'm quitting school, Becky, because it's for wimps and retards."

"No, you aren't," she said shortly. "I'm not working myself to death to watch you become a professional bum."

He glared at her dizzily. "You're just my sister, Becky. You can't tell me what to do."

"Stand and watch me," she said. "I don't want you hanging around with those Harris boys anymore. They're leading you right into trouble."

"They're my friends, and I'll hang out with them if I want to," he informed her. He felt wild. He'd smoked some crack, as well, and his head was about to explode. The high had been beautiful, but now that it was wearing off, he felt more depressed than ever. "I hate being poor!" he announced.

Becky glared at him. "Then get a job," she said coldly. "I did. I got one even before I graduated from high school. I worked at three before I found this one, and took night courses so that I could land it."

"Here we go again, Saint Becky," he said, slurring the words. "So you work. Big deal. What do we have to show for it?! We're dirt poor, and now that Granddad's ill, it'll get worse!"

She felt herself getting sick inside. She knew that, but having Clay fling it in her face didn't help. He was drunk, she tried to tell herself, he didn't know what he was saying. It hurt all the same.

"You selfish little boy," she said angrily. "You ungrateful brat! I'm working myself to death, and here you are complaining that we don't have anything!"

He swayed, sat down heavily, and took a slow breath. She probably was right, but he was too stoned to care. "Leave me alone," he muttered, stretching out on the couch. "Just leave me alone."

"What have you had besides beer and marijuana?" she demanded.

"A little crack," he said drowsily. "Everybody does it. Leave me alone—I'm sleepy."

He sprawled and closed his eyes. He was asleep at once. Becky stood over him in stunned agony. Crack. She'd never seen it, but she knew very well what it was from the news— an illegal drug. She had to stop him somehow before he got in over his head. The first step was going to be keeping him away from those Harris boys. She didn't know how she was going to manage it, but she'd have to find a way.

She covered him with a blanket, because it was simpler to let him sleep where he was than to cope with moving him. Clay was already almost six feet tall, and he weighed more than she did. She couldn't lift him. Crack, of all things. She didn't have to wonder how he'd gotten it, either. His friends had probably given it to him. Well, with any luck, it would only be this once and she'd stop him before he could do it again.

She went into her bedroom and lay down on the worn coverlet in her cotton gown, feeling old. Perhaps things would look better in the morning. She could ask Reverend Fox at church to talk to Clay—that might do a little good. Kids needed something to hold on to, to get them through the hard times. Drugs and religion were opposite ends of a security blanket, and religion was certainly preferable. Her own faith had taken her through some storms.

She closed her eyes and slept. The next morning, she got Mack off to school, but Clay wouldn't get up.

"We'll talk when I get home," she told him firmly. "You aren't going out with those boys again."

"Want to bet?" he asked her, his eyes challenging. "Stop me. What can you do?"

"Wait and see," she replied, mentally praying she could think of something.

She went to work worrying about it. She'd settled Grand-dad and asked him to talk to Clay, but he seemed to want to hide his head in the sand about Clay's difficult behavior. Per-haps it was the fact that he'd failed so miserably with Scott, his son, and couldn't admit that he was failing again with his grandson. The old man had a double dose of pride.

Maggie glanced at her as she sat brooding at her desk. "Anything I can do?" she asked softly, so that nobody else could hear.

"No, but thank you," Becky told her with a smile. "You're a nice lady, Maggie."

"Just a fellow human being," the older woman corrected. "Life has storms, but they pass. Just hang on to the tree until the wind stops, that's all you have to do. After all, Becky, no wind blows forever, good or bad."

Becky laughed. "I'll try to remember that."

And she did. Right up until that afternoon when the call came from the magistrate's office, informing her that Clay had been picked up for drug possession. Mr. Gillen, the magistrate, told her that he'd called the D.A. and they'd both talked to Clay, after which they'd sent him over to the juve-nile detention center while they decided whether or not to book him. He had a pocketful of crack when he'd been picked up, drunk, in the company of the Harris boys outside town.

The decision to press charges for felony possession was up to the D.A., Mr. Gillen said, and Becky could bet that if Kilpatrick had enough evidence, he'd go for a conviction. He was very hard on people who dealt drugs.

Becky thanked Gillen for telephoning her personally and walked immediately into Bob Malcolm's office to ask for advice.

Mr. Malcolm patted her absently on the shoulder after he'd closed the door, to spare her any scrutiny by people in the waiting room.

"What do I do? What can I do?" Becky asked him miserably. "They say he's got over an ounce and a half on him. That it could mean a felony charge."

"Becky, it's your father who should do something," he said firmly.

"He isn't in town right now," she said. Well, it was true. He hadn't been in town for two years, and he hadn't been responsible for his children ever. "And my grandfather isn't well," she added. "He has a bad heart."

Bob Malcolm shook his head and sighed. He said, after a minute, "Okay. We'll go see the D.A. and try to talk to him. I'll phone and make an appointment. Maybe we can make a deal."

"With Mr. Kilpatrick? I thought you said he didn't make deals," she said nervously.

"It depends on the severity of the charge, and how much evidence he has. He doesn't like to waste the taxpayer's money on a trial he can't win. We'll see."

He spoke to the D.A.'s secretary and was told that Rourke Kilpatrick had a few minutes free right now.

"We'll be right up," he told her and hung up. "Let's go, Becky."

"I hope he's in a good mood," she said, and glanced in the mirror. Her hair was neatly in its bun, her face pale even with its hint of pastel makeup. But her red plaid wool skirt showed its three years, and her black shoes were scuffed and scratched. The cuffs on her long-sleeved white blouse were frayed, and her slender hands showed the ravages of the work she did on the farm. She was no lady of leisure and there were lines in her face that should never have been noticeable in a woman her age. She was afraid she wouldn't make much of an impression on Mr. Kilpatrick. She looked what she was—an overworked, overresponsible country woman with no sophistication at all. And maybe that would work in her favor. She couldn't let Clay go to prison. She owed her mother that much. She'd failed him too many times already.

Mr. Kilpatrick's secretary was tall and dark-haired and very professional. She greeted Mr. Malcolm and Becky warmly.

"He's waiting for you," she said, gesturing toward the closed office door. "You can go right in."

"Thanks, Daphne," Mr. Malcolm replied. "Come on, Becky, chin up."

He knocked briefly at the door and opened it, letting Becky precede him. He shouldn't have. She stopped dead at the face she met across the big wooden desk piled high with legal documents.

"You!" she exclaimed involuntarily.

He put down the thin black cigar he was smoking and stood up. He didn't acknowledge the exclamation or smile or make any kind of attempt at a formal greeting. He looked just as intimidating as he had in the elevator, and just as cold.

"You didn't need to bring your secretary to take notes," he told Bob Malcolm. "If you want to plea bargain, I'll stick to what I tell you after I hear the facts. Sit down."

"It's the Cullen case."

"The juvenile." Kilpatrick nodded. "The boys he's running with are scum. The younger Harris boy has been pushing drugs in the local high school between classes. His brother deals everything from crack to horse, and he's already got one conviction for attempted robbery. That time he walked in and out of juvenile hall, but he's of age now. If I catch him again, I'll send him up."

Becky had been sitting stock-still. "And the Cullen boy?" she asked in a husky whisper.

Kilpatrick gave her a cold glare. "I'm talking to Malcolm, not to you."

"You don't understand," she said heavily. "Clay Cullen is my brother."

His dark brown, almost black eyes narrowed and he gave her a look that made her feel half an inch high. "Cullen is a name I know. Another Cullen was in here a few years ago on a robbery charge. The victim refused to testify and he got off. I would have gone for a conviction without parole if I'd gotten him to trial. Any kin to you?"

She flinched. "My father."

Kilpatrick didn't say a word. He didn't have to. His level

stare told her exactly what he thought of her family. *You're wrong,* she wanted to say. *We're not all like that.* But before she could even speak, he turned back to Malcolm. "Am I right in assuming that you're representing your secretary and her brother?"

"No," Becky began, thinking of the legal fees she couldn't afford to pay.

"Yes," Bob Malcolm interrupted. "It's a first offense, and the boy is a hardship case."

"The boy is a sullen, uncooperative young brat," he corrected. "I've already spoken to him. I don't consider him a hardship case," Kilpatrick said curtly.

Becky could imagine how Clay would react to a man like Kilpatrick. The boy had no respect at all for men—not with the example his father had set. "He's not a bad boy," she pleaded. "It's the company he's keeping. Please, I'll try to work with him..."

"Your father's done a great job of that already," Kilpatrick said, totally unaware of the real situation at home as he went for her throat with sickening ease, his dark brown eyes stabbing into hers as he leaned back with his cigar between his big fingers. "There's no point in letting the boy back on the streets unless his home situation changes. He'll just do the same thing again."

Her hazel eyes met his dark ones. "Do you have a brother, Mr. Kilpatrick?"

"Not to my knowledge, Miss Cullen."

"If you had one, you might understand how I feel. This is the first time he's done anything like this. It's like throwing out the baby with the bathwater."

"This baby was in possession of illegal drugs. Cocaine, to be exact, and not just cocaine—crack." He leaned forward, looking more Indian than ever, his level, unblinking stare faintly dangerous. "He needs guidance. You and your father quite obviously aren't capable of giving it to him."

"That was a low blow, Kilpatrick," Bob Malcolm said tautly.

"It was an accurate one," he returned without apology. "At this age, boys don't change without help. He should have gotten that in the beginning, and it may be too late already."

"But...!" Becky said.

"Your brother is damned lucky he didn't get caught peddling any of that poison on the street!" he said shortly. "I hate drug pushers. I'll go to any lengths to prosecute them."

"But he isn't a pusher," Becky said huskily, her big hazel eyes wet with tears.

Kilpatrick hadn't felt compassion in a long time, and he didn't like it. He averted his eyes. "Not yet," he agreed. He sighed angrily, glancing from Becky to Malcolm. "All right. Gillen, the magistrate, says he'll go along with whatever I decide. The boy denies possession. He says that he didn't know how it got in his jacket, and the only witnesses are the Harris boys. They, of course, back his story to the hilt," he added with a cold smile.

"In other words," Bob said with a faint smile, "you don't have much of a case."

"Chorus and verse," Kilpatrick agreed. "This time," Kilpatrick said with a meaningful glance at Becky. "I'll drop the charges."

Becky felt sick with relief. "Can I see him?" she asked huskily. She was too badly hurt to say any more, and this man hated her. She'd get no sympathy or help from him.

"Yes. I'll want Brady at juvenile hall to talk to the boy, and there'll be a condition for the release. Now, go away. I have work to do."

"Okay, we'll get out of the way," Malcolm said, rising. "Thanks, Kilpatrick," he said formally.

Kilpatrick got up, too. He stuck one hand in his pocket, staring at Rebecca's tragic face with mixed emotions. He felt sorry for her, and he didn't want to. He wondered why her father hadn't come with her. She was very thin, and the sadness in her oval face was disturbing. It surprised him that it bothered him. These days, very little did. She wasn't the cocky, amusing companion he'd had several elevator rides with. Not now. She looked totally without hope.

He saw them out the door and went back into his office without a word to his secretary.

"We'll go over to juvenile hall," Bob Malcolm was telling Becky as he put her into the elevator and pressed the sixth floor button. "Everything will be all right. If Kilpatrick can't prove his case, he won't pursue it. Clay can leave with us."

"He wouldn't even listen to me," she said huskily.

"He's a hard man. Probably the best D.A. this county's had in a long time, but sometimes he can be inflexible. Not an easy man to face across a courtroom, either."

"I can understand that."

BECKY WENT TO JUVENILE HALL to see her brother after work. She was ushered into a tiny meeting room to wait for him. Clay walked in fifteen minutes later, looking frightened and belligerent all at once.

"Hi, Becky," he said with a cocky grin. "They didn't beat

me, so you don't need to worry. They won't send me to jail.
I've talked with two other kids who know the ropes. They
say juvenile hall is just a slap on the wrist because we're un-
derage. I'll beat this rap sitting down."

"Thank you," she told him, stiff-lipped and cold-eyed.
"Thank you for your generous consideration of your grandfather's feelings and mine. It's nice to know that you love us
enough to become notorious on our behalf."

Clay was wild, but he had a heart. He toned down instantly
and dropped his eyes.

"Now, tell me what happened," she said shortly, sitting
down across from him after Mr. Brady, the juvenile officer
on Clay's case, joined them.

"Didn't they tell you?" Clay asked.

"You tell me," she countered.

He gave her a long look and shrugged. "I was drunk," he
muttered, twisting his hands over his jeans-clad legs. "They
said let's do some crack, and I just nodded. I flaked out in
the back seat and didn't come to until the police stopped us.
My pockets were full of the stuff. I don't know how it got
there. Honest, Becky," he added. His sister and brother and
grandfather were the only people on earth he loved. He
hated what he'd done, but he was too proud to admit it. "I
sobered up real good after Kilpatrick talked to me."

"Possession of illegal drugs alone could get you a prison
term of up to ten years, if the D.A. decided to try you as an
adult," Mr. Brady interjected with a level glance. "And you
may not be out of the woods yet. Mr. Kilpatrick, the district
attorney, would very much like to nail you to the wall."

"He can't. I'm a juvenile."

"Only for another year. And reform school wouldn't appeal to you, young man. I can promise you that."

Clay looked subdued, and a little less belligerent. He twisted his hands in his lap. "I won't go to jail, will I?"

"Not this time," the juvenile officer said. "But don't underestimate Kilpatrick. Your father was pretty arrogant when he beat the robbery charge, and that didn't endear your family to the D.A. He's a very moral man. He doesn't like lawbreakers. It would do you good to remember that. He still thinks your father threatened that victim to keep him from talking."

"Dad was arrested?" Clay began.

"Never mind," Becky said, stiffening her features.

He glanced at her, noticing reluctantly the strain in her face, the sadness. He felt a twinge of conscience.

"I'll say this once," Mr. Brady told Clay. "You've got a chance to keep your nose clean. If you throw it away, no one is going to be able to help you—not your sister or me. You may beat the rap for a while, as long as you're a juvenile. But you're seventeen. And if the crime is severe enough, the district attorney would be within his authority to have you prosecuted as an adult. If you keep messing around with drugs, inevitably you'll serve time. I wish I could show you what that means. Our prisons are overcrowded, and even the best of them are hellholes for young offenders. If you don't like being ordered around by your sister, you sure as hell aren't going to like being some older boy's imitation girlfriend." He stared at Clay. "Do you understand what I mean, son? They'd pass you around like a new toy."

Clay reddened. "They wouldn't! I'd fight...!"

"You'd lose. Think about it. Meanwhile, you're going to

get some counseling," the juvenile officer said. "We've set up appointments for you at the mental health clinic. You'll be required to go. I hope you understand that this is Kilpatrick's idea, and that he'll check on you periodically. I wouldn't advise you to miss a session."

"Damn Kilpatrick," Clay said harshly.

"That's not a good attitude to take," Brady warned quietly. "You're in a lot of trouble. Kilpatrick can be your worst enemy or your best friend. You wouldn't like him as an enemy."

Clay muttered something and averted his eyes to the window. He looked as if he hated the whole world.

Becky knew exactly how he felt. She wanted to cry. She clasped her hands together to keep them from trembling.

"Okay, Clay, you can go with your sister for now. We'll talk again."

"All right," Clay said tautly. He got up and reluctantly shook hands with the man. "Come on, Sis. Let's go home."

She didn't speak. She walked to the car like a zombie and got in behind the wheel, barely waiting for Clay to shut his door before she drove away. Inside, she felt sick all the way to her soul.

"I'm sorry I got caught," Clay said when they were halfway home. "I guess you're having a pretty hard time of it, being stuck with Granddad and me and Mack."

"I'm not stuck with it," she lied. "I love you all."

"Love shouldn't make prisons of people's lives," Clay said. He glanced sideways at her, with a crafty look in his eyes that she didn't see. "Really, Becky, I didn't know what I was getting into."

"I'm sure you didn't," she said, forgiving him anything, just as she always had. She managed a smile. "I just don't know what to do, how to cope. The district attorney was pretty rough."

"That Kilpatrick man," he muttered icily. "God, I hate him! He came to see me at that juvenile hall. He stared right through me and made me feel like a worm. He said I'd wind up just like Dad."

"You won't," she said stubbornly. "He had no right to say such a thing!"

"He didn't want to let me go," Clay said hesitantly. "He tried to talk Mr. Brady into putting me in reform school. He got upset when he couldn't get him to agree. He says anybody who fools with drugs deserves to go to jail."

"Mr. Kilpatrick can go to hell," she said fiercely. "We'll get by."

"Look," he began. "I could get a job—after school, you know. I could make some money…"

"I'm doing fine," she said, almost choking on the words. "You don't need to get a job," she added, missing the flash of anger on his face. "I'll take care of you, just like I always have. You finish school and go to work then. You've only got this year to go. That's not so much."

"Look, I'm seventeen!" he burst out. "I don't need looking after anymore! I'm sick of nothing but working around the farm and never having any pocket money. There's this girl I like and she won't give me the time of day. You won't even let me get a damned car!"

"Don't you cuss me!" she flashed at him. "Don't you dare!"

"Let me out." He reached for the door handle, his eyes daring her. "I'll do it, I swear. Stop this car and let me out!"

"Clay, where are you going?!" she demanded when he was on the pavement.

"Somewhere I can be what I want to be," he said harshly. "I'm not your little boy, Becky, I'm your brother! You just don't get it, do you? I'm not a kid you can order around! I'm a man!"

She slumped a little, stretched toward the open door, her hazel eyes weary, her face heavily lined. "Oh, Clay," she said heavily. "Clay, what am I going to do now?" She broke down, and tears ran down her cheeks.

He hesitated, torn between standing up for his independence and erasing that look from Becky's face. He hadn't meant to hurt her, but he wasn't quite in control of himself these days. He had these violent mood swings....

He slid back inside the car and closed the door, eyeing her warily. He felt suddenly older as he realized how much an act her strength really was. Guilt sat on him like a rock. He should never had added to her burden by acting like a stupid kid.

"Look, it will be all right," he began hesitantly. "Becky, please stop crying."

"Granddad will die," she whispered. She dug for a handkerchief in her purse and wiped her eyes. "He'll find out, no matter how hard we try to keep it from him."

"Hey. How about if we move to Savannah?" he suggested, and smiled. "We could build yachts and get rich."

That brightness lifted her spirits. She smiled back. "Dad would find out that we had money and come looking for us," she said with graveyard humor.

"They said he'd been arrested. Did you know?" he asked her.

She nodded her head.

He leaned back in his seat, glancing out the window. "Becky, why did he run out on us when Mama died?"

"He ran out on us long before that. You wouldn't remember, but he was always out with the boys, even when you and Mack were being born. I don't think he was ever around when we really needed him. Mama gave up eventually."

"Don't you give up, Becky," he said suddenly, turning his gaze back to hers. "I'll take care of things, don't you worry." He was already thinking of ways that he could make enough money to take some of the financial burden off her shoulders. The Harris boys had made one or two suggestions. He didn't have Becky's conscience, and there was plenty of money to be made. What she didn't know wouldn't hurt her, and he'd be careful not to get caught twice.

"Okay." She turned into the driveway, wondering how to break the news to their grandfather, how to cope with the future.

She hoped Clay would do what the juvenile officer had told him to. She hoped that being arrested had scared him. Maybe it would keep him straight.

She didn't know what to do. Life had become too complicated. She wanted to run away.

"What are you thinking?" Clay asked with dark perception.

"I was thinking about the chocolate cake I'm going to bake for supper," she hedged, and smiled at him. The smile took more effort than Clay would ever know.

CHAPTER THREE

Granddad took the news of Clay's arrest better than Becky had expected him to. It was a blessing that Clay had been arrested in town, and not at home. To his credit, he didn't balk at going to school, for once. He got on the bus without an argument, with Mack right behind him.

Becky settled Granddad in his armchair in the living room, concerned at his silence.

"Are you going to be all right?" she asked after she'd given him his pill. "Should I ask Mrs. White to come and sit with you?"

"I don't need fussing over," he muttered. His thin shoulders lifted and fell. "Where did I fail your father, Becky?" he asked miserably. "And where did I fail Clay? My son and my grandson in trouble with the law, and that Kilpatrick man won't stop until he's got them both in jail. I've heard all about him. He's a barracuda."

"He's a prosecuting attorney," she corrected. "And he's

only doing his job. He just does it passionately, that's all. Mr. Malcolm likes him."

Her grandfather narrowed one eye and looked up at her. "Do you?"

She stood up. "Don't be silly. He's the enemy."

"You remember that," he said firmly, his stubborn chin jutting. "Don't go getting soft on him. He's no friend to this family. He did everything in his power to put Scott away."

"You knew about that?" she asked.

He sat up straighter. "I knew. Saw no reason to tell you or the boys. It wouldn't have helped things. Anyway, Scott beat the rap. The witness changed his mind."

"Did he change it—or did Dad change it for him?"

He wouldn't look at her. "Scott wasn't a bad boy. He was just different; had a different way of looking at things. It wasn't his fault that the law kept hounding him, no more than it's Clay's. That Kilpatrick man has it in for us."

Becky started to speak and stopped. Granddad couldn't admit that he'd made a mistake with Scott, so he certainly wasn't going to admit that he'd made one with Clay. It wouldn't do any good to have an argument with him over it, but if left her holding the bag and Clay's future in her own hands. She could see that she'd get little help from Granddad now.

"Becky, whatever your father did or didn't do, he's still my son," he said suddenly, clenching the chair hard with his lean old hands. "I love him. I love Clay, too."

"I know that," she said gently. She bent down and kissed his leathery cheek. "We'll take care of Clay. They're going to give him some counseling and help him," she said, hoping she could make Clay go to the sessions without too much browbeating. "He'll come through. He's a Cullen."

"That's right. He's a Cullen." He smiled up at her. "You're one, yourself. Have I ever told you how proud I am of you?"

"Frequently," she said, and grinned. "When I get rich and famous, I'll remember you."

"We'll never get rich, and Clay's likely to be the only famous one of us—infamous, most likely." He sighed. "But you're the heart of the whole outfit. Don't let this get you down. Life can get hard sometimes. But if you see through your troubles, think past them to better times, it helps. Always helped me."

"I'll remember that. I'd better get to work," she added. "Be good. I'll see you later."

She drove to the office, inwardly cringing at the thought of the ordeal ahead. She had to talk to Kilpatrick. What Clay had said about Kilpatrick trying to put him in reform school frightened her. Kilpatrick might decide to pursue it, and she had to stop him from doing that. She was going to have to bury her pride and tell him the real situation at home, and she dreaded it.

Her boss gave her an hour off. She phoned the district attorney's office on the seventh floor and asked to see the man himself. She was told that he was on his way down, to meet him at the elevator and they could talk while he got his coffee in the drugstore.

Elated that he'd deigned to at least speak to her, she grabbed her purse, straightened her flowery skirt and white blouse, and rushed out of the office.

Fortunately, the elevator was empty except for the cold-eyed Mr. Kilpatrick in his long overcoat, his thick black hair ruffled, and that eternal, infernal choking cigar in one hand. He gave her a cursory going-over that wasn't flattering.

"You wanted to talk," he said. "Let's go." He pushed the ground floor button and didn't say a word until they walked into the small coffee shop in the drugstore. He bought her a cup of black coffee, one for himself, and a doughnut. He offered her one. But she was too sick to accept it.

They sat down at a corner table and he studied her quietly while he sipped his coffee. Her hair was in its usual bun, her face devoid of makeup. She looked as she felt—washed out and depressed.

"No cutting remarks about my cigar?" he prompted with a raised eyebrow. "No running commentary on my manners?"

She lifted her wan face and stared at him as if she'd never seen him before. "Mr. Kilpatrick, my life is falling apart, and I don't care very much about your cigar smoke or your manners or anything else."

"What did your father say when you told him about your brother?"

She was tired of the pretense. It was time to lay her cards on the table. "I haven't seen or heard from my father in two years."

He frowned. "What about your mother?"

"She died when the boys were young, when I was sixteen."

"Who takes care of them?" he persisted. "Your grandfather?"

"Our grandfather has a bad heart," she said. "He isn't able to take care of himself, much less anyone else. We live with him and take care of him as best we can."

His big hand hit the table, shaking it. "Are you telling me that you're taking care of the three of them by yourself?!" he demanded.

She didn't like the look on his dark face. She moved back a little. "Yes."

"My God! On your salary?"

"Granddad has a farm," she told him. "We grow our own vegetables and I put them up in the freezer and can some. We usually raise a beef steer, too, and Granddad gets a pension from the railroad and his social security. We get by."

"How old are you?"

She glared at him. "That's none of your business."

"You've just made it my business. How old?"

"Twenty-four."

"You were how old when your mother died?"

"Sixteen."

He took a draw from the cigar and turned his head to blow it out. His dark eyes cut into hers, and she knew now exactly how it felt to sit on the witness stand and be grilled by him. It was impossible not to tell him what he wanted to know. That piercing stare and cold voice full of authority would have extracted information from a garden vegetable. "Why isn't your father taking care of his own family?"

"I wish I knew," she replied. "But he never has. He only comes around when he runs out of money. I guess he's got enough; we haven't seen him since he moved to Alabama."

He studied her face quietly for a long time, until her knees went weak at the intensity of the scrutiny. He was so dark, she thought, and that navy pin-striped suit made him look even taller and more elegant. His Indian ancestry was dominant in that lean face, although he seemed to have the temperament of the Irish.

"No wonder you look the way you do," he said absently. "Worn out. I thought at first it might be a demanding lover, but it's overwork."

She colored furiously and glared at him.

"That insults you, does it?" he asked, his deep voice going even deeper. "But you yourself told me that you were a kept woman," he reminded her dryly.

"I lied," she said, moving restlessly. "Anyway, I've got enough problems without loose living to add to them," she said stiffly.

"I see. You're one of *those* girls. The kind mothers throw under the wheels of their sons' cars."

"Nobody will ever throw me under yours, I hope," she said. "I wouldn't have you on a half shell with cocktail sauce."

He lifted a dark eyebrow. "Why not?" he asked, lifting his chin to smile at her with pure sarcasm. "Has someone told you that I'm a half-breed?"

She flushed. "I didn't mean that. You're a very cold man, Mr. Kilpatrick," she said, and shivered at his nearness. He smelled of some exotic cologne and cigar smoke, and she could feel the heat from his body. He made her nervous and weak and uncertain, and it was dangerous to feel that way about the enemy.

"I'm not cold. I'm careful." He lifted the cigar to his mouth. "It pays to be careful these days. In every way."

"So they say."

"In which case, it might be wise if you stopped smearing honey over the mystery man who keeps you. You did say," he reminded her, "that you were the kept woman of one of your employers?"

"I didn't mean it," she protested. "You were looking at me as if I were totally hopeless. It just came out, that's all."

"I should have mentioned it to Bob Malcolm yesterday," he murmured.

"You wouldn't!" she groaned.

"Of course I would," he returned easily. "Hasn't anyone told you that I don't have a heart? I'd prosecute my own mother, they say."

"I could believe that, after yesterday."

"Your brother is going to be a lost cause if you don't get him in hand," he told her. "I came down on him hard for that reason. He needs firm guidance. Most of all, he needs a man's example. God help you if your father is his hero."

"I don't know how Clay feels about Dad," she said honestly. "He won't talk to me anymore. He resents me. I wanted to talk to you because I wanted you to understand the situation at home. I thought it might help if you knew something about his background."

He nibbled the doughnut with strong white teeth and swallowed it down with coffee. "You thought it might soften me, in other words." His dark eyes pinned hers. "I'm part Indian. There's no softness in me. Prejudice beat it out a long time ago."

"You're a little bit Irish, too," she said hesitantly. "And your people are well-to-do. Surely, that made it easier."

"Did it?" His smile was no smile at all. "I was unique, certainly. An oddity. The money made my path a little easier. It didn't remove the obstacles, or my uncle, who tolerated me because he was sterile and I was the last of the Kilpatricks. God, he hated that. To top it all off, my father never married my mother."

"Oh, you're..." she stopped dead and flushed.

"Illegitimate." He nodded and gave her a cold, mocking smile. "That's right." He stared at her, waiting, daring her to say something. When she didn't, he laughed mirthlessly. "No comment?"

"I wouldn't dare," she replied.

He finished his coffee. "We don't get to pick and choose, and that's a fact." He reached out a lean, dark hand devoid of jewelry and gently touched her thin face. "Make sure your brother gets that counseling. I'm sorry I jumped to conclusions about him."

The unexpected apology from such a man as Kilpatrick brought tears into her eyes. She turned her face away, ashamed to show weakness to him, of all people. But his re-action was immediate and a little shocking.

"Let's get out of here," he said curtly. He got her to her feet, purse and all, put the refuse in the appropriate container, and hustled her out of the coffee shop and into one of the elevators standing open and empty.

He closed the doors and started it, then stopped it suddenly between floors. He jerked her completely into his arms, and held her there gently but firmly. "Let go," he said gruffly at her temple. "You've been holding it in ever since the boy was arrested. Let it go. I'll hold you while you cry."

Sympathy was something she'd had very little of in her life. There had never been arms to hold her, to comfort her. She'd always done the holding, the giving. Not even her grandfather had realized just how vulnerable she was. But Kilpatrick saw through her mask, as if she wasn't even wearing one.

Tears tumbled from her eyes, down her cheeks, and she heard his deep voice, murmuring soft words of comfort while his hands smoothed her hair, his arm cradled her against his huge chest. She clung to the lapels of his coat, thinking how odd it was that she should find compassion in such an unlikely place.

He was warm and strong, and it was so nice for once to let someone else take the burden, to be helpless and feminine. She let her body relax into his, let him take her weight, and an odd sensation swept through her. She felt as if her blood had coals of fire in it. Something uncoiled deep in her stomach and stretched, and she felt a tightening in herself that had nothing to do with muscles.

Because it shocked her that she should feel such a sudden and unwanted attraction to this man, she lifted her head and started to move away. But his dark eyes were above hers when she looked up, and he didn't look away.

Electricity burned between them for one long, exquisite second. She felt as if it had knocked the breath out of her, but if he felt anything similar, it didn't show in that poker face.

But, in fact, he was shaken, too. The look in her eyes was familiar to him, but it was a new look for her and he knew it. If ever a woman's innocence could be seen, hers could. She intrigued him, excited him. Odd, when she was so totally different from the hard, sophisticated women he preferred. She was vulnerable and feminine despite her strength. He wanted to take her long hair down and open her blouse and show her how it felt to be a woman in his arms. And that thought was what made him put her gently but firmly away.

"Are you all right now?" he asked quietly.

"Yes. I'm...I'm sorry," she said unsteadily. She felt his lean hands pushing her from him, and it was like being cut apart suddenly. She wanted to cling. Perhaps it was the novelty, she tried to tell herself. She pushed back the wisps of hair that had escaped her bun, noticing the faint dark stains of his tan overcoat. "I've left spots on your coat."

"They'll dry. Here." He pressed a handkerchief into her hands and watched her dry her eyes. He found himself admiring her strength of will, her courage. She had taken on more responsibility than most men ever would, and was bearing up under it with enormous success.

Her face came up finally, and her red eyes searched his broad face. "Thank you."

He shrugged. "You're welcome."

She managed a watery smile. "Shouldn't we start the elevator up again?"

"I guess so. They'll think it's broken and send repair crews along." He snapped his wrist up and looked at the thin gold watch buried in thick hair over deeply tanned skin. "And I've got court in an hour." He started the elevator up, preoccupied now.

"I'll bet you're terrible across a courtroom," she murmured.

"I get by." He stopped the elevator at the sixth floor, his eyes faintly kind as he studied her. "Don't brood. You'll make wrinkles."

"On my face, who'd notice?" She sighed. "Thanks again. Have a nice day."

"I'll manage." He pushed the "up" button and was lifting the cigar to his mouth again when the doors swallowed him up. Becky turned and went down the hall in a daze. It was unreal that Kilpatrick had said something nice to her. Perhaps she was still asleep and dreaming it.

And she wasn't the only one feeling that way. She wore on Kilpatrick all day. He went to court and had to forcibly put her from his mind. God knew how she'd managed to get under his skin so easily. He was thirty-five years old and one bad experience with a woman had encapsulated him in solid ice. His women came and went, but his heart was impregnable, until this plain little spinster with her pale freckled face and wounded hazel eyes had started fencing with him verbally in the elevator. He'd actually come to look forward to their matches, enjoying the way she faintly teased him, the pert way she walked, and the light in her eyes when she laughed.

Amazing that she still could laugh, with the responsibility she carried. She fascinated him. He remembered the feel of her body in his arms while she cried, and a tautness stirred limbs that had banished feeling. Or so he thought.

The one thing he was certain of was that she wouldn't be a tease. She had a basic honesty and depth of compassion that would prevent her from deliberately trying to kill a man's pride. He scowled, remembering how Francine had created feverish hungers in his body and then laughed as she withheld herself, and taunted him for his weakness. The rumor was that she'd run away to South America with their law clerk, reneging on their engagement. The truth was that he'd found her in bed with one of her girlfriends, and that was when he had understood her pleasure in tormenting him. She had even admitted that she hated the whole male sex. She wouldn't have him under any conditions, she'd said. She was only playing him along, enjoying his pain.

He hadn't known such women existed. Thank God he hadn't loved her, or the experience might have killed his heart. At any rate, it kept him aloof from women. His pride was lacerated by what she'd done to him. He couldn't afford to lose control like that again, to want a woman to the point of madness.

On the other hand, that Cullen woman was giving him fits! He only realized how blackly he was scowling when the witness he was cross-examining began to blurt out details he hadn't even asked for. The poor man had thought the scowl was meant for him, and he wasn't taking any chances. Kilpatrick interrupted his monologue and asked the questions he needed the answers to before he went back to his seat. The black defense attorney, one J. Lincoln Davis, was laughing helplessly behind some papers. He was older than Kilpatrick—a big man with café au lait skin, dark eyes, and a ready wit. He was one of Curry Station's richest attorneys, and arguably the best around. He was the only adversary Kilpatrick had been beaten by in recent years.

"Where were you in court?" Davis asked him in a whisper after the jury had retired. "God, you had that poor man tied in knots, and he was your own witness!"

Kilpatrick smiled faintly as he gathered his material into his attaché case. "I drifted off," he murmured.

"That's a first. We ought to hang a plaque or something. See you tomorrow."

He nodded absently. For the first time, he'd lost his concentration in court. And all because of a skinny secretary with a mane of tawny hair.

He should be thinking about her brother. He'd had a long talk with his investigator at lunch, and there were some solid rumors that a drug-related hit was about to go down. Kilpatrick was working on a case involving crack peddling. He had two witnesses, and his first thought was that they might be the targets. The investigator had said that he was fairly certain Clay Cullen was involved somehow with the dealers because of his friendship with the Harrises. If the boy had that much crack on him, was it possible that he was starting to deal it?

Having to prosecute the boy wouldn't really bother him, but he thought of Rebecca and that did. How would she react to having her brother in jail and knowing that Kilpatrick had put him there? He had to stop thinking like that. Prosecuting criminals was his job. He couldn't let personal feelings get in the way. He only had a few months to go as district attorney. He had to make them count.

He went back to his office deep in thought. Would the drug dealers risk obvious murder to keep their territory intact? If they started blowing up people in his district, it was going to fall to him to get the goods on the perpetrators and send them away. He scowled, hoping that Rebecca Cullen's brother wasn't going to wind up back in his office as part of that fight over drug territory.

Rebecca was going through the motions of working herself. She typed mechanically, doing briefs on the electronic typewriter while Nettie fed precedents for another case into the computer. Nettie was a paralegal, qualified to do legwork for the attorneys as well as secretarial work. Becky envied her, but she couldn't afford the training that was required for paralegal status, even though it would have meant a salary increase.

She was worried about Granddad. His silence at breakfast had been disturbing. She phoned Mrs. White at lunch and asked the widowed lady to go over to the house and check on him. Mrs. White was always willing to look in on the old gentleman when she was needed. Besides that, she was a retired nurse, and Becky thanked her lucky stars for such a good neighbor.

If only Clay would straighten himself out, she thought. It was enough work trying to raise the boys without having to get them out of jail. Mack adored his older brother. If Clay kept it up, it might be only a matter of time before Mack emulated him.

It was quitting time almost before she realized it. She'd had a busy day, and had been grateful for it. Slow days gave her too much time to think.

She gathered up her purse and worn gray jacket and said her good-byes. The elevator would be full at this time of day, she thought, her heartbeat increasing as she went down the hall. Probably, Mr. Kilpatrick was still upstairs working, anyway.

But he wasn't. He was in the elevator when she got on it, and he smiled at her. She couldn't know that he'd timed it exactly, knowing when she got off and hoping that he'd encounter her. Amazing, he thought cynically, how ridiculously he was behaving because of this woman.

She smiled back, feeling her heart drop suddenly, and not from the motion of the elevator.

He got off with her on the ground floor and strode along beside her as if he had nothing better to do.

"Feeling better?" he asked as he held open the door for her on the way to the street.

"Yes, thank you," she said. She'd never felt so shy and speechless in all her life. She glanced up at him and blushed like a girl.

He liked that telltale sign. It made his spirits lift. "I lost a case today," he remarked absently. "The jurors thought I was deliberately badgering a witness and threw their decision in the defense's favor."

"Were you?"

"Badgering him?" His wide mouth pulled into a reluctant smile. "No. My mind was somewhere else and he got in the way."

She knew that black glare of his very well. She could certainly understand how a witness might feel under its pressure.

Her hands clutched her purse. "I'm sorry you lost your case."

He stopped on the sidewalk, towering over her, and looked down at her thoughtfully. He hesitated, wondering what kind of chain reaction he might start if he asked her out. He was crazy, he told himself shortly, to even contemplate such a thing. He couldn't afford to get involved in her life.

"How did your grandfather take the news?" he asked instead.

She was disappointed. She'd expected a different question, but it was probably just wishful thinking. Why would he want to take out someone like her? She knew she wasn't his type. Besides, her family would raise the roof—especially Granddad.

She managed a smile. "He took it on the chin," she said. "We're a tough lot, we Cullens."

"Make sure you know where that boy is for the next few days," he said suddenly. He took her arm and drew her to the wall, wary of passersby. "We've had a tip that something is going down in the city—a hit, maybe. We don't know who or when or how, but we're pretty sure it's drug-related. There are two factions fighting for dominance in the distribution sector. The Harris brothers are involved. If they tried to use your brother as a scapegoat, considering the trouble he's already in..." He left the rest unsaid.

She shivered. "It's like walking a tightrope," she said. "I don't mind looking out for my kin, but I never expected anything like drugs and murder." She shifted, wrapping her coat closer around her. Her eyes lifted to his, briefly vulnerable. It's so hard sometimes," she whispered.

His breath caught. She made him feel a foot taller when she looked at him that way. "Have you ever had a normal life?"

She smiled. "When I was a little girl, I guess. Not since Mother died. It's been me and Granddad and the boys."

"No social life, I guess."

"Something always came up—a virus, the mumps, chicken pox. Granddad's heart." She laughed softly. "There wasn't exactly a stampede to my door, anyway." She looked down at her handbag. "It isn't a bad life. I'm needed. I have a purpose. So many people don't."

He felt that way about his work—that it was necessary and fulfilled him. But with the exception of his German shepherd, he felt no real emotions except anger and indignation. No love. His whole work experience was based on moral justice, protection of the masses, and conviction of the guilty. A noble purpose, perhaps, but a lonely calling. And until recently, he hadn't realized how lonely.

"I suppose," he murmured absently. His eyes were on her soft mouth. It was a perfect bow, palest pink, with a delicate look that made him ache to feel it under his mouth.

She glanced up, puzzled by his frank stare. "Is it my freckles?" she blurted out.

His thick eyebrows lifted and he met her gaze with a smile. "What?"

"You seemed to be brooding," she murmured. "I thought maybe my freckles made you uncomfortable. I shouldn't have them, but there's just a hint of red in my hair. My grandmother was a flaming redhead."

"Do you take after your parents?"

"My father is blond," she said, "and hazel-eyed. We look a lot alike. My mother was small and dark, and none of us favored her."

"I like freckles," he said, catching her off guard. He checked his watch. "I've got to get home. The Atlanta Symphony is doing Stravinsky tonight. I don't want to miss it."

"The *Firebird?*" Becky asked.

He smiled. "Yes, as a matter of fact. Most people hate it."

"I love it," she said. "I've got two recordings of it—one avant garde and one traditional. I have to listen to it with earphones. My grandfather likes old Hank Williams records and both my brothers are into hard rock. I'm a throwback."

"Do you like opera?"

"*Madame Butterfly* and *Turandot* and *Carmen*." She sighed. "And I love to listen to Placido Domingo and Luciano Pavarotti."

"I saw *Turandot* at the Met last year," he remarked. His dark eyes searched her face warmly. "Do you watch those specials on public television?"

"When I can get the television to myself," she said. "We only have one, and it's small."

"They made a movie of *Carmen* with Domingo," he said. "I've got it."

"Is it good?"

"If you like opera, it's great." He searched her eyes slowly, wondering why it was so difficult to stop talking and say good night. She was pretty in a shy kind of way, and she made his blood sing in his veins.

She stared back at him, weak in the knees. This happened so quickly, she thought, and even as she was thinking it her mind was denying her the chance of any kind of relationship with him. He was the enemy. Now, of all times, she couldn't afford weakness. She had to remember that Kilpatrick was out to get her brother. It would be disloyal to her family to let anything happen. But her heart was fighting that logic. She was alone and lonely, and she'd sacrificed the best part of her youth for her family. Did she deserve nothing for herself?

"Deep thoughts?" he asked softly, watching the expressions cross her face.

"Deep and dark," she replied. Her lips parted on unsteady breaths. He was looking at her just as she imagined a man might look at a woman he wanted. It thrilled her, excited her, and scared her to death.

He saw the fear first. He felt it, too. He didn't want involvement any more than she did, and now was the time to cut this off.

He straightened. "I've got to go," he said. "Keep an eye on your brother."

"I will. Thanks for warning me," she said.

He shrugged. He pulled out a cigar and lit it as he walked away, his broad back as impenetrable as a wall.

Becky wondered why he'd bothered to stop and talk to her. Could he really be interested in a woman like her?

She caught a glimpse of herself in a window as she walked toward the underground garage where her car was kept. Oh, sure, she thought, seeing the thin, wan-looking face that stared back at her. She was just the kind of woman who would attract such a devastatingly handsome man. She rolled her eyes and went on to her car, putting her hopeless daydreams behind her.

CHAPTER FOUR

It was a beautiful spring morning. Kilpatrick stared out the window of his elegant brick home on one of the quieter streets of Curry Station, feeling a little guilty about spending a Saturday morning in his house, instead of at the office. But Gus needed some exercise and Kilpatrick had just shaken a bad headache. No wonder, because he'd had a late night going over briefs for upcoming trials.

Gus barked. Kilpatrick reached down to ruffle the big German shepherd's silver-and-black fur.

"Impatient, are you?" he asked. "We'll walk. Let me get dressed."

He was in jeans and barefoot, his hair-covered chest and stomach bare. He'd just finished a Diet Coke and a stale doughnut for breakfast. Sometimes he wished he'd kept Matilda on, instead of giving his former housekeeper notice when she'd started leaking news out of his office to the press. She was the best cook and the worst gossip he'd ever known.

The house was very quiet without her, and his own cooking was going to kill him one day.

He slipped on a white sweatshirt, socks and his sneakers, and ran a comb through his thick black hair. He stared at the reflection in the mirror with a raised eyebrow. No Mr. America there, he thought, but the body was holding its own. Not that it did him much good. Women were a luxury these days, with his job taking up every waking hour. He thought about Rebecca Cullen suddenly, and tried to picture her in his bed. Ridiculous. In the first place, she was almost certainly a virgin, and in the second, her family would come between her and any potential suitor. They had every reason not to want him around, too. No, she was off-limits. He was going to have to keep telling himself that.

He looked around at his elegant surroundings with a faint smile, thinking how odd it was that the illegitimate son of a socially prominent businessman and a Cherokee Indian woman should wind up with a house like this. Only someone as gutsy as his uncle, Sanderson Kilpatrick, would have had the nerve to push Rourke out into society and dare it to reject him.

Uncle Sanderson. He laughed in spite of himself. No one looking at the portrait over the fireplace of that staid, dignified old man would ever suspect him of having an outrageous sense of humor or a heart of pure marshmallow. But he'd taught Rourke everything he knew about being wanted and loved. His parents' death had been traumatic for him. His childhood had been a kind of nightmare—school, especially. But his uncle had stood behind him, forced him to accept his heritage and be proud of it. He'd taught him a lot about courage and determination and honor. Uncle Sanderson was a judge's judge, a shining example of the very best of the legal profession. It was his example that had sent Rourke to law school, and then catapulted him into the public eye as district attorney. Get out there and do some good, Uncle Sanderson had said. Money isn't everything. Criminals are taking over. Do a job that needs doing.

Well, he was doing it. He hadn't liked being a public figure, and the campaign after he'd served one year of his predecessor's unexpired term had been hell. But he'd won, to his amazement, and he liked to think that since then he'd taken some of the worst criminals off the street. His pet peeve was drug trafficking, and he was meticulous in his preparation of a case. There were no loopholes in Kilpatrick's briefs. His uncle had taught him the necessity of adequate preparation. He'd never forgotten, to the dismay of several haphazard public defenders and high-powered defense attorneys.

Uncle Sanderson had shocked Rourke by cultivating in him a sense of pride in his Cherokee ancestry. He'd made sure that Rourke never tried to hide it or disguise it. He'd pushed Rourke out into Atlanta society, and he'd discovered that most people found him interesting rather than an embarrassment. Not that it would have mattered either way. He had enough of Uncle Sanderson's spunk not to take insults from anyone. He was good with his fists, and he'd used them a few times over the years.

As he grew older, he began to understand the proud old man a lot better. Sanderson Kilpatrick's Irish grandfather had come to America penniless and his life had been one long series of disasters and tragedies. It had been the first-generation American, Tad, who'd opened the small specialty store that had become the beginning of the Kilpatrick convenience store chain. Sanderson had been one of only two surviving Kilpatrick children.

And then Sanderson had learned that he was sterile. It had been a killing blow to his pride. But at least his brother's only son had produced an heir—Rourke. The convenience store chain had slowly gone bankrupt. Uncle Sanderson had squirreled enough away to leave Rourke well-fixed, but the Kilpatrick name and generations of respect were about the sum total of his inheritance. And since Rourke was close-mouthed, that family secret didn't get much airing. He made a comfortable living and he knew how to invest it, but he was no millionaire. Uncle Sanderson's Mercedes-Benz and the elegant old family brick mansion, both unencumbered by debt, were the only holdovers from a more prosperous past.

Gus barked just before the doorbell rang. "Okay, hold your horses," he said as he returned to the living room, his bare feet landing silently on the luxurious beige carpet.

Kilpatrick opened the front door to Dan Berry, who grinned at him through the screen. "Hi, boss," his investigator said cheerily, flashing him a smile. "Got a minute?"

"Sure. Let me get Gus's lead and we'll walk and talk." He glanced at the heavyset man. "A little exercise wouldn't hurt you."

Dan made a face. "I was afraid you'd say that. How's the headache?"

"Better. Aspirin and cold compresses got rid of it." He attached Gus to the lead and opened the door. Early mornings in the spring were cool, and Dan shivered. The trees still sported bare limbs that would be elegant bouquets of blossoms only a month or so from now.

Kilpatrick moved out to the sidewalk, letting Gus take the lead. "What's up?" he asked when they were halfway down the block.

"Plenty. The sheriff's office got a complaint this morning about Curry Station Elementary. One of the kids' mothers called to report it. Her son saw one of the marijuana dealers having an argument with Bubba Harris at recess. It's just been marijuana, so far—until now."

Kilpatrick stopped dead, his dark eyes intent. "Are the Harrises trying to cut in on that territory with crack?"

"We think so," Berry replied. "We don't have anything, yet. But I'm going to work on some of the students and see what I can turn up. We're organizing a locker search with the help of the local police, too. If we find crack, we'll know who's involved."

"That will go over big with the parents," he murmured.

"Yes, I know. But we'll muddle through." He glanced at Kilpatrick as they began to walk again. "That Cullen boy was seen with Son Harris at one of the dives in midtown Atlanta. They're real thick."

Kilpatrick's face stiffened. "So I've heard."

"I know you didn't have enough evidence to go to trial," Berry said. "But if I were you, I'd keep a close eye on that boy. He could lead us right to the Harrises, if we play our cards right."

Kilpatrick was thinking about that. His dark eyes narrowed. If he got close to Becky, he could keep Clay Cullen in sight with ease. Was that it, he wondered, or was he rationalizing ways to see Becky? He had to think this through carefully before he made a decision.

"There's another complication, too," Berry went on, his hands in his pockets as he glanced up at Kilpatrick. "Your sparring partner's getting ready to announce."

"Davis?" he asked, because he'd heard rumors, too. Davis hadn't said anything in court to him about it. That was like the big man, to pull rabbits out of hats at the most unexpected time. He grinned. "He'll win, unless I miss my guess. There are plenty of contenders for my job, but Davis is pure shark."

"He'll be after your professional throat."

"Only to make news," Kilpatrick assured him. "I haven't decided yet about running for a third term." He stretched and yawned. "Let him do his worst. I don't give a damn."

"Want to round off your day?" Berry murmured with a dry glance. "One last tidbit of gossip. They're releasing Harvey Blair on Monday."

"Blair." He scowled. "Yes, I remember. I sent him up for armed robbery six years ago. What the hell's he doing out?"

"His lawyer got him a full pardon from the governor." He held up his hand. "Don't blame me. I don't hide your mail. Your secretary is guilty as hell. She told me she forgot to mention it and you were too busy in court to read it."

He bit off a curse. "Blair. Dammit. If ever a man deserved a pardon less...he was guilty as hell!"

"Of course he was." Berry stopped walking, looking uncomfortable. "He threatened to kill you if he ever got out. You might keep your doors locked, just in case."

"I'm not afraid of Blair," Kilpatrick said, and his eyes narrowed. "Let him try, if he feels lucky. He won't be the first."

That was a fact. The D.A. had been the target of assassins twice, once from a gun by an angry defendant who'd been convicted by Kilpatrick's expertise, and another time from a crazed defendant with a knife, right in court. Nobody present in the courtroom that day would ever forget the way Kilpatrick had met the knife attack. He had effortlessly parried the thrust and thrown his attacker over a table. Kilpatrick was ex-Special Forces, and as tough as they came. Berry secretly thought that his Indian ancestry didn't hurt, either. Indians were formidable fighters. It was in the blood.

Kilpatrick waved Dan off and he and Gus continued on their daily one-mile walk. He was fit enough, physically. He worked out at the gym weekly and played racquetball. The walk was more for Gus's sake than his own. Gus was ten years old and he had a sedentary lifestyle. With Kilpatrick away at the office six days out of seven—and occasionally, when the calendar was loaded in court, seven out of seven— he didn't get a lot of exercise in his fenced-in enclosure out back.

He thought about what Dan had told him and grimaced. Blair was going to be back on the streets and gunning for him. That wasn't surprising. Neither was the information about the Harris boys. A war over drug turf was just what he needed right now, with the Cullen boy in the middle. He remembered Cullen's father—a surly, uncooperative man with cold eyes. Incredible, that he could have fathered a woman like Rebecca, with her warm heart and soft eyes. Even more incredible that he could have deserted her like that. He shook his dark head. One way or another, her life stood to get worse before it got better—especially with a brother like hers. He tugged at Gus's lead and they turned back toward home.

IT WAS MIDNIGHT on Sunday, and Clay Cullen still wasn't home. He and the Harris boys were talking money, big money, and he was in the clouds over how much he was going to make.

"It's easy," Son told him carelessly. "All you have to do is give a little away to some of the wealthier kids. They'll get a taste of it and then they'll pay anything for it. Simple."

"Yeah, but how do I find the right ones? How do I pick kids who won't turn me in?" Clay asked.

"You've got a kid brother in school at Curry Station Elementary. Ask him. We might even give him a cut," Son said, grinning.

Clay felt uneasy about that, but he didn't say so. The thought of all that easy money made him giddy. Francine had started paying attention to him since he'd become friendly with her cousins the Harrises. Francine, with her pretty black hair and sultry blue eyes, who could have her pick of the seniors. Clay liked her a lot—enough to do anything to get her to notice him. Drugs weren't that bad, he told himself. After all, people who used would get the stuff from somebody else if not from him. If only he didn't feel so guilty....

"I'll ask Mack tomorrow," Clay promised.

Son's small eyes narrowed. "Just one thing. Make sure your sister doesn't find out. She works for a bunch of lawyers, and the D.A.'s in the same building."

"Becky won't find out," Clay assured him.

"Okay. See you tomorrow."

Clay got out of the car. He'd kept his nose clean tonight so Becky wouldn't get suspicious. He had to keep her in the dark. That shouldn't be too hard, he reasoned. She loved him. That made her vulnerable.

The next morning, while Becky was upstairs dressing for work, Clay cornered Mack.

"You want to make some spending money?" he asked the younger boy with a calculating look.

"How?" Mack asked.

"Any of your friends do drugs?" Clay asked.

Mack hesitated. "Not really."

"Oh." Clay wondered if he should pursue it, but he heard Becky's footsteps and clammed up. "We'll talk about it some other time. Don't mention this to Becky."

Becky came in to find Mack glum and quiet and Clay looking nervous. She'd put on her blue jersey dress and her one pair of black patent leather high heels. She didn't have a lot of clothes, but nobody at work mentioned that. They were a kind bunch of people, and she was neat and clean, even if she didn't have the clothing budget that Maggie and Tess had.

She touched her tidy bun and finished fixing Mack's lunch just in time to get him on the bus, frowning a little when Clay didn't join him.

"How are you getting to school?" she asked Clay.

"Francine's coming for me," he said carelessly. "She drives a Corvette. Neat car—brand-new."

She stared at him suspiciously. "Are you staying away from those Harris boys like I told you to?" she asked.

"Of course," he replied innocently. Much easier to lie than to have a fight. Besides, she never seemed to know when he was lying.

She relaxed a little, even if she wasn't wholly trusting of him these days. "And the counseling sessions?"

He glared at her. "I don't need counseling."

"I don't care if you *think* you need it or not," she said firmly. "Kilpatrick says you have to go."

He shifted uncomfortably. "Okay," he said angrily. "I've got an appointment tomorrow with the psychologist. I'll go."

She sighed. "Good. That's good, Clay."

He narrowed his eyes and stared at her. "Just don't throw any orders around, Becky. I'm a man, not a boy you can tell what to do."

Before she could flare up at him, he went out the door in time to see the Corvette roar up. He got into it quickly and it sped off into the distance.

A few days later, Becky called the principal of Clay's school to make sure he had been going. She was told that he had perfect attendance. He kept the counseling session, too, although Becky didn't know that he ignored his psychologist's advice. It had been three weeks since his arrest and he was apparently toeing the line. Thank God. She settled grandpa and went to work, her thoughts full of Kilpatrick.

She hadn't run into him in the elevator lately. She wondered if he might have moved back to the courthouse until she glimpsed him at a dead run when she was on her way to lunch. Curious the way he moved, she thought wistfully, light on his feet and graceful as well. She loved to watch him move.

Kilpatrick was unaware of her studied scrutiny as he retrieved the blue Mercedes from the parking lot and drove himself to the garage that the elder Harris, C.T. by name, ran as a front for his drug operation. Everybody knew it, but proving it was the thing.

Harris was sixty, balding, and he had a beer belly. He never shaved. He had deep circles under his eyes and a big, perpetually red nose. He glared at Kilpatrick as the younger, taller man climbed out of his car at the curb.

"The big man himself," Harris said with a surly grin. "Looking for something, prosecutor?"

"I wouldn't find it," Kilpatrick said. He paused in front of Harris and lit a cigar with slow, deliberate movements of his long fingers. "I've had my investigator checking out some rumors that I didn't like. What he came up with, I didn't like even more. So I thought I'd come and check it out personally."

"What kind of rumors?"

"That you and Morrely are squaring off for a fight over territory. And that you're moving on the kids at the local elementary school."

"Who, me? Garbage! It's garbage," Harris said with mock indignation. "I don't push to kids."

"No, you don't have to. Your sons do it for you." He blew out a cloud of smoke, aiming it into the man's face with cold intent. "So I came to tell you something. I'm watching the school, and I'm watching you. If one kid gets one spoon of coke, or one gram of crack, I'm going to nail you and your boys to the wall. Whatever it takes, whatever I have to do, I'll get you. I wanted you to get that message in person."

"Thanks for the warning, but you're talking to the wrong guy. I'm just not into drugs. I run a garage here. I work on cars." Harris peered past Kilpatrick to the Mercedes. "Nice job. I like foreign makes. I could fix it for you."

"It doesn't need fixing. But I'll keep you in mind," Kilpatrick said mockingly.

"You do that. Stop in any time."

"Count on it." Kilpatrick gave him a curt nod and climbed back into his car. Harris was glaring after him with a furious expression when he pulled out into traffic.

Later, Harris took his two sons aside. "Kilpatrick's getting to me," he said. "We can't afford any slip-ups. Are you sure that Cullen boy's dependable?"

"Sure he is!" Son said with a lazy grin. He was taller than his father, dark-haired and blue-eyed. Not a bad-looking boy, he outshone his chubby, red-faced younger brother.

"He's going to be expendable if the D.A. comes too close," the elder Harris said darkly. "Do you have a problem with that?"

"No problem," Son said easily. "That's why we let him get caught with his pockets full of crack. Even though they didn't hold him, they'll remember it. Next time we can put his neck in a noose if we need to."

"They can't use his record against him in juvenile court," the youngest Harris reminded them.

"Listen," the man told his sons. "If Kilpatrick gets his hands on that boy again, he'll try him as an adult. Bet on it. Just make sure the Cullen boy stays in your pockets. Meanwhile," he added thoughtfully, "I've got to get Kilpatrick out of mine. I think it might be worthwhile to float a contract, before he gets his teeth into us."

"Mike down at the Hayloft would know somebody," Son told his father with narrowed eyes.

"Good. Ask him. Do it tonight," he added. "Kilpatrick's term is up this year; he'll have to run. He may use us as an example to win the election."

"Cullen says he isn't going to run again," Son said.

The older Harris glared at him. "Everybody says that. I don't buy it. How about the grammar school operation?"

"I've got it in the bag," Son assured him. "We're lining up Cullen for that. He's got a younger brother who goes there."

"But will the younger brother go along?"

Son looked up. "I've got an angle on that. We're going to let Cullen go on a buy with us, so that the supplier gets a good look at him. After that, he's mine."

"Nice work," the older man said, smiling. "You two could swear he was the brains of the outfit, and Kilpatrick would buy it. Get going, then."

"Sure thing, Dad."

ONE AFTERNOON Becky noticed Clay talking earnestly to Mack as she walked in after work. Mack said something explosive and stomped off. Clay glanced at her and looked uncomfortable.

She wondered what it was all about. Probably another quarrel. The boys never seemed to get along these days. She started a load of clothes in the washing machine and cooked supper. In between, she daydreamed about the district attorney and wished that she was pretty and vivacious and rich.

"Got to go to the library, Becky!" Clay called on his way out the front door.

"Is it open this late...?" she began, but there was the slam of one door, then another, then a car roared away.

She ran to the window. *The Harris boys,* she thought, furious. He'd been told to stay away from them. Mr. Brady had warned him; so had she. But how could she keep Clay away unless she tied him up? She couldn't tell Granddad. He'd had a bad day and had gone to bed early. If only she had someone to talk to!

Mack was doing his math homework at the kitchen table without an argument, strangely silent and uneasy.

"Anything I can help you with?" she asked, pausing beside him.

He looked up and then away, a little too quickly. "No. Just something Clay asked me to do and I said no." He twirled his pencil. "Becky, if you know something bad's going to happen, and you don't tell anybody, does that make you guilty, too?"

"Such as?"

"Oh, I didn't have anything in mind, really," Mack said evasively.

Becky hesitated. "Well, if you know something wrong is being done, you should tell. I don't believe in being a tattletale, but something dangerous should be reported."

"I guess you're right." He went back to work, leaving Becky no wiser than before.

Clay went with the Harris boys to pick up their load of crack. In the past three weeks, he'd learned plenty about how to find customers for the Harrises. He knew the kids who were hassled at home, who were having trouble with schoolwork, who were mad for anything outside the law. He'd already made a sale or two and the money was incredible, even with a small commission. For the first time, he had money to flash and Francine was all over him. He'd bought himself a few new things, like some designer shirts and jeans. He was careful to keep them in his locker at school so that Becky wouldn't know. Now he wanted a car. He just wasn't sure how to keep Becky in the dark. Probably he could leave it with the Harris boys. Sure, that was a good move. Or with Francine.

He was still seething about Mack. He'd asked him to help him find customers at the elementary school, but Mack had gotten furious and told him he'd do no such thing! He threatened to tell Becky, too, but Clay had dared him. He knew things about Mack that he could tell—like about those girlie magazines Mack hid in his closet, and the butterfly knife he'd traded for at school that Becky didn't know he had. Mack had backed down, but he'd gone off mad, and Clay was a little nervous. He didn't think his brother would tell on him, but you never knew with kids.

They were at the pickup point, a deserted little diner out in the boonies, with two suppliers in a four-wheel drive jeep. The Harris boys were acting odd, he thought, noticing the way their eyes shifted. They'd left the motor running in the car, too. Clay wondered if he was getting spooked.

"You go ahead with the money," Son told Clay, patting him on the back. "Nothing to worry about. We're always careful, just in case the law makes a try for us, but we're in the clear tonight. Just walk down there and pass the money."

Clay hesitated. Up until now, it had just been little amounts of coke. This would label him as a buyer and a dealer, and he could go up for years if he was caught. For a moment he panicked, trying to imagine how that would affect Becky and Granddad. Then he got himself under control and lifted the duffel bag containing the money. He wouldn't get caught. The Harris boys knew their way around. It would be all right. And this supplier wouldn't be too anxious to finger him, either, because Clay could return the favor.

By the time he got to the black-clad figure in the trendy sports coat, standing beside a high-class Mercedes-Benz, he was almost swaggering with confidence. He didn't say two words to the supplier. He handed over the money, it was checked, and the coke, in another satchel, was given to him. He'd seen dealers on TV shows test the stuff, but apparently in real life the quality was assured. The Harris boys didn't seem bothered at all. Clay took the goods, nodded at the dealer, and walked back to where Son and his brother were waiting, his heart going like a drum, his breath almost gasping out of his throat. It was an incredible high, just overcoming his own fear and doing something dangerous for a change. His eyes sparkled as he reached the car.

"Okay." Son grinned. He took Clay by the shoulders and shook him. "Good man! Now you're one of us."

"I am?" Clay asked, hesitating.

"Sure. You're a dealer, just like us. And if you don't cooperate, Bubba and I will swear that you're the brains of the outfit and that you set up this deal."

"The supplier knows better," Clay argued.

Son laughed. "He isn't a supplier," he said, studying his

nails. "He's one of Dad's flunkies. Why do you think we didn't test the stuff before you handed over the money?"

"If he's just one of your father's men…" Clay was trying to think it through.

"There was a surveillance unit across the street," Son said easily. "They made you. They couldn't pick you up because there wasn't enough time to get a backup and they knew you'd run. But they've got a tape, and probably audio, and all they need is testimony from eyewitnesses to have an airtight case against you. You bought cocaine—a lot of cocaine. Dad's flunky won't mind doing the time, either, for what he'll get paid. We can always buy him out later. You won't get the same consideration, of course."

Clay stiffened. "I thought you trusted me!"

"Just some insurance, pal," Son assured him. "We want your little brother to do some scouting for us at the elementary school. If he cooperates, you don't do time."

"Mack said no. He already said no!" He was beginning to feel hysterical.

"Then you'd better make him change his mind, hadn't you?" Son said, and his small eyes narrowed dangerously. "Or you're going to end up in stir for a long, long time."

And just that easily, they had him. He couldn't know that the so-called surveillance people were just friends of the Harrises, not heat. Or that Francine was being persuaded to be nice to him to help keep him on the string. Yes, they had the poor fish doubly hooked, and he didn't even know how caught he really was. Yet.

CHAPTER FIVE

Becky was trying to balance making photocopies for Maggie with typing a desperately needed brief for Nettie, one of the paralegals, and going out of her mind in the process. It had been a rough few days. Clay had been more belligerent than ever—withdrawn, moody, and openly antagonistic. Mack had been withdrawn, too, avoiding his brother and refusing to tell his sister why. It was worse than an armed camp. Granddad was living on her nerves. Becky was, too. She came to work vibrating, wishing she could just climb in the car, drive away, and never look back.

"Can't you hurry, Becky?" Nettie begged. "I've got to be in court at one, and it's a forty-five-minute drive in lunch-hour traffic! I won't get to eat as it is!"

"I'm hurrying—really, I am," Becky assured her, frowning as she tried to make her fingers work even faster.

"I'll do my own copies," Maggie said, patting Becky's shoulder as she walked by. "Just calm down, darlin'. You're doing fine."

The sympathy almost brought tears to Becky's eyes. Maggie was such a love. Becky gritted her teeth and put everything she had into it, finishing in good time to get Nettie off to court.

"Thanks!" Nettie called from the door, and grinned. "I owe you lunch one day!"

Becky just nodded, and paused to catch her breath.

"You look terrible," Maggie noted as she passed by on her way back from the copying room. "What's wrong? Want to talk?"

"It wouldn't do any good," Becky said with a gentle smile. "But thanks just the same. And thanks for doing those."

Maggie held up the copies. "No problem. Don't try to take on too much at one time, will you?" she added seriously. "You're the junior here and that puts you in a bad position sometimes. Don't be afraid to say no when you can't make a deadline. You'll live longer."

"Look who's talking," Becky chided gently. "Aren't you the one who always volunteers for every charity project the firm takes on?"

Maggie shrugged. "So I don't listen to my own advice." She checked her watch. "It's almost twelve. Go to lunch. I'll take second shift today. You need a break," she added with a worried glance at Becky's thin figure in the plain pink shirtwaist dress, her hair all over her face and shoulders, her makeup long gone. "And tidy up first, darlin'. You look like something the cat dragged in."

"I look like a little green snake?" Becky asked, aghast.

Maggie stared. "I beg your pardon?"

"Well, snakes are all MY cat ever brings in." She looked down at herself. "I can see me as a giant pink mushroom, maybe. A little green snake? Never!"

"Get out of here," Maggie muttered.

Becky laughed. Maggie was like a tonic. Pity she couldn't bottle her and take her home at night. Home was a worse ordeal than work had ever been, and she knew she was losing ground.

She went downstairs to the cafeteria around the corner, surprised to find herself in line with the county district attorney, Kilpatrick himself.

"Hello, Counselor," she said, trying not to sound as shell-shocked as she felt. He was just dynamite at close quarters, especially in that watered gray suit that emphasized his broad shoulders and dark complexion.

"Hello, yourself," he mused, glancing at her with faint interest. "Where have you been hiding? The elevator is beginning to bore me."

She looked up at him with raised brows. "Do tell? Why not try the staircase and see if you can smoke the janitors out of hiding?"

He chuckled. He wasn't smoking one of those hideous cigars, but she was sure he had one tucked away.

"I've already smoked him out of hiding," he confessed. "Caught the trash can on fire this morning. Didn't you hear the fire alarm go off?"

She had, but Maggie had checked and it was a false alarm. "You're kidding," she said, not sure how to take him.

"No joke. I was on the phone and not paying too much attention to where the ashtray was. A mistake I won't make twice," he added. "My secretary had the fire chief make a personal call and give me some literature on fire safety." He pursed his lips and his dark eyes sparkled. "She wouldn't be a relative of yours, by any chance?"

She laughed. "I don't think so, but she sounds like my kind of secretary."

He shook his head. "You women. A man isn't safe." He glanced ahead at the long line with resignation and flipped his wrist to check his watch. "I had two hours when I started, but I had to have my notes typed and pick up another brief before I could get time for lunch." He shook his head. "Having my office halfway across town from the courthouse isn't working out too well."

"Think of the exercise you're getting," she said. "That has to be a fringe benefit."

"It would be, if I needed to lose weight." He studied her slender body. "You've lost some. How's your brother?" he asked pointedly.

She felt nervous when he looked at her like that. She wondered if he had microscopic vision, because he certainly seemed to see beneath the skin. "He's all right."

"I hope he's keeping his nose clean," he said evenly. "The Harris boys are up to their collective necks in trouble. Running with them could get him into a scrape you won't be able to talk him out of."

She looked up. "Would you send him to prison?"

"If he breaks the law," he said. "I'm a public servant. The taxpayers expect me to earn the salary I'm paid. Somebody must have told you how I feel about drug pushers."

"My brother isn't one, Mr. Kilpatrick," she said earnestly. "He's a good boy. He's just fallen in with a bad crowd."

"That's all it takes, you know. The jails are full of good boys who played follow the leader one time too many." His eyes narrowed. "Do you remember I told you that something big was going down? Maybe a hit? Don't forget it. Keep your brother at home nights."

"How?" she asked, spreading her hands. "He's bigger than I am and I can't even talk to him anymore." She drew a hand over her eyes. "Mr. Kilpatrick, I'm so tired of holding up the world," she said, half under her breath.

He took her arm. "Come on."

He drew her out of line, to her astonishment, and right out the door.

"My lunch," she protested.

"To hell with this. We'll eat at a Crystal."

She'd never set foot in a Mercedes-Benz in her life until then. It had real leather seats, gray ones, with a headrest and plush comfort. It even smelled like real leather. The dash had wood panels, and they were probably real, too. The car had a polished metallic blue finish, and she caught her breath at the beauty of the carpeted interior.

"You look shocked," he murmured as he started it.

"The engine really purrs, doesn't it?" she asked as she fastened her seat belt automatically. "And I guess the seats are real leather? Is it automatic?"

He smiled indulgently. "Yes, yes, and yes. What do you drive?"

"A renovated Sherman tank—at least, that's what it feels

like early on a cold morning." She smiled across at him. "You don't have to take me out to lunch. I'll make you late."

"No, you won't. I've got time. Is your brother a pusher, Rebecca?"

She gaped. "No!"

He glanced at her as he eased into the turning lane. "Fair enough. Try to keep him out of it. I've got my sights on the Harris family. I'm going to nail them before I get out of office, no matter what it takes. Drugs on the street, that's one thing. Drugs in grammar school—not in my county."

"You can't be serious!" she exclaimed. "In midtown, maybe, but not in Curry Station Elementary!"

"We found crack," he said, "in a student's locker. He was ten years old and a pusher." He looked across at her, scowling. "My God, you can't be that naive. Don't you know that hundreds of grammar school kids are sent to jail every year for pushing narcotics, or that one kid out of every four has addicted parents in Georgia?"

"I didn't," she confessed. She leaned her head against the window. "Whatever happened to kids going to school and playing with frogs and having spelling bees and sock hops?"

"Wrong generation. This one can dissect a bee and the hops are in the beer they drink. They still go to school, of course, where they learn subjects in grammar school that I didn't get until I was in high school. Accelerated learning, Miss Cullen. We want our kids to be adults early so that we won't have the bother of childhood traumas. We're producing miniature adults, and the latchkey kids are at the top of the class."

"Mothers have to work," she began.

"So they do. Over fifty percent of them are out there in

the work force, while their kids are split up and locked up and divided into stepfamilies." He lit a cigar without asking if she minded. He knew that she did. "Women won't have total equality until men can get pregnant."

She grinned. "You'd have one horrible delivery, I imagine."

He chuckled softly. "No doubt, and with my luck, it would be a breech birth." He shook his head. "It's been a rotten day. I've been prosecuting two juveniles as adults this week and I'm bitter. I want more parents who care about their damned kids. It's my favorite theme."

"You don't have any children, I guess?" she asked shyly.

He pulled into a Crystal hamburger place and parked. "No. I'm old-fashioned. I think kids come after marriage." He opened his door and got out, helping her out before he locked it. "Feel like a hamburger or chili?"

"Chili," she said instantly. "With Tabasco sauce on the side."

"You're one of those, are you?" he mused, his dark eyes teasing.

"One of those what?" she asked.

He let his hands slide down to enfold hers, and she caught her breath audibly. He paused at the door and looked down again, catching the shocked delight that registered on her soft oval face, in her hazel eyes with their flecks of gold. She looked as surprised as he felt at the contact that ran like electricity through his hand, into his body, tautening it with unexpected pleasure.

"Soft hands," he remarked, frowning slightly. "Calloused fingers. What do you do at home?"

"Wash, cook, clean, garden," she said. "They're working hands."

He lifted them and turned them in his lean, warm ones, studying the long, elegant fingers with their short, unpolished nails. They looked like working hands, but they were elegant, for all that. Impulsively, he bent and brushed his mouth softly over the knuckles.

"Mr. Kilpatrick!" she burst out, flushing.

His head raised and his eyes danced. "Just the Irish side of me coming out. The Cherokee side, of course, would have you over a horse and out of the country by sundown."

"Did they have horses?"

"Yes. I'll tell you all about them one day." When he linked his fingers with hers and led her inside the hamburger shop, she felt as if she were sleepwalking.

They got their food, found an unoccupied table, and sat down. Becky spooned chili into her mouth while he wolfed down two cheeseburgers and two orders of French fries.

"God, I'm starved," he murmured. "I never can find enough time to eat these days. The calendar's overflowing; I'm working most weekends and nights. I even argue cases in my sleep."

"I thought you had assistants to do that."

"Our caseload is unbelievable," he said, "despite plea-bargaining and guilty pleas. I've got people in jail who shouldn't be, waiting for their cases to be put on the court calendar. There aren't enough courts, or enough judges, or enough jails."

"Or enough prosecutors?"

He smiled at her across his chocolate milk shake. "Or enough prosecutors," he said. His dark eyes slid over her face and back up to catch her eyes. The smile faded and the look grew intimate. "I don't want to get involved with you, Rebecca Cullen."

His bluntness took a little getting used to. She swallowed. "Don't you?"

"You're still a virgin, aren't you?"

She went scarlet.

His eyebrow jerked. "And I didn't even have to guess," he said ruefully. He finished the milk shake. "Well, I don't seduce virgins. Uncle Sanderson wanted me to be a gentleman instead of a red Indian, so he taught me exquisite manners. I have a conscience, thanks to his blasted interference."

She shifted in her seat, unsure if he was serious or teasing. "I don't fall into bed with strange men," she began.

"You wouldn't fall, you'd be carried," he pointed out. "And I'm not strange. I do set fire to my office occasionally, and stand on my dog's tail, but that isn't so odd."

She smiled gently, feeling warm ripples up and down her body as she looked at him, liking the strength of his high-cheekboned face, the power and grace of his body. He was a very sensuous man. He was stealing her heart, and she couldn't even save herself.

"I'm not the liberated type," she said quietly. "I'm very conventional. I was raised strictly, despite my father, and in the church. I suppose that sounds archaic to you…"

"Uncle Sanderson was a deacon in the Baptist church," he interrupted. "I was baptized at the age of ten and went to Sunday school until I graduated high school. You aren't the only archaic specimen around."

"Yes, but you're a man."

"I hope so," he sighed. "Otherwise, I've spent a fortune on a wardrobe I can't wear."

She laughed with pure delight. "Is this really you? I mean, are you the broody man I met in the elevator?"

"I had plenty of reason to be broody. They moved me out of my comfortable office into a high-rise airport and took away my favorite coffee shop, flooded me with appeal cases—of course I brooded. Then, there was this irritating young woman who kept insulting me."

"You started it," she pointed out.

"I defended myself," he argued.

She fingered her Styrofoam coffee cup. "So did I. I'll bet you're scary in court."

"Some people think so." He gathered up the remains of his lunch. "We have to go. I don't want to rush like this, but I've only got half an hour to get back to court."

"Sorry!" She got up at once. "I didn't realize we'd been here so long."

"Neither did I," he confessed. He stood aside to let her precede him to the trash can and then out of the building. It was warming up, but still a cold day, and she pulled her jacket closer.

His eyes fastened on it. It was worn and probably three or four years old. Her dress wasn't new, either, and her black high heels were scuffed. It disturbed him to see how little she had. And yet she was so cheerful usually—except when her brother was mentioned. He'd known women with wealth who were critical of everything and everyone, but Becky had practically nothing and she seemed to love life and people.

"You've perked up," he commented as they drove back to the office building.

"Everybody has problems," she replied easily. "I handle mine fairly well most days. They're no worse than anyone else's," she added with a smile. "Mostly I enjoy life, Mr. Kilpatrick."

"Rourke," he corrected. He glanced at her and smiled. "It's Irish."

"No!" she said with mock surprise.

"What did you expect I'd be named? George Standing Rock, or Henry Marble Cheek, or some such outlandish thing?"

She covered her face with her hands. "Oh, my gosh," she groaned.

"Actually, my mother's name was Irene Tally," he said. "Her father was Irish and her mother was Cherokee. So I'm only one-quarter, not one-half Cherokee. All the same," he said, "I'm pretty damned proud of my ancestry."

"Mack keeps trying to get Granddad to say he's got Indian blood," she mused. "His class is studying Cherokee Indians this semester, and he's gung-ho to learn how to use that blowgun they hunted with. Did you know that the Cherokee were the only southeastern tribe to hunt with a blowgun?"

"Yes, I knew. I am Cherokee," he pointed out.

"Only one-quarter, you said so, and the quarter you are might not have known about it."

"Stop splitting hairs."

"*Au contraire,* I have never whacked a rabbit in half," she assured him haughtily.

He did a double take. "My God." He whistled through his teeth. "You're quick, lady."

"Quick, but not fast, sir," she drawled.

He chuckled. "I had that much figured out. Tell Mack that the Cherokee didn't use curare on their darts. Only the South American Indians knew about the poison."

"I'll tell him." She glanced down at the purse in her lap. "He'd like you."

"Think so?" He wanted so badly to ask her out for an evening, to meet her family. It would work to his advantage, because Clay was close to the Harrises, and it would give him a pipeline. But he didn't want to hurt Becky, and he would if he played on her interest. It was better to let it ride, for now. "Here we are."

She had to fight down disappointment. He'd taken her out to lunch, after all. She should be grateful for crumbs and not resentful because he hadn't offered her a banquet. So she gave him a brilliant smile when she wanted to cry.

"Thanks for the chili," she said softly when they were standing beside the car.

"My pleasure." His lean hand lifted to her face, and his thumb traced under her lower lip with expert deliberation. "If this weren't such a very public place, Miss Cullen," he said, letting his dark eyes fall to her mouth, "I'd take your mouth under mine and kiss you until your knees gave way under you."

She caught her breath. Those dark eyes were hypnotizing her, and she had to do something before she threw herself at his feet and begged him to do just that. "Do cheeseburgers often affect you like this?" she whispered, trying to salvage her pride.

He lost it. He burst out laughing and dropped his hand. "Damn you, woman!" he ground out.

She was proud of herself. She'd managed to regain her balance without denting his pride too much. She made him laugh. She wondered if it was as easy as it seemed.

"For shame, cursing a lady in public, Mr. District Attorney," she said pertly. She smiled. "Thank you very much for lunch, and for the shoulder. I don't often get depressed, but lately, things have been rather hectic at home."

"You don't have to explain anything to me," he said gently. She made him feel protective. It wasn't a feeling he was accustomed to.

"I'd better go in," she said after a minute.

"Yes." His dark eyes held her hazel ones, and time seemed to stand still. He vibrated with the need to pull her against him and kiss her. He wondered if she felt the need, too, and that was why she'd countered his move with one of her own.

"Well...see you."

He nodded.

She managed to get her feet to move, but she was sure they didn't touch the ground all the way back into the building. She didn't know that a curious pair of eyes had watched her leave with Kilpatrick and come back with him.

"Your sister is thick with the D.A., Cullen," Son Harris said to Clay that night. "She had lunch with him. We can't let that situation develop. He might get to us through her."

"Don't be stupid," Clay said nervously. "Becky isn't interested in Kilpatrick—I know she isn't!"

"He and his investigator are getting too close. We may have to get rid of him," Son said, his small eyes pinning Clay's disbelieving ones. "We've got a major load coming in here in the next few weeks. We can't afford any complications."

"You don't think killing the D.A. would cause complications?" Clay laughed, because Son loved to exaggerate.

"Not if somebody else gets blamed for it."

Clay shrugged. "Well, count me out. I can't shoot straight."

Son stared at him levelly. "We were thinking about something a little less dangerous than that. You know, like wiring his car." He smiled at Clay's dubious expression. "You're real good in science, aren't you, Clay? And you did that paper on explosives for the science fair last year. Not hard for a good investigator to dig out that information, you know. Not hard at all." Son patted his arm. "So you be a good boy, Clay, and get to work on your brother. Or we may just have to bomb the D.A. and pin the rap on you."

"Mack won't budge," he said hesitantly. Son was high already. Maybe this was his idea of a drunken joke. Surely they didn't mean to do something that stupid. No, he assured himself. It was just talk. They were afraid Becky might say something to Kilpatrick, that's all. They were trying to scare him. God, they couldn't be serious!

"Mack had damned well better budge," Son said in that soft voice that meant trouble. His dilated eyes met Clay's. "You hear me, Clay? He'd better budge, soon. We want that business at the elementary school and we're going to have it. So get busy!"

Becky went home floating on a cloud, her mind full of Kilpatrick, her problems far away. She didn't notice that Mack and Clay were missing for several minutes while she was working on supper, and Granddad was watching the news.

Mack came into the kitchen white-faced, but he didn't say a word. He mumbled something about not being hungry and he wouldn't look Becky in the eye.

She followed him into his bedroom, wiping her wet hands on a dish towel. "Mack, is something wrong?"

He looked at her and started to speak, then looked behind her and abruptly closed his mouth.

"Nothing's wrong. Is there, Mack?" Clay said, and smiled easily. "What's for supper?"

"Are you actually going to be here for supper?" Becky asked.

He shrugged. "Nothing better to do—not tonight, anyway. Thought I might play Granddad a game of checkers."

She smiled with relief. "He'd like that."

"How did you day go?" he asked as they went back to the kitchen and she checked on the homemade rolls she was baking.

"Oh, very nice," she said. "Mr. Kilpatrick took me out to lunch."

"Getting chummy with the D.A.?" Clay asked, his eyes narrowing.

"It was nothing to do with you," she said firmly. "He's a nice man. It was just lunch."

"Kilpatrick, nice?" He laughed bitterly. "Sure he is. He tried to put Dad in jail, now he's after me. But he's nice."

She went red. "This has nothing to do with you," she repeated. "For God's sake, I have the right to some pleasure in my life!" she burst out. "I cook and clean and work to support us. Don't I even have the right to go to lunch with a man? I'm twenty-four years old, Clay, and I've hardly ever been out on a date! I—"

"I'm sorry," he said, and meant it. "Really, I am. I know how hard you work for us," he added quietly. He turned away, feeling small and ashamed. There was so much he couldn't tell her. He'd meant to bring in some extra money, he'd told himself, to help out. But he'd known he couldn't show Becky any of it because she'd want to know where he got it. He'd made a god-awful mess of everything.

Son Harris had him over a barrel. He didn't want to go to jail, either. He sighed and looked out the window at the night sky. Maybe there was another kid he could work on—somebody with fewer scruples than his little brother.

Clay glanced at Becky. She liked the D.A. He didn't. But to think the Harrises had talked about killing him....

God, what a mess! He went back into the living room while she worked on supper. He could always call Kilpatrick and warn him. But what if it was a joke? Son made sick jokes. He couldn't be sure that the hit wasn't one. After all, he rationalized, where would Son Harris find a hit man? Right. He was getting worked up over nothing. He relaxed then, because without a hit man, Son wasn't going to do anything. It was all just a sick joke, and he'd fallen for it! What a laugh on him!

"How about a game of checkers after supper, Granddad?" he asked the old man on the couch, and forced a smile.

Becky fed them quickly and went to bed, determinedly not noticing Mack's despondency, Clay's unnatural cheeriness, and Granddad's lack of enthusiasm for life. It was time she had a life of her own, even if she had to harden her heart to get it. She couldn't go on sacrificing forever. She closed her eyes and saw Rourke Kilpatrick's face. She'd never wanted anyone enough to fight her family before. Until now.

CHAPTER SIX

Kilpatrick wondered sometimes why he kept Gus around. The big German shepherd climbed into the Mercedes and leaped back out. It took him five minutes to get the big animal settled, and he was already running late. He'd planned to drop Gus off at the kennel for some remedial obedience training. He would be lucky if he reached his office before lunch at this rate.

"You blessed troublemaker," he grumbled at the dog.

Gus barked. He was oddly restive, as if he sensed something. Kilpatrick didn't see anybody else near the car.

He felt for his cigar case, couldn't find it, and with a frustrated sigh, got of the car to go back for it. He slammed the door, leaving Gus inside. As he reached the front door the bomb went off, turning the sleek Mercedes into twisted metal and charred leather.

Becky could tell something was wrong by the hectic rush of people in the building. She saw policemen coming and going, and the sound of sirens was almost constant.

"Do you know what's going on?" she asked Maggie as she tried to peer down to the street below through the curtained window. It was lunchtime and the lawyers were all out, along with the paralegals. Maggie and Becky were alone in the office, since the other secretaries and the receptionist were taking an early lunch.

Maggie joined her, small and dark and curious. "No. But something is, I know that," she asserted. "That's the bomb squad. I recognize the vehicle." She frowned. "What would the bomb squad be doing here?" she wondered.

Mr. Malcolm came into the office at a dead run. He was preoccupied and unsettled. "Have they been here?" he asked.

"Who?" Maggie asked with lifted brows.

"The bomb squad. They're going all over the building. My God, haven't you two heard yet? Somebody tried to kill the district attorney this morning! They set a bomb in his car!"

Becky fell back against the wall, her face white. Rourke! "Is he dead?" she asked, and stopped breathing while she waited for the answer.

"No," Malcolm replied, watching her curiously. "Got his dog, though." He went toward his office. "I've got to make a couple of calls. Don't worry, I don't think there's anything to worry about in the building. It's better to be safe than sorry, though."

"Yes, of course," Maggie said. She put a thin arm around Becky when the boss was in his office and the door closed. "Well, well," she said with a gentle, knowing smile. "So that's how things are."

"I don't know him really well," Becky hedged. "But he was kind about my brother, and I've…seen him around the building."

"I see." Maggie hugged her gently and then moved away. "He's indestructible, you know," she said with a smile. "Go fix your face."

"Yes. Of course." Becky went to the rest room in a daze, and stayed there while the bomb squad combed through the office. They found nothing. By the time they finished, it was time for Becky and Maggie to go to lunch. Becky held back, making excuses. The minute Maggie was out of sight, Becky went up to the next floor and straight to Kilpatrick's office.

He was talking to some men, but when he saw her white face and huge, frantic hazel eyes, he dismissed them and, taking her arm without a word, pulled her into his private office and closed the door.

She didn't think or pause to consider the consequences. She went into his arms and clung to him, shivering with reaction. She didn't make a sound, not a sob or a gasp. She held him close, rocking against him, her arms under his jacket, her eyes tightly closed, and inhaled the exquisite scent of his cologne in the silence that kindled around them.

Kilpatrick, never lost for words, was without them for the first time in recent memory. Becky's headlong rush, the horror in her soft eyes, humbled him. His arms contracted. "I'm all right," he said softly.

"That's what they said, but I had to see for myself. I only just found out." She pressed closer. "I'm sorry about your dog."

He drew in a steadying breath. "So am I. He was a damned pest, but I'll miss him like hell." His jaw clenched as his dark head bent over hers. He hugged her close and his lips pressed into her soft neck. "Why did you come?"

"I thought...you might need someone," she whispered. "I know it was presumptuous, and I'm sorry I came barreling in like that..."

"I don't think you have to apologize for caring," he replied, his voice deep and slow. He lifted his head and searched her soft, worried eyes. "My God, it's been years since anyone worried about me." He scowled and brushed her long hair away from her face. "I'm not sure I like it."

"Why?" she asked.

"I'm a loner by nature," he said simply. "I don't want ties."

She smiled sadly. "And I can't have any. My family is all the responsibility I can handle. But I'm sorry about your dog, and I'm glad you weren't hurt."

"Those damned cigars you hate so much saved me," he murmured, finding bitter amusement in the thought. "I'd gone back inside to get them. Apparently the mechanic who wired my car wasn't very expert. There was a loose connection on the timer."

"Oh. It wasn't connected to the door or the gas pedal?"

He glowered at her. "You don't know beans about C-4 plastic explosives and electronic timers, do you?"

"Actually, I've never wanted to do anybody in, so I neglected to learn," she replied.

"Pert miss," he murmured. His dark eyes fell suddenly to her mouth. He bent without thinking and kissed her, hard. His mouth left hers seconds later, long before she had time to savor the warmth of it, and he was back to normal. He put her away from him with firm, strong hands. "Go away. I'm up to my knees in investigators and federal agents."

"Federal agents!"

"Terrorist acts," he replied. "Organized crime. It's federal in this instance. I'll explain it to you one day."

"I'll go. I hope I didn't embarrass you," she began, a little shy now that she'd recovered from her blatant fear.

"Not at all. My secretary is used to hysterical blondes bursting in here to throw their bodies at me." He chuckled, the first ripple of humor he'd felt since the grief and anguish of the morning. His eyes were still sad, even though he smiled down at her. "Softhearted little scrap. Go back to work, Miss Cullen. I'm not bombproof, but somebody up there likes me."

"I'm inclined to agree." She moved away from him reluctantly, and paused in the doorway. "Good-bye."

"Thanks," he added gruffly, and turned away. It had touched him all too much that she cared if he lived or died. It had been a damned long time since anyone had cared like that about him. In fact, no other woman ever had. It was a sobering thought.

He was still brooding over it when Dan Berry came in and pointedly closed the door.

"Wasn't that the Cullen boy's sister who just left?" he asked Kilpatrick. "Did she come to see if he scored?"

He stood very still. "Explain that," he asked curtly.

"The Cullen boy's a whiz with electronic stuff," Berry said. "He won a science fair last year with a timed explosive. I guess the Harris boys helped him set it up. We're sure they're involved, but we can't prove it."

Kilpatrick lit a cigar and leaned back against his desk, feeling depressed and frustrated. Was that why Becky had come running? Had Clay perhaps confided in her? Did she know something? It took some of the pleasure out of her headlong rush into his arms, and now he had to ask himself if she was involved.

He looked up at Berry. "What have you found out?"

"It was a primitive timer. Nothing professional, that's a fact. If you'd had an out-of-town mechanic after you, you'd be dead. The whole thing was botched. It shouldn't even have gone off."

He blew out a cloud of smoke, his dark eyes narrowed thoughtfully, his elegant length propped against the edge of the desk while he thought. "Work with the police and see if the detectives can trace any of the explosive materials. I want to keep an eye on the Cullen boy."

"A wiretap?"

Kilpatrick swore. "We can't ask for that. Dammit, we don't have anything to go on except suspicions. Without some kind of evidence to back it up, we can't get a wiretap, or surveillance, or anything else. Not on Cullen, not on the Harrises."

"Then, what do we do?"

"Let the feds handle it," Kilpatrick said reluctantly.

"With their caseload? Sure. They've got all kinds of time to follow two amateur dope dealers around Atlanta."

Kilpatrick glared at him. "I'll think of something."

Berry shrugged. "Too bad you don't like the Cullen girl a little. She'd make a dandy source—especially if she liked you." He glanced at the taller man knowingly. "Just a thought."

"Get to work," Kilpatrick said curtly, and without looking at the other man. He'd been thinking the same thing himself about Becky, but it was underhanded and dishonest. He'd lived his life by a rigid code of honor. This went against it. Did the end justify the means? Did he have the right to pump Becky for information that might put her own brother in jail? He turned back toward his desk with an exclamation of pure disgust.

Becky, blissfully ignorant of the conversation Kilpatrick was having with his investigator, went home that evening in a state of panic. She was worried now. If someone had tried to kill him once, wouldn't they try again?

Granddad and the boys noticed her somber withdrawal over supper.

"What's wrong?" Clay asked.

"Somebody tried to blow up Mr. Kilpatrick this morning," she said without thinking.

Clay went a pasty white. He got up and made an excuse about having a stomach bug and left the table. Mack just sat there, all eyes.

"I can understand that his enemies might want him out of the way," Granddad said. "But that's a pretty cowardly way to kill a man. And blowing up his pet—damned cowardly."

"Yes," Becky said quietly. She glanced toward the living room, where Clay had gone. "Clay looks bad. Do you suppose he's all right?" she asked slowly.

"Sure he is," Mack said quickly. "I'll go check on him for you, okay?"

"Mack, you didn't eat your spinach…"

"Later!" he called back.

"Coward!" she called after him.

Granddad exchanged a speaking glance with Becky. "I wish

we could keep Clay away from the Harris boys," he said miserably.

"So do I, but how—tie him to the porch?" She put down her napkin and rested her face in her hands.

"You aren't going soft on Kilpatrick?" Granddad asked suddenly, his eyes sharp. "You sounded pretty upset about what happened to him."

She lifted her head. It was the last straw. "I have a perfect right to like anyone I please," she said. "If I like Mr. Kilpatrick, that's my business and nobody else's."

Granddad cleared his throat and looked away. "How about passing me some more corn? It sure is good."

Becky began to feel guilty because of what she'd said. But it was getting too difficult to make all the sacrifices she did and have them just taken for granted. She was brewing inside like a fermenting vat of grapes. She felt reckless and wild, and for once, she didn't really care if her attitude upset anybody.

CHAPTER SEVEN

Clay was still lying in bed the next morning when Becky stuck her head in the boys' room to remind him to get up. Mack was already at the table, eating pancakes as fast as Becky could cook them, but Clay mumbled something about a stomachache and wouldn't get up.

"Do you need me to take you to the doctor?" she asked, frowning.

"No. I'll be fine. Granddad's here," he reminded her.

She sighed. Fat lot of good that would do, when he could hardly get from bed to the living room by himself. But she didn't argue. Clay had been quiet since she'd mentioned Kilpatrick's close call. She didn't understand why, unless it was because he'd wished something terrible on the D.A.

"Well, take care of yourself," she said firmly, and closed the door. She went back to the kitchen, wishing she knew more about teenagers.

"You look nice," Mack said unexpectedly.

Her eyebrows rose. She was wearing an old red plaid skirt with a white blouse and black pullover sweater, and her long hair was pulled back in a neat bun. "Me?" she asked.

He grinned. "You."

She bent and kissed his cheek. "You'll be a lady-killer in four more years," she assured him.

"Monster killer," he corrected. "I hate girls."

She pursed her lips. "I'll remind you of that in four more years. There's the bus," she said, nodding out the window. "Get cracking."

"What about Clay?" He hesitated at the back door, his eyes worried. "Is he okay?"

"He's got a bellyache," she said. "He'll be fine."

Mack hesitated again, then shrugged and went out the door.

Becky hadn't thought a lot about it that morning, but it haunted her all day at work.

"Problems?" Maggie asked gently as they got things put away in time for lunch.

"Always, these days, it seems," Becky said with a sigh. "My brother's home with an upset stomach. Seventeen, and already in trouble with the law. I don't know what I'm doing wrong. He's so difficult!"

"All boys are difficult, in various degrees," the older woman assured her. "I raised two of my own, but they were Ivy League kids, I guess," she added with a warm smile. "You know, chess club, band, drama club—that kind of kid. Thank God they never had wild streaks."

"Thank God is right. My brother Mack is like that. But Clay makes up for him, I'm sorry to say."

"It's been quiet today," Maggie noted. "Nice not to have bomb squads crawling all over the building."

Becky nodded, glancing at the brown bag she'd brought along. It contained a lemon pound cake she'd baked for Kilpatrick. She'd dithered all morning, wondering how she was going to get up enough nerve to give it to him. She thought he needed a little pampering after his upset yesterday, and losing his dog.

"You'd better go ahead," Maggie said absently. "It's ten minutes to twelve, but I'm going a little later today so that I can meet one of my ex-husband's sisters for lunch. Incredible how well I get along with his family after all this time." She shook her head. "Pity I couldn't get along with him."

"I'll be back by one," Becky promised, grateful for being allowed to leave early. Maybe she could give the cake to Kilpatrick's secretary without saying who it came from.

"Sure," Maggie said. She noticed the brown bag, but she didn't say a word. She just smiled as Becky left the office.

Becky was sure she looked her absolute worst. She pushed two stray wisps of hair back into her bun, but it was trying to come down because her fingers had worried it so much this morning. Her skirt was askew and there was a run in one leg of her panty hose. She paused at Kilpatrick's office door and almost turned around and ran. Then she realized that her appearance was going to be the least of his worries, so she opened the door and went in.

His secretary looked up from her desk and smiled. "Hi. Can I help you?"

"Yes," Becky said, taking the opportunity to avoid a confrontation. Her heart was beating in her ribs as it was, and her nerve was gone. She put the sack on the desk. "It's some lemon pound cake," she blurted out. "For him."

An investigator, a paralegal, and three assistant district attorneys were in the office, all male, but the secretary knew who Becky meant. "He'll appreciate it," she told the younger woman. "He's partial to cake. It was nice of you."

"I was sorry about his dog," Becky murmured. "I had a dog myself. The mailman ran over him last year. I'd better go."

"He'll want to thank you..."

"No need. No need at all," Becky said, smiling as she backed toward the door. "Have a nice...oops!"

Her back collided with a tall, strong body. Big, lean hands, very dark, caught her arms, and a deep voice chuckled behind her.

"What have you done now?" he asked. "Robbed a bank? Held up a grocery store? Are you here to plea-bargain?"

"Yes, sir." His secretary grinned at him. "She brought you a bribe. Lemon pound cake." She leaned forward. "It smells delicious. I'd settle out of court, if I were you."

"Good idea, Mrs. Delancy," he replied. "I'm taking you into protective custody, Miss Cullen. We'll discuss terms at the nearest café."

"But..." Becky began.

It was no good protesting. He was already guiding her out the door. "I'll be back in at one," he told Mrs. Delancy.

"Yes, sir."

Kilpatrick was wearing a cream and tan sports coat with tan slacks, and he looked twice as tall as usual as he guided her to the elevator, his eternal smoking cigar in his hand.

"Nice of you to bake me a cake. Is it a bribe, or do you just think I'm undernourished?" he asked with a faint smile as he hit the "down" button with a big fist.

"I thought you might have a sweet tooth," she replied. She was still tense, but being with him was like going on the wild rides at a carnival. She felt as if she glowed. She glanced up at him, her big hazel eyes radiant. "I guess you're probably a better cook than I am."

"Because I live alone?" He shook his head. "I can't boil water. I buy things at the deli and heat them up. Someday I'm going to have to break down and hire another housekeeper, before I poison myself."

She studied him covertly while they waited for the slow ascent of the elevator. He looked all right. Amazing that he could walk away from a car bombing and look so cool and collected. "Were you in the armed forces?" she asked absently.

He lifted an eyebrow. "Marine Corps," he said. "Does it show?"

She smiled. "You don't get rattled very easily."

He stuck the cigar in his mouth and stared down at her. "Neither do you, as a rule. Living with two brothers, you've probably had advanced combat training."

"Living with my brothers feels like it," she agreed. "Clay, especially."

He had to bite his tongue not to ask questions. He averted his eyes to the elevator as it arrived. He put Becky inside, making room for the two of them, because it was crowded with office workers heading to lunch.

Becky was crushed backwards. She felt his lean arm snake

around her with delicious subtlety, drawing her back so that she leaned against his hard, broad chest. She could feel him breathing against her, smell the cigar smoke and cologne that clung to him. Her knees went weak, so it was a good thing that the elevator went straight down without stopping. It was almost a relief to get off on the ground floor.

"Does the café suit you today?" he asked. "We could drive across town."

"But, your car!" she said and stopped dead, her face paling as she realized how close a call he'd had.

He paused and lifted an eyebrow, searching her wide eyes. "My car was a total loss, but the insurance payments were current, thank God. It will be replaced. I'm driving a city car right now. It's not the flashy piece of metal my own was, but it's comfortable and functional."

She lowered her eyes to his chest and swallowed. "I'm glad you smoke cigars, Rourke."

His lean hand smoothed down the worn sleeve of her white blouse. "So am I," he said hesitantly. His fingers clenched suddenly, enclosing her arm in a warm, rough grasp. He towered over her, so close in the hallway leading to the café that she could feel the heat and power of his body all the way to her toes. "Say my name!" he said huskily.

"Rourke." It came out as a breathless whisper. She looked up, then, and the world narrowed to the darkness of his eyes in a face like honed steel. "Rourke." She said it again, achingly.

His gaze fell suddenly to her mouth and his jaw clenched. The hand on her arm bit into it until he turned suddenly and drew her along with him toward the line forming at the café door. "I can't imagine how you've escaped being ravished on the lobby floor."

Her eyes widened. She wasn't sure she'd heard him.

He glanced down at her and laughed in spite of himself at the look on her face. "You don't understand, do you?" he mused, lifting the cigar to his lips. "You have the sexiest damned eyes I've ever seen. Bedroom eyes. Long lashes with golden tips and a way of looking up at me that makes me want to..." He shook his head. "Never mind." He looked over her head. "Looks like fish and liver and fried chicken," he murmured to change the subject. His body was tautening in a way that made him uncomfortable.

"I hate liver," she murmured.

"So do I."

She made a face as the cigar fired up curls of smoke.

"Did you know that there's a city ordinance against smoking down here?" she asked him.

"Sure. I'm a lawyer," he reminded her. "They teach us stuff like that at law school."

"You're not just a lawyer, you're the county district attorney," she replied.

"I'm setting an example," he explained. "If there are people who don't know what smoking looks like, when they see me, they will." He stuck the cigar between his teeth and grinned.

She laughed and shook her head. "You're just impossible!"

But when they reached the inner doors of the cafeteria, he did put out the cigar. And despite her protests, he bought her lunch. She felt guilty, because she'd added a dessert and a salad that she wouldn't have if she'd known.

"Please, you shouldn't have..." she protested as they sat down at a table for two near the window.

"Shut up. Here, let me have your tray." He took it with his and handed it to a passing waitress, flashing a smile at her. "Now eat," he told Becky as he picked up his fork. "I don't have time to argue with you."

"Actually, I hate arguing," she murmured between bits of fish.

He stopped in the middle of spearing a mouthful of salad. "You?"

"I do enough of it at home," she explained with a rueful smile.

"There are legal ways to force your father to meet his responsibilities," he said quietly.

"Dad is the last complication I need right now," she said with a heavy sigh. "You can't imagine what it's like, to have him turn up and demand to be helped out of some jam. I spent my whole life doing that up until two years ago. It's been like another world since he went to Alabama. I just hope he stays there," she said, and shivered. "I've got all I can handle."

"You shouldn't have to handle it," he said shortly. He put down his fork. "Look, there are social agencies..."

She touched his lean hand where it lay on the table. "Thank you," she said, and meant it. "But my grandfather is too proud to accept any kind of help. My brothers would run away and live on the streets before they'd stay with anyone else. The farm is all we have, so I have to keep it going as best I can. I know you mean well, but there's only one way to do things, and I'm already doing it."

"In other words," he said bluntly, "you're trapped."

She went white. She averted her eyes, but his hand turned over and grasped hers in its hard, warm grasp.

"You don't like the word, do you?" he demanded, his eyes narrowing as they compelled hers to meet them. "But it's the truth. You're as much a prisoner as any criminal I send to jail."

"A prisoner of my own pride and duty and honor and loyalty," she agreed. "My grandfather taught me that those words are the foundation of any decent upbringing."

"And he's right," he said. "I can't fault his teachings. But guilt is no substitute for them."

She shifted uncomfortably in her chair. "I don't stay out of guilt."

"Don't you?" He toyed with her hand, sliding his big, strong fingers in and out of hers in an intimacy that made her tremble. His eyes came up and caught hers. "Have you ever had a love affair?"

"Even if I believed in that sort of thing, there's no time," she began, flustered.

"You're attractive. You could have a husband and family of your own if you wanted it enough."

"I don't," she began.

His thumb circled her damp palm sensuously. "Don't what?" he asked, his voice deep and slow and exciting. His eyes fell to her lips and lingered there until she was drowning. "You've never had a lover, Becky?" he whispered.

"No."

He looked up, seeing the feverish reaction he'd kindled, the mingled fear and hot excitement in her face. He felt her hand tremble as his touched it. His own body clenched with a sudden fierce need. She was slender, but her breasts were firm and high and her waist small, narrowing just above flaring hips and long legs. He could imagine that she was exquisite under her clothes, and his imagination went wild as he let his gaze fall to the soft rise and fall of her chest.

"Rourke," she groaned, flushing.

He forced his gaze back up to hers. "What?"

She tugged at her hand and he let it go with obvious reluctance. She put a mouthful of fish on her fork and almost dropped it getting it to her lips.

Kilpatrick watched her with detached satisfaction. She was vulnerable to him, all right. She was attractive and innocent, and it would be like shooting ducks in a row to win her trust.

Part of him disliked the idea of using her to get to her brother, and through him, the Harris boys. But another part was excited by her and hungry for her, and that part convinced him that he was helping to liberate her from a smothering lifestyle. After that, it was easy enough to rationalize his intentions, all the way to noble intervention. He simply refused to consider any other ideas.

"We could do this again tomorrow," he said, leaning back in his chair to watch her. "I don't like eating alone."

She was almost pulsating with excitement. Imagine, a man who looked like Kilpatrick actually noticing her, wanting her company! She didn't question his motives or his intentions. She was too infatuated with him to care about them. It was enough that he was interested.

"I'd like to have lunch with you," she stammered. "Are you sure?" she added uncertainly.

He let his gaze wander over her oval face, down to her soft mouth. "Why wouldn't I be?" He scowled. "You seem to have some crazy idea that no normal man would find you attractive."

"Well, I'm not very," she said with a faint smile.

"You have beautiful hair and eyes," he said. "Your figure is enchanting, and I like your sense of humor. I enjoy being around you." He smiled wickedly. "Besides, I'm partial to lemon pound cake."

"Oh, I see," she said, all too ready to lighten the atmosphere. "You're allowing yourself to be bribed."

He nodded. "That's it, exactly. I can't be bought with money, but food is another matter. A starving man and a good cook are a match any jury could understand."

"That's in case I poison you accidentally?" she asked, all eyes.

"Of course."

"I'll stomp my hemlock patch to death this very night," she said, placing a hand on her heart. "I only kept it to feed traveling salesmen carrying vacuum cleaners."

"Good girl. Eat your dessert."

She did, but she never knew what she'd put in her mouth. She was too busy staring at Kilpatrick to notice.

She floated around the office for the rest of the day, half in and half out of her mind. Maggie noticed and teased her, and she didn't even care. Having a man notice her was so new that she could hardly believe it had actually happened.

Once she got home, she was careful not to mention Kilpatrick. It wouldn't do to borrow trouble, and she knew already how her family felt about him. Clay would hate the whole idea, and so would her grandfather. The only ally she might have was Mack, and he wouldn't be enough. She groaned inwardly as she wondered how she was going to keep her sanity and Kilpatrick.

She fed the chickens and gathered eggs with her mind only half on what she was doing. With her long, tanned legs in cut-off jeans and her breasts emphasized by the green tank top, her long hair veiling her face, she was the picture of a country girl. Her legs were her best asset, long and elegant and tanned from hours working in the sun. But her thoughts were a long way from her appearance. She was thinking about Kilpatrick and allowing herself to dream for the first time in her life.

The loud drone of an engine pulled her up short and she watched Clay climb out of a very expensive sports car, laughing as he waved off the driver. *That's not the Harris boys,* she thought, watching. *It's a girl.* His stomachache had improved pretty rapidly! She glared toward him with pure rage.

Clay was walking toward the house when he spotted Becky. He hesitated and then joined her. He was wearing designer jeans and a designer shirt. Becky caught her breath.

"A stomachache, wasn't it?" she asked icily. "And where in the world did you get those clothes?"

"My clothes?" he murmured. His mind was on Francine and the fever that was burning between them. They were getting real thick now that he had some neat clothes and a little pocket money, but he'd blown it by letting Becky see the clothes. Now she was going to give him hell about them. Not to mention the bigger trouble he was in for laying out of school again.

"Designer clothes," she said heavily. "Oh, Clay!"

"I got them on time," he said, thinking fast. "I've got a part-time job working nights at a convenience store in Atlanta," he added. "That's where I've been. I wanted to surprise you."

She studied him with patent disbelief. Clay didn't like work. She couldn't even get him to clean up his room, so this revelation came as just a little too much of a surprise. "Really?" she asked. "Exactly where are you working?"

He couldn't think of a quick reply. He wondered if Mack had spilled the beans, and decided probably not, or Becky would be doing more than guessing. He'd held his breath over that, because he'd really put some pressure on his brother. But Mack wouldn't give an inch, so Clay had found himself another contact at the elementary school. Now the Harrises had a real business going over there. Clay hadn't allowed himself to feel any guilt. After all, the kids were going to get the crack anyway, so they might as well get it from him as anybody else. And it wasn't as if he was actually dealing. He just handed the stuff out to the dealers. That was his only part of the action. He couldn't get in any real trouble.

"What does it matter where?" he asked belligerently. "Now that I can afford good clothes, I've got a girl."

Becky stiffened. "Listen, buster," she said, lifting her head, "a girl who looks at the cost of your clothes before she looks at what's inside them isn't a girl you want."

"Baloney!" he shot back with narrowed eyes and a reddening face. "Girls look at that sort of thing! Francine wouldn't even talk to me before, and now she's asking me for dates!"

"The lady in the fancy sports car?" Becky asked.

"Yes, if it's any of your business," he said icily.

"If?! Who got you out of jail?" she demanded, glaring at him. "As long as you live here, everything you do is my business. And I want to know more about this job of yours."

"Dammit, that's enough! I'm going to pack my stuff and get out!"

"Fine!" She emptied the feed bowl on the ground. "Go ahead. I'll tell Kilpatrick you've welshed on the bargain to remain in my custody and you can damned well go to jail!"

He sucked in his breath. That didn't sound like sweet, forgiving Becky. His eyes almost popped.

"I'm sick of you," she continued, almost shaking with pent-up rage. "I've given you and Mack and Granddad all my attention, all my free time, for what seems forever. And what have I got to show for it? One brother who lays out of school, half in and half out of prison, another one who thinks homework is done by elves, and a grandfather who wants to dictate who I spend my spare time with! Not to mention a father with no sense of honor at all!"

"Becky!" Clay exclaimed.

"Well, you can go to hell," she raged at him. "You and your dope-peddling friends can land yourselves in prison and get yourselves out, as well!"

Tears were pouring down her cheeks. Clay felt helpless and guilty and angry all at once. He couldn't think of anything to say.

He let out a furious curse and stormed off toward the house.

"Where do you think you're going now?" she demanded, beyond trying to reason with him.

"Make a guess!" he ground out over his shoulder.

She slammed the bowl down in the dirt, shaking with rage. He was just too much for her to handle. Everything was too much these days. Now he was going to upset Grand-dad and she'd have her hands full listening to him rage for the rest of the night. She hoped he didn't have another heart attack in the process. If only she could throw up her hands and go away, just drop it all in somebody else's lap and quit. But life wasn't that simple. She shouldn't have started accusing Clay the minute she opened her mouth, but he had no business laying out of school, running around with girls in expensive sports cars, and wearing designer clothes when she could hardly afford to buy seconds for the rest of the family on her salary. Clay had expensive tastes and now she was going to worry herself sick wondering how he was feeding them.

She picked up the bowl she'd slammed to the ground, amazed that the heavy stoneware hadn't broken. She wouldn't have cared much, in her present mood. If only there was someone she could go to for help—someone who could advise her on how to handle Clay before he did get into so much trouble that he couldn't be saved.

But there is someone, she thought, stopping in her tracks. There was Kilpatrick, who'd invited her out to lunch again and who seemed to actually care a little bit about her. He enjoyed her company, at any rate, and that had to mean he'd be willing to listen to her problems.

She wouldn't impose on him, either, she promised herself, brightening as she thought about asking him for advice. He'd dealt with problem kids before, and surely he wouldn't mind telling her what he thought. If Clay didn't like it, that was just too bad. Maybe it was time Clay had a little less indulgence and a lot more responsibility.

By the time she had supper on the table, Clay had vanished out the front door without a word. Becky didn't mention it. Mack and Granddad seemed as disinclined to talk about Clay as she did, so the conversation stayed off the topic. Bedtime came, but Clay didn't return. Becky lay awake, wondering where she'd gone wrong with him. The only positive thing was that he'd sobered up lately. Maybe it was a good sign.

CHAPTER EIGHT

Kilpatrick picked Becky up at her office for lunch, causing raised eyebrows all over the floor. He smiled gently at her faint embarrassment while his dark eyes slid down her slender body, admiring her flowered shirtwaist dress and loose hairstyle. She looked younger and prettier than ever; the soft flush of her cheeks gave her a new radiance.

"Not as easy as you thought it would be?" he asked, glancing back toward one of the secretaries, who was blatantly staring after them. "I don't have a steady date," he added. "Consequently, when I start taking a lady out to lunch, people notice."

"Oh." She was lost for words. She'd wondered if he had a mistress or the significant other of modern life, but she'd been afraid to ask, in case he had. Now she was stunned to find how much it mattered to her that he didn't.

She was still analyzing her attitude when they sat down in the café with their trays. She glanced up as he emptied his and put it aside with her own. He was so handsome. He caught her watching him and smiled faintly.

"How are things going with you?" he asked casually as he started on his salad.

"All right," she lied. She smiled, forcing herself not to cry on his shoulder about Clay. She could handle it. To mention such a thing might make him think there were ulterior motives in her interest in him. He might even believe that she was chasing him on Clay's behalf. She couldn't let that happen—not at this fragile stage of their relationship. "How about you?" she asked. "Have you...well, have you found out who tried to kill you?"

His dark eyes narrowed slightly as they searched hers. "Not yet," he said after a minute. "But I will." He lifted a forkful of salad to his mouth.

She thought about what a close call he'd had and shivered. He saw the faint movement and misunderstood it for fear because of what he'd said. He wondered how deeply her brother was involved and how much she knew. Perhaps if he could win her trust, she might tell him one day.

"The pound cake was good," he said unexpectedly, and smiled. "I thought it would last at least a week, but I finished it off last night."

"All of it?" she exclaimed and stopped as she realized how it would sound.

He laughed, though, not taking offense. "What was left of it," he corrected. "My secretary and my investigator got into it while I was in court." He leaned forward. "In fact, I understand that Mrs. Delancy actually used a slice of it to entice her husband into a compromising situation."

"I'm shocked!" she said, biting back a grin.

"Well, it was a rather exquisite morsel," he said. He finished his salad.

"I'm glad you and the people in your office liked it," she said with a smile. She toyed with her own salad. "Are you safe now?" she asked, her voice unsteady as she forced the question out. She lifted eyes that gave away more of her fears than she realized. "They won't try again?"

"I don't think so," he replied, meeting her eyes. "It's made every local newspaper and television station, and was even picked up by the national wire services. Hit men, even unprofessional ones, don't like that kind of heat. They'll lie low until the publicity dies down, at least."

"Maybe by then you'll have caught them," she said fervently.

"Worried about me, Becky?" he asked with a lazy grin.

"Yes," she said honestly. Her big hazel eyes searched his, and there was a wan look to her cheeks. "You do look under your hood, at least, don't you?"

"When I think about it," he murmured dryly. "Stop looking like that. I'm not suicidal."

"Going after drug dealers certainly is that," she said stubbornly. "I was reading this article in *National Geographic* about some drug lord overseas who killed off everybody who tried to stop his operation. He had billions of dollars. How do you fight somebody with that kind of money and power?"

"The best way is to attack the reason people use drugs," he said seriously. "The market exists because of the pressure of living. People have to have an escape. Crack is cheap— about fifty dollars for half an ounce, compared to fifteen hundred dollars an ounce for cocaine, street level. It's more expensive than booze, but it's the in thing right now. Marijuana is dirt cheap on the streets, and it wards off the nausea of too much beer or wine." He sighed. "Prohibition didn't stop the sale of alcohol. You have to cut the demand I order to affect the market." His dark eyes narrowed. "How do you help a kid cope with an alcoholic father who beats his mother, or a kid whose mother or father sexually abuses him? How do you put food in the bellies of a family of five supported by a mother who works in a garment factory? How do you bail out a family on relief when they can't afford transportation to a job? How do you get a homeless man off the streets and out of the cardboard box he's living in? We're talking about hopelessness, Becky. People who can't bear reality have to have a way out. Some people read books, some people watch movies, some people watch TV. A larger number turn to a bottle or a coke spoon. The pressure of modern life is just too damned much for a segment of society. When the pressure gets too much, they break out. That's when they fall into my lap."

"By using drugs, you mean," she said.

"By doing what it takes to afford drugs," he corrected. "Even the nicest people will steal to support a hundred-dollar-a-day habit."

"A hundred dollars a day!" she burst out, horrified.

"That's a small habit," he said gently. "It can go as high as a thousand a day for somebody who's really addicted."

Becky felt the nausea rise in her throat. She knew that Clay had used coke, because he'd told her he had. She didn't think he was still using it, but she wondered if he was selling it to afford those designer clothes.

"Do dealers make a lot of money—small-time dealers, I mean?" she asked hesitantly.

"If you mean the Harris boys, that Corvette Son drives should tell you what kind of money they're into."

"I've seen it," she said wearily. "Cocaine is terribly addictive, isn't it?" she asked, thinking about the people it was sold to. She was almost certain that Clay was cold sober these days.

He pursed his lips. "Do you know how an alcoholic behaves?"

"Sort of," she admitted, because she'd seen Clay when he was drunk once or twice. "They giggle and act odd, their eyes are bloodshot, and they slur their words."

"That's about the size of it."

"Can it be cured?" she asked.

"In the early stages, but the cure rate isn't reassuring. Addiction isn't easy to face or defeat." He toyed with his coffee mug, searching her face. "It's better not to start."

She hesitated. "I'm sure it is," she said. "Do little children get addicted, just like adults?" she added.

"Some of them are actually born addicted," he said quietly. "It's a hell of a world, isn't it, when parents care that little about their own children?"

"It's an even worse one when they sell that stuff to grammar school children. Mack said they actually searched lockers at his school and found crack."

He glanced at her sharply. "There's something of a turf war going on there," he replied. "Marijuana dealers slugging it out with much tougher crack dealers."

"Oh, lord." Her nails were picking at her napkin, almost

shredding it. His lean hand came out and covered them, dark against the soft pink of her nails.

"Let's find something more cheerful to talk about."

She forced a smile. "Suits me."

He nodded, removing his hand. "I think this steer died of old age before they brought it in here," he murmured, scowling over his steak. He prodded it with his fork. "See? No life left in it at all. It doesn't move."

She laughed. "You're kidding, aren't you? I mean, you don't really want your steak to move around by itself?"

He glared at her. "Why not? A good piece of meat should be robust, full of fight. I hate to eat anything this dejected." He prodded it again and sighed, laying down the fork. "To hell with it. I'll eat Jell-O instead."

She just shook her head. He was fun to be with. And she'd imagined him so stern and brooding, but he was nothing like that. He had a dry wit and a no-nonsense attitude to life. She enjoyed his company as she'd never enjoyed anyone else's.

In the week that followed, Becky ate lunch with Kilpatrick every day. She'd never been so happy in all her life. The only drawback was having to keep the fact from her family. She'd had enough headaches the other time she'd had lunch with Kilpatrick, so she didn't tell them anything about how often she was seeing him.

Meanwhile, Clay was gone every night to his supposed job and spending most of the weekend in the company of Francine, the dark-haired beauty in the sports car. Clay never brought her in the house. Probably he was ashamed to have her see the cracked linoleum and poorly painted walls, Rebecca thought angrily. But Francine picked him up for work and brought him home, so that was one small blessing to be thankful for, she supposed. At least he wasn't demanding a car to go with his designer clothes. And he stayed sober.

She'd asked him where he worked, but all he'd tell her was that it was at a convenience store on Tenth Street downtown. She hadn't pursued that because she didn't want to know if he was lying. If he was, and she caught him, it would mean more trouble. She'd had so much that she felt cowardly about going looking for more. It was easier to believe that he'd reformed, that his interest in Francine had straightened him out. But a teenage girl driving a new Corvette bothered Becky especially since she'd found out inadvertently that Francine's folks were just mill workers.

Mack was quiet these days, too. He studied his math without being told, and he avoided Clay. Rebecca noticed that, and other subtle differences. They all bothered her, but she was beyond knowing what to do. She couldn't even confide in Kilpatrick now, because if she mentioned anything about the company Clay was keeping or the designer clothes he was sporting, it just might land her little brother in jail.

She couldn't talk to Clay anymore, so she tried to pretend everything was all right. She was just beginning to feel alive for the first time. She didn't want her happiness marred by anything unpleasant. So if she just ignored what was going on around her, it didn't exist.

Kilpatrick had started to watch her in a way that she found deliciously exciting. His dark eyes spent more and more time lingering on her breasts and her mouth, and even the timbre of his voice seemed to be changing. The way he spoke to her was different from the way he spoke to anyone else. Even Maggie had noticed.

"He seems to purr when he talks to you," the older woman had mentioned just that morning, grinning wickedly at her colleague. "When he called to ask you to meet him in the parking lot, I could hear his voice change when you came on the line. Oh, he's interested—really interested. Imagine that—our shy little wallflower carrying off the sexy D.A."

"You stop that." Becky laughed. "I haven't carried him anywhere. And having lunch together is just convenient. I baked him a cake, you know."

"Everybody knows you baked him a cake," Maggie informed her. "The people he didn't tell found out from his secretary. I'm surprised the news people haven't dropped in to interview you on your baking skills."

"Will you stop?" She groaned.

"Don't mislay that program disk," Maggie warned. "And if I were you, I'd go home late this afternoon and do some shopping in town. I have a feeling you're going to need some party duds real soon."

Becky frowned, brushing back her hair. She was wearing it long all the time now, because Kilpatrick liked it that way. She was taking more care with her makeup, too, and wearing the prettiest and most feminine clothes in her closet to work. It must have impressed him, because he certainly stared at her these days.

"Party duds?"

"Kilpatrick is being wined and dined by the political powers that be," Maggie explained. "They're trying to talk him into running for a third term. I'm sure you'll enjoy the parties."

"I'm not sophisticated enough for that kind of thing."

"You don't have to be sophisticated, child. You only have to be yourself," Maggie said firmly. "You don't put on airs. That's why people like you. You're just yourself. Don't worry, you'll do fine."

"Do you really think so?" she asked, all eyes.

"I really do. Now, powder your nose and go to lunch. We wouldn't want to upset the D.A., when we have all these big cases coming up in court next month," she added with a mischievous smile.

"Heaven forbid," Becky agreed. Impulsively she hugged Maggie, then escaped before things got embarrassing.

Kilpatrick was leaning on the hood of a black sedan, his long legs crossed, whistling faintly. He had on gray slacks and a light sports coat with a cheery red tie. Becky sighed at the sight of him.

He looked up as she approached, smiling. His dark eyes ran down her figure in the trim white suit and pink blouse she was wearing, her long legs in dark hose that ran into spiked white high heels. With her honey-colored hair long and loose around her shoulders and her face radiant with happiness, she was frankly pretty.

He whistled at her, and laughed when she blushed.

"Where are we going?" she asked.

"It's a surprise. Get in."

He put her inside and went around to climb in under the wheel. He reached for the key, then stopped when he saw the expression on her face. "I checked it," he whispered, leaning toward her. "The wiring, the hood, everything. Okay?"

She buried her face in her hands. "I'm an idiot."

"No, you're just human. And if my secretary wasn't leaning halfway out the window watching, I'd kiss you until you screamed for mercy," he added with a rakish grin.

She felt her cheeks go hot, and her eyes dropped involuntarily to his hard, chiseled mouth. She remembered the one kiss he'd given her and how it had felt—how her mouth had tingled all day with the memory of it. She wanted it again, but it wasn't wise to let him know how much.

"I like your secretary," she said to break the tension.

He chuckled, seeing her diversion for what it was. "So do I. We'd better go."

He cranked the car and drove off.

The restaurant he took her to was a creperie. Becky gasped with delight at the menu. It was the fanciest place she'd ever been to, and she was busy for several minutes drinking in every detail to share with Maggie when she got back to the office. Maggie probably had been to places like this so often that she took them for granted, but the café at work and the local fast food joints comprised the total extent of Becky's knowledge of prepared food.

"Haven't you been to a creperie before?" Kilpatrick asked gently, frowning at her evident delight.

"Well, no." She shifted and smiled self-consciously. "My budget doesn't run to places like this, and even if it did, I'd have to bring my whole family along. It could get expensive. Mack could eat what you're having and what I'm having and still ask for dessert."

"Mack?"

"My youngest brother," she explained. "He's just ten."

"Does he look like you?" he asked gently.

"Oh, yes," she said, smiling. "He loves to help me in the garden. He's the only one who does, these days. Granddad can't and Clay's...got a job," she blurted out.

He lifted an eyebrow. "Good for him."

"He has a girlfriend, too, but I haven't been given the opportunity to meet her," she added nervously. "He never brings her inside."

"She may not be the kind of girlfriend he wants to bring inside," he mused, watching her puzzled expression. "Becky, at his age, sex is new and exciting, and boys don't like having adults know what they're up to. It isn't surprising that he doesn't bring her home."

She felt a surge of relief. Could that be it? Could Clay be embarrassed to have his sister know that he was sleeping with someone? That was easy to answer. Clay knew that Becky was old-fashioned in her outlook and that she went to church. No wonder he didn't want her to meet Francine!

"Could it be that simple?" she asked absently. "Oh, I thought he was ashamed of us!"

He scowled. "Ashamed? Why would he be?"

She hesitated. Her eyes fell to her coffee cup. "Rourke, we're farm people. The house is old and falling apart, and we don't have anything fancy in it. A boy trying to impress a girl might not want her to know how...frugally...he lived."

"I imagine any house you kept would be neat as a pin," he said after a minute, his dark eyes quiet and soft. "And I can't imagine anyone being ashamed to show you off."

She flushed and then smiled. "Thank you."

"I meant it," he said simply. He studied her for a long moment, yielding finally to a temptation he couldn't put off any longer. "I'd like to take you out to dinner Saturday night. Will that be convenient?"

She knew she hadn't moved an inch. She stared at him while her heart shook. "What?"

"I want to take you out on a date. Dinner and a movie, or a nightclub, if you prefer," he said. "If you're not afraid to go," he added. "I could be a target again. I'll understand if you want to wait until this blows over."

"No!" she interrupted breathlessly. "Oh, no, I don't... I mean, I'm not afraid. Not at all. I'd love to go!"

He picked up his cup and sipped rich black coffee. "Your family won't like it."

"Then they can dislike it," she said stubbornly. "I'm entitled to go out once in a while."

"I'm flattered that you're willing to fight them over it," he said, a peculiar light in his dark eyes.

She flushed. "What time?"

"About six," he murmured, chuckling at her expression. "Wear something sexy."

"I don't have anything sexy," she confessed. She smiled wickedly. "But I will have, by Saturday night."

"That's my girl." He finished his coffee. "Now, how about dessert?"

The rest of the week went by in a flash. Becky stayed late and went shopping with Maggie for just the right dress to wear out to dinner. They found it in a small boutique, marked down fifty percent, and Becky couldn't believe that she was actually the owner of such a grand party dress.

It was black, with spaghetti straps and a fitted, low-cut

bodice and a full, flaring crepe skirt. It was the witchiest dress she'd ever seen in her life.

"I've got just the shoes to go with it," Maggie added. "Fortunately, you and I wear the same shoe size, and there's no need to buy a pair when I've got an almost new pair I can loan you."

Becky hesitated. "You're sure you don't mind?"

"I've got an evening bag that will match, too," she continued. "Do you have any jewelry?"

"A gold cross my mother left me," Becky said.

"The perfect accent." Maggie grinned. "It will keep Kilpatrick honest."

"You devil, you!" Becky gasped.

"Kilpatrick's the devil, and don't you forget it. Any man will take as much as you'll give, no matter how nice he is. Don't let yourself get carried away under the moon."

"I won't," Becky promised, but without a lot of conviction. She had a feeling that if Kilpatrick ever turned on the heat, she wouldn't have a prayer.

Maggie stopped by her apartment and produced a pair of spiked, strappy black velvet high heels and a black beaded evening bag for Becky. She lived in a spacious apartment overlooking the Hyatt Regency hotel in downtown Atlanta.

"I love your view." Becky sighed, looking out the picture window at the busy streets below. "But not your pet," she added with a grimace at the baby python Maggie kept in an aquarium.

"He won't bite. Ignore him. You should see my view at night," the older woman replied, smiling. "It's magic. You need an apartment of your own, Becky. A life of your own."

"What can I do?" Becky asked gently. "My grandfather can't manage the boys alone. If I leave, there's no money for a housekeeper or a nurse." She shook her head. "They're my family and I love them."

"Love can build prisons, and don't you forget it," Maggie said firmly. "I know. I'll tell you about it one day."

She looked haunted for a minute, and Becky felt a surge of affection for her.

"Why are you being so kind to me?" she asked Maggie.

Maggie smiled. "Because it's easy to be kind to someone as nice as you are, my darling. I don't make friends easily. I'm too independent and I like my own way. But you're special. I like you."

"I like you, too," Becky said. "And not just because you're staking me to shoes and a purse."

"That's nice to know," Maggie said, laughing. "Okay, I'd better drive you back to the parking lot to get your car. But you'll have to come over one Saturday afternoon and go shopping with me. I'll show you where all the best bargains are."

"I'd really like that," Becky said.

"So would I."

Maggie dropped her off at the parking lot and Becky drove home with pure reluctance. Well, she had until the next night to break the news to her family about her date with Kilpatrick. Maybe she'd work up enough nerve by then.

She got supper and only Granddad and Mack were there to share it.

"Is Clay at work?" she asked.

Granddad lifted an eyebrow. Mack shrugged.

"Well, did he come home at all?" she asked.

"He came by," Mack said. "He and his girlfriend came in to get something out of his room. He said he'd be home late, if he came home at all." He scowled. "I didn't like her. She had on these tight jeans and a see-through tank top, and she looked down her nose at the house."

Becky felt as if she were sitting on hot coals. "From what I hear, she doesn't come from money."

"She doesn't have to," Granddad said. "She's old man Harris's niece."

Becky felt her knees go weak. "Really?"

He nodded. He cut his steak and ate it slowly. "Clay's going to get into big trouble if he doesn't look out."

"Maybe it's just infatuation," Becky said hopefully.

"Maybe it ain't," Granddad replied. He put down his utensils. "Why don't you talk to him, Becky? Maybe he'll listen to you."

"I've tried talking to him," she said. "He just blows up and walks off. I can't do any more than I've already done. I can't protect him forever."

"He's your brother," the old man said grumpily. "You owe him."

"I owe everybody, it seems," she said irritably, glaring at him. "I can't go around picking up after him forever. He has to grow up."

"The way he's going about it, he'll never make it. You might give a party for him. Invite some of the nice kids around."

"We tried that once, don't you remember? He left right in the middle of it."

"We could try again. Or you could have a talk with him tomorrow night."

"I won't be here tomorrow night," she said slowly.

Granddad gaped at her. "What?"

"I have a date."

"A date? You? Wow!" Mack burst out enthusiastically. "Who with?"

Granddad scowled fiercely. "I know who with. That damned Kilpatrick man! It is, isn't it?!" he demanded.

"Becky, you wouldn't, would you?" Mack asked, his hazel eyes accusing and wide. "Not that man, after all he's done to Clay?"

"He's done nothing to Clay," she reminded him. "He's the one who turned Clay loose, if you remember. He could have prosecuted him."

"He didn't have a damned shred of proof. He wouldn't have dared take him to court," Granddad scoffed. "Well, you listen here, girl. You're not dating any lawyer…"

"I'm going out tomorrow night with Mr. Kilpatrick," she told her grandfather firmly, even though her heart was beating uncomfortably fast and hard and her hands were shaking with nerves. It was the first time in her life that Becky had ever deliberately defied him.

"Turncoat," Mack muttered.

"You can shut up," she told him. "I don't answer to you, or to anybody else," she added with a speaking glance at her grandfather. "I like him. I'm entitled to one date every five years. Even you have to admit that."

Granddad hesitated when he realized that anger wasn't going to work. "Listen, sugar, you need to stop and think what you're doing. I know you need to go out occasionally, to get away from housework and your job. But this man...he might actually be using you to spy on Clay."

He'd said something of the sort before, but this time Becky was ready for him.

"I've had lunch with him every day this week. He hasn't even mentioned Clay, not once."

Grandad looked outraged, but he camouflaged it. He started to speak again, but Becky got up and started gathering the dishes together.

"Oh, go ahead," he said angrily. "I can't stop you. But mark my words, you're going to regret this."

"No, I'm not," she said firmly. She took the dishes into the kitchen, her cheeks blazing with bad temper. Oh, lord, I hope I'm not, she amended before she started filling the sink with soapy water.

Clay came in just as she was finishing up in the kitchen and about to lock up for the night.

"It's after midnight," she told him. "Have you been working?" she asked flatly.

"Yes," he blurted out. Of course he was, but not at the kind of job Becky thought he had. It wasn't a total lie, he reassured himself.

"Exactly where?" she asked.

He arched his eyebrows. "Why do you want to know—so that you can have me checked out? As long as I'm working and going to school, what business is it of yours?"

Her jaw clenched. "I'm legally responsible for you, that's what business of mine it is," she said icily. "I don't like this cocky attitude of yours, and from what I hear of your new girlfriend, I don't think much of her, either."

His hands clenched at his sides. "I don't care what you think of her, or me," he said. "I'm tired of having you try to run my life. Why don't you find yourself a man?"

"In fact, I have," she said hotly. "I'm going out with Rourke Kilpatrick tomorrow night."

He paled. "You can't," he began, thinking of the hell he was going to catch when his friends found out that his sister was dating their worst enemy. "Becky, you can't!"

"Oh, yes, I can," she returned. "I've had enough of being everybody's mother and keeper. I'm going to have a little fun of my own for a change."

"Kilpatrick's my worst enemy!" he shouted.

"He isn't mine," she replied quietly. "And if you don't like it, that's just tough. I've worn myself out trying to get you to see what kind of people you're associating with. You won't listen, so why should I? Your friends won't like having me go out with the district attorney, will they?" she asked him flatly. "Well, that's just tough. You can't stop me, can you, Clay?"

He looked, and was, shaken. She didn't sound or look like his easygoing sister. She looked…different.

"Well, you'll be sorry," he said, backing away. "You hear me, Becky? You'll be sorry!"

"So everybody says," she murmured to herself after he'd slammed into his room. She closed her eyes. "Oh, lord, if I thought I had fifty more years of this to look forward to, I'd throw myself under a truck."

She contemplated that for a minute and decided that, given the way her luck was going, Clay would be driving the truck and it would be full of illegal drugs. She began to laugh almost hysterically. Life, she thought, was getting too complicated. Despite her attraction to Kilpatrick, and her hunger to be with him, just the fact of dating him was going to make things so much worse at home. But as she'd told her family, she was entitled to a little pleasure, even if she had to fight tooth and nail to get it. And she would, she promised herself. She would!

CHAPTER NINE

Becky didn't see Clay at all the next day. Well, let him sulk, she thought angrily. It was about time he faced the fact that she had rights, too. But she was on pins and needles all afternoon, worrying that something was going to go wrong and spoil her one big evening. But Granddad managed not to have a sick spell and Mack didn't give her any trouble. Both of them brooded, naturally, but it looked as if they weren't going to try to stop her from going out with Kilpatrick.

She put on the black dress and arranged her hair in an elegant coiffure. She drew on dark hose to wear with the spiked heels, and transferred the contents of her handbag to Maggie's evening bag. It was a good thing, she thought, that Kilpatrick wouldn't see what was under her dress. Her slip was several years old and white, not black. It had faint stains that wouldn't even bleach out, and her underwear, while clean, was hardly exciting—cotton, with raveled lace. Thank

God she wouldn't have to take any of it off. It would be just too embarrassing to have him see how poor she really was.

The dress was an extravagance, and she felt slightly guilty. But that only lasted until Kilpatrick came to pick her up and saw how it looked on her. His eyes said enough, even without the faint whistle and the husky exclamation.

"Will I do?" she asked breathlessly.

"You'll do just fine," he murmured, and smiled warmly.

He was wearing a dinner jacket, and the white shirt looked even whiter against his dark skin.

"Come in," she stammered, embarrassed by the shabby furniture and the tattered rug as much as by Clay's furious glare. He'd shown up at the house only minutes before, and he looked as if he would like to shoot Kilpatrick on the spot. He didn't even bother with a greeting. He turned on his heel and left the room.

That didn't seem to bother Kilpatrick. And he didn't stare, or seem to really notice his surroundings. He shook hands with a reluctant Granddad and a nervous Mack with careless ease.

"I'll have her home by midnight," he assured Granddad.

Granddad allowed Becky to kiss his cheek. "Have a good time," he said tersely.

"Thanks, I will." She winked at Mack, who managed a reluctant smile and went back to watching television.

Kilpatrick closed the door behind them. Becky could have burst into tears. She knew that it was Clay's lead that had influenced Granddad and Mack; they were trying to show their support for him. But Mack had been withdrawn and moody all day, and he hadn't even spoken to Clay when his brother had come in. In fact, she realized, his behavior toward Clay was more hostile than his attitude toward Kilpatrick.

"Stop brooding. I didn't expect fireworks and flags waving," he said dryly as he helped her into the front seat of his car—a new one. It was not a Mercedes, either, but a Thunderbird turbo coupe. It was white with a red interior—a streamlined beast of a machine. "Well, how do you like it?" he asked impatiently.

"I love it," she said gently. He walked around to the driver's side. "I'm sorry, anyway, about my family," Becky added when he was in the car and they were driving away.

"No apology needed." He glanced at her in the glare from the streetlights and smiled. "Is that a new dress, and for my benefit?" he asked.

She burst out laughing. "Yes, it is, and I hope you aren't going to get conceited."

"Child, a man who looks like I do, and with my obvious charm and modesty, has a hell of a lot to be conceited about," he informed her with a wicked grin.

She felt as if she were floating, dreaming. "Oh, you're so different from what I thought you were!" she said, thinking out loud. "You're not stern and unapproachable at all."

"That's my public face," he informed her. "I have to keep the voters convinced that I'm one step down from public enemy number one. A good D.A. should look worse than Scarface." He scowled thoughtfully. "Maybe I could get a makeup kit and work on myself. Of course, I'm not too thrilled at the prospect of a third term in office."

"How in the world did you get to be a district attorney?" she asked, really interested.

"I got tired of seeing victims who suffered more than the criminals," he said simply. "I thought I could do something about it. And I have, in a small way." He glanced her way. "There's a lot wrong with the world, little one."

"I've noticed." She leaned her head back on the headrest, her eyes searching over his hard, lean face in the glare of overhead streetlights. "You look tired," she said, aware of new lines in his face.

"I am tired," he said. "I spent most of last night in a hospital emergency room."

"Why?" she asked gently.

All the lightness went out of his expression. "I was watching a ten-year-old boy die of a drug overdose," he said with brutal candor.

"Ten?!"

"Ten." He bit off the word, his face hardening even as she watched. "He was a fifth grader at Curry Station Elementary. He overdosed on crack. It seems the boy's parents are well-to-do and he got a substantial allowance. He wasn't making good grades, and the other kids were giving him a hard time. It's amazing how kids seem to be able to find any weakness in another child and attack it."

"My little brother goes to Curry Station Elementary," she said in a stunned voice. "And he's in fifth grade."

"He'll hear all about it Monday, I'm sure," Kilpatrick said angrily. "It's going to be a media holiday, and guess who's on the hot seat?"

"You and the police," she made a shrewd guess.

He nodded. "He was an only child. His parents were pretty torn up. I promised them I'd find the perpetrators if it was the last thing I did. I meant it, too," he added coldly. "I'll get them. And when I do, I'll send them up."

She clenched her hands in her lap, refusing to think that Clay might somehow have been involved. Her eyes closed. "Ten years old."

He lit a cigar and cracked a window for Becky's benefit. "Mack doesn't do drugs, does he?" he asked, glancing at her.

She shook her head. "Not Mack. He's much too sensible. He's more like me than Clay ever was. I never did drugs in my whole life. In fact, I only ever had a drink once and I hated it." She smiled wistfully. "I'm a real square. I guess it comes from living out in the sticks and having little contact with the modern world."

"You aren't missing much," he murmured as he executed a sharp right turn out of the growing weekend night traffic. "From what I see every day, the modern world is going straight to hell."

"You must think there's hope for it, or you'd have quit your job long ago."

"I still may," he informed her. "The political powers-that-be are leaning on me to go for a third term, but I'm sick of it. I take criminals to court and the judges and juries turn them loose. The first drug supplier I prosecuted was sentenced to life and he got out in three years. How's that for having your eyes opened?"

"Does it always work that way?"

"It depends on the perp's connections," he replied. "If he works for some drug lord who considers him valuable enough, there are always political strings that can be pulled and palms that can be greased. Nothing is black and white these days. Corruption is more widespread than you'd ever believe. I'm tired of politics and plea-bargaining and over-crowded jails and courts."

"They say the courts are backed up really bad," she mentioned. "I know it sometimes takes months for us to get a case calendared."

"That's true. I average several hundred cases a month, of which only about twenty or thirty ever get to trial. No joke," he said when he saw her expression. "The rest are plea-bargained out or dropped for lack of evidence. You can't imagine how frustrating it gets when you're trying to handle so many cases without adequate manpower. And then, when I finally get a case together and get it into court, two out of three times the defense attorney or the public defender is called away or we can't get a crucial witness to show up for court, and we have to have the trial put off again. I've had one case get to the bench three times and the man I'm prosecuting is still in jail waiting to be tried." He gestured angrily with the hand that was holding the cigar. "What hurts the most is having to send off a first-time offender and having him land in stir with older criminals. He gets an education money can't buy, and that isn't the worst of it." He stopped for a traffic light. "I suppose you know that some men are used like women in prison?" he added, glancing at her.

She nodded. "Yes. The juvenile officer mentioned that when I picked up Clay."

His dark eyes narrowed. "Trying to frighten him, I suppose. I hope it worked. He wasn't telling lies."

"Clay's something of a hardcase," she murmured, her hands

tightening on the evening purse Maggie had loaned her. "He doesn't scare easily."

"Neither did I, at his age," he replied. "It's a shame that your father wasn't more of a father, Becky. What that boy needs most right now is a man he can look up to."

"If Granddad was the man he used to be, he might have been able to do something with Clay," she said. "But he's been in bad health for the past year, and I'm just not up to coping with a boy bigger than I am. I can't very well put him over my knee and spank him."

He chuckled softly as the light changed and the powerful car sped off. "I can imagine that. But at his age, spanking is hardly the answer. Can he be reasoned with?"

"Not since he started hanging out with his new friends. I have no influence over him at all now. He's even stopped going to counseling." She studied her hands in her lap. "He's got a job, at least. Or so he says."

"Good for him." He took another draw from the cigar. "I hope he does well at it." He didn't push his luck. He wondered if Clay really had a job or if that was just what he'd told his sister to explain his nocturnal activities. It would be worth checking out.

She laid her head against the headrest and stared at him openly, smiling. "I'm glad you asked me out."

"So am I. And you still haven't told me what you want to do after we eat," he reminded her. "What's it going to be—a movie or dancing?"

She shook her head. "I don't care," she said, and meant it. It was more than enough just to be with him.

"In that case, we'll go dancing," he said. "I can watch a

movie by myself, but dancing alone is rough. People stare, and it plays hell with my credibility."

She laughed with pure delight. "You're a lunatic," she told him.

"Absolutely," he informed her as he turned into the parking lot of one of the better restaurants in Atlanta. "No sane man would do my job." He parked the car and cut off the engine, turning to study her with blatant interest in the light from the overhead streetlights. "I do like that dress," he remarked. "But your hair would look better if you took it down."

"No, it wouldn't," she protested with a laugh. "It took me the better part of a half hour to get it in this condition in the first place."

"It wouldn't take half as long to take it down, now, would it?" he murmured dryly, his dark eyes mischievous as they held hers.

"But..."

He traced her mouth with his forefinger, creating havoc with her pulse and her makeup. "I like long hair," he murmured.

This wasn't fair at all. Of course, she couldn't have expected him to give up before he finally got his own way. He had a reputation for being worse than a bulldog in court. She sighed with audible defeat and reached up to take the pins out of her high coiffure. So much for trying to look elegant for him.

"That's better," he said when she finished dragging her hairbrush through her long tresses so that they waved softly around her bare shoulders. His lean, dark fingers smoothed down it and tangled in its silky softness. "It smells like wild-flowers."

"Does it?" she whispered. It was hard to get her breath with his face so close to hers. She looked up into dark eyes that seemed to see right through her and her heart skipped.

He was doing some looking of his own. Becky had a quality that he'd never known in any other woman—an exaggerated empathy, a way of feeling the pain of people around her. She had spirit and she was strong, but it wasn't those qualities that attracted him to her. It was her warmth, her soft heart, her capacity for opening her arms to the whole world. Love had been singularly lacking in Kilpatrick's life. Except for his uncle, he'd never been really close to anyone. His one brief brush with being engaged had soured him on women for a long time, but Becky was opening doors in his heart. He scowled, a little uncomfortable at the thought of being vulnerable again.

"Is something wrong?" she asked huskily, because she didn't understand the scowl.

He searched her hazel eyes with quiet discomfort, then smiled faintly and drew his hand away from her thick, silky hair. "Just thinking," he said carelessly. He leaned forward and stubbed out his cigar in the ashtray. "We'd better get going."

He helped her out and escorted her into the restaurant—one so fancy that the place setting had half a dozen assorted forks and spoons—and Becky ground her teeth together, hoping she wasn't going to embarrass him.

The menu, to add insult to injury, was in French. She blushed, and Kilpatrick, seeing her face, could have kicked himself. He'd meant to give her a special evening, not make her feel out of place.

He plucked the menu out of her cold, nervous hands with a quiet smile. "Which do you prefer, fish, chicken, or beef?" he asked softly.

"Chicken," she said immediately, because it was usually less expensive in the restaurants she'd been to before and she didn't want to strain his pocket.

He leaned forward, staring at her. "I said, which do you prefer," he emphasized.

She colored delicately and dropped her eyes. "Beef."

"All right." He motioned to the waiter, who came immediately, and he gave the order in what sounded to Becky like flawless French.

"You speak French?" she asked.

He nodded. "French, Latin, and a little Cherokee," he said. "It's a knack, I suppose—kind of like the ability to make a mouthwatering lemon pound cake."

She smiled at him. "Thank you."

"Believe it or not, I didn't bring you here to make you uncomfortable," he said. His dark eyes narrowed. "Something else bothers you, besides the menu," he said abruptly. "What?"

She couldn't seem to fool him. Anyway, why bother, she thought recklessly. He'd seen where she lived; he must have some idea of her background. "All these utensils," she confessed, gesturing toward them. "At home we have a knife, a fork, and a spoon, and I only know where they go because of home economics class at school."

He chuckled. "Well, I'll try to educate you." He did, amusing her with the various salad and dessert forks and the collection of spoons until the waiter came with their orders.

She watched him to see which utensils to use. By the time they reached dessert—a scrumptious pecan pie with vanilla ice cream on top—she felt as if she'd had an education in the culinary arts.

"What did we eat?" she asked in a whisper when they'd finished dessert and were having a second cup of strong black coffee with real cream.

"Boeuf bourbonnaise," he informed her. He leaned forward and lowered his deep voice. "It's an uptown French beef stew."

She laughed softly. "Is it, really?"

"Really. It's made with the kind of spices we put in pies and with a good red wine."

"I'll have to dig out my cookbooks and try it on the family," she mused. "I'll bet Granddad would slip his to the dog."

"Do you have a dog?" he asked.

She remembered his big German shepherd and felt sorry for him. "We did have; an old hound we called Blue. But the mailman ran over him last year. I'm sorry about Gus. I guess you really miss him."

He moved his coffee cup in its thin china saucer absently. He nodded. "The house is pretty quiet. Nobody needs to be taken for a walk anymore."

"Rourke, why don't you get another dog?" she asked gently. "Really, it's the best thing to do. There are pet shops all over Atlanta. You could find any breed you liked."

He searched her soft eyes. "What breed do you like?"

She smiled. "I like collies," she said. "But I've heard that they don't do well here in the South because it gets so hot. And they're long-haired, so the fur gets everywhere."

He leaned back in his chair. "I like basset hounds."

She laughed. "I like them, too."

"You'll have to come with me when I go looking for one," he said idly. "After all, it was your idea."

Becky felt as if she'd been shot through with pleasure. "Oh, I'd enjoy that," she said.

"So would I. Maybe next weekend. I've got a pretty full calendar during the week, but we'll find time."

She wondered what he'd say if she told him that she was falling in love with him. Probably he'd grin and think she was joking, but it was the truth. He appealed to her in so many ways.

"Let's go over to that new nightclub in Underground Atlanta and dance for an hour or so," he murmured, checking his watch. He raised an eyebrow. "You said once that you liked opera."

"Well, yes," she began.

"They're playing *Turandot* at the Fox next month. We can go."

"To a real opera?" She caught her breath.

"Yes. You can wear that dress, as a matter of fact," he added with a long, meaningful look. "You're dishy, Becky."

She smiled at him. "Not really, but thank you for saying so."

"Come on."

He got up and helped her up, watching her with warm curiosity while he waited to pay the bill. She seemed to find the restaurant fascinating. He found her the same way. He was looking forward to introducing her to a new world of luxury and culture, even if it only lasted for a few weeks. He enjoyed being with her. Loneliness was beginning to wear on him. He liked having someone to go places with. Even an evening out was a treat for him, and Becky's delight with her surroundings made it all worthwhile.

One unpleasant thought marred his pleasure in the evening. He'd become a target, and they still hadn't found out who'd put the bomb in his car. He could be putting Becky at risk just by being seen with her, and that bothered him. He didn't want her hurt. But if it was just him the perpetrator was after, perhaps Becky wouldn't be at risk. He wouldn't allow himself to think about her brother or the Harrises at all.

He took her to Underground Atlanta, to one of the newer clubs, and Becky found herself in another world. This was the Atlanta she'd never seen—the bright and sparking nightlife that made friends of total strangers.

"It's beautiful," she exclaimed when they were seated near the dance floor. "But I don't think I can do that." She gestured toward several couples who seemed to be human contortionists as they danced to the throbbing rhythm of the music.

"Neither can I," he murmured dryly. He'd ordered ginger ale for himself and Becky, forgoing his usual scotch and water. He didn't want to give her the impression that he was a hard-drinking man. In fact, he wasn't. He liked the occasional scotch and water, but that was about the extent of his interest in alcohol.

"Do they ever play slow music?" she asked.

Just as she made the remark, the music stopped and a slow, bluesy melody began to build. Kilpatrick got to his feet and held out his hand. Becky put hers into it and followed him onto the dance floor.

He was much taller than she was, but they melted together as if they'd been especially designed to fit. He
smoothed her hand onto his chest and held it against the soft
fabric of his dinner jacket with his own big, lean hand warm
over it. His other hand slid around her waist and drew her
completely against him so that her body rested against his as
they moved, her cheek against his chest.

She felt like heaven in his arms. Her body was soft and warm,
and the smell of her was like wildflowers in his nostrils. He
looked down at her, so vulnerable and trusting in his arms, and
thought that he'd never felt quite so content. But with the contentment was a fierce awareness of her as a woman, a heated
need to have her even closer than this, to bend his head and take
her soft mouth under his, to teach her passion.

Becky was unaware of his deep hunger, but she was feeling one of her own. His body was taut and fit, and the feel
of it was making her heart beat fast. He smelled of spicy cologne and soap—masculine smells that acted like a drug on
her emotions. It had been years since she'd danced with anyone, and never with anyone like Kilpatrick. He led her
around the floor with consummate ease, as if dancing was
second nature to him. It probably was. He knew a lot about
women, and this nightclub seemed to be his kind of place.
That meant he'd probably taken other women out to similar places, and gone dancing like this, except that at the end
of the evening, he hadn't taken his date straight home. Her
face burned as she saw unwanted images of Kilpatrick with
other women and she stiffened slightly in his arms.

"What is it?" he asked at her forehead, his voice deep and
slow and lazy.

"Nothing," she whispered.

His hand at her back pulled her closer, sliding up to the flesh left bare by the cut of her dress, warm and sensuous on her bare skin. "Tell me, Becky."

She sighed softly and looked up at him. She hadn't realized his face was so close. In the dim light, it seemed darker than ever, harder, and his superiority in age made him seem a world away from her. "Why did you ask me out?" she whispered.

He didn't smile. His dark eyes held hers and he almost stopped dancing. His body moved slowly against her as the music blared around them and other couples drifted past. "Don't you have any idea?" he asked quietly.

Her lips parted on a held breath. "Because of the lemon pound cake?" she ventured.

His hand slid up into the thickness of her hair and grasped it, holding her face at just the right angle as he bent toward her. "Because of this," he breathed.

She couldn't believe what he did. Her eyes widened with faint surprise as his hard lips brushed across hers once, twice, in a lazy exploration that was pure seduction.

The lean fingers in her hair contracted, making her gasp so that her lips parted. He made a sound deep in his throat and began to move again to the music. His mouth didn't touch hers, but hovered just above her lips, making her head spin as they danced.

Her eyes met his shyly as she felt his coffee-scented breath on her lips.

"Exciting, isn't it?" he whispered huskily and his fingers began to move in her hair, caressing movements that made her body react fiercely. "Half of Atlanta around us, and I'm making love to you on a dance floor."

"You...aren't," she managed.

"No?" He smiled. It was a different smile from any she'd ever seen on a man's face before. It threatened and seduced at the same time. He tugged her head back farther on his shoulder and executed a turn that brought one long, powerful leg in between both of hers, a contact that made her gasp out loud even as his mouth moved closer and she breathed him.

She was hardly aware of the music. He did it again, and again, his eyes blazing into hers, his body an instrument of the most exquisite torture. She caught at his arm when the contact worked on her so deeply that her knees went weak.

"Are you going to faint on me, Becky?" he whispered, sliding his cheek against hers so that his breath was warm on her ear. He nibbled the lobe delicately. "If it's this affecting on a dance floor, try to imagine how it's going to feel on your front porch when I kiss you good night. I can promise you, I won't be this gentle."

She shivered. He laughed softly and stopped as the music ended. She couldn't look at him as he escorted her back to their table; she was overwhelmed by the sensations she'd felt. Sensuality was new to her. So was desire, but surely that was what she'd felt shivering through her body at the veiled threat in his words.

"Look at me, you coward," he taunted when they were sipping piña coladas a little later.

She lifted her eyes, and a shock of pleasure ran through her as she met that dark, knowing gaze.

"Tell me you don't want my mouth, Becky," he murmured, letting his gaze fall to her parted lips.

"If you don't stop that, I'm going to melt on the floor," she said in a husky whisper. "Shame on you."

He chuckled over his drink. "Dewy-eyed innocent," he murmured. "You're a refreshing change, Rebecca Cullen. At least I know what kind of woman I'm dealing with this time," he added, half to himself.

She stared at him curiously. "What do you mean?"

He finished his drink and stared at the empty glass with narrowed eyes. "Did you know that I was engaged once, when I was in my twenties?"

"Yes," she said.

He lifted his gaze to hers. "She was a lesbian."

She didn't know what to say. She knew what a lesbian was, but it puzzled her that he'd become engaged to one.

"Did you know?" she asked finally.

"Good God, no!" he returned curtly. "She was beautiful and sophisticated, and considered in my circles to be a good catch. She came from old money. I was crazy about her." He twirled the empty glass in his hands, smarting from the memory. "She teased me and provoked me until I was wild to have her. We got engaged, and one night she invited me over after a dinner I had to attend."

His eyes narrowed. "I was two hours late. I guess she'd given me up, but her door was unlocked, so I assumed she was waiting. I'd worked myself into a frenzy. She was mine, and that night all my dreams were going to come true. I pushed open her bedroom door and got the shock of my life." He put the glass down. "She was in bed with her female law clerk, and the situation spoke for itself. I took my ring back and she begged me not to give her away. After that, I didn't trust women very much. I've had my flings, but nobody's gotten close enough to touch my heart again. It was a hard lesson," he concluded with a wry smile.

"Yes, I imagine it was. Do you…still love her?" she asked hesitantly.

He shook his head. "It would be a waste, don't you think? Sexual preferences don't change. It wouldn't have worked."

"I suppose not." She felt his pain. Her soft hazel eyes searched his hard face, and she wondered at the vulnerability she saw there. "Is that what you meant when you said you knew what kind of woman I was?"

He nodded. "The way you react to me is comforting, Rebecca," he mused, smiling gently. "At least your responses are normal ones for a woman. I never noticed it until the engagement was past history, but she always seemed to suffer me on the dance floor or anywhere else that called for intimacy. I don't think she could have surrendered to me under any circumstances."

Becky flushed. This was a kind of plain speaking she'd never experienced. "I see."

He chuckled. "Embarrased? I don't suppose you've ever discussed such things at home."

"No," she replied with a faint smile. "You see, my grandfather is rather old-fashioned. I can talk to Maggie at the office, but not about that sort of thing," she added.

He studied her with open curiosity. "Did you never get to go on dates?"

She shrugged. "When?" she asked gently. "There were the

chores to do——the cooking and cleaning and helping Grand-dad on the farm. Since last year, I've had to look after him, as well. And Clay…" She broke off, staring down at the tablecloth. "Well, I guess you can imagine how that's complicated things. Now Granddad worries about him, too. Mack's gone broody." She shook her head. "I used to wonder, you know, if life was this complicated for everybody. The girlfriends I had at school used to talk about their families and about things they did together, but nobody had as many chores as I did. I guess I grew up young."

"You shouldn't have had to," he said quietly, feeling anger toward her father for putting her in such a position. "My God, it's too much for one young woman."

"Not really. I'm used to it, you see. I love them," she said helplessly, her big hazel eyes searching his. "How do you desert people you love?"

"I wouldn't know," he replied. His face hardened. "I don't know a lot about love. I live alone. I have for a long time."

"But, who takes care of you when you get sick or hurt?" she asked suddenly, concerned.

That concern made his teeth clench. "Nobody."

She smiled at him gently. "I'd look after you, if you did."

"Becky," he groaned. He shot back his cuff and looked at his watch. This was getting totally out of hand. "We'd better go. I promised to have you home by midnight."

Becky got up, flustered. She'd said too much. She should have known how he'd react to being fussed over. She wanted to apologize, but she didn't know what to say, so she said nothing at all.

He paid the check and led her out to the car. He put her

inside absently while he tried not to be affected by what she'd said. He couldn't let her go soft on him. It would be the very worst thing that could happen to both of them. He didn't want her on his conscience. He wouldn't ask her out again. He didn't dare.

The house was dark when Rourke pulled up at the front steps. He helped Becky out of the car and escorted her to her door.

"I'm sorry," she said gently, breaking the silence for the first time since they'd left the nightclub. "I shouldn't have said anything."

He sighed heavily, looking down at her in the faint light from the full moon. His lean hands framed her face, and she looked so vulnerable, so hurt, that he was driven to comfort her.

"It's all right," he said softly. His gaze fell to her mouth. He bent, touching his hard lips to hers, and the contact went through his tall body like lightning.

He lifted his mouth just briefly and then nudged her lips with it with faint roughness, biting at them, teasing them. The fires burned high in him. It had been too long since he'd had a woman in his arms. Becky was catching the fallout. He heard her gasp as he teased her soft lips. His fingers speared into the hair at her temples, holding her still. She smelled of flowers, of innocence. She tasted that way, too. It drove him mad.

She gasped and a faint moan escaped her lips as he tugged at her soft lower lip with his teeth and then slowly teased her mouth with his, biting at it, steadily increasing the pressure and the rough contact until her mouth was blindly following his, desperately hungry. She whispered his name pleadingly and reached up to him, on fire with sensation that frightened her even as they took control of her body.

As he felt her give in to him, his hands left her face and slid around her, bringing her body into his so that she could feel the length of him against her. Then the teasing stopped, as his mouth parted hers ruthlessly and ground into it with a pressure that forced her head back into his broad shoulder.

She hadn't been kissed often, and never like this. She was trembling all over as he gave her what her mouth had been begging for. She felt the fierce possession of his lips with aching joy. She breathed in the smoky taste of his mouth, drowned in the unbridled fervor of his kiss. She moaned and reached up to hold him, her mouth answering his in a frenzy of shaken emotion.

He felt her tremble and abruptly drew back. His own breath came roughly as he stared down at her rapt, stunned face. Her wide hazel eyes mirrored the aroused confusion she was feeling. He felt guilty.

"I'm sorry," he said gently. "I shouldn't have done that."

"I don't understand," she whispered, grateful for his hands on her arms, because she was weak enough to slide to the floor without support. Her whole body throbbed.

"Becky, a man kisses a woman like that when he's trying to entice her into bed," he said heavily. His lean hands slid up and down the soft flesh of her arms. "It was the last way I should have kissed you. I suppose it's been longer than I realized."

"It's all right," she said softly.

He let her go slowly, watching her with mingled emotions

of his own. His body felt taut and uneasy, but he was going to have to get it under control. Becky wasn't the kind of woman he could satisfy his hungers with. She needed a marrying man, not a confirmed bachelor.

"Thank you for tonight," she said after a minute. "I enjoyed it very much."

"I enjoyed it, too. Good night." He sounded abrupt and not in the best of moods.

She watched him go down the steps with a feeling of loss. He wouldn't be back. She'd overstepped the boundaries of their fragile relationship and brought emotions into it. She knew instinctively that he wouldn't want a woman who could get inside his emotional armor. No, he wouldn't be back.

She watched him get into the car and drive away without even glancing toward her. *Cinderella,* she thought with faint amusement. The clock strikes twelve and the spell dies.

Well, I'm just lucky I didn't turn into a pumpkin, I suppose, she thought to herself. With a long, hurting sigh, she turned and unlocked the door.

The house was dark and nobody was stirring. She hoped Clay was in bed, and not still out carousing with his slinky girlfriend or his awful male friends. But she'd had one lovely night that she could tuck away in her memory. Maybe it would help get her through the rest of her life.

She went to bed determined not to cry, but she did.

CHAPTER TEN

Kilpatrick brooded all night long, and barely slept. Occasionally on Sundays, he made an attempt to get to church. This morning wasn't one of those times. He'd had two neat scotch whiskeys when he had gotten home the night before, and his head was hurting.

Becky had looked at him with eyes so soft they haunted him. She'd said that she'd take care of him if he got sick. His own eyes closed and he groaned out loud. Even his uncle, who'd cared for him, hadn't been an openly affectionate man. Kilpatrick didn't know how to handle affection. He'd never had to. Becky was changing that, and he couldn't let her. He was totally wrong for such an innocent. He wanted her badly, almost enough to seduce her. He couldn't let that happen. Becky had too many burdens.

He made coffee and drank it while he read the Sunday paper. It was so quiet now that Gus was dead. He missed the dog terribly. Perhaps it would be a good idea to get a puppy.

He remembered what Becky had said about a basset hound and smiled. He'd like one. Well, he could do worse than go looking in pet shops. He couldn't take her with him, of course. Odd how that put a damper on his enthusiasm. But he couldn't let her get attached to him. She was so vulnerable, dammit—not the kind of woman who could take an affair in stride.

He put down the paper and pulled out his briefcase, stuffed to the top with briefs he needed to look over before court began the next day. If he was going to brood, he might as well work, he told himself firmly.

Becky dressed to go to church after a long and sleepless night. It was probably just as well that Kilpatrick had walked away without a backward glance, she told herself. It would make her life less complicated. But that didn't make it any easier to swallow.

She knew that Granddad wasn't up to church, and Clay never went, despite her best efforts to encourage him there. But Mack enjoyed Sunday school and he alone was always up and dressed when she went out the door.

With reluctance, she knocked at Clay's door and poked her head around it.

"Keep an eye on Granddad while we're gone, if you can," she said coolly, noticing that he looked hungover. She wasn't going to ask when he had gotten home.

He raised himself up on one elbow sleepily, glaring at her. "You're a turncoat, Becky," he accused coldly. "How could you go out with that man after what he did to me?"

She didn't blink an eye. "After what *he* did to *you*?" she asked. "How about what you did to get yourself in trouble—or doesn't that count?"

"If you bring him here again, I'll...!" he began.

"You'll what?" she demanded in a driven tone. "If you don't like the conditions here, you know where the door is. But don't expect me to stand up for you in court a second time. If you leave, I'll be sure to let the juvenile authorities know."

He actually paled. She'd threatened that once before and she looked determined. He felt sick. The Harrises had him well under their thumbs with what they'd threatened, and his own infatuation with Francine kept him there. He didn't want to lose her or his new wealth, and he sure didn't want Kilpatrick on his neck. But to let the man hang around here was to invite disaster.

"Becky," he began.

"A ten-year-old boy at Curry Station Elementary died of a coke overdose," she said, watching his face carefully.

Clay seemed to stop breathing. His face gave nothing away, but there was a flash of pure fear in his eyes and Becky wanted to scream. She'd tried not to believe he had any connection with drug pushing, but that look made her nervous.

"Do you know anything about it?" she demanded.

He looked away. "Why would I? I told you, I don't want to go to jail, Becky."

She didn't really relax. She couldn't. She just gave him a long look and went out, closing the door.

Mack suddenly appeared behind her. Becky turned to notice that his face was flushed, his eyes wide and troubled. "It was Billy Dennis," he said. "The boy who died. He was a friend of mine. John Gaines called me while you were gone last night and told me about it." His eyes lowered. "Billy never hurt anybody. He was a loner. Nobody much liked him, but I did."

"Oh, Mack," she said softly.

Mack glanced toward Clay's room and started to speak, but he couldn't bring himself to tell her. He sighed and turned away.

Becky said good-bye to Granddad after she settled him, and she and Mack drove to the small Baptist church she'd attended since childhood. In rural Georgia, Baptist was the predominant church, and had been for over a hundred years. Fire and brimstone rained down from the pulpits of all but the most citified churches, and on Sunday morning, the pews were always full.

Becky loved the little white country church with its tall spire and picturesque setting. But mostly she loved the peace and security she felt inside its spartan walls. Her mother, her grandmother, and her great-grandparents were buried in the graveyard behind the church. One of her cousins had donated a large chunk of the cash it had taken to build the structure, which was over seventy years old. Becky knew that the sense of tradition and continuity that made the rural South so closeknit was part of the reason local residents came to church each Sunday and supported its outreach programs. They might curse their cats and each other during the week, but on Sundays they at least made the effort to reach for a nobler self than they possessed.

"You look very handsome," Becky told Mack as they climbed out of the car and moved toward the door.

"You, too." He grinned. He was wearing dress slacks, the only pair he had, with one of his two white shirts and his only tie. He wore sneakers, because they didn't have the money for leather dress shoes.

Becky had on her one white suit, which she wore with a blue knit blouse and faintly scuffed white high heels. Fortunately, nobody here made an issue of how people dressed, or looked down on less fortunate members of the congregation. These were the people who'd come rushing out to the house when Becky's mother died, with plates full of food and offers of help. They were people who lived what they believed in. She felt as much at home here among them as she did in her own living room. Perhaps that was what made church fun, instead of a weekly chore undertaken only for show.

As she listened to the sermon, she thought about Clay and hoped that he wasn't beyond help. She didn't know what to do. Giving in to his threats wouldn't accomplish anything, but what if by refusing she pushed him too far and he wound up in prison? She ground her teeth together. If only she could ask Kilpatrick for help. She'd tried, but her emotions had gotten in the way. Now she was going to have to manage alone, somehow.

Monday morning came all too soon. She'd spent the rest of Sunday cooking and getting everyone's clothes ready for the week and watching television with Mack and Granddad. Clay had been gone when she and Mack returned from church. He didn't come in until late Sunday night, after everyone had gone to bed.

"Are you going to school today?" she asked him coldly as she hustled Mack down the hall.

Clay shrugged. "I guess so," he said. He looked and sounded subdued. In fact, he was. The child's death had worn on him. He'd never expected anything like that to happen. It was worse than anything he'd ever done before, even if he hadn't given the stuff to the kid. He'd just asked one of the older boys he knew for some tips, and the Dennis boy was known to somebody's younger brother. Bubba had done the actual selling. But Clay couldn't say anything about that without implicating himself, and the Harris boys had already made some nasty threats about what they could do to Clay with their combined testimony. He was well and truly hogtied, and matters were worse now since Mack had refused flatly to have any part of what they were doing. He'd sweated it out, expecting Mack to tell, but the boy hadn't. But Mack wouldn't even speak to him now, and since the Dennis boy's death, Mack looked at him as if he were some nauseating piece of garbage. It really hurt to have his hero-worshiping little brother hate him. Becky, too, seemed to have stopped caring about him. He was like a whip without a wheel, drifting deeper and deeper toward the shallows and sandbars, with no one he trusted enough to confide in.

Francine had comforted him last night. Don't worry, she'd said, nobody will know you had anything to do with it. But even that hadn't given him peace. He wondered if he was ever going to know it again. He had to go to school because he'd go crazy if he stayed home.

Becky went to her office equally subdued. Granddad had looked a little peaked this morning, and she was worried about him, too. He hadn't said two words about Kilpatrick since Saturday, but that wasn't his usual style, either. He said exactly what he thought, except when he was too sick to care. She hoped he wasn't headed for a relapse.

"Well, how did it go?" Maggie demanded under her breath when Becky walked into the office.

"We had dinner and danced, and it was great fun," she lied, smiling. She handed the beaded bag and shoes back to Maggie in the paper bag she'd carried them in. "Thanks so much for the loan of those. I was dishy. He said so."

"I'm glad that you enjoyed yourself. You're entitled to some fun."

Becky tucked a strand of loose hair back into her bun and straightened her plaid shirtwaist dress. She looked neat and clean, but not spectacular. "This is more my style, I guess—country and fundamental." She sighed. "Oh, Maggie, why is life so complicated?"

"I'll have to tell you later," Maggie whispered, nodding toward her boss's office. "He's in a mean mood. Court starts this morning, you know, and he's got two cases—one of them against your friend Kilpatrick. He's boning up on new decisions for all he's worth, but I'll bet Kilpatrick is already two steps ahead of him. He thinks so, too."

Becky's heart jumped at the sound of Kilpatrick's name, but it wouldn't do to get overenthusiastic. That interlude was over. And grand though it was, she had to live in the real world, not in the dreamy past. She uncovered her typewriter and got to work.

It was late afternoon when Kilpatrick returned from court. He'd handled one case himself that involved drug trafficking, while his colleagues had been parceled off into other courtrooms, prosecuting cases ranging from child molestation to attempted murder. He was tired and out of humor, and it didn't do his temper any good to find Dan Berry waiting for him.

He put his briefcase down beside his desk and stood erect, stretching, his body aching from hours of sitting in one position.

"Well, what is it?" he asked heavily.

Berry got up and closed the door gently. "Something personal," he replied. "It's about the bomb."

Kilpatrick sat down on the edge of his desk and lit his cigar. "Shoot."

"You know I told you Harvey Blair was out of prison and had threatened to waste you when he was released?" he began.

Kilpatrick nodded.

"The state fire marshal's office has traced the timer in the bomb to a local radio parts shop. The owner was a good friend of Blair's, as it turns out."

"Which doesn't mean that he made the bomb or ordered it made. And most electronics shops carry the makings of a bomb." He shook his head, his dark brows drawn together in a scowl. He smoked his cigar absently. "No, I think it's old man Harris and his boys. I'm damned near sure of it."

"You haven't forgotten what I told you about the Cullen boy and his electronics knack?"

"I haven't forgotten. I just don't think he's quite that stupid."

Berry's eyes narrowed. "Look, we all know you've been seeing the Cullen boy's sister…"

"Which doesn't have a damned thing to do with the way

I handle this office," Kilpatrick said in a hot, angry tone. "I won't turn a blind eye to anything that kid does just because I take his sister out occasionally. If he was involved, I'll prosecute him. All right?"

"All right!" Dan said, saluting. "You've convinced me— honest!"

Kilpatrick glared at him. "And I don't think it's Blair, either. But if it will make you feel better, I'll go by and have a chat with him."

"Unarmed?" Berry burst out.

Kilpatrick's dark eyes flashed. "He won't off me in broad daylight in his own house. Even Blair has more brains than that." He got up and checked his watch. "I'll do it now. My next case isn't until morning. Have you done any more checking into the Dennis case?" he asked.

Berry nodded. "I've interviewed several kids who knew him at the elementary school, including a young man named Mack Cullen, who was one of his friends."

Kilpatrick's jaw clenched.

Berry saw that telltale movement. "You didn't know, I gather? I thought the Cullen woman might have mentioned it."

He shook his head. "But I'll make a point of asking," he said, agreeing to something he'd sworn he wouldn't do. He'd promised himself he'd leave Becky alone, but the weekend had dragged by and he missed her company, her smile, the sound of her voice. He'd almost picked up the phone early this morning, but he'd managed enough willpower not to. Now, it seemed that he had a good excuse to satisfy his conscience. His whole mood lightened.

"Please check under your hood before you drive away," Berry cautioned wearily. "We don't want you blown to bits before we get the goods on the perp who wired you. Okay?"

"I'll do my best," Kilpatrick assured him, sticking the cigar in his mouth and grinning around it. "I'd look like hell in pieces, I'm sure."

Berry started to speak but Kilpatrick was already out the door, headed directly for Becky's office. To hell with noble principles, he told himself.

He opened the door and walked in, finding Becky bent over her typewriter. The other women stopped working to stare at him.

He perched himself on Becky's desk and waited until she looked up, her face first astonished, then radiant with delight.

He grinned. "Glad to see me? I'm glad to see you, too. I'll be tied up all week in court, but we can have dinner Friday night. Chinese or Greek? I'm partial to a good moussaka and resinated wine, but I like sweet and sour pork almost as much."

"I've never had Greek food—or Chinese," she confessed, sounding as flustered as she felt.

"We'll work it out as we go. I can't stay. I'm going to interview a man who threatened to pull out my guts and knot them around a telephone pole."

She gasped.

"No problem," he said, getting to his feet. "I don't think he did it. He doesn't know beans about electronics, and he wants to stay on the outside too much to complicate things."

"Do you check your car..." she began again.

"You and Berry," he muttered, glowering down at her. "Honest to God, don't you people think I like living? Of course I check my car, and my door, and my bathroom, and I even had a cat imported to check my food before I eat. Satisfied?"

She laughed in spite of herself, and noticed Maggie smothering a giggle.

"I've lived almost thirty-six years all by myself," he murmured. "I'll make forty yet. Did you catch hell at home?"

"I started to, until I told Clay he could move out and handle his own bail from now on. He was in a snit the rest of the weekend. And even Mack went broody. He knew the little boy who died," she said with a long sigh. "Poor little guy. What a rotten age to die."

"Any age is a rotten age, if it's senseless." He searched her face, reading the pain there. *She even feels for strangers,* he thought, and wondered if he might have read too much into her words the other night. That bothered him. He was beginning to realize that he wanted a lot more from Becky than distant compassion.

"I've got to go," he said abruptly. "See you later."

"Yes," she said with her heart in her eyes as she watched him walk away. It was a good thing that he didn't look back. She smiled and then she laughed. She'd been blue all weekend, thinking he'd said good-bye to her, and it had only been hello.

"Well, well—Cinderella, right here in my office," Maggie chuckled. "I think he likes you."

"I hope he does," Becky said softly. "Time will tell."

The next few days sped by. With court in session, Becky

went mad filing and typing, and so did Maggie and the other girls in the office. But in a way it was good, because it diverted her thoughts from Kilpatrick.

At home it was a different matter. Becky found herself daydreaming regularly. It was amazing to her how bright and new the world seemed now that she had someone to dream about. Granddad and Mack didn't say anything when she announced that she was going out with Kilpatrick on Friday. Neither did Clay, although his blood went cold. He didn't know what was going to happen, but having the district attorney hanging around his sister was going to cause him a hell of a lot of trouble. When the Harrises got wind of it, he didn't know what they might do. If anybody got in trouble, he'd be the first person they'd suspect.

KILPATRICK HAD BEEN fairly certain that Harvey Blair wasn't out to kill him, and he was even more certain once he'd been out to see the ex-con.

Blair, a huge, ham-fisted man with dark hair and light eyes, didn't even seem hostile when he answered the door in his run-down housing project apartment and found Kilpatrick standing there.

"I don't want any trouble, Kilpatrick," he said instantly. "I read the papers. I know what's happened to you. But I didn't do it."

"I never thought you did," he replied easily. "But it's part of the job to check out all the leads. How are things going?"

Blair stood aside to let the taller man enter. The apartment was neat and clean, but noisy. A thin woman and three preschoolers were sprawled on the floor playing with building blocks. They looked up and smiled shyly before they went back to their amusement.

"My daughter and my grandkids," Blair said with a beaming smile. "They're letting me live with them. My son-in-law was killed on the job last year, so I'm sort of taking care of them. Amazing, isn't it, how responsibility takes the wild streak right out of you?" He sighed heavily and stuck his hands into his pockets. "I got a job driving a truck for the city. Pays good, and they don't mind that I'm an ex-con. I even get insurance and retirement." He grinned at Kilpatrick. "How's that for making crime pay?"

Kilpatrick actually chuckled. "I'm glad things worked out for you," he said. "Of all the cases I ever prosecuted, I regretted winning yours the most."

"Thanks. But I was guilty as hell, even if I did finally get pardoned. The thing is, I want to make this work," he said seriously. "I've got a second shot at respectability. I won't waste this one."

"No. I don't think you will." Kilpatrick stuck out his hand and the other man shook it. He left the apartment, sure that Blair hadn't wired his car. The man had too much to lose. But that still left Clay Cullen a suspect, and he couldn't tell Becky how much evidence pointed to his involvement—even if it was only as an accessory—to that and the Dennis boy's death. God, some days were rough!

The rest of the week found him sitting wearily in court going through voir dire until he thought he was going to scream. The process required him to question each panel of jurors with regard to the matter under judicial consideration. Are you related to the defendant, any of the witnesses, or any of the attorneys? Are you familiar with the case in question? Do you have any relatives who were involved? On and on the questions went for each of five panels of twelve prospective jurors and an alternate, for most of the day. He had to remember each juror's name and jot down every bit of information he got that would go against his case. Then came the silent strike, where he and the public defender ran through the jurors and struck those prejudicial to their case until they were both satisfied that they had an impartial jury.

An impartial jury was important, but so was an impartial judge. He was fortunate to have drawn Judge Lawrence Kentner, an older man who knew law from the ground up. He was a credit to the bar, and Kilpatrick respected him. If he got a conviction in Kentner's court, there was very little chance of any sharp defense attorney finding a loophole in improper courtroom procedure.

J. Lincoln Davis had turned up in court during a recess in proceedings to present a motion for continuance on one of his own cases. He'd stopped by Kilpatrick's chair, looking smug.

"I guess you heard that I'm ready to announce," he remarked.

Kilpatrick grinned. "I heard. Good luck."

"At least give me a good fight," Davis muttered.

"Why, Jasper. Don't I always?" he asked innocently.

"Don't use that name," the other man groaned, looking around quickly to make sure the bailiffs and the junior attorney talking to the clerk of court hadn't heard. "You know I hate it."

"Your mother didn't. Shame on your for hiding it in an initial."

"Just wait until I get you on television in a debate," Davis said, smiling as he considered the prospect. "I'm having my staff research all your past cases."

"Tell them to have fun," Kilpatrick said amiably.

"For a man seeking reelection, you certainly are insufferably casual about it."

Kilpatrick wasn't seeking reelection, but why spoil Davis's fun by admitting it now? He only grinned. "Have a nice day, now."

Davis made a face and walked out, his briefcase dangling from one big hand.

Kilpatrick felt vaguely ashamed for baiting the other man. Davis was a good egg, and a hell of a good attorney. But he could be a real pain sometimes.

He packed up his papers and left the courtroom. It was five o'clock and he still had two hours' work in his office on routine matters before he could go home. But it was Friday night and he'd promised to take Becky out. He groaned inwardly. He hated disappointing her, but there was nothing he could do. The job had to come first.

He stopped by her office on his way to his own. Everyone else was getting ready to leave, but Becky was still at her typewriter. He spoke to Bob Malcolm and then settled himself on the desk beside Becky.

"I've got two hours more at least in the office," he said irritably. "It's been a hell of a week."

"And you can't go out tonight," Becky guessed, smiling so that her disappointment wouldn't show. "It's all right, really."

He sighed angrily. "No, it's not. Go home and feed your family." He studied her wan face. "It would be a late supper," he began hesitantly, "but if you want to drive back here and sit with me while I finish up, we can still have a bite to eat."

Her heart leapt and the sadness lifted from her eyes. "I'd like that very much. Unless you're too tired…"

"I have to eat, too, Becky," he said. "I'm not that tired. Lock your doors when you come back. I'll follow you home when we're through."

"All right. I won't be long."

He got up, chuckling at her expression. She looked like a kid at the circus. "Don't let them lock you in a closet, either."

"No chance," she murmured, and meant it.

She went home spoiling for a fight. She'd already told them the night before that she was eating out with Kilpatrick. This time, Granddad had a sick spell and moaned and groaned for all he was worth.

Becky panicked. She helped him to bed and then wrung her hands worrying about what to do. The doctor would come if she asked him, but it would take a chunk out of the budget she didn't want to use if Granddad was just pretending. She didn't know whether or not he was.

Clay, they told her, had gone out for the evening. They didn't know where he was. Mack was watching television and couldn't be budged from the screen. It looked as if Becky wasn't going to have a date.

CHAPTER ELEVEN

Becky sat down beside Granddad's bed with her face in her hands. Every time he had sick spells, her nerves got worse. It was terrifying to have the full responsibility for another person's life. If she did the wrong thing, he might die, and she'd never forgive herself. On the other hand, she couldn't be certain that he wouldn't use his bad health to keep her away from Kilpatrick, whom he disliked.

"It's all right, girl," he said, grimacing at the look on her face. "I'm not going to die."

She shook her head. "I know. It's just…" Her thin shoulders lifted and fell. She smiled gently. "I've never had a real beau, you know. Nobody ever looked at me and liked me enough to ask me out two times. Kilpatrick knows that I'm not modern, and he still likes me." She lowered her eyes to the bedspread. "It's nice, having him want to take me out."

Granddad sighed angrily. "It will lead to heartache," he said stiffly. "He could be using you to get to Clay. Clay's up to something, Becky. We both know it, and I'll lay odds your friend Kilpatrick does, too. You're the best and most obvious way to keep Clay under tabs."

"So you keep saying. But if that's so, why doesn't he ever ask me anything about Clay?"

"That I can't answer." He sat up and rubbed a hand through his white hair. "I'm all right now. You go on. Mack can get me a doctor if I have to have one. He's a good kid."

"Yes, I know."

She hesitated, and he looked guilty for a moment. "I said I'm all right. I don't approve of you going out with this man, but I have to admit it's nice to see you smile for a change. I can bite the bullet while you get him out of your system. You just make sure he doesn't play you for a sucker, in any way," he added firmly.

"I will." She beamed. She leaned over and kissed him. "I'll finish getting supper before I go. And I'll be home on time."

"You're a good girl," he said, frowning as she opened the door. "I guess it's been pretty hard on you. I've taken you for granted, Becky, and you shouldn't have let me."

"Somebody has to look after you and the boys," she said gently. "I don't mind. I love you," she added and smiled.

"We love you, too," he said gruffly, averting his gaze. "Even Clay, but he's got to learn what love is."

"Let's hope it isn't too painful a lesson," Becky replied. She went out and closed the door.

As she finished fixing supper, she suddenly realized that she was an hour later than she'd promised to be. Kilpatrick would give her up, and worse, it was already too late to get a meal out unless it was a hamburger. A man who worked as hard as he did needed a balanced meal.

Becky pulled out the old worn wicker picnic hamper and packed some buttered biscuits, potato salad, and baked ham in it, along with two slices of the apple pie she'd made earlier in the week. She fed Mack and Granddad and added a thermos of hot coffee to the basket before she left. They were amiable enough—especially Mack, who didn't seem to be miffed at her at all. And Granddad was almost cheerful. She allowed herself to wonder if they'd had time to poison Kilpatrick's part of the meal.

Kilpatrick was waiting for her. He glanced pointedly at the clock, because it was past the two hours he'd said he'd need to finish his work.

"Sorry," she said sheepishly, as she stood with her old coat wrapped around her. It had rained and become chilly outside. "Granddad had a bad spell and I had to sit with him a little bit until I was sure he was all right."

"Is he?" he asked.

"Just fine," she said. "But I'm sorry I was late. Had you given me up?" she asked, dangling the hamper beside her purse.

He stood up, smiling. His jacket was off and his shirt-sleeves were rolled back to his elbows. "No, I hadn't given you up. You'd have phoned long ago if you weren't coming."

"You know me pretty well already," she said with a laugh.

"Not as well as I want to. What's it going to be, Chinese or Greek?"

"How about home cooking?" she asked with a smile, and

produced the hamper. "I guessed it would be too late to eat out, except for hamburgers or something. I thought you might like ham and potato salad and apple pie better."

"You angel!" he exclaimed as she put the hamper on the desk and opened it. The delicious smells filled the office. "I'd resigned myself to a hamburger. This is a feast."

"Leftover supper," she corrected as she produced two plates, along with cups, saucers, and utensils. She saw him frowning at the unbreakable dishware and flushed a little. She couldn't admit that she wasn't able to afford disposable paper plates and plastic utensils.

Kilpatrick had worked that out already for himself, though. He smiled gently as he cleared enough space for her to put out the food.

"This is delicious," he sighed when they reached the apple pie stage. He leaned back, sipping black coffee, as she unwrapped the pie and put it in saucers. "Becky, you're quite a cook."

"I like cooking," she confessed. "My mother taught me. She was super."

"It must have been a terrible blow for you when she died," he remarked, watching her as he ate.

"The end of the world," she agreed, "at the time. Mack was only two years old, you see. Clay was nine. Dad was never at home much—he sort of came and went. It was Granddad who kept things going. I managed to finish high school. Mrs. White down the road would keep Mack. Granddad was still working on the railroad then." She smiled wistfully. "It was fun, looking after a toddler. Mack and I are pretty close because I'm more like a mother than a sister. But Clay...well, he was always into trouble, even as a youngster. He's just gotten worse. He hates authority."

"I imagine he's given you hell about seeing me?" he asked.

"Of course. He and Granddad both. Mack's the only one who seems to think about me," she added as she finished her own coffee and pie.

"Were you a tomboy?" he asked, picturing her up in trees and playing baseball.

She laughed. "Yes. Having two brothers sort of disposes you that way. I can still pitch hay and drive the tractor, although I don't like to." The laughter fell away as she thought about spring planting. "It's getting to be hard this year, without Granddad to help plant. We've always had a small truck garden as well as our kitchen garden, but this year I don't know. Clay's just no help at all, and Mack's still too young."

"Your father contributes nothing toward the boys' support?" he asked.

She shook her head. "He has no sense of responsibility. He always wanted easy money."

He toyed with the white mug he was holding. "I remember him, barely. He was a lot like Clay."

"Disrespectful, arrogant, and totally uncooperative," she guessed.

He burst out laughing. "Yes, as a matter of fact."

"That's Dad." She cleared away the plates and cups, glancing wryly at Kilpatrick. "I'm glad I take after my mother. She was painfully honest. Mack's going to be like that. He already is. He was furious about the little Dennis boy."

"How do he and Clay get along?" he wondered aloud.

"They don't, lately," she replied as she filled the hamper

with the leftovers and closed it. "Mack won't even speak to him since the weekend." She frowned. "I can't get him to tell me why."

"Brothers always fight, they say," he said, smoothing things over. It was much too soon to start probing.

"You don't have brothers or sisters, do you?" she asked gently.

He shook his head. "No. I've always been a loner. I guess I always will be." He stood up, stretching lazily, so that his white shirt strained against the muscular expanse of dark-shadowed chest under it. He was hairy there. Becky could see curly black hair peeking out of the opening at his throat. The sight made her shy and she averted her eyes.

"Next time, we'll eat out," he said, smiling lazily at her. His gaze fell to her soft mouth and lingered there as he remembered how it had felt to kiss her.

"You could come out to the farm for Sunday dinner," she suggested hesitantly, and blushed as she realized how forward it probably sounded. "That is, if you want to. It would be kind of like marching into an enemy camp unarmed."

"I'm never unarmed," he replied. "I'd enjoy that. What time?"

"About one?"

"Will that give you enough time to get the meal together after church?" he asked.

"If it doesn't, you can always sit in the kitchen and talk to me while I work."

"Saving me from the rest of the family, I gather?" he chuckled. "Okay. I survived two years in Vietnam. I guess I can survive an afternoon of Clay and your grandfather."

"You served in Vietnam?" she asked.

"Yes. I don't talk about it, beyond that," he added gently.

She smiled. "I won't ask, then. Do you liked fried chicken?"

"Very much." He moved toward her, the very slowness of his steps a threat, considering the smile and the dark warmth of his eyes. He caught her by the waist and pulled her against him, his smile fading as his gaze moved from her wide eyes, over her straight freckled nose, down to her soft mouth. "I didn't frighten you the other night, did I?"

She didn't pretend not to know what he was talking about. "No," she replied softly. She could feel his coffee-scented breath on her mouth, almost taste it in the sudden silence of the closed room. His lean hands smoothed her back, bringing her breasts hard against his broad chest.

"I was determined that I wasn't going to see you again," he said, suddenly serious as he met her eyes. "You and I are worlds apart, and I don't just mean financially."

"But you came back," she whispered.

He nodded. His hands contracted, bringing her closer, and his head bent. "Because no matter how hopeless it is," he breathed against her mouth, "I want you, Becky!"

Her breath caught as his mouth opened on hers, forcing her lips apart with its expert pressure. Her eyes closed and she slid her arms under his and around him. He was powerfully built. She could feel the muscles rippling as he held her, feel the strength of him. She floated between heaven and earth, and her body began to tauten until it was almost painful with a tension she'd never experienced before.

As if he sensed it, his hand slid to the base of her spine and jerked, dragging her hips against his so that she felt for the first time in her life the blatant reality of a man's physical arousal.

She gasped against his mouth. He lifted his head. His eyes were darker than ever, narrow, intense. She tried to move back, but his hand increased its intimate pressure on her hips, holding her.

He watched the blush cover her cheeks, watched her freckles stand out vividly against it. His eyes held hers relentlessly until he felt her tremble.

Then he bent again and his mouth teased, brushed, and lifted until she relaxed against him and gave in completely. She no longer fought against his hold on her. Her mouth opened to the persuasion of his lips and she breathed him, lived through him, in a state of mindless pleasure.

When he lifted his head again, her eyelids would barely open. She looked up at him dazedly. Her full lips were swollen, her face devoid of expression, her eyes yielding and gentle.

His hands had fallen to her hips while he was kissing her. He held her gaze and moved her deliberately against him, his dark eyes studying her helpless reaction.

"Thank your lucky stars that I have a conscience," he said, his voice huskier than usual, deeper. "Because when it gets this bad, most men will invent an excuse to go the whole damned way."

"Do you really think that I could stop you?" she whispered.

He smiled gently. "You wouldn't want to," he corrected. "But afterward...what about afterward, Becky?"

Her whirling mind clung to that thought, and she realized

what he was getting at. Guilt. Shame. Those would come afterward, because her particular code of honor didn't allow for intimate interludes. To her, sex and marriage and love were intermingled, indivisible. She lowered her eyes and he let her go, if a little reluctantly, and moved away to light a cigar.

"Did your mother ever have little talks with you about men?" he asked finally, staring out his window toward the streetlights below.

"I wasn't dating then, so I guess she didn't see the need. Granddad said to be good and we got lectures in school about the hazards of promiscuity." She shrugged. "I learned more from reading romance novels than from anyone in my family. Some of them were *very* educational," she added with a faint grin.

He turned around, chuckling at the expression in her eyes. Pure witchery. He was aching like mad, but she had a positive gift for making him laugh. "But you still don't want to be modern and liberated?"

She shook her head. "Not when I'm thinking properly, no." She traced a pattern on the skirt of her dress. "I don't know very much about men, or things I'd need to know to be liberated."

"Prevention, you mean," he said quietly, his eyes narrowing.

"Yes."

"I wouldn't want to create a child any more than you would, Becky," he said after a minute. "I'm sure you know that a man can prevent it, just as a woman can."

She felt hot all over. It was a very intimate thing to talk

about, especially with a man. She sat down in the chair in front of his desk. "Nothing is foolproof, they say. And there are...other things."

"Diseases."

She nodded.

He chuckled. "You're as cautious as I am." His eyebrows lifted at her sharp glance. "You don't think men concern themselves about it? Think again. I don't sleep around."

She stared at him. She'd assumed that his experience had been gained with a number of women. At his age, he was certainly no virgin.

"I used to," he continued, puffing on his cigar as he moved to the edge of his desk and perched himself on it. "But a man gets wiser with age. Sex without emotional involvement is about as satisfying as cake without sugar in it. These days I'm careful, and damned particular."

"Maybe I just appeal to you because I'm not experienced," she ventured, lifting soft, worried eyes to his.

"Maybe you appeal to me because you're you," he replied, his voice deep and measured. He let his eyes slide boldly over her, from her long, honey-brown hair, to her big hazel eyes and soft mouth, down over the thrust of her breasts and her narrow waist. "I think you and I are eventually going to sleep together, Becky," he said softly. "But whether we do or not, we're going to be friends. I've been alone for a long time. I've reached the age where I don't enjoy it anymore. We can hang out together, at least."

Her heart sang. "I'd like to hang out with you," she said, smiling up at him. "But the other..." She frowned worriedly. "I'm a coward. You see, if something happened, if something went wrong. I'm not the kind of person who could have an abortion. I don't even like to kill bees when they've stung me."

He caught her hand and pulled her up from the chair, so that she was standing between his thighs, her eyes on an unnerving level with his. "I don't believe in abortion, either," he said quietly. "I believe in prevention. Let's take it one day at a time. Okay?"

"Okay."

He slid his arm around her and drew her close. His mouth found hers easily in a kiss as soft and tender as his other ones had been passionate and fierce. He let her go then, smiling, and moved away.

"I'd better follow you home," he said gently. "It's been a long day for both of us, and we need our rest."

"You don't have to go all the way to the farm," she began.

"I said, I'll follow you home," he replied.

She threw up her hands. "No wonder you're such a good D.A. You never give up."

"Count on it," he replied, without a smile.

He followed her home, watched from the car as she opened the front door, and then sped off with a wave of his hand.

Becky went straight to bed. Fortunately, everyone else seemed to be in their own already.

At breakfast, she announced that Rourke was coming to Sunday dinner. Clay didn't say a word. He was afraid to, after what she'd already threatened. He just shrugged. He had a date with Francine that night and knew he would have some hard explaining to do to the Harris boys about Kilpatrick.

He'd find some way to convince them that it was an advantage. After all, he'd know what the D.A. was up to through Becky. He brightened. Sure he would! The Harrises would love it! He relaxed and began to enjoy his breakfast.

"Dinner?" Granddad muttered. He sighed heavily. "Well, I guess I can stand it," he added when he saw Becky's face. "Just don't expect sparkling conversation."

She smiled at him. "Okay. Thanks, Granddad."

"I could show him my electric train set," Mack murmured. He was proud of the old Lionel O-scale trains. They'd belonged to a friend of Granddad's, who'd given them to him unexpectedly three Christmases ago. Becky had cried, because she'd never have been able to afford to give them to the boy, who loved trains almost as much as his grandfather did.

"I'm sure he'd like that, Mack," Becky replied. "He's not a bad man," she told Granddad and Clay. "He's funny when you get to know him, and in his own way, he cares about people."

"I've got to go," Clay said, getting up from the table. "I'm helping Francine's father work on his car today."

"Have fun," Becky said. "How's the job?"

Clay glanced at her, his eyes worried, his face vulnerable. "It's fine," he lied. He glanced at Mack and watched the younger boy's face harden with dislike. He turned away. "See you later."

Becky glanced at Mack, puzzled by his expression. "Have you and Clay argued?" she asked him.

"He wanted me to do something for him and I said no," Mack said curtly. "Well, he isn't my boss," he added defensively. He put down his fork. "Want me to milk for you?" he asked. "I've been practicing. I'm really good, Becky—you ask Granddad if I'm not."

"He is," Granddad had to admit. He smiled at the boy. "I've been teaching him. Thought it might help you out a bit if he could do that much," he murmured uncomfortably.

"It would," she replied. She got up and kissed Granddad's cheek. Life was getting sweeter by the day! "Thank you!"

"Nice to see you looking so pert," he added, smiling. "You glow."

"She sure does," Mack agreed. He grinned. "It must be love." He struck a pose, his hands over his heart. "Oh, Romeo!"

"Get out of here before I throw the rest of the eggs at you," she muttered. "Shakespeare must be whirling like a top by now!"

"With jealousy," Mack called as he grabbed the milking pail and rushed out the back door.

She shook her head and got up to wash the dishes. Granddad sat in his chair, looking frailer than usual. "Worried?" she asked gently.

His thin shoulders rose and fell. "About Clay," he admitted. "He and Mack used to be so close. Now they don't speak." He lifted his eyes. "The boy's into something, Becky. He looks just like your dad used to when he'd done something real bad."

"Maybe he'll decide that he's in over his head and get out," she said hopefully, not believing it herself.

Granddad shook his head. "Not now that he's got that girl. She's a bad girl—the sort who'll use any persuasion to keep a boy in her clutches. You mark my words, Harris put her up to it. There's no telling what those boys are doing, and Clay's going to catch the blame for it sooner or later. He can't see what they're up to. By the time he does, it may be too late."

"What can we do?" she asked.

"I don't know," he replied. He got up slowly from the table. "I'm an old man. I'm glad I don't have a long time left to live. It's not a good world anymore, Becky. Too much self-ishness and dirt out there for me. I grew up in a gentler time, when people had honor and pride, when a family name meant something. It's the pressure and pace of life, don't you see? Back when people worked the land, they depended on God. Now they work for machines and depend on them." He shrugged. "Machines stop when the power goes off. God doesn't. But maybe they have to learn that for themselves. I'm going to go lie down for a spell."

"Do you feel all right?" she asked hesitantly.

He stopped in the doorway and smiled back at her. "I'll do, despite all those pills you and the doctor shove into me. I'm not done for yet."

"Good for you," she said, smiling.

He nodded and ambled back into his bedroom. Becky did the chores inside and went out to feed the chickens. It was warm now, early spring, and easy on the bare arms. She was in jeans and a tank top, with her hair in a long pigtail, and she felt like a million dollars. Just for today, her problems didn't exist. And tomorrow, Rourke was coming to dinner!

"WHAT DO YOU MEAN, the D.A.'s coming to your house for dinner?" Son demanded furiously when he met Clay and Francine at the garage.

"He likes my sister," Clay said, trying to sound nonchalant. "It's great! Becky talks about him all the time. He'll tell her what he's working on and she'll tell me." He glanced at Son to see how this information was taking. "It's like having our own pipeline into the D.A.'s office."

"It hasn't occurred to you that he might be on to us, and keeping tabs on you through your sister?" Bubba added, his red face even redder than usual.

"She won't have anything to tell him," Clay replied. "Besides, she's so goofy over him that she'd have let it slip if he suspected us."

"Listen, Cullen, you're lucky we didn't phone in a tip about you and the D.A.'s car," Son said, ice-cold. "Your baby brother wouldn't play ball. If it hadn't been for that friend of yours who gave us a tip on the elementary school, we could have lost the whole territory!"

"A kid died because of the crack," Clay began.

"So a kid died. He did too much stuff—it happens all the time. Don't you go bleeding heart on us," Son scoffed. "If you don't have the guts to get your fingers dirty, you're no good to us. And if we decide to turn you out, we'll do it in style, all the way to your sister's boyfriend—so good that you'll never get out of stir."

"That's right," Bubba added.

Francine clung to Clay's arm, tossing her long black hair. "Leave him alone. He's no fink," she said.

"I haven't told anybody anything," Clay agreed. "Look, I like having a little money in my pocket and some decent clothes to wear," he muttered, feeling a little guilty because he knew how hard Becky had worked for him and the others.

"Then don't rock the boat," Son replied. "Hold up your end. There's a deal going down in a couple of weeks. We'll expect you to help get the stuff to the local dealers."

"Sure. I'll do my part," Clay agreed. He smiled, but it wasn't easy. He'd discovered that it was a lot easier to get into lawbreaking than it was to get out. He'd closed all the doors behind him now. He slid an arm around Francine and walked her back to the car.

"It's okay," she told him gently when he opened the door for her, but she looked worried. "They won't tell on you."

"Won't they?" he asked. He drew in a heavy breath. "My God, if they turn me in for wiring Kilpatrick's car, Becky will never forgive me. She'll never believe I didn't do it. I didn't, Francine—you know I didn't!"

She glanced over her shoulder at her cousins. In the beginning, she had wanted to help them out. Now she saw Clay for another reason entirely. He treated her like a lady; he bought her things. Nobody had ever been that kind to her before.

"Listen, I'll help. Somehow, I'll help. But Clay, don't do anything stupid, you know?" Her dark eyes pleaded with him. "Don't go off the deep end and tell your sister anything. If they even suspected, they'd both point a finger at you and send you up for life."

"They'd send themselves up, too," he argued.

"No. They'd be out in no time. They've got the money to buy people, Clay. Don't you understand what this is all about? They can buy policemen, city councilmen, judges—there's nobody they can't get to! But you don't have that kind of pull. You'd do the time. Please, Clay, keep your nose clean!"

He smiled at her. "Worried about me?"

"Yes, you idiot," she said furiously. "God knows why, but I love you!" She kissed him fiercely, got in the car, and drove off before he had time to react.

Clay was over the moon. He walked back to the garage to talk to Son, but heard only half of what Son said to him about setting up the buy.

Clay went home in a daze. He hadn't touched drugs in quite a while now, except as a middleman. He didn't need them since Francine had come along.

Clay arrived to find Mack working on his trains. He stepped into the bedroom to watch, but Mack just ignored him. "Look, can't you forgive me?" he asked the younger boy.

"You and your sleazy friends killed a buddy of mine," Mack said, glaring at him.

"It wasn't me," Clay muttered, glancing toward the open door to make sure nobody was near enough to hear him. "Listen, I've got myself in a hell of a fix. I let them talk me into making a buy, and now they're threatening to put me in jail for good. I didn't mean to hurt anybody. I got a lot of money."

"Money won't bring my friend back," Mack said coldly. "And if Becky knew what you were doing, she'd throw you out of the house."

"She probably ought to," Clay said wearily. He felt old. One mistake, and it had led to so many that he didn't know when it would ever stop. He stuck his hands in his pockets. "Mack, I didn't sell any crack at your school. You've got to believe that. I'm bad, but I'm not that bad."

Mack picked up his locomotive and fiddled with it. He felt sick. "You're a pusher. I don't want you in my room."

Clay started to speak, gave up, and left as quietly as he'd come. He couldn't remember ever feeling so alone or so ashamed of himself.

CHAPTER TWELVE

Becky was all thumbs as she prepared Sunday dinner. She was just home from church, still in the gray jersey dress she'd worn to services, her hose-clad feet in faded blue mules while she puttered around the kitchen trying to put together a meal.

She'd suspected Kilpatrick would be early, and he was. When she heard his car she ran to let him in, ignoring the gravy bubbling on the stove. But Mack had beat her to the door and was being, of all things, polite.

"She's in the kitchen, Mr. Kilpatrick," Mack began.

"No, she's right here," Becky returned, flustered. She smiled at Rourke, approving of the way he looked in tan slacks, a yellow knit shirt, and a trendy tan plaid sports coat.

"Go back and watch your dinner, girl. Mack and I will entertain Mr. Kilpatrick," Granddad yelled from his seat, but the look in his eyes said a lot more, not much of it complimentary.

"You could come in the kitchen with me," Becky said weakly.

"Nonsense. You'll burn the gravy," Granddad scoffed. "Sit down, Mr. Kilpatrick. It's not what you're used to, but you won't fall through the chairs just yet."

Kilpatrick stared at the old man with pursed lips. "You don't pull your punches. Good. Neither do I. Are you allowed to smoke, or does the doctor think a cigar will kill you?"

Granddad looked taken aback. Becky disappeared back into the kitchen. *Silly me,* she thought, *worrying about Rourke being savaged by Granddad.*

She got the meal together as quickly as possible. Raised voices drifted over from the living room briefly, then there was silence, then muffled conversation. When she poked her head around the door to call them to come to the table, Granddad looked out of humor and Rourke was smoking his cigar quietly and smiling.

No need to ask who'd come out on top, she told herself. She put everything on the table and had Granddad say grace. Clay was nowhere in sight. He'd probably decided that the D.A. was more than he could swallow along with lunch. It was just as well, too, because it was hard enough with Granddad.

They ate in silence, mostly, except for a few kind words from Rourke about the food. Afterward, Granddad excused himself and shut himself in his room. *So much for his promise not to make waves,* Becky thought miserably. Mack went out to feed the chickens, leaving her and Rourke alone in the kitchen while she washed dishes.

She bent her head over the sink, her long hair half obscuring her face. "I'm sorry," she said with a heavy sigh. "I thought they were going to behave. I guess it was too much to ask."

"They're afraid of losing you," he said perceptively, glancing down at her while he dried the plates and utensils she'd washed and rinsed. "I don't suppose you can blame them. They're used to having you around to do the work."

She looked up at him, her eyes more eloquent than she knew. "Even housekeepers get days off," she replied.

He reached down and kissed her gently. "You're a lot more than a housekeeper. They don't want you to fall into the clutches of a man with nothing more than sex on his mind."

"Are you?" she asked softly, searching his eyes.

Those eyes, he thought achingly. *Those soft, seductive eyes.* They played havoc with his nervous system. "I have law on my mind most of the time," he murmured dryly. "Sex has its place, I suppose. But I've already told you that I have evil designs on you, haven't I?"

She laughed delightedly. "So you have. Honesty above all?"

"That's right. I plan to lure you to my secret hideaway and have my way with you."

"How exciting. Do we take your car or mine?" she asked.

He glowered at her. "You aren't supposed to go willingly," he said. "You're a girl of high principles and I'm a rake."

"Oh. Sorry." She tilted her chin. "Which car would you like to abduct me in, yours or mine?" she amended.

He whacked her over the head with the drying cloth. "Get to work, you unbalanced female."

She giggled—something she hadn't done since childhood. "That puts me in my place."

"Be careful that I don't put you in your place," he mused. "Honest to God, I never dreamed that you'd try to seduce me over a sink of dirty dishes. Don't you have any finesse?"

"No. Is there a better place?"

"Certainly. I'll explain it to you one day. You missed a plate."

"So I did." She washed and he dried in silent contentment for several minutes. "Was Granddad hard going?" she asked eventually.

"Yes. He doesn't like having me here. I can't say I blame him. I've been instrumental in unsettling his life several times, even if it was unavoidable."

"You were just doing your job. I don't blame you," she said.

He smiled down at her. "Yes, but your grandfather doesn't enjoy kissing me as much as you do, so he blames me more."

She flushed and then hit him. "No fair."

He chuckled. "Do you know that I laugh more with you than I ever have with anyone else?" he asked. "I thought I'd forgotten how. Prosecution is a dark job. It's easy to lose your sense of humor after a while."

"I used to think you didn't have one," she said, grinning up at him.

"Because I baited you in the elevator?" He smiled back. "Oh, I had a ball doing that. It got to the point where I deliberately tried to run into you. It was such a refreshing change."

"From what?"

"From having women tear their clothes off and throw themselves across my desk," he told her with a straight face.

"I'll bet!"

"You were a ray of sunshine, Becky," he said then, and he didn't smile. "The nicest part of my day. I wanted to ask you out the day you told me the truth about your home situation, but I didn't want complications in my life."

"And now you do?"

He shrugged. "Not really." He glanced at her while he dried the last plate and put it on the stack. "But I don't have a choice anymore. Neither do you, I imagine. We've gone beyond the point of no return. We're getting used to each other."

"Is that bad?" she asked.

"I'm a target," he reminded her. "Doesn't it occur to you that being seen with me could make you one?"

"No. I wouldn't care anyway."

"It could also have consequences in other ways," he continued. "The Harris boys might think Clay was feeding me information, since I spend so much time with you."

She caught her breath. That possibility hadn't occurred to her.

"Don't brood," he said gently. "I think Clay could convince them otherwise. But I can see things you don't. Then, too, there's the stress I'm putting on you by creating dissent in your family. Your grandfather and your brothers don't want me around. That's going to make life harder on you."

"I have a right to go out when I like, and I've told them so," she said firmly. "The one thing you've done is show me that people can make slaves of you if you let them. I've been a slave here most of my adult life, because I allowed my family to become totally dependent on me. Now I'm paying the price. Guilt isn't a nice weapon, but people will use it when all else fails."

"You can bet on it," he agreed. "What do you want to do when we finish here?"

"Well, if we try to sit and watch television, Granddad will come back in and smoulder through whatever we watch." She finished the last plate. "I could show you around the farm. There isn't a lot to see, but it's been in our family for over a hundred years."

He smiled. "I'd enjoy it. I like the outdoors, but I've lived in town for a long time. If it wasn't a quiet neighborhood, I think I'd go stir crazy. I feed the birds and put out birdhouses. When I have time, I look after my roses."

"Ah, that's the Irish in you," she teased gently. "The love of the land and growing things, I mean. My great-grandmother was an O'Hara from County Cork, so I come by mine honestly."

"Both my grandmothers were Irish," he replied.

"One of them was Cherokee, wasn't she?" Becky asked.

"My grandfather was Irish. He married a Cherokee lass, and my mother was the result. But she looked more Cherokee than Irish. I barely remember her, or my father. Uncle Sanderson said they loved each other very much, but my father wasn't a marrying man." He sighed heavily. "I don't mind so much being illegitimate now, but it was hell when I was a kid. I wouldn't want that to happen to a child of mine."

"Neither would I," Becky replied. "Here, I'll hang that cloth up. Then we'll go out and wander around."

"Don't you need to change first?" he asked, nodding toward her pretty jersey dress.

She laughed. "And leave you at Granddad's mercy?" she exclaimed.

"It's okay, Becky, I'll protect him," Mack volunteered as he appeared in the doorway. "Do you like electric trains, Mr. Kilpatrick? I've got some real old Lionel O-scale cars and a locomotive that one of Granddad's friends gave me."

"I like trains," Rourke said, noticing again how much Mack looked like Becky. "Nice of you to sacrifice yourself on my account, young Mack."

Mack laughed. "That's okay. Becky sacrificed herself for me a time or two. Come on."

Becky watched them go, pleased with Mack's attitude. She went off to her room to change into jeans and a yellow knit pullover sweater that had seen better days. She didn't mind now, though. Kilpatrick didn't seem to mind what she wore, or how often she wore it.

Mack started up the trains, and Rourke sat in the chair by the table and watched them with gleaming eyes.

"They're beauts," he told the boy. "I used to love trains when I was your age, but my Uncle Sanderson ran a tight ship. He didn't think a boy needed things to divert him from his studies, so I didn't get many toys."

"Didn't you live with your parents?" Mack asked, curious.

Kilpatrick shook his head. "They died when I was pretty young. Uncle Sanderson was the only relative I had who wanted me. It was that or live on the Cherokee reservation. I don't know, it might have been more fun living with my mother's people, at that."

"You're an Indian?" Mack exclaimed.

"Part Cherokee," he nodded. "On my mother's side. The rest is pure Irish."

"Wow! We're studying about the Cherokee! They had

these blowguns to hunt with, and Sequoya gave them their own alphabet and written language." He sobered. "They were forced out of Georgia in 1838 on the Trail of Tears. Our teacher said they were just gotten rid of because there was gold on their land and the greedy white men wanted it."

"Simplified, but accurate enough. The Supreme Court decided in favor of letting the Cherokee stay in Georgia, but President Andrew Jackson forced them out anyway. Supreme Court Chief Justice John Marshall attacked the president publicly for refusing to obey the law. It was quite a story."

"And President Jackson's life had been saved by a Cherokee Indian named Junaluska," Mack added, surprising Kilpatrick with his knowledge of the subject. "Some gratitude, huh?"

Rourke chuckled. "You've got a sharp mind," he murmured.

"Not sharp enough," Mack said, his shoulders hunching as he absently ran the train around the tracks. "Mr. Kilpatrick, if you know somebody's doing something wrong, and you don't tell, are you really as guilty as they are?"

Rourke studied the boy quietly for a long moment before he answered. "If somebody's commiting a felony, and you know about it, that makes you an accessory. But remember, Mack, there are extenuating circumstances sometimes. The court takes those things into consideration. Nothing is truly black and white."

"Billy Dennis was my friend," he said, lifting concerned hazel eyes to Rourke's dark face. "I never even knew he used drugs. He didn't seem the type."

"There isn't really a type," Rourke replied. "Anyone can get into a state of mind that makes them vulnerable to crutches like drugs or alcohol."

"Not you, I'll bet," Mack said.

"Don't you believe it. I'm human, too. When my Uncle Sanderson died, I spent half the night in a downtown bar and drank myself into a stupor. I don't drink, as a rule, but I was fond of the old buzzard. I hated losing him. He was the only family I had, by that time. None of my mother's people are still alive, and Uncle Sanderson was the last of my father's line."

"You mean, you're alone in the world?" Mack asked, frowning. "You haven't got anybody?"

Rourke got to his feet and stuck his hands in his pockets, absently watching the train run. "I had a dog, until that bomb went off in my car," he said. "He was my family."

"I'm real sorry about that," Mack told him. "We were all sad when the mailman ran over Blue. He was part of our family."

Rourke nodded. He wanted so much to ask Mack what he knew, because the boy obviously had something on his mind that was really bothering him. But it was too soon. He didn't dare risk it now.

"I'm ready," Becky called from the door.

Rourke glanced at her, his dark eyes smiling as he took in the picture she made in her leisure clothes, with her hair loose around her shoulders. She looked young and carefree, and pretty, freckles and all.

"Mr. Kilpatrick likes trains," Mack said.

"He sure does," Rourke agreed. "He just might go out and buy a set of his own, too."

Mack and Becky chuckled. Kilpatrick then caught her hand in his and knocked the laughter right out of her, replacing it with heated excitement.

"We're going out to look at the farm," Rourke told Mack. "Want to come?"

"Sure. But I have to listen out for Granddad," Mack said importantly. "I'm the doc when Becky's not here. I know how to give him his medicine and everything."

"I know he's glad to have you around," Rourke said. "Thanks for letting me see the trains. They're neat."

"Any time," Mack told him. "Uh, if you get some," he added hesitantly, "think I could come and watch you run them?"

"You bet," the man said easily, and he smiled.

"Wow!"

"We'll be within yelling distance," Becky told Mack. "Call if you need me."

"I will."

Becky led Rourke out back, where the chickens and the two cows shared the barnyard. Hay from last year dribbled down from the hayloft onto the floor of the ramshackle barn, but it was almost all gone now. Becky stared at it worriedly, wondering how she was going to get the fields hayed without Granddad to help.

"Do you milk the cows?" Rourke asked.

"Yes. Mack helps. He's pretty good at it, too. We churn and make our own butter and buttermilk."

He stopped and looked down at her, still holding her soft hand in his lean, strong one. "By choice?" he asked.

She smiled and shook her head. "Necessity. We have to

budget like mad, even with Granddad's pension. I used to make most of my own clothes, but now it's cheaper to buy them, with the cost of material so high. I can food in the summer and put it up in the pantry. We buy a side of beef for the freezer. I make my own breads. We get by."

"I can imagine that keeping the boys in school clothes is a full-time job," he said.

"Mack's, yes. Clay's buying his own now," she said with unexpected bitterness. "Designer things. He wasn't satisfied with the things I could afford for him."

"He's old enough to buy his own," he reminded her. "And that's one financial burden you don't have."

"Yes, but..."

His eyes narrowed speculatively. "But, what?"

She looked up. She wanted so much to trust him, but she couldn't tell him her suspicions. Whatever else Clay was, he was her brother. "Oh, nothing," she said, and forced a smile. "The barn dates back to the early 1900s. The original one burned about 1898. We have a photograph of it, and so does the local historical society. This one is a duplicate of the original, but not quite so old."

He let her change the subject without an argument, smiling to himself as she walked alongside him. There was time, he thought. Meanwhile, he was enjoying himself. Most Sundays he spent alone, working. This was a refreshing change.

She led him through the dry brush of the field and into a grove of pecan and oak trees to a small creek. An old oak stump sat near it, and Becky patted it.

"This is Granddad's pouting stump," she explained as she sat on it, tugging Rourke down beside her. There was plenty of room, because it had been a huge tree. "He cut it down because he wanted someplace to sit and fish from, but he used to tell us that it was his pouting stump. He'd come out here and sit when Grandma made him mad. Eventually he'd get hungry and come back to the house," she added with a laugh.

"What was your grandmother like?" he asked.

"Like me, mostly," she recalled. "She wasn't pretty, but she had a good sense of humor and she was a terrific cook. She liked to throw things at Granddad when she got mad at him. Pots, pans—once she threw a bowl of oatmeal and hit him with it. He was a walking mess."

He threw back his dark head and roared. "What did he do?"

"He took a bath," she replied. "Afterward, he and Grandma went off into their room, and it got quiet for a long time." She sighed. "They were so happy. I think the fact that my father and mother were so miserable together hurt them. My father was always in trouble with the law or somebody he owed money to, or some woman's husband. He ran around on Mama. That was what killed her, I think. One day she got pneumonia and she just lay there and died. The doctor came and we gave her the medicine, but she had no will to live."

"Some men don't take to marriage, I guess," Rourke said gruffly. He lit a cigar and blew out a cloud of smoke. "It's a pity he didn't realize it before he took the plunge."

"That's what Granddad used to say." She smiled wistfully. "He's still my father, you know, no matter what he's done. But I used to dread having him turn up. He always needed money and expected us to cough it up. Sometimes, he took the very food out of our mouths, but Granddad never refused him." She studied her jeans-clad legs, unaware of Rourke's murderous expression. "I guess I'd feel that way about my children, so I can't really blame Granddad."

He didn't say anything. He was looking at Becky, trying to imagine how hard it had really been for her. She never complained about her lot in life, and she could even defend a man like her father. Incredible. He was less forgiving and far less understanding. He'd have enjoyed putting the man away for life.

"You do blame him, don't you?" she asked suddenly, looking up to see the hardness in his face, his dark eyes. "You're very rigid in your principles, Mr. Prosecutor."

"Yes, I am," he agreed without argument. "Inflexible, I've been called. But someone has to take a stand against lawlessness and not back down, Becky. Otherwise, criminals would rule the world. These bleeding-heart liberals would have you believe that we'd have a better world if we made everything legal. But all we'd have is a jungle. Do I have to tell you who comes out on top in any jungle or wilderness?"

"The predator who's the strongest and most bloodthirsty," she said without thinking, and shivered inwardly at the images that ran through her mind. "It's hard for me to imagine the kind of person who can kill without compunction, but I guess you've seen plenty of them."

He nodded. "Fathers who've raped daughters, women who've strangled their own children, a man who shot and killed another man for taking his parking space." He smiled at her striken expression. "Shocked? So are most decent people when they hear about such crimes. In fact, some of them sit on juries and bring in a verdict of innocent in those kinds of cases, because they simply can't believe that any human being would do that to another human being."

"I can understand that." She felt a little sick. "It must be hard for you sometimes, when you prosecute some of those people and they get turned loose."

"You can't imagine what it's like," he said. His eyes kindled with memories. "King Henry the Eighth had a Star Chamber—a group of men who were thought of as the law beyond the law. They had the power of life and death over criminals who were turned loose even though they were guilty. I don't approve, but I can see the rationale behind such courts. My God, the corruption you see in public office is almost beyond belief."

"Why doesn't somebody do something?" Becky asked innocently.

"Now, that's a good question. Some of us are trying to. But it can get hairy when the power and wealth is all in the hands of the people you're trying to convict."

"I begin to see the light."

"Good. In that case, let's talk about something more cheerful," he said, taking a puff from the cigar. "Where do you want to eat tomorrow?"

"Lunch, again?" she asked softly.

He chuckled. "Tired of me already?"

"Oh, no," she said with such fervent emotion that he felt ashamed for baiting her. He stared down into her soft eyes, and felt himself being pulled into them. Bedroom eyes. Hazel fires that could burn a man for life. He had no desire to escape them anymore.

He got up slowly, grinding out the cigar under his shoe.

The woods were so quiet that only the bubbling of the creek could be heard above the pounding of Becky's own heart as he reached for her. She went willingly, her hands flat against his broad chest under his jacket, feeling warm muscle beneath his knit shirt. She could feel his heartbeat, almost as hard and quick as her own. She lifted her face, unnerved by the fierce darkness of his eyes, the hardness of his lean face above her.

His hands bit in at her waist, holding her against him. He prolonged the look until she felt as if she'd caught a live wire in her hands. "No, don't look away," he said roughly when she tried to.

"I can't bear it," she whispered shakily.

"Yes, you can." His breathing became audible. "I can almost see your soul."

"Rourke," she ground out.

"Bite me," he whispered against her mouth as he took it.

He'd kissed her before, but this hunger was new. He made her want to bite and claw. He aroused something inside her that he hadn't been able to touch before. She obeyed him, nipping his lower lip, catching it in her teeth. Her nails scored down his knit shirt and he shuddered.

"Get it out of the way," he said huskily. "Touch me…"

His mouth bit into hers with a ferocity that might have frightened her only a week before. But now she was hungry, as he was—hungry to know him in every way there was, beginning with this way. She tugged at his shirt until the hem came out of his slacks. Her hands fumbled their way under it and up until they tangled in the thicket of curling black hair that covered his warm, hard chest. She moaned at the intimacy of it, her mind scrambling for reason as her body denied the need for it. She moved closer without the urging of his hands, her legs against his, her stomach registering the sudden hardness of him, the urgency of the mouth invading hers.

"Becky," he groaned in anguish. His hands slid to the back of her thighs and pulled, lifting her into total contact with his blatant maleness.

She gasped, but she didn't protest. She couldn't. It was like pure electricity bonding them there, sending her into a sensual oblivion that made her tremble in his arms.

He let her slide to the ground all at once and turned away to lean his hands against a big oak trunk. He dragged her into his lungs and shivered with frustrated desire. It was getting harder and harder to draw back. He couldn't remember ever having to before, except with his damned fiancée. But Becky wasn't like her. Becky would give him anything he wanted—right here, right now, standing up if he wanted it that way. She was his for the taking. But she wasn't that kind of woman and he didn't want to force her into doing something that would torment her later. He could keep his head, if he just recited points of law until the pain stopped.

Becky sat down heavily on the stump with her arms wrapped around herself, staring down at the leaf-littered ground. She knew that they were headed for disaster. It was hurting him to deny his need, even though he respected her enough not to ask her to satisfy it. She felt guilty. It certainly wasn't fair to him to continue a dead-end relationship with her. Friendship wasn't going to be enough. He'd said he hadn't been with a woman in a long time, and that fact alone was going to fan the fire until he couldn't bear it any longer.

"You shouldn't see me again, Rourke," she said in a barren tone, and without looking at him. "This isn't going to work."

He pushed himself away from the tree and turned to face her. He was pale, but well in command of himself. "Isn't it? I thought I'd just proved that it would."

"It isn't fair to ask a man to torture himself, just for companionship." She kept her eyes on the ground. "I've got all I can handle right now, you know. Granddad and Clay—and Mack. If it was just myself, principles and all, I don't think I'd be strong enough to deny you. But…"

He sat beside her and turned her to face him with gentle hands. "I'm not asking you for anything, Rebecca," he said softly. "We'll muddle through." He smiled crookedly. "I've never enjoyed anything as much as I enjoy your company. Except maybe your cooking," he added ruefully. "I can handle my glands. When it gets too much for me, I'll say so."

She frowned, unconvinced. "It's hurting you," she said. "Don't you think I know? Rourke, I'm a dinosaur. I wasn't ever prepared for the real world, and I've lived like a recluse all these years. You deserve so much more than me."

"Do I?" He framed her face in his hands and kissed her warmly, his smoky breath mingling with hers. "You'll do, thanks. But we'd better not spend too much time alone, from now on."

Her eyes searched his, her heart in them. "Rourke, are you sure?" she whispered.

He nodded, and his face was solemn. "Oh, yes, I'm sure," he said fervently. "Now, will you stop agonizing for me and start thinking about seconds of that great pound cake you made for lunch? I'm starving!"

She laughed. All the tension drained out of her. "Okay." She put her hand in his and they walked back to the farmhouse, and for the rest of the afternoon, they didn't mention what had happened in the woods.

Becky dreamed about it, though. Only in her dreams, they didn't stop. Rourke laid her down in the leaves and took off her clothes. She lay there, breathless and hungry, watching him take off his own. This part was a little hazy, though, because she'd never seen a naked man. What came next was, too. She'd seen a racy movie once with Maggie, but it had been two bodies under a sheet making loud gasping and moaning sounds and clenching their hands together. She had a feeling that it involved a little more than that. Somewhere in the middle of it, she fell asleep.

CHAPTER THIRTEEN

Except for Clay's unusual silence at home, the next few weeks were the happiest of Becky's whole life. She ate lunch with Rourke whenever his schedule permitted. One sour note sounded when the decorators finished his office in the courthouse and he had to move, with his staff, out of Becky's building. But he was as somber about it as she was, and he promised her that they'd have just as much time together. She hadn't believed him, but it was true. He managed to arrange his schedule so that he could take her to lunch at least twice a week. And, as he said, they had the weekends together. It bothered her sometimes that he never invited her to his house. Now that she knew him, she was curious about every aspect of his life. She wanted to see where he lived, the kinds of books he read, the kinds of things he collected, and even the furniture he sat on. They seemed to spend their time sightseeing or just riding. Often she packed a picnic lunch and they drove up to Lake Lanier in Gainesville, or to the

Barvarian motif of Helen, GA., up on the Chattahoochee.
Once he took her to the Civil War battlefield at Kennesaw,
in Cobb County near Marietta. It was great fun, and she was
falling deeper and deeper in love with him.

It touched her that he never said anything about the lack
of variety in her clothes. He knew she was on a limited
budget. He took her to places that wouldn't embarrass her,
and he made sure that they were never completely alone for
long at a time. Since that day in the woods when he'd kissed
her so hungrily, there had been little passion in their relationship. Becky missed the sensual pleasure of his touch, but she
didn't want to make things any harder for him than they already were. It was enough that he enjoyed being with her.

And he did seem to enjoy that, she reflected. They went
to a pet shop one weekend and bought him a new dog. It
wasn't a basset hound, because they hadn't been able to find
one. It was, instead, a Scottie. The little bundle of black
curly fur was precious. Even Rourke had laughed at his antics, and had immediately named him MacTavish. Despite his
busy schedule during court weeks, Rourke had managed
time for the dog and Becky. Now when they went on picnics, MacTavish went, too.

Once or twice, when Clay was at home to stay with
Granddad, Mack had joined them on sightseeing trips. Mack
had been excited about the treat, and had told all his friends
at school about it.

He and Rourke were becoming friends. Mack looked up
to the man and listened to what he said with flattering at-
tentiveness. Mack and Clay were still at odds, but Clay was
so deep in his own misery these days that he hardly paid at-

tention to anything around him, including Becky's fascination with the D.A. He was caught in a trap, with no way out. And he'd long since cut his ties with Becky. He told her nothing these days, not even where he was going when he left the house. He treated her like a stranger.

ATTORNEY J. LINCOLN DAVIS announced his candidacy for district attorney with pomp and fanfare, giving a huge barbecue for the occasion. He even invited Rourke, who told Becky that he didn't relish becoming the entrée and wouldn't go near the place.

It did no good. Immediately after his announcement, Davis began to court the press. His initial jab was at Rourke—that he was easing up on drug dealers and that he hadn't made any progress in his investigation into the grammar school child's death from crack cocaine. Drugs became Davis's platform, and Rourke his whipping boy. Rourke characteristically ignored every barb and kept right on doing his job. He was frustrated by his own lack of progress in the Dennis boy's death. His investigators and the police together hadn't yet been able to link the Harris boys to the elementary school trafficking in drugs.

He'd long since forgotten his earlier motive in dating Becky, which had been to keep tabs on Clay. He was more enchanted with her by the day, and although she mentioned her brother from time to time, it was never anything serious.

Mack, however, had confided something to him that he hadn't even told Becky.

It happened one weekend while he was at the farm.

Rourke had gone to watch Mack run his trains while he waited for Becky. Mack had gotten up suddenly, peeked out into the hall, and quietly closed the door. He sat back down beside Rourke.

"I can't tell Becky," he said after a minute, fiddling with a tiny rail joiner while he spoke. "She's worried enough already. But I have to tell somebody." He looked up, his thin face drawn with worry. "Mr. Kilpatrick, Clay tried to get me to tell him who might buy drugs at my school. I wouldn't, and he got real mad." He bit his lip painfully. "He's my brother. I love him, even if he is a rat. It's just, I don't want any more kids to die." He put the rail joiner down. "He doesn't talk to me or anything, but I heard him talking to Son Harris on the phone. He's supposed to meet them at the Quick-Shop parking lot next Friday night at midnight. It's something big and Clay sounded like he didn't want to do it. I heard him try to back out." Tears formed in his eyes. "He's my brother! I don't want to hurt him, but it sounded like Son was threatening him."

Rourke pulled the boy into his arms and held him tight while he cried. He didn't know much about children, but he was learning fast. This one had a big heart and a lot of courage. He didn't want to sell out his brother, but he was afraid for him.

"I'll do what I can for Clay," he told Mack quietly, producing a handkerchief to dry the boy's eyes with rough tenderness. "And nobody, especially not Becky, will ever know where I got the information. Fair enough?"

Mack nodded. "Did I do the right thing?" he asked miserably. "I feel like a stool pigeon."

"Mack, doing the right thing takes a lot of courage sometimes. It's hard to choose between a member of your own family and a principle. But if these pushers keep up what they're doing, more kids are going to die. That's a fact. The Harrises are responsible for most of the junk going into the schools. If I can put them away, a lot of innocent lives will be spared the anguish of addiction. I'll give your brother the best deal I can. If you're right, and the Harris boys have threatened him to keep him on the payroll, I may be able to offer him a plea-bargain in return for his testimony. We'll see. Is that fair enough?"

"I guess. But I still feel like a jerk," he muttered.

Rourke sighed heavily. "How do you think I feel when I help send somebody to the electric chair, Mack?" he asked quietly. "Even if he's guilty as sin?"

"Do you really have to do that?" the boy asked.

"Once or twice in the past seven years, yes, I have," he replied. "It never gets easy. It never should. Anyone is capable of murder, given the right incentive."

Mack didn't understand that, but he nodded. He felt as if a great weight had been lifted from him, but it hurt to think that his betrayal might send his brother to jail.

Rourke made it back into the living room before Becky reappeared, so she knew nothing about their conversation. But he had thought of nothing else all week.

He sat at his desk with a stack of file folders in front of him, all cases that had to be dealt with by him or his associates. He and his secretary went crazy trying to get them all calendared, subpoenaing witnesses and making sure they showed up in court, getting briefs together. It was a nightmare of paperwork and meticulous detail that sometimes paid off handsomely. And sometimes it was a hopeless confusion of misplaced witnesses and hung juries and overzealous defense attorneys. Kilpatrick sat among the ruins of his late lunch, a cigar standing in two inches of cold coffee in a Styrofoam cup, with the phone ringing off the hook and appointments overlapping. And he thought with malicious delight that J. Lincoln Davis would deserve this job.

By the time Friday arrived, Rourke had tipped off a contact in the local police department about the meet in the parking lot—a man he knew he could trust not to be bought. He put his investigator wise just as a precaution, and then went to pick up Becky.

Clay was there. The family was just finishing supper, and Clay looked thinner than ever and nervous. He glanced at Rourke warily, his whole demeanor antagonistic and baiting.

"You back again?" he chided as he got up from the table, ignoring Becky's furious glare. "Why don't you just move in?"

"I'm considering it," Rourke said imperturbably, smoking his cigar with casual indifference to Clay's behavior. "It seems to me that Becky could do with a little more help than she gets around here."

Clay flushed. He stared to say something, but decided against it. He threw up his hands and went out the back door, slamming it viciously behind him.

"You've got no call to bait my grandson," Granddad said hotly.

"I don't?" Rourke said innocently. "Or have you already forgotten who threw the first punch?"

Granddad got up from the table with visible effort. He

didn't look at Rourke. "I'm going to bed, Becky. I don't feel well."

"Do you want me to stay home with you?" Becky asked worriedly. "Will you be all right?"

For God's sake, stop it, Rourke wanted to rage. *Stop letting yourself be used like this!* But he couldn't interfere. She had every right to care about her family. That loving concern was part of her.

Granddad glanced at her, and then at Rourke. He'd have loved to say that he needed her to stay. But the look on her face even as she offered stopped him. "No. I'm just a little puny today. Mack and I will play checkers, won't we?" he asked the boy.

Mack smiled wanly. "Sure we will. You have a good time, Becky."

"I'll be home early," she promised. She got her sweater, because it was chilly for late spring, and pulled it around her shoulders. She was wearing the old flowered shirtwaist dress with low-heeled shoes and a pink sweater, her hair flowing down to her shoulders. She felt very young when she was with Kilpatrick, despite the fact that he was only twelve years her senior. Tonight he seemed preoccupied, and he hadn't yet mentioned where they were going.

He'd phoned earlier to tell her that he wouldn't be able to get there until after supper, because he had some last-minute work to finish. When he showed up, he was wearing jeans, a checked shirt, and boots. He looked much more casual than she was used to seeing him even when they went on picnics.

"I've been helping my neighbor move," he explained as he

put her into the white T-bird. "I promised him a month ago that I'd be available when he was ready, and tonight he called in the marker. I hope you aren't too disappointed about dinner."

"I'm not disappointed at all," she said gently. "I'm amazed that you haven't run off screaming long before now, having to look at me every day."

He glanced at her with raised eyebrows. "What's wrong with you?"

"If you don't know, I'm not about to tell you," she laughed. "Where are we going?"

"To my place," he said. "I thought you might like to see where I live."

Her eyes searched his profile, and she wondered if he was feeling the need for a little physical closeness as keenly as she felt it. She ached to lie in his arms and make love with him—an unashamed reaction to the emotional state she was in. She loved him. It was the most natural thing in the world to want to be intimate with him, but she wanted him to make a commitment, to say that he cared about her, to start talking about a future, before she took that giant step. He'd never said anything about marriage or a permanent relationship, but she knew he wasn't seeing anyone else. And he seemed to care about her, even if he wouldn't admit it.

He pulled into a long driveway that led off a quiet suburban street into a garage. The house was brick, very elegant, and had a garden out back, complete with fountain and birdbaths. She imagined that in the daylight, the house looked striking against that manicured lawn and the tall hedges that lined the property and protected it from the prying eyes of neighbors on both sides.

He unlocked the door inside the garage and led her into a thickly carpeted den. Beyond it was a formal living room, a dining room, and a hall.

"It's huge," she remarked slowly.

"Much too big for me," he agreed, "but it's been home for a long time. Hello, MacTavish!" he greeted the Scottie, who came running, barking enthusiastically as he jumped on Kilpatrick's jeans-clad leg.

Rourke picked up the dog, petted him, and laughed as he put him back down. "I managed to get him paper-trained the first week, or we'd be in real trouble here," he told Becky. "Come on. We'll leave this turkey in the kitchen with the rest of his supper. I usually make him go to bed long before I do, so that I can concentrate on my work. He can be a real pain when he wants attention." He didn't add that he was too attached to the pup to refuse him that attention.

"Do you bring work home a lot?" she asked, pausing to pet MacTavish before he was closed up in the kitchen with his food, water, and doggy bed.

"I have to," he said. "Davis thinks he wants this job, but he's in for a real shock when he finds out how little leisure time he's going to have to spend with his girlfriends."

He led her into the living room, with its antique furniture and open fireplace.

"How beautiful," she exclaimed. "Do you use the fireplace in winter?"

"No. Those are gas logs in the fireplace," he replied, smiling at her. "I don't have the leisure to keep wood chopped to burn in it, as mundane as that sounds. Would you like a drink?"

"Of what?" she asked demurely.

"Scotch and water is about all the bar runs to around here," he chuckled as he pulled out a squat crystal bottle and two squatty square glasses to go with it. "I'll make sure yours is mostly water, though, Little Bo Peep."

He poured the drinks and handed hers to her, then sat down beside her on the wide, cushy sofa.

She took a sip of her drink and made a face. It was pretty strong stuff, even watered down. She glanced up at his profile and smiled. "You really haven't got the hang of this rake thing," she said. "You're supposed to get me drunk and lure me into bed."

"I am?" He scowled. "Damn! Why don't you tell me these things?"

"I'm doing my humble best," she assured him. She took off her sweater and slipped out of her shoes, then drew her feet up under the full skirt of her dress with a sigh. It felt so nice, being here with him like this—as if the world were very far away.

But when she looked at Rourke, he was staring into space and brooding, his brows drawn together, the drink hanging absently from his lean fingers.

"What's wrong?" she asked gently.

"Sorry," he murmured, glancing down at her. "I hate my job from time to time, Becky. Tonight I'd like to forget I ever wanted it."

"Would you?" She searched his eyes, her heart going wild at the expression she found there. With nervous deliberation, she set her drink on the side table. She coaxed the glass from his hand and put it beside hers. Then, with pure bravado, she eased herself into his lap and looped her arms around his neck.

He looked down at her, still brooding, the soft, scented warmth of her body seducing him. He'd wanted her for a long time. Tonight he'd had all he could take. Clay was bothering him, she was bothering him, the job was bothering him. He'd reached flashpoint and he wanted her enough to risk anything. He felt reckless tonight. He didn't seem to be the only one, either. Her eyes were a little apprehensive, but her lips were already parted, and the look on her face spoke volumes.

"Feeling brave, are you?" he asked in a deep, husky whisper. "All right. Let's see how brave you really are."

His hand went to the buttons on her dress. He opened the top one at her collarbone. Then the next, at the soft beginning slope of her breasts. He opened another one between her breasts. She caught his hand nervously, staying it.

"Not so brave after all," he chided gently.

"It's...it's not that." She bit her lip and dropped her gaze to his broad chest. "I guess you're used to women who can afford frilly, pretty things to go under their clothes. All I have is old and worn. And it's cotton, not silk and lace. I didn't want you to see it."

He caught his breath. He couldn't believe what he was hearing. He tilted her chin up, making her look at him. "Do you really think that matters to me?" he asked softly. "Or that I'd even notice? Sweet innocent, what I want to see is your pretty breasts, not your bra." Her face flamed. She felt her breath shuddering out of her as she looked up at his solemn, quiet face. He looked very adult and masculine, very much in control of what was happening. She knew then, without asking, that he was no novice. And then the excitement of what he'd said, of what they were doing, burned in her blood.

"You're blushing," he whispered, pushing her hand gently aside while he completed what he'd started. He unbuttoned the dress to her waist, his eyes holding hers as he did it with sensual slowness. "Is it shocking, to let me do this?"

"Yes," she whispered back, her eyes wide with excited pleasure. She moved, wanting him to do something, anything. But he paused with his hand at her waist, toying with the open buttonhole.

His blood was raging through his veins. He'd thought about doing this for weeks. He'd hardly thought of anything else. Becky was a virgin. She'd done nothing intimate with a man, but here she lay in his arms, waiting for him, eager for his touch. It made him feel sensations he'd left behind in his boyhood.

His lips parted as he breathed, trying to hold back as long as he could, to savor every second of it. "Is it hard to breathe?" he asked, his voice velvety smooth, deep.

"Yes," she whispered, managing a smile.

His fingers trailed up her rib cage to just below her breast and back down again, a lingering torment that he repeated again and again, watching her with arrogant pleasure, until she began to lift toward his fingers in a rhythmic arching of her body. She bit back a moan, but not in time.

His free hand clenched in the long, thick hair behind her

head and contracted while his other hand continued its slow
arousal. She hardly felt the tension on her hair. Her whole
body was involved in a mad race to make him touch her
breast. She gasped and lifted one last time toward that tormenting hand, shivering as she held the arch.

And then his hand moved the rest of the way, finally,
smoothing up over her breast, cradling the hard nipple. And
she moaned, sobbing, her body convulsing helplessly at the
tiny culmination.

Rourke was shocked. He hadn't really believed that a virgin could be this easily aroused, this sensual. But he recognized what he saw in her face, and it sent him reeling. With
a rough murmur, he jerked the dress off her shoulders and
fought the catch of her bra, feeling her hands helping him as
she breathed feverishly.

His mouth was on her breasts, on her nipples. She felt a
horrible dragging sensation in her lower stomach—a sensation that grew worse and worse until it was as tension that
hurt. She gathered handfuls of his thick hair and pulled his
head even closer, feeling his teeth and loving the faint abra-
sion of them on her soft skin. He suckled at one breast until
the very heat of the suction sent her arching upward in another tiny consummation.

Rourke was on fire. He'd never known anything as mad
and uncontrollable in his whole damned life. He stripped her
without a thought in the world except getting her under him.
His hands trembled on her soft skin, his mouth ate her, savored her, in the silence of the room that was broken only
by her soft gasping cries and his own harsh breathing.

His jeans were too tight, and he cursed as he forced

them down his taut legs. He fought out of his shirt and underwear, socks and shoes, and the whole time, his mouth was feverish on Becky's body, keeping her in thrall until he was nude.

His mouth was one long, aching pleasure on her hot skin. She felt the air on it with a feeling of thankfulness, relief. She was burning, and he was thorough, slow and fierce and expert, his hands finding her as no hands ever had, his mouth on the inside of her thighs, making her cry out.

She was on her back on the carpet, shuddering as his mouth and body began to move again. His lips traveled with sensual slowness up her belly, over her breasts, to find her mouth. His tongue slid inside it delicately, tenderly, while his powerful body slid upward until it covered hers. He was hairy, and the hair was abrasive against her soft skin, but it was arousing, heaven. His cool skin covered the heat of her body. She felt him between her thighs, probing. She opened her legs, too far gone to deny him when she was aching to know him, aching to be filled. The need was anguish now.

Her hands pulled at him. He lifted his head and looked into her eyes, holding their wildness.

"Look down," he said huskily. "Look at us."

He coaxed her feverish eyes down and his followed them. And then he pushed, hard.

The shock of seeing it happen, of seeing man joined to woman in such a shattering way, took the sting out of the sudden penetration. She gasped, but even as the sound left her lips, he filled her completely in one smooth thrust.

He lay against her, his elbows catching his weight, and he held her eyes.

The shock was in her face, in its sudden color, and in the tensing of her body under his.

"Relax," he whispered. One hand came up to smooth back her disheveled hair, to gentle her. He could feel her tensing around him, increasing his pleasure, but he knew it could cost her her own. "Relax, Becky. Relax for me. I won't have to hurt you anymore."

His voice was soft, even with the tension she felt in him. She swallowed, only just realizing what she was letting him do. And now it was much, much too late to stop.

"You're...inside me," she said huskily. "Inside my body."

The words wrenched him. His eyes closed and his jaw clenched as he fought for control, shivering. "Yes," he whispered. He groaned. "Oh, God, it's so sweet!"

He was moving. He hadn't meant to, so soon, but her husky observation sent him beyond his own limits. He moved down in a slow, deep rhythm that was pure feverish hell, his teeth grinding together as he looked into Becky's wide eyes the whole while.

"Fever," he said. "You burn me up. Got to have you, Becky, got to...have you!"

She felt him buffet her. She felt a sharp twist of pleasure and gasped.

"There?" he whispered, holding her eyes as he did it again.

"Yesss!" She gasped again.

"Hold on," he managed with his last bit of breath. "Let me take you up to the sky!"

Everything seemed to burn red, like fire. She closed her eyes finally as the anguish built. Sounds climbed out of her throat that she'd never heard before—high-pitched sounds that were more like screaming than moans. She lifted up to him as the pleasure became so unbearable that she begged him to end it, and then begged him not to.

She was gasping for breath. She heard a heartbeat so loud and quick that it was frightening, and it seemed to be his and hers. She was drenched in sweat. So was he. Her hands were on his broad back, and it was slick. She felt his body between her legs, felt the lax weight of it, with a sense of wonder.

"Can you forgive me?" he whispered wearily.

She moved her hands to his shoulders, touching him. He was still part of her body, part of her soul.

"Oh, my goodness," she said huskily.

He heard the note of wonder in her soft voice and lifted his head. His hair was as damp as the rest of him, his eyes dark with remorse and fatigued satisfaction. Her face was flushed, her lips swollen from the pressure of his mouth. His eyes drifted down farther, to the faint marks on her soft pink breasts that his lips had left there. They were pretty breasts. He'd been too aroused to look at them properly, but now his eyes savored their soft thrust, the mauve nipples that were relaxed and swollen now.

"I wanted you too much to pull back," he said quietly. "I tried. But it had been a long time, Becky——a hell of a long time. And I don't think I've ever wanted anything as much as I wanted you tonight."

"I wanted you, too," she confessed. She couldn't quite meet his eyes. She looked down the length of their bodies, fascinated by the intimacy she'd never experienced before.

He saw her stare and abruptly lifted himself, giving her a sight that shocked her speechless.

He chuckled as he sprawled on his back beside her, the carpet soft and faintly abrasive against his damp back. "You might as well get used to it," he mused. "You're going to find that sex is worse than eating peanuts. Once is never enough."

She sat up, feeling shy and faintly uncomfortable and a little embarrassed.

"The bathroom is that way," he said, understanding her expression.

She nodded, grabbing up her dress and underthings without looking at him again. Whatever she thought she knew about sex was past history now. She had a shocking knowledge not only of the mechanics, but of the feverish, uncontrollable hunger that preceded it. She'd been so confident that she could refuse her own need, that she could hold back. Now she knew what true helplessness was. She'd given in without a single protest. What must he be thinking of her now?

She blushed as she laid her things out in the bathroom and searched for a washcloth and a towel. Would he mind if she took a shower?

Just as she pulled out the towel and cloth, he opened the door and walked in, smiling gently at her shy withdrawal.

"It's all right," he said softly. He pulled her to him, and she was aroused all over again, just by touching him.

She gasped. She couldn't believe what was happening.

He drew back a little and looked down at her, his lean fingers touching her suddenly hard nipples with quiet satisfaction. "I want you again, too," he said gently. "But we'll have a shower first. This time, we're going to have each other in bed, and I'm going to take a hell of a long time with you. I want you screaming mad before I take you the second time."

She shivered with the impact of the words, and before she could say anything, he was kissing her. She moaned against his mouth, clinging to his powerful body, feeling his arousal with a fierce pride in her own womanhood.

When he turned on the water and took her into the shower, she didn't protest. They bathed each other quietly, without words. He turned off the water and toweled them dry, his hands lingering on her soft body as he dried it, whispering things that made her tremble with desire.

He picked her up then, carried her into the bedroom, and laid her gently on the thick quilted bedspread. He stood over her for a long moment, looking down at her. And for the first time, she looked at him properly, too. He was tan all over—the kind of tan that doesn't come from the sun. Thick hair curled over his broad, muscular chest and down over his flat stomach to his thighs. He was everything a man should be, she thought, finding the courage to look at him intimately and not flinch as his body reacted violently and blatantly to her fixed stare.

He did some staring of his own, letting his eyes slide from her peaked, full breasts, down over her narrow waist and rounded hips to her long, slender legs. She was beautiful nude, he thought—beautiful and desirable. Tomorrow they could pay the piper. Tonight, he was going to make her glad that she was a woman.

He slid down beside her on the bed, arching over her with smiling intent.

"The lights," she whispered, glancing at the table lamps.

"We made love with them on the first time," he reminded her. He slid his lean, dark hand down her creamy body, into a place he hadn't had the time or patience to touch before. She gasped and caught his hand, but he shook his head. "You gave yourself to me," he told her. "It's much too late to set limits, little one."

"Yes, but...oh!" She arched, shivering, as he touched her and found the key to her fulfillment.

"That's right," he whispered, his eyes heated with pleasure as he watched her respond to his touch, first shyly, and then with pure abandon, arching, moaning, and writhing under his touch. "That's right, let me satisfy you. I want you to know exactly what I'm going to give you this time. Like that. Yes, little one, like that, like that!"

She cried out and the spasms lifted her helplessly while he watched, his eyes glittering with pride and excitement, until she lay exhausted and trembling, her eyes finding his and widening with shock.

"Did you think you'd reached a climax before?" he whispered. "Now you know you hadn't. But you will, this time. You will, I promise you."

His mouth eased over her breasts and he began to kiss her lazily, waiting until she was relaxed again and responding to the touch of his warm mouth on her skin. She began to tense. Her nipples budded under his tongue. She moaned jerkily.

He took his sweet time, drawing it out, teasing her body and her mouth with lazy movements that eventually had her racked with frustrated desire. She sobbed, writhing under his tormenting hands, whispering things she knew she was going to be ashamed of, but helpless to stop them under her lips. He laughed while he roused her, glorying in her headlong response, her feverish pleading.

When he had her mindless and in anguish, he moved over her and inside her in one long, slow, downward drive, and she convulsed instantly. He'd never seen it happen so quickly for a woman before.

He drove for his own fulfillment, confident that she was already past hers before he even began. It took him a long time, all the same, and she went with him every step of the way, her own satisfaction wrung out of her time and time again before the one, final thrust that sent him arching above her in a convulsion that tore an agonized groan from his throat. He couldn't remember ever crying out before, but this time the pleasure had all but knocked him unconscious.

He collapsed on her, shivering in the aftermath, too shaken to move, almost too shaken to breathe.

"Baby," he whispered huskily, rolling onto his side to gather her totally against him and cradle her in his arms. His eyes closed as he held her. "God, I need you, Becky," he groaned.

She heard him, but she didn't say anything. Rourke wondered if she realized that he'd never admitted to needing anyone in his life, or that saying it all but amounted to a declaration of love from him.

In fact, she didn't. She managed a weary smile and nuzzled her face into his damp throat, kissing him there, tasting salt and cologne and pure man. "I love you," she whispered sleepily.

His breath stilled in his throat. Nothing had ever sounded so sweet to him before, even if she was saying it to justify giving in to him. His arms contracted. He couldn't stop shaking. "It was never this good," he whispered, almost to himself. "Never so violent that I thought I might die of it, that I lost control enough to cry out."

"You tortured me," she murmured.

"I aroused you to the point of madness," he corrected, drowsy himself. He wrapped her closer. "That's what made it so good for both of us. I couldn't take long enough with you, the first time. I lost control."

"So did I," she confessed. "I wanted you. Oh, I wanted you." She shivered. "I still want you, even now. Rourke!" she moaned, moving helplessly against him as the fever caught again.

"I want you, too," he groaned. "But we can't. My God, you're much too new to this for an all-night session. I'd hurt you, sweetheart."

"You never called me sweetheart before."

"I never made love to you before," he whispered at her ear, kissing it gently. He frowned as a sudden nagging thought invaded his mind. "Becky," he added unsteadily.

"What?" she whispered softly.

His lips slid down her cheek. "I didn't use anything," he breathed into her lips.

Three things happened at once. She jerked back to reality with a start as she realized that neither of them had been rational enough to take precautions. Rourke lifted his head, came wide awake at his own words, and realized the same thing. And the phone rang, stridently and starkly.

He stared down at Becky's shocked face, scowled, and reached over to pick up the receiver.

"Kilpatrick," he said huskily. He listened for a minute, during which his face changed, paled. He looked at Becky with faint horror. "Yes. Yes, I understand. I'll be over first thing in the morning. That's right. Yes, it was. Good night."

"What is it?" she asked, sitting upright with dawning fear in her eyes.

He didn't know how to say it, especially after what had just happened. He didn't want to say it. But there was no way to avoid it now.

"They've just picked Clay up," he said quietly. "He's been charged with three counts of felony possession of cocaine, including one count of possession with intent to distribute. He's also been charged with aggravated assault."

"Aggravated assault? What's that?" she whispered blankly.

"In this instance, attempted murder," he said flatly. "The police searched his girlfriend's car. They found some of the plastic explosives that was used to blow up my car," he said through his teeth. "They found it in a toolbox she said belongs to Clay. They think he planted the bomb under my hood."

Becky got to her feet shakily. She started toward her clothes, but she never made it. She passed out in a heap at Rourke's feet.

CHAPTER FOURTEEN

When Becky came to, Rourke was dressed and leaning over her with a jigger of scotch, his expression one of anguished concern.

She pushed the glass away and sat up. Her clothes were on the bed beside her. With a furious blush, she turned away and began to dress with fumbling, clumsy fingers. When she had her things on again, she stood on wobbly legs, barely comprehending where she was. She didn't really care what condition she was in, anyway. The world had just come down and hit her on the head.

"It will kill Granddad," she whispered.

"No, it won't," he replied. "He's tougher than you think. Come on, Becky. I'll take you home."

She pushed back her disheveled hair and walked into the living room, flushing as she put her shoes back on and picked up her sweater from the floor. She couldn't bring herself to look at the carpet where they'd made love.

Becky turned back to Rourke with a pathetic kind of pride. "How did they catch Clay?" she asked, quite aware that he was holding something back.

He'd promised not to betray Mack's trust. That only left him one alternative, to take all the blame. "I told them," he replied, adding coldly, "Clay let something slip one day while I was at the house. He was overheard." That was true, even if he hadn't been the one who'd overheard him.

She closed her eyes, almost in tears. "Was that why you took me out, why you spent time with me?"

"Do you really need to ask me that, after tonight?" he demanded shortly, remembering his own voice whispering how desperately he wanted her, needed her.

But Becky was thinking about Clay's arrest, not Kilpatrick's whispered endearments, which he probably hadn't meant anyway. She'd read and heard that men would say anything to get a woman into bed.

"No," she said with quiet defeat. "I don't need to ask."

She turned and went out the door. Kilpatrick followed her, locking up. Her attitude bothered him. She wasn't acting like the Becky he knew.

"Those charges," she said when they were in the car and headed back to the farm. "They're felony counts, aren't they? And drug dealing carries a minimum of ten years and some awful fine, doesn't it?"

"You don't have to worry about it tonight," he replied tersely. "Tomorrow morning will be soon enough. Clay's being processed now, and you won't be able to get a bail bondsman until he's arraigned and bail is set."

"He isn't at the juvenile detention center?" she asked huskily.

"God, I hate to have to tell you this," he replied after a minute. "Becky, these charges are major felony counts. I didn't have any choice. I have to prosecute him as an adult."

"No!" she burst out, tears rolling down her pale cheeks, making her freckles stand out violently. "No, you can't! Rourke, you can't, he's just a boy! You can't do this to him!"

His jaw tautened and he didn't look at her again. "I can't change the rules. He broke the law. He has to pay for it."

"He didn't try to kill you. I know he didn't. He's not a monster. He's just a boy who didn't have any advantages, who didn't have a father to help him grow up. You can't put him away for life!"

"It isn't up to me," he tried to reason with her.

"You could tell them he's not guilty," she said frantically. "You could refuse to prosecute him!"

"They've got hard evidence, dammit! What do you want me to do, overlook it? Turn my back and let him loose?"

The icy cut of his tone sobered her. She took deep breaths until she got herself together. She stared out the window, shivering. "You knew they were going to arrest him tonight, didn't you, Rourke?" she asked. "You knew before we left the farm."

"I knew they were going to try," he was wearily. He lit a cigar and opened the window. He'd never realized how it was going to feel when he had Clay in jail. He hadn't realized how it was going to hurt when Becky thought of her brother before she thought of him. Clay was accused of trying to kill him, but it was Clay that Becky was worried about. The fact that the bomb might have killed him didn't seem to bother her.

"Doesn't it matter that he tried to kill me?" he asked after a minute.

"Yes," she said with unnatural calm, her own pain making her strike out blindly. "He should have tried harder."

He felt the shock of those words like a physical blow. He didn't say another word. He smoked his cigar and drove.

When he pulled up at the farmhouse door, Becky got out and started toward the porch without saying anything. It wasn't until she saw him beside her that she realized he'd parked the car and cut off the engine.

"Where are you going?" she asked coldly.

"I'm going with you," he replied doggedly, his eyes narrow on her face. "You may need help with your grandfather."

That had occurred to her, too, but she didn't want Rourke's help and she said so.

"Hate me, if it helps," he said, staring down at her without flinching. "But I'm coming in."

She turned and unlocked the door.

She didn't have to tell anyone what had happened. Granddad was on the floor, groaning and clutching his chest, and Mack was bending over him with a tiny white pill.

"It was on the news about Clay," Mack said, tears rolling down his cheeks. He looked helplessly at Rourke instead of Becky. "Granddad had a spell and fell down. I can't get the pill in him!"

"Oh, no," Becky whimpered. "Oh, no!"

Rourke took her by the arms and eased her gently down on the sofa. He had a feeling she was at the end of her rope.

He knelt beside Mack and took the pill from him. "Come on, Mr. Cullen," he said quietly, lifting the old man and propping him against his knee. "Come on, you have to have your medicine."

"Let me die," the old man groaned.

"Like hell I will," Rourke said gruffly. "Come on. Get this under your tongue."

Granddad opened his eyes and glared at Rourke even as he grimaced with the pain. "Damn you!" he whispered.

"Damn me, by all means, but take the pill. Here."

Amazingly, the old man did as he was told. He took the small pill and tucked it under his tongue, grimacing with even the slight movement of his hand that was required. Rourke didn't move him immediately. He asked Mack to fetch a cushion, and he elevated the old man's head and chest.

"Just lie there and breathe," Kilpatrick said curtly. "I'll phone for an ambulance."

"Don't need that," Granddad gasped. "It will pass."

"You and I both know that it should have passed already," Rourke said, meeting the tired, pain-filled eyes. "Nitroglycerin acts instantly. My uncle had angina pectoris."

"I won't go!"

"Hell, yes, you will," Kilpatrick said doggedly. He walked to the phone and lifted the receiver.

Becky was numb—so numb that she couldn't even protest. An ambulance and a hospital bill were nothing. What was the fine for narcotics possession—something like fifty thousand dollars? Compared to that, the hospital and ambulance together were chicken feed. She'd have to sell the farm and her car and have her wages garnisheed to even afford a lawyer for Clay, much less absorb the fine and Granddad's doctor bill. She began to laugh hysterically.

"I'm sorry, Becky." The voice came from a long way off. She felt the sting of a hand on her cheek and sat erect, holding her face.

Rourke was kneeling just in front of her. "Hang on," he said quietly. "Everything will be all right. Don't start worrying about it tonight. I'll take care of it."

"I hate you," she whispered, and at the moment she meant it.

"I know," he said softly, humoring her. "Just sit there and try not to think."

He got to his feet, pausing to put a comforting arm around Mack before he went back to sit beside Granddad.

It seemed to take forever for the ambulance to come. Rourke let the paramedics in and waited while they did the necessary things before they loaded Granddad into the ambulance and sped away toward Curry Station General.

"Somebody has to go with him," Becky protested weakly.

"You can go and see him in the morning. I've told the paramedics the circumstances and they'll inform your family doctor. You need rest," he said firmly. "Go to bed."

"Mack," she managed as Rourke got her to her feet.

"I'll take care of Mack. Get in there."

She went into the bedroom and put on her gown, too ashamed to look at herself as she did it, because she didn't want to see the faint marks Rourke had left on her. She thought she'd die of shame every time she remembered what she'd let him do. And she deserved to, she told herself angrily. Stupid woman. Why hadn't she realized that he was only seeing her to get to Clay? Granddad had even warned her, but had she listened? No! She was too flattered by his attention. All he'd wanted was Clay's head in a noose, and she'd given it to him, fool that she was. Her brother was going to be in jail for the rest of his life, and it would be her fault.

She cried until her eyes and nose were red. Then she slept. By the time Rourke went in to see about her, she was sound asleep, her long hair spread out on her pillow.

He looked down at her with aching tenderness. *Such a gentle, sweet woman to be so passionate and generous in bed,* he thought, sighing. She was everything he'd ever wanted in a woman. But it was going to take some work to convince her of that after tonight. He shook his head, foreseeing anguish ahead.

He closed her bedroom door and went back to get Mack to bed.

"Stop brooding," he told the boy, hugging him. "You probably saved his life, although I don't expect you to believe that now. Will you and Becky be all right if I leave? I want to make sure your grandfather's settled and stable. I'll phone if there are any complications."

"You don't have to do that," Mack said.

Rourke put his lean hands on Mack's thin shoulders, and looked down at him with quiet determination. "Mack, Becky's the only family I have now. She hates my guts, and maybe I deserved it, but I can't leave her to face this alone.'

Mack nodded. "Okay. Thanks."

Rourke shrugged. "Lock the door after me. Then go to sleep. No late movies. Becky's going to need all the help she can get in the morning."

"I'll help all I can. Good night, Mr. Kilpatrick."

"Good night."

Rourke walked out to his car and lit another cigar, feeling tired and wounded. It had been one hell of a night, and it was just beginning.

He went by the hospital to make sure that Granddad was settled and spoke to the attending physician.

"I can't tell you how he'll do," the doctor said curtly. "He's old and he doesn't have much strength left. If he makes it past the next seventy-two hours, there's hope. But I'll need to run tests and keep him in for several days, and that's going to hurt Becky's budget. The old man is too young for Medicare, and he doesn't have any hospitalization insurance."

"I'll take care of the bill," Rourke said easily. "Or the major part of it," he added with a grin. "Enough to make Becky think she's holding up her end."

The doctor stared at him. "You're the district attorney, aren't you?"

Rourke nodded.

"I heard on the news that Becky's brother was arrested. You'll be prosecuting him, I guess?"

"I don't know yet."

"Tough break for you. For the whole family. Those Cullens are tough, and the old man's as honest as a dollar. So is Becky. I'm sorry for them."

"So am I," Rourke said quietly. "Becky will be in tomorrow to see about her grandfather. Tonight, she's had just about all she can take."

"I can imagine. Yes, I can imagine she has."

And he doesn't know half of it, Rourke thought. He drove back home with his heart feeling like lead in his chest. Of all the damned stupid things to do, he hadn't taken any precautions—none at all. Neither had Becky. Now she had the threat of pregnancy to add to all this, because he'd lost his head and given in to his need of her.

The fact that she'd given in, too didn't help his conscience. She'd hate them both when she woke up. She'd hate him most of all because she thought he was using her to get to Clay. That might have been true in the beginning, but not now. He'd made love to her because he loved her, because he wanted the oneness that came from two souls joining. It had been the most exquisite experience of his life, and he'd told Becky that he loved her. She'd said she loved him, too, but maybe she'd only said it to appease her conscience, to assuage her guilt at giving in to desire. Women were odd creatures— they needed excuses for having sex. He'd never needed one, but this time he had an extreme one—he was crazy about her.

He shook his head. He didn't know what he was going to do, about Clay or Becky. Maybe a good night's sleep would give him a better perspective on things.

It didn't. He opened the morning paper and there, spread across the front page, was a vicious attack by J. Lincoln Davis, accusing the Curry County district attorney of trying to cover up the drug dealing at the elementary school to protect the brother of his girlfriend!

He crumpled it in his hand, blazing with rage. Well, if Davis wanted dirty fighting, he could have it. He went back inside and phoned the *Atlanta Times*.

THE AFTERNOON DAILY CARRIED its own banner headline, as Rourke accused Davis of exploiting an arrest that had put a helpless old man in the hospital. Before the day was out, Kilpatrick's phone was ringing off the hook with sympathy calls blasting Davis for his lack of compassion.

Becky couldn't decide whether to go to the hospital or the jail first. She went to see Granddad, putting off the trip to see Clay because she didn't know what to say or do. She felt sick all over, remembering the night before.

Granddad was asleep. They'd given him painkillers, and he looked pale and helpless. Becky sat down beside him in the semiprivate room and bawled, grateful that the other bed in the room was empty. So much anguish, in so short a time, had broken her spirit. She'd never flinched from her duty and obligations, but she'd never had such a burden on her thin shoulders before. She sat with the old man for several minutes and finally decided that Clay needed her more.

She drove to the county jail with cold apprehension. It was going to be terrible, she knew, having to confront her brother. He'd blame her and Rourke for his predicament. She didn't feel up to another fight.

She was surprised to find the young man totally subdued. He hugged her gently, looking wan and wounded and unlike the Clay she'd come to know in the past months.

"How are you?" she asked, staring around at the stark bare cell with its white commode, steel bunk, and steel bars. She shivered as the voices of other prisoners came floating down the corridor, harsh and crude.

"I'm all right," Clay said. He sat down on the bunk, inviting Becky to join him. He was wearing blue prison clothing, and he looked washed out and fatigued. "It's almost a relief to get it over with. I'll go to prison and the Harris boys will leave me alone. At least I'll be shed of them."

"What do you mean?" she asked.

"They got me drunk and doped up and stuffed my pockets with coke. You know about that," he said. "Well, afterward they set me up on a buy with one of their father's cohorts and started me dealing as a middleman. I never actually pushed the stuff myself, but they said they'd swear I did if I didn't help them find contacts at the elementary school."

"Oh, my God," Becky whispered. She buried her face in her hands. "The Dennis boy."

"I didn't give them his name, Becky, I swear," he said quickly. "It wasn't me." He lowered his eyes. "You might as well know it all. They tried to make me get Mack involved, and I leaned on him. He didn't give an inch. It's why he won't talk to me. He thinks I'm scum. He blames me for his friend's death. And who knows, maybe I am. But I never wired Kilpatrick's car, Becky. I'm a stupid idiot, but I'm not killer. You've got to make him understand."

"I can't make him understand anything," she said tightly. "He was only seeing me to get to you."

Clay cursed. "That son of a...!"

"I let myself be taken in. It's not all his fault," she interrupted. "We dig our own graves, don't we?" She drew in a slow breath. "Granddad's in the hospital. They think it was a mild heart attack."

Clay groaned, his face in his hands. "I'm sorry! Becky, I'm so sorry!"

She patted him awkwardly on the shoulder. "I know."

"Hospital bills, planting time with nobody to help you, and now me." He looked up, his eyes dark and hurting. "God, I'm so sorry! How the hell are you going to manage the bills?"

"The same way I've always managed," she said proudly. "By working."

He flushed. "Honestly, you mean." He looked away. "I convinced myself that I was doing it to help you, that I was earning money to put into the kitty, but I was just lying to myself. When I finally laid off the drugs and the booze and saw what I'd done, I was horrified. But they wouldn't let me out, Becky. They wouldn't let go. They'll all testify that I masterminded the whole setup—that I gave the dope to the Dennis boy, that I wired Kilpatrick's car. I haven't got a prayer."

"Yes, you have. I'll talk to Mr. Malcolm and ask him to represent you, and I'll get a bail bondsman..."

"And try to pay for that, too? No, you won't, Becky," he said. "Listen, Sis, I've got a lawyer—a public defender. He's young, but he's good. He'll do for me. No defense on the face of the earth is going to stop me from serving time, Becky. You have to face that. As for bail, I don't want it."

"It's not fair!" She groaned.

"That's beside the point. I broke the law. Now I have to pay for it. You go home and get some rest. You've got enough to worry about with Granddad. I'm perfectly safe here."

"Oh, Clay," she whispered tearfully.

"I'll be fine. Francine's coming to see me. She's on my side, even though it's going to get her in big trouble with her uncle." He smiled. "She's not bad, once you get to know her. I don't think you've ever seen her the way she really is."

"I've never seen her at all," she reminded him dryly.

He cleared his throat. "Well, you will. One day."

She nodded. "One day." She kissed him good-bye and called to the guard to let her out of the cell. It was a long, cold walk back to freedom. The sound of that cell door closing echoed in her mind all the way home.

CHAPTER FIFTEEN

Sunday morning, Becky got up to go to church. Just after she dressed, however, Mack brought in the Sunday paper. When Becky read the headline, she sat down and cried.

"Don't, Sis," Mack said. He seated himself beside her, and tried awkwardly to comfort her. "Don't."

She couldn't stop. It was so horribly embarrassing to see J. Lincoln Davis's accusations that Rourke had covered up the elementary school drug dealing to protect his girlfriend's brother. The paper did everything but call Becky Rourke's mistress, and said that protecting Clay was Rourke's motive for dragging his heels in the investigation over the Dennis boy's death. There, in glorious print, was her name and Clay's, for her neighbors, friends, and, worst of all, her employers, to see.

"I'll lose my job," she said miserably, wiping away the tears with her fingers. "My bosses won't want this kind of notoriety. They'll have to let me go. Oh, Mack, what will we do?" she burst out, eaten up by panic for the first time in memory.

"Becky, you're just upset," Mack said, trying to sound calm. The sight of Becky crying frightened him. She was always the strongest one of them. "It's been a bad two days. It will get better. You always say that."

"Our names on the front page of the paper," she groaned. "Granddad will never get over it, if he even lives."

"He'll live," Mack said. "And Clay will be all right. Becky, I'll get my clothes on. We're going to church."

She gaped at him. Ten years old and full of authority. He looked like a human bulldog.

"Come on," he said. "Nobody will point at us or talk about us. Church is good medicine. You always say that, too," he added with a grin.

She laughed in spite of her misery. "Yes, sir, Mr. Cullen, I do. And I'll be very proud to go to church with you."

"That's more like my sister," he told her. He winked and went off to put his Sunday clothes on.

So Becky went to church. And, as Mack had said, nobody gossiped. There were offers of help, however, and when they went home, she was glad Mack had talked her into it. She found the strength she needed to face whatever came.

Monday morning, Becky drove to work. When she entered the lobby, she pressed the elevator button. For the first time, she was glad that Rourke had moved back into his renovated office in the courthouse. It spared her the embarrassment of having to talk to him. He hadn't called. Or perhaps he just hadn't called when they were home. She'd taken Mack with her to the hospital the previous evening.

Well, why should he call, she asked herself miserably. He'd only taken her out to get next to Clay. He'd caught him and now he was going to prosecute him, so what did he need with Becky? If he'd harbored any dark desire for her, now it was satisfied and he wouldn't come around anymore. She groaned inwardly at what had happened. She'd given in without a struggle. In fact, she'd started it herself. Her principles had been sand writing on a low-tide beach—only good until the first wave came along. She felt ashamed. With the shame came another idea. What in the world was she going to do if she became pregnant because of it?

She pushed that thought away as she walked into her office. It wouldn't do any good to worry about it now. If her employers wanted to fire her, let them. She could type and take dictation, so she'd be able to get another job, even if it didn't pay as much. With that thought firmly in mind, she uncovered her typewriter and went into Mr. Malcolm's office to face the music.

"There you are," he said with a kind smile. "I'd expected to hear from you Saturday morning. I'll be more than glad to take Clay on as a client, and you can pay me a dollar a month if it comes down to that."

She had to fight back the tears. She'd done enough crying. "Oh, Mr. Malcolm, you're so kind," she said gently. "I thought you might want to fire me."

His eyebrows lifted. "You can type a hundred and five words a minute and you're afraid I might fire you? My God!"

"The newspapers painted me as a scarlet woman yesterday morning, and Clay was branded a child killer…"

"Damn the newspapers," he said calmly. "It's just Lincoln

Davis out trying to scalp Kilpatrick before they get to the polls. And you obviously haven't read Kilpatrick's rebuttal. Look at that," he added, pushing the afternoon daily across the desk toward her.

She read the story with stark fascination. Rourke didn't mind hitting below the belt himself, she thought. He put his adversary's accusations in perspective, accusing him of political exploitation and sensationalism. He did it coolly and very concisely, every quote short and terse and guaranteed to turn Mr. J. Davis any way but loose. He mentioned Granddad's heart attack and added that he was a bachelor and free to date whom he pleased. Furthermore, he told the reporter who interviewed him, Miss Cullen was a lady, and if Davis didn't retract his insinuation about her character, Rourke would be pleased to quote him the statutes on defamation of character across a courtroom. At the end of the long article was a quote by the aforesaid Mr. Davis, accusing the morning newspaper of misquoting him and publicly apologizing to Miss Cullen.

"For heaven's sake!" she said huskily.

"Formidable, is our Mr. Kilpatrick," Mr. Malcolm said with a smile. "Even if I hate his guts in court, I have to give him credit for occasional eloquence. He put the estimable Mr. Davis's posterior in a sling."

"It was kind of him to defend me," she said, thinking that she hardly fit Rourke's description of her anymore. Davis's insinuation was much more accurate after the way she'd behaved on Saturday night.

"He likes you," Malcolm remarked, puzzled by the look on her face. "We've all begun to think of the two of you as an item. You've been inseparable for weeks."

She looked down at the newspaper without seeing it. "Well, that isn't likely to continue," she replied dully. "I won't be seeing him again."

"You don't have to make that kind of sacrifice," her boss said quietly. "Not just to placate Davis. He'll find something besides your brother to hit Kilpatrick with—you wait and see. Staying away from Kilpatrick because of your brother's arrest isn't going to affect his chances at reelection, even if it is a noble thought," he added, smiling.

He'd totally misread her motives, but before she could even try to set the record straight, the phone began to ring and half the staff walked in. It was back to work, and she was grateful for the diversion. She hadn't thought that Rourke might suffer politically because of his association with her and her family. He'd said he wouldn't run again, but she knew there were people trying to make him change his mind. Surely, if his only thought had been to keep tabs on Clay, he wouldn't have sacrificed his reelection hopes by connecting himself with her, would he? Not if he was sure Clay was going to be arrested?

The more she thought about it, the more muddled she became. She only wished Rourke would call her. She remembered telling him she hated him when he'd taken her home. She grimaced. He'd looked after all of them that night—he'd even gone to the hospital to see about Granddad—and she hadn't even thanked him. Despite what had happened between the two of them, it was wrenching to have lunch alone. It was like being half a person suddenly, more so now that she knew him so intimately. She could close her eyes and feel him, taste him, experience him as she had that night. Her mind rebelled at the memories, but her body wanted them. It wanted him. But he'd betrayed her and she'd never be able to trust him again. Clay could go to the electric chair or to prison for life. She had to remember that Rourke had put him in jail and would be fighting to keep him there.

Besides, she thought bitterly, *if he really cares about me, he'd have said something by now. He'd have contacted me.* She finished her solitary lunch and went back to the office. At least she still had a job. She was grateful for that.

Maggie had been supportive and quietly sympathetic all day. "Kilpatrick's the worst of it, isn't he, Becky?" she asked at quitting time, her dark eyes sympathetic. "I suppose you've convinced yourself that he only saw you to get to your brother."

"It's true," Becky replied wearily. "He hasn't even phoned me since that night."

"Perhaps he's gnawing on some guilt of his own," the older woman suggested. "He may think you don't want to hear from him. Who could blame him? He had your brother arrested and he's prosecuting him. He has to know that your grandfather is furious at him, and sick besides. It could be to protect you that he's staying away, Becky," she added solemnly. "The newspapers are all over him, thanks to Mr. Davis. Reporters will be attached to him like cockleburs until the heat dies down. He's sparing you the limelight, honey."

That was another thought that hadn't occurred to Becky. It was the most comforting of the lot.

A WEEK WENT BY. Rourke shepherded his cases through court with a stoic demeanor and black humor. Davis was his adversary in one case, and the two of them turned the atmosphere of the courtroom so static that the judge called them into his chambers during recess and read them both the riot act.

Rourke didn't dodge the press, but then, he didn't need to. Davis was capturing the limelight with the skill of a born showman, manipulating every confrontation with him to his advantage, waving crime statistics and conviction records under the noses of Atlanta's news media. Twice he made the six o'clock news. Rourke fed MacTavish a hamburger patty and squirted catsup at the screen. Personally, he thought a red beard did wonders for the esteemed counselor.

But under his relatively calm exterior, he was still stinging from Becky's angry words. Apparently her family was more important to her than he was ever going to be. He didn't know how to handle being last on her list of priorities. He'd thought they were growing so close that their world centered on the two of them, but Clay's arrest had taught him different. She immediately put Clay's welfare above his own, as if what had happened here in his house was of no importance at all.

He sipped black coffee with a cold glare out the window. She'd been a virgin and he'd betrayed her trust. He'd allowed things to progress too far, but she'd helped him, dammit—he hadn't gone the whole way alone!

He got up and poured himself some more coffee, idly watching MacTavish eat. He'd spent so much of his life alone that it was odd to feel uncomfortable. He and Becky had done so much together. He'd looked forward to her company with real delight. And after the feverish way she'd responded to him in bed, he was certain that she loved him. He knew he'd heard her whisper it to him. But afterward, all she'd felt for him was hatred. Even now, she was probably cursing him for seducing her and blaming him for Clay's arrest.

He'd wanted to call her. In fact, he'd tried once or twice last Sunday, but there had been no answer. After that, he'd convinced himself that she didn't want his interest. He knew she'd read the newspaper accounts, and if she wanted to think that he'd jettisoned her to salvage his job, let her. He'd go on by himself, as he always had, and she could...

He sighed heavily, closing his eyes. She could what? She was holding up the whole world. She'd told him that once, so long ago. She was the sole support of her family, the morale booster and cut-bandager and housekeeper who held it all together. There was nobody else to do for Clay now, except Becky. She'd have Granddad to visit every day, in addition to her job and her chores and the worry of Clay's trial. He'd seen her break once already. What would happen to her if Granddad died, if Clay was convicted?

He knew already that he was going to disqualify himself as prosecutor when Clay's case was calendared. But if he gave it to one of his colleagues, that was going to cast doubts on the whole office, because Davis could accuse him of pressuring his people to throw the case on Becky's account.

His eyes narrowed. Well, maybe there was a way out. He could have the governor appoint a special prosecutor for the case and that would satisfy everyone. But there was still the matter of Clay's guilt or innocence. Mack had said that Clay was being threatened and coerced into what he'd done. If that was true, and the boy really wasn't the ringleader, could he let him go to prison? It was certainly possible that Clay hadn't wired his car or sold crack to the Dennis boy. If that was true, the Harrises might be using Clay as a scapegoat to keep their own noses out of jail.

It did gall him to let the pushers get away with it. He might be able to dig a little deeper. But even if he did, the public defender was overloaded and underpaid. So how would Clay have a chance anyway? A good defense attorney could make all the difference in the world, but Becky couldn't afford that kind of representation. The public defender was the best the Cullens could hope for. He sat back down, pushing a restless hand through his dark hair. He lit a cigar and sat back in his chair, his eyes narrowing in thought. Clay's preliminary hearing was two weeks away. The grand jury had already handed in a true bill against him. Bail had been set at his arraignment, but he'd waived it. Apparently Clay wasn't going to let Becky pay it. And he was safe from the Harris boys now.

He cursed roundly. Life had been so simple three months ago. The world was going sour, and all because of a backwards little country girl who baked him lemon pound cakes and made him laugh. He wondered now if he would ever laugh again.

BECKY HAD BEEN GOING TO SEE Granddad every night, but he continued to lie in the hospital bed without showing the slightest interest in life. The doctor knew she was going to have fits trying to pay the bill, even though Rourke Kilpatrick had promised to absorb the lion's share. Finally, he recommended moving the old man to an intermediate-care nursing facility.

"It would be the best thing, for the time being," he told Becky. "I think we can get some funding for him. I'll look into it. He isn't responding as fast as I'd like, and I don't think you can handle him at home right now."

"I could try," she began.

"Becky, Mack's in school. Clay's in jail. You're trying to hold down a job. And frankly, you don't look well," he added with a keen glance at her pinched face and pale complexion. "I'd like to see you in my office for a routine physical."

She swallowed, trying to stay calm. There were plenty of reasons why she didn't want him to examine her, the main one being that her period was two weeks late and she'd brought her breakfast back up this morning. She'd had a lot of stress, which could account for those symptoms, but she was willing to bet it wasn't purely an emotional state that she was in.

"I can't afford it right now, Dr. Miller," she said quietly.

"We'll put it on the tab, Rebecca," he said doggedly. "I won't take no for an answer."

"I'm just run down and tired," she tried again.

"I delivered you," he interrupted. His keen blue eyes saw right through her. "Whatever I find will be between you and me and Ruthie," he added. Ruthie had been his nurse for thirty years, and even if she knew where all the bodies were buried, nobody would get it out of her.

"All right." Becky gave in wearily. "I'll make an appointment."

"See that you keep it," he muttered. "Now, about your

granddad. I think we can get him in at HealthRex—that new nursing home the county built. It's modern and not too expensive, and a few weeks there might be just the thing for him. He'll be around people his own age. Maybe the change will make him want to live."

"And if it doesn't?" she asked.

He shrugged. "Becky, the will to live isn't something you can prescribe. He's had a hard life, and his heart isn't good. He needs a reason to get well. He doesn't seem to think he has one."

She grimaced. "I wish I knew what to do."

"Don't we all. You take care of yourself. I'll expect you to make an appointment Monday. I'll let you know about your grandfather as soon as I can get some information on the possibilities. All right?"

"All right." She smiled. "Thank you."

"I haven't done anything yet. You can thank me later. Try to get some rest. You look exhausted."

"It's been a very long two weeks," she said, "but I'll try."

"How's Clay?"

She shook her head. "Depressed and defeated. I met his public defender." She made a face. "He's young and energetic, but his caseload is ridiculous. He won't have time to prepare a proper defense and Clay's going to pay for it. I wish I could afford a good attorney."

"You work for some," he said.

She nodded. "But I can't let Mr. Malcolm sacrifice that kind of time if I can't pay him for it." She clenched her hands at her side. "The world runs on money, doesn't it?" she asked bitterly, glancing down the hall at the poor people, black and white and Hispanic and Oriental, old and young, waiting at the charity emergency room until they could see a doctor. "Look at them," she said. "Some of them will die because they can't afford medicine or a hospital or a good doctor. Some of them will wear themselves out nursing their relatives because they can't afford any help. Most of them will die in a charity ward." Her brows drew together in pain. "It's like jail. If you're poor, you do time. If you're rich, you get a good lawyer and a good chance. What kind of world is that?"

He put an arm around her shoulder. "Tell me about Mack and cheer me up."

She managed a smile for him. "Well, he's actually passing math," she began.

"Mack? Amazing!"

"That's what I thought myself," she replied. Inside, her emotions were sitting on a knife-edge. She talked almost mechanically, but her thoughts were on Granddad and Clay and that inevitable medical examination that was going to change her life. She didn't know how she was going to bear it all. Somehow, she was going to have to find the strength to get through the next few months.

Fortunately, when she called Dr. Miller's office for an appointment, she discovered that it would be a month before he could see her. That suited her very well. It was cowardly to be happy about putting it off so long, but until then, she could pretend that everything was all right. She wouldn't have to face it until she heard the words, and a miracle might happen. She might not be pregnant. It gave her something to hold on to.

ROURKE WASN'T SURE WHY he did it, but he went to Becky's office the following Monday. Bob Malcolm had asked to see him about a plea bargain. Malcolm usually went to Rourke, not the reverse, but it had been almost three weeks since Rourke had seen Becky, and Clay's hearing was set for Friday. He wanted to see her, to find out how she was coping.

When she looked up from her typewriter and saw him, she went first scarlet, then a ghostly kind of pale. She looked gaunt, he thought, as if she wasn't eating properly. Her gray dress was familiar—one she'd worn when they went out together. Her honey-brown hair was in a loose bun and she had on just a bare minimum of makeup that didn't even camouflage her freckles. He filled his eyes with her.

Becky could barely breathe. She hadn't even considered that Rourke might actually come to the office. She couldn't move at first. She just sat there looking at him, blind to everything around her. He didn't look worn at all, she thought miserably. He didn't look as if he missed her or thought about her. He looked the same as he always had—dark and faintly somber and threatening.

He perched himself on her desk. "The preliminary hearing is Friday," he said. "There are other public defenders."

She let her eyes fall to his mouth and cringed inwardly, remembering how hungrily they'd kissed that night. She swallowed down the bitterness. "He's a very good lawyer," she said. "He suits Clay."

"Does he suit you?" he asked abruptly. "Your brother's life may hang in the balance."

"What do you care?" she asked rawly, looking up with angry, hurting hazel eyes. "You're the one who's trying to send Clay to prison! Why should it matter to you who defends him?"

"Oh, I like a good fight," he said tautly. "I hate to win a case too easily."

Her lower lip trembled. She looked away. "You needn't worry. Clay will be just another statistic for you to use against Mr. Davis in your campaign. He tried to kill you, remember?"

He picked up a paper clip and turned it in his lean, dark hands, oblivious to the curious stares of Becky's co-workers. "You don't think he did."

"No," she said simply. "I may be blind as a bat in some respects, but I do know my brother and what he's capable of. He could never take another life."

He opened the paper clip, bending it. "How is your grandfather?"

"We've moved him into a nursing home," she said dully. "He's given up."

His eyes lifted and caught hers. "How are you?"

She felt her cheeks go hot. His eyes didn't match the words. There were dark memories in them—sensual ones that struck an answering chord in her—but she didn't dare give in to them. "I'm all right," she said evasively.

"If you aren't all right, I expect to be told," he said sternly. "Do you understand me, Rebecca?"

Her jaw set. "I can take care of myself!"

He sighed angrily. "Oh, certainly you can. We both found out how careful two people can be, didn't we?"

She went scarlet. Her hands twisted together and she didn't dare look around to see if anyone was watching. "Please go," she whispered.

"I came to see your boss, actually," he said carelessly and stood up. "Is he in?"

She shook her head. "He's in court this morning."

"Then I'll phone him before I make the trip again." He stuck his hands in his pockets and stared down at her with narrow, brooding eyes. "You said you hated me. Did you mean it?"

She couldn't look up. Her fingers clenched in her lap. "Are you going to prosecute my brother as an adult?" she asked.

His face hardened. "Is that your condition for a ceasefire?" he asked with quiet mockery. "Sorry, Rebecca, I don't use bribes. Yes, I'm going to prosecute him as an adult. Yes, I think he's guilty. Yes, I think I'll get a conviction."

Her eyes blazed with dislike. She hated that arrogant, mocking smile. She'd underestimated him all the way along, and now she and Clay were paying for it. "The jury may not agree with you."

He shrugged. "That's possible, of course, but not probable." His jaw tautened. "A little ten-year-old boy died because your brother got greedy. I'm never going to forget that."

"Clay didn't do it," she said huskily. "He didn't!"

"He even tried to involve Mack. Did you know that?" he asked.

She closed her eyes to blot out the accusation in his face. "Yes," she whispered. "Clay told me." She didn't question how Rourke knew that. The anger in his voice diverted her.

"You're welcome to rationalize his behaviour all you like," he said after a minute. "But the fact is this—Clay knew exactly what he was doing, and the consequences if he were caught. He's going to do time, and he deserves to. I won't apologize for my part in his arrest. Given the same set of circumstances, I'd do the same damned thing again—exactly the same, Becky."

"Clay didn't wire your car," she said spiritedly. "He didn't sell drugs to the Dennis boy. He may be guilty of every other charge, but he isn't guilty of those."

"You just won't quit," he said roughly. "The Harrises and two other eyewitnesses saw him dealing. They'll swear to it. There was an eyewitness who saw him sell the crack to the Dennis boy, as well," he added gruffly. He hated to tell her that, but Dan Berry had brought that tidbit back from an interview with some teenagers at the high school.

"It's a lie," Becky said. She looked up at him levelly. "I don't care how many people swear they saw it. Clay told me he didn't do it. He can lie to anybody else, but I could always see right through him. He wasn't lying."

He just shook his head. "God, you're stubborn," he muttered. "All right, hang on to your illusions."

"Thank you for your permission, Mr. Kilpatrick," she said sweetly. "Now, if you'll excuse me, I have work to do."

She turned back to her typewriter. Rourke stood and watched her for several long seconds. He'd wanted to smooth things over, but he'd only made them worse. She was never going to believe Clay was guilty.

He turned and walked out of the office. But as he drove back to his own, her words nagged him. They nagged him so much that he drove right past the courthouse and on to the county jail, where Clay was being lodged.

He hadn't planned to see the boy. Becky didn't know that he'd disqualified himself from prosecuting the case, and he'd been too angry to tell her. He still thought Clay was guilty, but maybe he was allowing himself to be prejudiced because of his run-in with their father years ago. Like father like son might not be the answer here. He'd always seen things in black and white, but now he was involved with the family, whether he liked it or not. Since he'd been instrumental in putting Clay here in the first place, maybe it wouldn't hurt to assure himself that he'd been justified.

Clay reddened at the sight of him. His angry eyes flashed at Rourke when he walked into the cell, a smoking cigar in his hand.

"Hail the conquering hero," Clay said as the guard left him alone with Rourke. "I hope you're satisfied, now that you've got me where you want me. I hear I'm being accused of everything short of actual murder, as well as being a notorious dope dealer. Why don't you just send in a cop with a loaded gun and let him save the taxpayers some money?"

Rourke ignored the tirade and sat down on the bunk. He was used to these outbursts. He'd spent most of the past seven years dealing with angry men.

"Let's put things in perspective," he told Clay. "I think you're guilty as hell—by association, if nothing else." His dark eyes pierced Clay's. "I've seen kids like you come and go. You're too lazy to work for what you want, and too impatient to wait. You want everything right now, so you opt for the easy money. It doesn't matter to you how many lives you destroy, how many innocent people suffer. It's *your* needs, *your* comfort, *your* pleasure that counts." He smiled without humor. "Congratulations. You hit the jackpot. But this is the price."

Clay leaned against the wall with an angry sigh. "Thanks

for the lecture. I already had one from Becky, and our minister came to put another nail in my coffin." He looked away. "They tell me my little brother won't even talk about me."

"That isn't true," Rourke said slowly. His jaw set as Clay glanced at him with poorly concealed hope. "Mack tried to convince me that the Harris boys threatened you into this last deal. I wouldn't listen."

"Why should you?" Clay asked, looking away. At least Mack didn't hate him completely, maybe, if he'd defended him to Rourke. He stared at the floor blankly. "It was just beer and a little crack at first," he said dully. "I didn't have much luck making friends at school. Everybody knew my dad had been in trouble with the law, and a lot of families wouldn't let their kids associate with me. The Harris boys seemed to like me. They started letting me hang around with them. First thing I knew, I was drinking and doing drugs. Things were so damned lousy at home," he said harshly. "Granddad had a heart attack and was sick all the time. Becky did nothing but work and fuss at me about schoolwork, and there was never any money—never anything but work and cutting corners to make ends meet."

He looked up at the ceiling. "God, I hate being poor! There was this girl I liked, and she wouldn't even look at me. I wanted nice things. I wanted people to stop looking down their noses at me because my dad was a criminal and my people had no money."

Rourke scowled. "Didn't you think about Becky?" he asked.

"Oh, I thought about her when I got arrested," he laughed bitterly. "I thought about how hard she'd worked for us, the sacrifices she'd made. She hadn't even had a real date until you came along, but we ruined that for her, too. We gave her hell, because I was sure you were just seeing her to get to me." He looked at the older man. "You were, too, weren't you?" he asked.

"In the beginning, maybe," Rourke agreed. "Afterward..." He lifted the cigar to his mouth. "Becky's not like most women. She's got a big heart. She's a natural-born fusser. She makes sure you wear a jacket when it's cold, and don't get your feet wet when it's raining. She makes you hot soup when you feel bad, and tucks you in at night." He averted his face. "She hates my guts. That ought to compensate you a little."

Clay didn't quite know what to say. He'd seen Rourke's eyes before the taller man could avert them, and he was shocked at the fierce emotion in them.

He moved away from the wall. "I didn't wire your car," he said hesitantly.

Rourke looked up, his piercing gaze missing nothing. "You had reason to."

"I like dogs," Clay muttered. "I hated you, but I wouldn't have blown up your dog."

Rourke's face broke into a reluctant smile. "My God."

"I know a lot about electronics," he added. "But plastic explosives are tricky, and I don't know a lot about them." He stared at Rourke, wanting to make him believe. "I didn't sell crack to the Dennis boy, either. Mack thinks I did," he said honestly. "I wasn't rational while I was on the stuff, and I tried to rook Mack into helping me find contacts at his school. That's the truth, but I didn't sell any myself." He shrugged helplessly. "I didn't want to do it, after the first time, when they set me up as a go-between on a buy. That was how they got me. They say undercover cops saw me passing the money. Then they wired your car and told me they were going to make it look like I did it. They said if I didn't get Mack to help them, they'd turn me in and...oh, what's the use?" He threw up his hands and went to the barred window. "Nobody's going to believe me." His fingers gripped the cold iron bars. "Nobody in the world is going to believe that I was forced into it, or that I'm just the fall guy. The Harrises bought enough witnesses to get me the electric chair. They're going to fry me, and you'll pay the electric bill, won't you?"

Rourke smoked his cigar quietly, thinking. "What did you do, exactly?"

"I was a go-between that first time, and then I handed out the stuff to the dealers."

"Did you ever sell it yourself?" he asked shortly, staring at Clay.

"No."

"Did you ever give away samples to get potential clients hooked?"

"No."

"But you used it?"

Clay grimaced. "Yes. Just a little. Mostly I drank beer and smoked joints. I only did a little crack, and I never got hooked. I didn't like how out of control I was getting, so I stopped."

"Did you ever have more than an ounce in your possession at any time?"

"Well, I did that night I was arrested. You remember. They'd crammed my pockets full of the stuff."

"Besides that night."

Clay shook his head. "I never had more than enough for one smoke, ever. I'm sorry I even tried it."

Kilpatrick smoked some more, blowing out a gray cloud, his dark brows knitted as he concentrated. "Were you in on the buys regularly?"

"Only that once, when the set me up. They made sure I knew next to nothing about what they were doing. I only knew one thing, and not even that for certain—they said they were going to hit you. But I thought it was just talk, you know. I didn't realize they meant to do it until Becky came home and told us about it. My God, I've never been so sick or so scared…and they told me that night that they'd made sure I'd be connected with it if I didn't do exactly what they said." He stared at Rourke. "That makes me an accessory to attempted murder, doesn't it?"

"No," Kilpatrick said slowly. He paced the small cell for a minute and then paused by the cell door. "But unless you get a damned good attorney, all the honesty on earth won't keep you out of Reidsville, even if they did decide not to charge you in the Dennis boy's death."

"I can't ask Becky to sacrifice any more," Clay began.

"Oh, to hell with that," he muttered. "I'll take care of it. But this is between you and me. I don't want Becky involved in this in any way, do you understand?" he added curtly. "She isn't to know anything about the details."

"What can you do, for God's sake? You're the prosecutor!" Clay burst out.

Rourke shook his head. "I disqualified myself and my office. The governor's appointed another district attorney for this case."

"Why?"

"If I lost the case, Davis would swear I threw it because of Becky," Rourke told him. "The same thing could apply if I let one of my staff handle it. That puts Becky right in the middle, and she's had enough nastiness from the press on my account."

Clay's hazel eyes narrowed as he studied the older man. "She got to you, didn't she?" he asked shrewdly.

Rourke's face closed up. "I respect her," he said. "She's got enough problems to cope with as it is. I don't see how she's managed this long."

"She's tough," Clay said. "She's had to be."

"She isn't invulnerable," Rourke reminded him. "If you manage by some miracle to get out of this, you might consider giving her a hand."

"I wish I'd done that before," Clay confessed. "I told myself I was doing what I was doing to help Becky, but I wasn't. It was to help me."

"At least you've learned something." Rourke called for the guard. "Someone will be in touch," he said before he left. "Don't tell Becky I was here, or that I've had any part in this. That's the condition."

"All right. But, why?"

"I've got my reasons. And for God's sake, don't talk to the press," he added curtly.

"That's one promise I can make," Clay said.

Rourke nodded and left the cell. After he was gone, Clay remembered that he hadn't even thanked him. Incredible, that Kilpatrick would try to help him. Could it be because of Becky? Perhaps the prosecutor was more emotionally involved than he wanted to be.

CHAPTER SIXTEEN

It had been a slow day for J. Davis. He was grateful to have time to catch up on his law journals. He was sipping coffee and munching on a doughnut with his feet propped up on his desk when his secretary announced that Rourke Kilpatrick was in the waiting room.

Davis got up and went to the door. This he had to see for himself. Why would his worst political enemy to seek him out—unless he had a gun.

He opened the door and stared at Rourke. Rourke glared at him.

"I want to talk to you," he told Davis.

Davis raised both eyebrows. He looked much more like a wrestler than a lawyer, both in size and demeanor. "Only talk?" he probed, cocking his head to look pointedly at Rourke's open jacket. "No knives, pistols, clubs?"

"I'm the district attorney," Rourke pointed out. "I'm not allowed to kill colleagues."

"Oh. Well, in that case, you can have a cup of coffee and a doughnut. Right, Miss Grimes?" he added, smiling at his secretary.

"I'll bring them right in, Mr. Davis," she said, smiling back.

Davis motioned Rourke into the plush visitor's chair and realigned himself behind his desk in his former position.

"If you didn't come here to attack me, what do you want?" he asked.

Rourke reached for a cigar just as Mrs. Grimes came in with a cup of coffee and a doughnut for him. He thanked her and put the cigar back in his jacket pocket. "You won't believe why I'm here," he said after a bite and a swallow.

"You're going to offer to concede," Davis said and grinned effusively.

Rourke shook his head. "Sorry. It's too soon in the race. I have my reputation to consider."

"Oh."

"Actually, I want you to defend Clay Cullen."

Coffee went everywhere and so did the rest of Davis's doughnut.

"I was afraid that might be your reaction," Rourke said.

"You were afraid...my God, Rourke, the boy's guilty as sin!" Davis exclaimed as he mopped coffee from his desk and his law journals with his white handkerchief. "Clarence Darrow couldn't save him now!"

"Probably not. But you might be able to," Rourke replied. "He says the Harris boys coerced him into a buy, and that the rest of the charges are all trumped up ones to make him the scapegoat for their crimes."

"Listen, Rourke, everybody knows that you've been seeing Cullen's sister," Davis began earnestly.

"And because of her I've gone soft on her brother. That's what you insinuated in print, you back-stabbing glory-seeker," Rourke said hotly. "But it's not true. I'm an officer of the court. I don't deal under the table and I don't turn my back on drug dealing and murder. In case you've forgotten, the attempted murder he's accused of is mine."

"I haven't forgotten, and I'm not a back-stabbing glory-seeker. I just want your job," Davis defended. "I am sorry about dragging Miss Cullen into it, however. I honestly didn't mean to do that."

"I didn't think so," Rourke replied, and smiled as he finished his doughnut. "You're not a bad sort, for a defense attorney."

"Thanks a hell of a lot," Davis muttered. "And here you sit eating my doughnuts and drinking my coffee."

"Takes guts," Rourke said.

Davis studied Rourke quietly. "There are times when I like you. I fight it in my saner moments, of course," he added wickedly.

"Of course." Rourke lit a cigar, ignoring Davis's glare. "I happen to know that you have a smokeless ashtray in your left desk drawer," he pointed out smugly.

"Judge Morris has been talking again, I see." Davis sighed. "He smokes those big black cigars. Here, you pirate. Now, why do you want me to represent Cullen?"

Rourke turned on the smokeless ashtray. "Because I think he's telling the truth about the Harris boys. I've been trying for years to put them away. You know as well as I do that most of the drug traffic in the local public schools can be traced to them. Other dealers try to cut in and get put away, because the Harrises have the local syndicate boss on their side. That's the one reason I've never been able to get them to trial. Cullen may be the key. I think he'll cooperate. If he turns state's evidence, it may be just the spur I need to ride the Harris family out of town."

"Nobody would mourn them," Davis agreed. "But it could be political suicide to take on a case like this."

"Only if you lose it. I don't think you will. And think of the news value," he added with a shrewd smile. "It's a case Perry Mason might think twice about, but here you are risking your neck because you think this poor, underprivileged boy whose father was in trouble with the law is innocent. It's a dream case!"

"Of course it is," Davis agreed. "That's why you've disqualified yourself so you won't have to get involved with it."

"I knew you'd accuse me of throwing it if I lost." Rourke shrugged. "That wouldn't have done Becky's reputation any good."

"Or yours," Davis added. He thought carefully. "It's a political hot potato, all right. But if I could get him off and tie the Harrises into trafficking at the same time, we could sweep the streets clean."

"You'd be hailed as a crusading candidate, saving the innocent while punishing the guilty." Rourke chuckled.

"Why are you offering this to me?" Davis asked then. "It can only hurt your chances of reelection if I pull it off."

"If you want the truth, I don't know that I want to run for a third term," Rourke told him seriously. "I haven't quite made up my mind."

Davis leaned back in his chair. "I'm going to have to think this through."

"Think fast," Rourke replied. "The hearing is Friday."

"Thanks a lot." Davis stared at him, frowning. "The Cullens aren't wealthy people. They've got a public defender."

Rourke nodded. "I'll be paying your salary on this one."

"Like hell you will," Davis said with a laugh. He shook his head firmly. "Every lawyer takes a pro bono case now and again. This is going to be mine. Having you for a boss would be the living end. I'd rather go bust."

"I love you, too," Rourke said.

"God, what a ghastly thought! Why don't you go back to work and let me do the same? I'm a busy man."

"So I noticed," Rourke murmured dryly.

"Reading law journals is hard work."

"Right. But now that you mention it, I could do a bit of that myself. Anyway, this was my last cigar." He put it out and stood up. He extended his hand and Davis shook it. "Thank you," he said with genuine feeling. "I didn't believe Cullen at first, but I do now. I'm glad he's got a chance."

"We'll see about that. I'll go and talk to him this afternoon."

"If you need any information, I'll give you whatever I have. Cullen can fill you in on the rest."

"That'll do for a start." He followed Rourke to the door. "I heard you and the Cullen girl have split. I hope it wasn't because of anything in the papers."

"It was because she thought I was using her," he replied. "And at first I was."

"She'll get over it when she finds out what you've done for her brother."

"She won't know," Rourke said easily. "Clay promised not to tell, and you can't, either. That's the condition."

"May I ask why?" Davis asked.

"Because if she comes back to me, I don't want it to be out of gratitude," Rourke said simply.

"That's very wise," Davis told him. "Love is hard enough when you don't have doubts. It takes a lot of work."

"You're speaking from experience, I gather?"

Davis grimaced. "Well, not really. I don't have a lot of luck keeping women in my life. Henry sort of keeps me single."

"Henry?"

"My python," Davis explained. "He's twelve feet long and weighs about ninety pounds." He shook his head as Rourke stared at him. "You just can't get women to understand that they're harmless. They don't eat people."

"A man who keeps a giant snake is not likely to get many dates," Rourke murmured.

"I've noticed that. Odd, isn't it?"

Rourke chuckled. "I guess he's good company, anyway."

"Great. Until I need something repaired." He whistled softly. "The TV repairman was working on my audio when Henry crawled into the living room to see what was going on. Did you ever see a grown man faint?"

"If word gets around, you'll go through life without electricity, a telephone, or any working appliances."

"That's why the repairman and I made a deal," Davis said in a loud whisper. "I won't tell if he won't tell."

Rourke was still laughing when he went out the door.

Becky was given time off work to go to court for Clay's hearing.

Mr. Malcolm had a case himself that morning and needed to confer with his client, so he gave her a lift. She sat in the courtroom with her emotions tied in knots while she tried to unravel the puzzle of what she was seeing.

For one thing, the public defender wasn't sitting with Clay—J. Lincoln Davis was. And from what he'd said about her and Clay in the newspapers, she couldn't imagine why. In the second place, Rourke wasn't at the prosecutor's table— there was an older man, whom Becky had never seen before.

The people behind her had noticed, too. "Where's the district attorney?" one of them asked. "Wasn't he supposed to be trying this case?"

"He disqualified himself," the man's companion whispered loudly. "This is an out-of-town district attorney. Would you look at who's defending the boy! Isn't that J. Davis?"

"It sure is," came the reply. "He replaced the public defender this morning."

"He doesn't come cheap. I wonder how the Cullen boy's going to pay him?"

"These dope dealers stick together," the man said with disgust, and Becky cringed at the contempt and the insinuation that Clay was guilty before he was even tried. "They've got all kinds of money."

"There's the judge," someone else whispered.

Becky clenched her hands in her lap as the judge came in and everyone rose. Clay had just been brought in. He didn't look around at all. Becky had wanted to go see him that morning, but she hadn't had the opportunity.

Part of her had been hungry for the sight of Rourke in the courtroom this morning, but he wasn't here. Why hadn't he told her that he was disqualifying himself? Or had it been a spur-of-the-moment decision? She was so confused that the proceedings were over by the time she got her thoughts organized. Clay was bound over for trials in superior court, as she'd expected, and he waived bail. He was escorted out of the courtroom and Becky got up, feeling old and worn as she walked down the long hall alone to find Mr. Malcolm.

Rourke's office was on the way. She couldn't help glancing in the open door as she went past. Rourke saw her, but he didn't even acknowledge her presence. He deliberately lowered his eyes to the paperwork in front of him.

Becky quickened her steps, inflamed. Ignore her, would he? Well, he could just sit and wait until she said one word to him. She wanted to know why he'd refused to try the case. She'd entertained a dim hope that it might have been because he finally believed Clay was innocent. But that couldn't be the reason. The real puzzle was why J. Davis had taken on Clay as a client, and how his salary was being paid. Those were questions she intended to have answers to by the end of the day, one way or another.

She waited until she got off work to go see Clay. He was brighter than he had been, and enthusiastic about his new attorney.

"How did you get him?" Becky asked eagerly.

"I don't know," Clay confessed. "It's more a matter of how he got me. He just showed up here this morning early and told me he was representing me."

"He's about the best there is, Mr. Malcolm says," Becky told him. "How are we going to pay him?"

"Don't start fretting about money," Clay said tersely. "He told me that he takes on a case once in a while if he believes in the client's innocence, and waives the fee. He doesn't think I did it, Becky," he said quietly, and had to look away. He wished he could tell her about Kilpatrick's part in all this—that he believed in his innocence, too—but he'd promised.

"I never thought you did, either," she reminded him. "Neither did Mack."

He sighed wearily. "I guess it's hell on Mack. All the kids in school will be on him, because of me."

"Only a few, and school's out next week," Becky reminded him. "Your English teacher phoned me," she added. "She said to encourage you to finish high school when you can, even if it means a correspondence course."

"Time enough for that later on," Clay said. "Right now I've got to beat this rap." He sat down beside her and took her hands in his. "Becky, they want me to think about turning state's evidence."

She sat very still. "In other words, turn in the Harris boys."

"That's about the size of it."

Becky's eyes flashed. "I can imagine whose idea that was, even if he did refuse to prosecute you!"

"Mr. Dais says there's a possibility of a reduced sentence on the possession and dealing charge if I do it."

"They'd kill you," she said. "Don't you know that? If you do it, they'll have you killed, just like they tried to kill Rourke!"

"They botched that, good and proper," Clay replied. "They did it on their own, too, which didn't make them too popular with the big boys in town. It brought a lot of heat down on everybody."

"All the same, it's such a risk."

"Listen, Becky, if I don't do it, I could go up for ten to fifteen years of hard time."

She blanched. She'd faced this before, but never so graphically, in a jail cell with bars all around. "Yes, I know."

"I told Mr. Davis I'd think about it," he said. "If I decide to do it, we'll have to make some kind of provisions for you and Mack and Granddad—to make sure they don't try to threaten any of you."

The possibility that the Harrises would go after her whole family was scary, but it was better than having Clay spend years in prison for something he wasn't guilty of. She lifted her chin. "Cullens survived the Civil War and Reconstruction," she said proudly. "I suppose we can survive the Harris boys."

"That sounds more like the old you," Clay said, smiling at her. "You've been puny lately."

"I've had a lot on my mind," Becky said. "But the worst is almost over now. I just want to have you back home again. We miss you."

"I miss you all, too," Clay said. "But if I get out of here, I'm not coming back home."

Becky almost gasped. "What?"

He got up and stood against the wall, looking much older than seventeen. "I've been a burden at home long enough. You've got all you can take with Mack and Granddad. I think you should consider letting Mack go to a foster home and putting Granddad in a nursing home or a retirement home."

"Clay!" Becky felt herself go white. "What are you saying?"

"You're twenty-four," he reminded her. "Your whole life has been us. Well, none of us realized how it was for you until it was almost too late, but there's still time. You need to start thinking about a family of your own, Becky. Maybe, in time, you and Kilpatrick…"

"I don't want anything to do with Mr. Kilpatrick," she said hotly. "Never again!"

Clay hesitated. She looked venomous. "He was doing his job," he said quietly. "I didn't like him. I thought he was my worst enemy and I fought having him around. But it's how you feel about him that matters, Becky. You can't spend your whole life being a slave to the three of us."

"But it's not like that," she protested. "Clay, I love all three of you!"

"Sure. We love you, too. But you need something we can't give you anymore." He smiled. "I'm crazy about Francine, you know. She's taught me a lot about coming to terms with life. I care about her enough to want to go straight, and she's going to help me. She's in big trouble with her uncle and her cousins over me, but she's already promised to testify for me."

"Well," Becky exclaimed. "That's nice of her."

"She loves me," he said with faint wonder. "I want to give her the world. But next time, I'll try to do it in a conventional way. I think I might turn my life around now, if I try."

"I'm glad you want to try," Becky said. "I'll help, too."

"You already have, just by believing in me." He folded his arms across his chest. "Becky, how's Granddad?"

"No change," she said. "None at all. He just lies there. He hasn't said a word."

He grimaced. "What a mess I made."

"Granddad's old and tired," she replied. "Mack and I are lonely without him, and you, but we're bearing up."

"No crop, though," he guessed shrewdly. "Nobody to help you plow and plant and hay. Nobody to look after the livestock, either. If you asked Kilpatrick, he'd find you somebody."

Her face closed up. "I'd starve before I'd ask him for anything."

"Why?" Clay asked. "Just because he was having me watched and I got caught?"

She refused to look at him. Of course that wasn't the reason. The real reason was that Rourke had betrayed and seduced her and then abandoned her once he had Clay in hand. He'd taken all she had to give and thrown her over. That was why. Added to that was the growing threat of pregnancy. And about that she wouldn't think, not yet.

She got up from the bunk and smoothed the skirt of her plaid shirtwaist dress. "I'm glad you've got a good attorney," she said. "I'll help in any way I can. Will you tell him that?"

"I will, but he knows that already." He hugged her impulsively, and then moved away with faint embarrassment. "Thanks for coming to see me. I'm sorry I landed you in this predicament. There's going to be more publicity, too, I'm afraid. Mr. Davis is running for office, you know, and he's sure to use this case to his advantage. It's probably the reason he agreed to take it."

"Yes," Becky agreed. She'd reasoned that out herself already. She searched his eyes quietly. "Take care. If you need anything, just have somebody call me, okay?"

"Okay. Get some rest, Sis," he added quietly. "You look… bad."

"I'm just tired," she said, and forced a smile to her lips. "I go to see Granddad every day, even though he doesn't notice me. I still have meals to get, and the house to see to."

"They ought to put Dad in here," Clay said suddenly, scowling. "It's where he belongs for leaving us all in your lap."

"That's something we won't worry about. It's years too late to matter. Anyway, I think I've done a pretty decent job on you guys," she said with a grin. "Even you turned out good, eventually."

He chuckled. "Not as good as I needed to," he sighed. "Think about what I said, Becky, will you? Life is passing you by."

That was what he thought. Life had caught up with her. "I'll think about it, but I won't adopt Mack out. I've invested too much time in him."

He shook his head. "No man is going to want to take on your burden, you know," he said seriously. "It's too much to ask."

Becky felt her heart rock. She'd thought about that, too—far too often since Rourke had started taking her out to lunch. He wouldn't have wanted the responsibility for her entire family. Probably that was one reason he hadn't come back, even after he'd seduced her. Sex was one thing, but committing himself to years of looking after in-laws wouldn't appeal to most men. She'd accepted years ago that she'd have her family to look after all her life. What a pity she hadn't refused Rourke's first offer of coffee and made the best of her lot in life. Her desire for freedom and love had taken a terrible toll.

She mumbled something appropriate and kissed Clay good-bye. When she left the courthouse, she made sure that it didn't involve going past Rourke's office again. One snub was all he was going to get.

CHAPTER SEVENTEEN

Rourke left the restaurant where he'd had lunch in no better humour than when he'd arrived there. After Becky had gone past his office and he'd seen how worn and thin and pale she looked, his conscience had hurt him so much that he'd given everybody hell for the rest of the morning. He was lonely without her, and hurt because she thought more of Clay than she did of him. He was jealous of her fervent defense of her brother and her loyalty to her family. He wanted that kind of unconditional love himself, but he knew he'd ruined things by backing her into an emotional corner with seduction. He knew how old-fashioned and conventional she was. If only he'd kept his glands in check that night, things might have worked out for them. But he'd wanted her so badly, needed her. He'd been without a woman for a long time, and Becky's response had simply been too much for him to cope with. That was no excuse, of course, and now he'd given her the additional burden of a possible pregnancy that she wouldn't want.

He'd allowed himself some impossible dreams about that condition. Rourke had been alone all his life, except for Uncle Sanderson. He'd thought about a family many times, but he'd never found a woman he wanted it with. Then Becky came along with her mischievous personality, ready smile, and generous heart, and he found himself thinking about shared things instead of solitary ones. Even that night they'd slept together, he'd thought of the possibility of pregnancy with delight instead of dread. He'd been so smitten that he'd deliberately put precautions out of his head.

That hadn't been fair to Becky. As ignorant as she was about men, she wouldn't have known what to do anyway. But he wasn't ignorant, and he hadn't given her a choice. She wasn't the type who could have an abortion without beating herself to death mentally for it, and to bear an illegitimate child would scar her just as much.

He wouldn't mind marrying her, he decided. No, he wouldn't mind at all. The question was going to be how to get her to agree in her present venomous state of mind.

It had only been about four weeks. They couldn't detect pregnancy, as far as he knew, until six weeks. He'd have to bide his time and work out a strategy. He wished he'd spoken to her when she'd gone past his office, but just the sight of her had lacerated his conscience. He'd put a wall between them that was going to be hard to tear down.

He was still thinking about it when he got back to his office, and not paying too much attention to what he was doing when he opened the office door.

Mrs. Delancy had heard him coming and called the other

members of his staff. They were all standing at attention in front of her desk, waving white handkerchiefs.

Rourke burst out laughing. He hadn't done much of that since he'd stopped seeing Becky. He shook his head. He hadn't realized he'd been that irritable.

"You idiots," he said, chuckling. "All right, I get the message. But you'd all better get back to work, because even with unconditional surrender, I don't take prisoners."

"Yes, sir," Mrs. Delancey said with a grin.

He waved the others away and sat down behind his desk. He had a lot of work to get through, and he'd spent a good deal of his day thinking all too much about the future. The present was more than enough to keep him busy during court weeks.

Becky came back from the doctor's office two weeks later with blank eyes.

Maggie, who'd suspected what was going on all along, drew her gently into the rest room and closed the door.

"What did he say?" she asked the younger woman.

Becky was very pale. She'd tried to convince herself that all her symptoms added up to was fatigue, but Dr. Miller had gently cut the ground from under her feet.

"They did tests, and the results won't be in until tomorrow," Becky said absently.

"But?" Maggie prompted.

She met the smaller woman's dark eyes levelly. "Can't you guess?"

Maggie smiled gently. "Do we cry or celebrate?"

"I don't know. I just don't know. I'm scared to death." Becky wrapped her arms around herself. "It's not the scandal that worries me; it's the thought of being responsible for a little human being. I was responsible for Mack when Mama died. But this one is different. This one is going to be part of me."

"It's part of someone else, too," Maggie said. "Even if you hate him, he has a right to know."

Becky's face colored angrily. "He knew there was a risk, but he hasn't called or written or said one word to me since that day he came to the office. He doesn't care. He never did. It was because of Clay that he took me out, just as I thought once."

"Don't underestimate Kilpatrick," Maggie said. "He's not stupid. I'd bet anything I have that he knows the exact date you'll know for sure about your condition, and that he'll either be on the phone or sitting on your doorstep by the end of the day."

Becky hated having her heart jump at that prediction. She didn't want Rourke to call or visit. She didn't, she assured herself. He was a traitor and she was well rid of him.

Then she thought about the baby and wondered which one of them he or she was going to favor. Would the baby's eyes be dark like his or hazel like hers? She forced herself not to think about it. She couldn't have this child, she told herself. And then she thought about the only alternative to having it, and got so sick that she had to sit down. A woman who couldn't even kill a bee that had stung her was an unlikely candidate for a drastic alternative. Besides, when she thought about holding the tiny thing in her arms, she burned with delighted pleasure. Having a baby of her very own, to love and nurture and raise, was...awesome.

Rourke was thinking the same thing as he sat on the front porch of the Cullen home, making himself at home in the porch swing. Six weeks to the day, and she'd know for sure by now. He'd phoned Dr. Miller's office to see if she had an appointment, and sure enough, she'd made one. He smoked his cigar, feeling a pleasant sense of anticipation. She hated him, but that was just a minor obstacle. He was stubborn. He'd wait her out.

Her car drove up to the porch, and he saw the flash of shock on her wan face when she saw him there. She got out of the car alone, and he wondered idly where Mack was.

Becky came toward him, wearing a loose blue sleeveless overdress with a soft, short-sleeved pink blouse, her hair in a ponytail. She looked trendy and very young, and radiant despite her gaunt face.

She stopped on the porch facing him, her hand curled around the faded paint of the banister. "Did you want something, Mr. Kilpatrick?" she asked coldly.

He let out a cloud of smoke and his dark eyes slid over her with soft pleasure. "Just the usual things," he said carelessly. "Fabulous wealth, regular meals, an island of my own, a Rolls-Royce or two." He shrugged. "But I'll settle for coffee and conversation."

"I don't have any coffee and I don't want to converse with you," she said belligerently. "You said some horrible things to me the last time we met, and when I walked past your office in the courthouse at Clay's hearing, you snubbed me."

"You looked like hell and I felt guilty," he said quietly. "I still do."

"Thank you, but there's no need. Clay's got a good attorncy, Granddad's in a nice nursing home where he's getting care and government assistance, and Mack and I are doing fine."

"Where is Mack?" he asked, glancing at her empty car.

"Spending the day with one of his friends at Lake Lanier. They have a boat."

He eased his tall frame out of the swing, the smoking cigar in his hand. It was a weekday, and he was still wearing a pale tan suit with a nice brown and tan speckled tie. His black hair had been neatly trimmed. He looked elegant and dangerous, and when he moved closer to Becky, he smelled of luxurious cologne. It brought back some wounding memories and she wouldn't look at him.

"Why are you really here?" she asked curtly.

He tilted her chin up and searched her hazel eyes. "You saw Dr. Miller today. I want to know what he said."

"You haven't been very interested up until now," she said with bitterness.

"There wasn't any use asking until now," he replied. His dark eyes slid down her body to her flat stomach and back up again to her eyes. She jerked back from him, and that in itself was almost answer enough.

She turned away and unlocked the door, powerless to prevent him from following her inside. She turned on the lights, because it was already almost dusk, and went straight into the kitchen to make coffee. But only because she wanted a cup of it, she assured herself mentally.

Rourke found himself an ashtray before he pulled up a chair and straddled it. Then he sat and watched Becky move around the room, his heart lighter than it had been for the weeks they'd been apart. It hit him all at once how very alone he'd been without her.

"You haven't answered me, Becky," he said after she'd filled the percolator and started it.

"He ran some tests," she said tersely. "I didn't get the results today."

"My God, you're stubborn," he sighed, shaking his head. "You and I both know that tests are just a formality by now. There are unavoidable symptoms. Shall I name them? Fatigue, nausea, swelling, being hardly able to stay awake at night…"

"How many times have you been pregnant?" she asked irritably.

He chuckled, his white teeth flashing against his dark complexion. "This is my first time," he murmured dryly. "But I bought a book about pregnancy and it gave the symptoms."

"If I am pregnant, it's mine," she informed him.

"If you're pregnant, it's ours," he corrected imperturbably. "I helped you make it."

She went scarlet. "There's a good chance that I'm not," she muttered, glancing away. "There are a lot of things that have those symptoms, including fatigue, overwork, and worry."

"Sure." He lifted the cigarette to his lips and smiled smugly. "When was your last period?"

"You…!" She grabbed up a cup and threw it at him, missing his head by inches. The pottery shattered against the clapboard wall, a sound that echoed violently in the high-ceilinged room.

"At least six weeks overdue, I gather by the evidence," he murmured, clicking his tongue at the shards on the floor. "What a mess!"

"I wish your head was lying beside it!" she raged at him.

"That's no way to talk to the father of your child," he told her. "When are we getting married?"

"I'm not marrying you!" she shot back, furious that he was taking such a profound subject so lightly. It didn't occur to her that he was feeling his way as he went, trying not to let her see how delighted and awed he really was.

"Yes, you are," he replied. "Illegitimacy is no easy thing. I know. I've carried it around all my life."

"I'll marry someone else!"

"Really? Who?" he asked. He looked genuinely interested.

She went to fill two cups with black coffee. She was so rattled that she almost upended both of them as she put them on the worn wood tabletop.

"Thank you. You make good coffee," he said.

She didn't answer. She sipped her own, trying not to look at him. After a minute she raised her eyes. "Marrying me would hurt your career," she said. "Not to mention that it would put us both in the limelight again. I've got my family to think about, besides. I have to take care of Mack and Granddad."

His eyes kindled with anger. "Your family could take care of itself if you'd let it. You won't let them be independent. You want them to lean on you. It's a hell of a lot easier than trying to let *yourself* depend on someone for a change, isn't it?"

"I've never had anybody I could lean on," she said shortly. Her face flushed with temper and her freckles stood out vibrantly against her nose. "And there isn't anyone on earth I trust enough to depend on myself, especially you! I trusted you once, and look what happened!"

His dark eyes narrowed on her flushed face. "Tell me you weren't willing," he invited. "Tell me I forced you."

"You could have taken precautions!" she raged.

She had him there. He couldn't deny that. "Accidents happen," he said curtly. "We made a mistake. Now we have to live with it."

That wasn't what she wanted to hear. She wanted him to say that he loved her, that he wanted a child with her, that he was happy bout it. Words like *accident* and *mistake* and *live with it* weren't quite what she had in mind.

"You don't have to live with it," she said proudly. "I can take care of a baby. I don't need you to make any sacrifices on my account."

His eyebrows lifted. "You might at least give me credit for being interested in my own child."

She averted her eyes. "I'm sorry. Yes, I can give you credit for making the most of a bad situation. I don't imagine you really want it any more than I do," she lied.

He went pale. His jaw tautened. "I want it, all right. If you don't, I'll take care of it myself. All you have to do is carry it to term."

She'd regretted the words the minute they were out. She regretted them even more when she saw his expression. "No, I didn't mean..."

He got up and towered over her. "I'm not totally insensitive," he said gruffly. "I know you've got all you can handle with your brothers and your grandfather. A baby is the last thing you need." He rammed his hands into his pockets, and his eyes were terrible as they met hers. He didn't want to say it, but she had rights, too, and he was putting his own beforc hers. He had to be fair, despite his own prejudices. He ground his teeth together and forced the words out. "I can't force you to have the child, of course," he added stiffly. "Your body is your own. So if you think an abortion is the only sensible way to go—if you really want one—I'll pay for it," he added between his teeth. Inside his pockets, his hands were clenched so hard the knuckles were white.

"Oh, my God!" she breathed in total disbelief. She drew a shaky breath and lowered her gaze to the tabletop. She'd never meant to give him that impression. He was trying to be fair, she realized that, but the way he looked when he said it cut her to the heart.

"You can let me know what you decide," he said, mistaking her attitude for relief as he turned toward the door. "I'll assume the financial responsibility, either way. As you said, I didn't take precautions, so it is my fault."

He was gone before she could utter another word, or correct the wrong impression he'd assumed from her poorly worded explanation. She put her face in her hands. It had gone wrong from the very beginning, but she did want the child. She wanted it terribly. If only she could make him understand what she was feeling. He'd looked at her with pure dislike. It would make it even harder for her to face him in the future. Meanwhile, she had another responsibility to add to her growing list. The next day the tests came back, and they were conclusive. She was pregnant.

Prenatal visits were expensive. So were the vitamins her new obstetrician prescribed. She had an HMO at work, but there were things it didn't cover, and pregnancy was one. She'd asked them to delete pregnancy coverage because she hadn't thought she'd ever need it. What an irony. The small monthly cost of the coverage would have more than paid for itself, but she'd burned her bridges. Now that Mack was out of school for the summer, she had to pay a neighbor to keep him while she was at work. The car needed a tune-up. And in between, there were these new medical bills.

In desperation, she took on a morning newspaper route. She had to be up before daylight to get her papers in the boxes, but it meant that she could still get to her job on time. Mack raised the roof when he found out, but he wasn't in any position to fight her.

Granddad was losing his grip on life, or so it seemed to Becky when she visited him. He was slipping away, a little more every day.

Clay, on the other hand, was spouting information to Mr. Davis to help with his defense. He was still nervous about turning state's evidence, though, and he hadn't entirely made up his mind to do it. Becky was uneasier than ever about having him do it, in her present condition. She didn't mind risking herself, but she couldn't risk the baby.

As the days passed, the baby became her reason for living. She loved the very idea of it, and she blossomed. If it hadn't been for her two jobs and the worry for Clay and Granddad, she might have breezed through the first trimester, but the strain took its toll on her strength. She began to lose weight, and she was sicker in the evenings than she'd ever been in the mornings.

Rourke showed up on Friday evening looking like the first cloud of a summer storm. He was disheveled and wearing jeans and a pullover white cotton knit sweatshirt with traces of grease all over it. His dark hair was down in his eyes, and he was sweaty and irritable and tense.

But when he saw Becky lying on the sofa with her face gaunt and thin, pinched with nausea, the irritation left.

He put his hands on his hips and glared down at her surprised face. "My God, you look like death. Can you eat an omelet?"

"No!" She groaned and buried her face in the cold wet cloth Mack had brought her.

"Then you're out of luck, because that's the only thing I can cook that's edible. Mack said you missed lunch, too."

She glanced at a sheepish Mack, who was watching a game show on TV. "Traitor," she accused.

"I couldn't think of anybody else who'd care if you died," Mack said simply.

Becky flushed and wouldn't look up. "What makes you think Mr. District Attorney would?" she muttered.

"Well, after all, Becky, it's his baby," Mack said simply.

She sat up, gasping with outraged shock. "*What* did you say?" she exclaimed breathlessly.

"Oh, there was this show about babies," Mack explained eagerly, getting up to join her and a fascinated Rourke. "It told all about how ladies act when they get pregnant. You went to the doctor and he sent you to an obstetrician, and Mr. Kilpatrick is the only guy you ever went out with." He shrugged. "Figuring it out was a piece of cake."

Becky put her embarrassed face in her hands. "What is the world coming to?"

"I don't know," Rourke said shortly, glowering down at her. "When a woman won't marry the father of her child, I'd say it's a pretty lousy world."

"Becky won't marry you?" Mack exclaimed.

"See?" he muttered at Becky. "You've shocked your innocent little brother. You scarlet woman."

She flushed. "Stop talking that way around him."

"The baby won't have a name." Mack sighed.

"Sure he will," Rourke assured him, putting an affectionate arm around the thin shoulders. "We'll wait until she goes into labor and sneak a minister into the delivery room." He grinned. "She'll marry me."

"Never!" she said fervently, and turned green. "Oh, no!"

Rourke slipped his arms under her, lifted her gently, and carried her down the hall to the bathroom. He astonished her by knowing exactly what to do. He took care of her until the wave of nausea had passed, then mopped her up and helped her douse the taste with mouthwash. He carried her back to her room and laid her gently down on the faded quilt.

"You need rest," he said. "Mack told me about the paper route." He shook his head. "I'm sorry, honey, but you're fired. I just told your boss you couldn't risk the baby."

"You didn't!" she exclaimed weakly.

"I did. I'll take care of the obstetrician and the pharmacy," he told her. "I've got a man coming over to see about the haying and looking after the livestock on a regular basis. The garden will have to wait until fall now, but I'll have the plot turned over and fertilized so it will be ready." He glanced around the house, ignoring Becky's wan protests. "The house needs some work, too. I might as well give that a shot."

"Rourke, will you listen to me…" she began.

He looked down at her, smiling gently. "I'm glad you remember my name."

"You can't," she wailed.

"Yes, I can." He bent and drew his lips slowly over her eyes, closing them. "I'll get Mack some supper. Try to sleep a little while. I'll check on you later."

"You can't take over," she tried again.

"No?" He chuckled gently. "Good night."

He turned off her light and went out, closing the door softly behind him.

"It's just because of the baby," she murmured out loud and closed her eyes. "You don't really care about me—you just want him. Well, you won't fool me into losing my wits a second time."

And having settled that, she went to sleep.

CHAPTER EIGHTEEN

Becky slept until morning. She woke up still in her lounging clothes, but under the sheet. Rourke no doubt, she thought bitterly. Well, at least he hadn't undressed her while she was helpless. And why should he, she asked herself then, when he'd already seen everything she had? It wouldn't be interesting for him anymore!

Mack was up watching Saturday cartoons when she stumbled to the kitchen to make toast and coffee for herself and fix cereal for him. She almost fell over Rourke, who was sitting in a chair with his long legs spread out in front of him.

"What are you doing here?" she gasped. "Didn't you go home last night?"

"Obviously," he said nonchalantly, indicating his gray slacks and blue pin-striped shirt. He was freshly shaven as well, and a delightfully masculine cologne emanated from him as she paused uncertainly by his chair. "You can eat and then we'll all go and see Granddad."

Her mouth fell open with horror. "You're going, too? You can't! He'll have a heart attack and die if he sees you with me!"

"We can bet on that later," he informed her.

He looked stubborn and determined, and she didn't feel like fighting. She gave in—only temporarily, she promised herself. She pushed back a tangle of golden-brown hair. "Well, I suppose I could eat a little cinnamon toast," she murmured. "I'll make it."

"I've already made it," he told her. "There's a plate of it on the stove. Mack and I left you a couple of slices. Coffee's in the percolator," he added, lifting a mug of steaming black coffee to prove it. "Of course, I'd be delighted to fix it for you, but I hesitate to offer," he said with a slow grin. "I don't want another cup thrown at my head."

She cleared her throat. "I can't afford to lose any more crockery," she said. She pulled her worn blue robe closer around her with tattered pride. "I'm sorry about that," she apologized stiffly. "My emotions are sort of ragged right now."

He nodded. "The book said that a woman's emotions get a little strained in pregnancy because of all the metabolic changes," he replied easily. "Eat something."

She started to speak, but he lifted an eyebrow and looked as if he might do something unpredictable, so she shrugged and went to put toast on a saucer and pour coffee into a cup.

He watched her sit down across from him, smiling faintly at her reluctant submission.

If she'd had the stomach, she'd have said something cutting in answer to that smug grin, but her insides were churning. She stared at the toast and wasn't sure that it would stay down.

She glanced up at him and back down again after she'd taken a nibble of toast and a sip of coffee and was waiting to make sure it stayed down before she took another nibble. He was the handsomest man she'd ever known. Looking at him made tiny shivers of pleasure run down her spine. He could belong to her, if she'd just agree to marry him. It was a tremendous temptation. But she couldn't be sure of his motives. He might just want the baby, or feel guilty about his treatment of her. Maybe both, because he'd said some hurtful things to her, although she had to admit that she'd said some hurtful things back.

He shifted in his chair. "Doing okay?" he asked, and she nodded.

"Good." He sipped more coffee and drew out the inevitable cigar, but he didn't light it. He laid it next to his saucer. "I'll wait until I'm outside," he said when he noticed her curious glance. "I don't want to make you any more nauseated than you already are."

"How kind," she murmured.

"Have you decided what you want to do about the baby?" he added, and didn't look at her.

His stillness was more eloquent than any expression would have been. She stared at his averted profile and could almost feel the pain emanating from him. He seemed so self-sufficient and well-adjusted to being alone that she'd never imagined him as a family man even in her fondest dreams. But just lately he was giving every appearance of being a man who wanted a child of his own.

She wrapped her cold fingers around the coffee cup. "I go out of my way not to step on ants," she began hesitantly. "Once I tried to patch up a garter snake that the hoe hit, even though I'm deathly afraid of snakes." She stared into her reflection in the coffee cup, aware of his intent scrutiny. "I couldn't live with an abortion. Some women can, I guess, especially if they don't want a child. I want this baby—very much."

He made a sound deep in this throat—such an odd one that she looked up. But he was out of his chair and moving toward the living room before she could see his face. He didn't come back. She ate a little more toast and drank a little more coffee. She didn't want to think about his reaction, so she left the rest of her small breakfast and went to get dressed.

Rourke was sitting in the front porch swing smoking a cigar when Mack went out to find him.

"Becky's getting dressed," he said. He didn't quite know what to say to Rourke. He looked different somehow—shaken, pale. Mack didn't understand why he looked that way at all. "Are you okay?" he asked warily.

Rourke took a puff on the cigar. "I'm all right. Sit down."

Mack plopped into the swing beside him and leaned back. "Why is Becky so mad at you?"

His broad shoulders rose and fell. "Wait until you're Clay's age and I'll explain it to you."

"Oh. It's because of the baby, right?"

"More than likely." He sighed wearily and ran a restless hand through his thick, dark hair. He glanced down at the boy with a smile more tender than he realized. "I remember being your age. I liked to go fishing with my best friend's family and read comic books sprawled across my bed. It was a good time. Uncomplicated."

"Yeah." Mack propped a sneakered foot up on the swing and leaned his chin on his knees. "Isn't it better to be big, though? At least nobody bosses you around and tells you what to do."

"Think so?" Rourke leaned back with a long sigh and took another draw on the cigar. "Mack, my boy, I've got thousands of bosses. Everybody from John Q. Public to the presiding judge on every case tells me what to do. If you get a job, you get a boss."

Mack thought about that. "Well, yes." He grinned up at the older man. "But you get to pick the job."

"I can't argue with that," Rourke replied.

"Will Becky get big, like in the movies?"

He nodded, smiling a kind of secret smile that puzzled Mack. "Big as a pumpkin."

"Will it be a boy or a girl?"

"We don't know yet," he said gently. "I'm not sure I want to know," he added with a gin. "I like surprises, don't you?"

"Nice ones," Mack agreed. "But Becky won't marry you, Mr. Kilpatrick."

"Oh, she will," he murmured absently, seeing in his mind pictures of himself carrying a gently restrained Becky into a church past shocked spectators at their wedding. "She'll do it for the baby's sake, even if she won't do it for mine," he added.

"That means you'll be family," the boy said.

Rourke took another draw from the cigar. "Irrevocably."

Mack studied his sneakered foot without really seeing it. "What about Clay, Mr. Kilpatrick?" he asked. "I turned him in."

Rourke put a careless arm around the boy's thin shoulders. "You and I are the only two people on earth who know that. And nobody will hear it from me. Okay?"

"But…"

Rourke turned his head. His dark eyes lanced into the boy's. "Okay?" he asked levelly.

"Okay. Thanks," Mack added uneasily.

"A man has to look out for his youngest brother-in-law, doesn't he?" Rourke asked with a grin. He wouldn't let himself think about how much that promise might hurt his relationship with Becky, when they finally sorted things out.

Inside the house, Becky put on a pair of jeans that were suddenly very tight and added a colorful puffy-sleeved loose striped top that overlapped the waistband. She brushed her hair, put on a minimum of makeup, and went to join Mack and Rourke on the front porch.

They looked very natural sitting in the swing together, Rourke smoking his eternal cigar and gently moving the swing with one long leg while he and the boy talked as if they were old friends.

"Ready?" Rourke asked, getting to his feet with Mack right beside him. "I'll drive."

"Good idea," Mack nodded. "Becky's car goes sometimes and doesn't go sometimes—you can never be sure."

"It's a good car," Becky protested.

"It's not a new car," Mack said, making enthusiastic noises as he got into the back seat of Rourke's car. "Wow! Radical!"

he exclaimed, examining everything from the ashtrays to the pull-down armrest.

"Don't you get bored in the waiting room?" Rourke asked with a frown as he glanced back at Mack, remembering that the boy was probably too young to visit in Granddad's room.

"Oh, he can go in, too," Becky said, quickly understanding his train of thought. "Granddad's in the HealthRex nursing home now; they moved him. I told you, remember?"

"I've had a lot on my mind," he murmured. "I'd forgotten. Is he any better?" he asked.

She glanced at Mack, who was looking out the window, then back at Rourke and quickly shook her head.

He grimaced. "He's giving up."

"That's right. I've tried talking to him, but he just closes his eyes and shuts me out." She lifted the hem of her blouse and examined the stitches in it. It was one she'd made herself last year, and not a bad job if she did say so.

"He needs something to liven him up," he mused.

"No. He needs rest."

"Rest isn't going to get him out of there." He didn't say anything else, leaving an excited Mack to talk nonstop to Becky while she puzzled over what Rourke had said.

"You won't get him stirred up, will you?" she asked warily when they were walking down the long, spotless hall to the room the old man shared with another patient.

"Of course not," he said innocently.

She didn't believe him for a minute. The three of them went in. The other bed was bare, but there were the remains of a breakfast tray on it, so presumably somebody was berthed there. Becky took one of the chairs and Rourke took the other while Mack went to the old man's bedside and held his hand.

"Hi, Granddad," he said. "How are you today? We sure do miss you at home."

The old man's eyelids flickered. He didn't open them.

"It's lonely, all right," Becky added. "Are you feeling any better?"

Still there was no response.

Rourke glanced at the two of them and then got up and moved to the bedside.

"You missed a good breakfast at the house," he said calculatingly, putting a finger to his lips when Becky started to speak. "Not to mention the great coffee I made."

The old pale blue eyes levered open and he glared up at Rourke. "What were you…doing in my house?"

"Trying to take care of Becky and Mack," he said simply.

Mr. Cullen struggled to sit up. "Oh, no, you don't, you cold-eyed scalawag!" He fought out from under the sheet. "You aren't hanging around my granddaughter without a chaperone. You've done enough damage to my family."

"It sounds as if he knows already, doesn't it?" Rourke asked a horrified Becky with maddening carelessness while he stared at the older man.

Granddad stopped in the act of getting up. "What do I know already?" he asked.

"About the baby Becky's carrying," Rourke said, shocking Becky speechless.

Granddad went red. He scowled furiously at Rourke. "You blackguard! If I only had my cane, I'd thrash you!"

"You'll have to start eating and get your strength back

first," the younger man said with apparent indifference. "And come home, too, of course."

"I'll come home all right," he muttered. He glanced at a red-faced Becky. "How could you?!" he demanded. "Your grandma would roll over in her grave!"

She lowered her face, feeling faintly ashamed and embarrassed. Now everybody would know what she and Rourke had done. She was walking proof.

"Don't do that," Rourke said curtly, scowling at her. "A baby is nothing to be ashamed of. And you can stop, too," he told Granddad, focusing his dark eyes on the old man before he could speak. "Becky and I both want this child. It got made too soon, but neither of us wants to get rid of it."

"I should hope not!" Granddad shifted and grimaced, his pale blue eyes wary. "She won't marry you, will she?" he asked and managed a grin. "You played her for a fool over Clay. She knows it."

"I started taking her out partly because I wanted to keep tabs on Clay," he said quietly, hating the admission even as he made it.

"Thought so."

Becky wouldn't look at him. She'd known that already, but it was painful to have it confirmed.

Rourke saw the wounded look on her pale, freckled face and was sorry he'd ever thought that way about her. His feelings for her had changed dramatically over the weeks they'd been dating, and now he regretted the way they'd started off. But it was much better to tell the truth, in the long run. She'd be more likely to believe him when he told her the real reason he wanted to marry her. But she wouldn't believe anything he told her in her present angry state of mind, so it was going to take time. He had to win her trust all over again, make her see how he felt, before he made any confessions. And they had big priorities right now——Granddad and Clay.

Granddad, though, was rapidly becoming less of a problem——or more of one, depending on your point of view.

"I want out of here," Granddad raged, and struggled to get his feet over the side of the bed, panting with the effort. He'd half starved himself trying to die, so he was weak. "I'll be damned…if you're going to get away with this."

"With what?" Rourke asked politely as he gently restrained the old man and tried not to grin at the show of spirit.

"Compromising my granddaughter!" he said loudly.

"I didn't compromise her, I…"

"Don't you dare say it!" Becky gasped when she saw the look in Rourke's mischievous dark eyes.

He shrugged. "All right. I was only going to tell him that you forced yourself on me."

"I did not!"

"You've ruined my reputation," Rourke said with a dogged expression, looking comically wounded, so that Mack stifled a giggle. "Stood me up to public ridicule. Everyone will think that I'm easy. Women will write my telephone number in public rest rooms. I'll be attacked at work. And it's all your fault. You knew how weak-willed I was!"

Granddad didn't exactly know how to take that. In his day, if a woman displayed her ankle, it was considered indecent. Here were Rourke and Becky talking about a child they'd made together, and they weren't even married. The only consolation he could find was that they both wanted the child. And there was something about the way Rourke looked at Becky, when she wasn't watching.

He lay back down slowly, still smarting from the idea of Rourke moving in and taking over his household. But he felt more alive than he had since he'd gone to the hospital that horrible night Clay was arrested.

"Are you all right?" Becky asked gently.

He nodded and took a long breath. "My heart's fine. They said I'd recover nicely. I'm sorry about the expense, Becky," he added, a little ashamed now that he'd cost her this long confinement for nothing. He'd hoped he might die, but God seemed to have something else in store for him.

"Don't worry about the money," Becky said gently. "Everything's all right."

"That being the case, suppose we bail you out of this place Monday and take you home?" Rourke said, changing the subject. He didn't want Granddad asking any more questions about paying the bill. Becky might start wondering about that nonexistent government assistance and find out that he was helping on the expenses. He didn't want her told about that, or what he'd done for Clay, just yet.

"I want to go home, but you can't hang around," Granddad said firmly.

"Sorry, but I'll have to," Rourke said conversationally. "The house is falling apart. I've got painting to do, doors to fix, screens to put in...I can't have my future wife living in a run-down house."

"I am not your future wife!" Becky raged.

"It's my house!" Granddad fumed.

"How *do* you stand it?" Rourke asked Mack with a theatrical sigh. "My God, you poor kid."

Mack chuckled. He liked Rourke a lot, and he didn't think Becky had a chance of getting away unmarried.

The arguing went on, but Rourke ignored them until they fell to talking about Clay and his trial. Mack went down the hall to the drink and snack machines in the waiting room with a pocketful of change Rourke gave him.

"Who is the Davis man that's going to defend him?" Granddad wanted to know.

"A black attorney..." Becky began.

"Black?!" Granddad burst out.

"Black," Rourke said in a tone that dared the old man to continue. "It isn't a dirty word. J. Davis is one of the finest defense attorneys in the country. He makes in the neighborhood of half a million dollars a year, and he's the best there is. He's waiving his fee to defend Clay, so you might consider putting aside your prejudices for the duration of the trial."

Granddad's pale blue eyes narrowed. "We can agree to disagree on the matter of prejudice. I don't imagine either of us is going to give an inch on our points of view. If you say this Davis man is a good lawyer, that's all that counts. I don't want Clay to go to jail."

"He'll do time," Rourke replied quietly. "I hope you understand that. He broke the law. There's no way he's going to avoid some penalty for being involved in drug trafficking, and it won't matter who defends him. The most damaging charge is the attempted murder rap, and there's substantial evidence to connect him with it."

"I don't care about the evidence," Becky said stiffly. "I know Clay, and he wouldn't do something like that."

Rourke didn't think so, either, because of what Clay had told him. But he wasn't going to share that information just yet.

"The drug dealing might be plea-bargained down to a lesser charge, however," he continued as if Becky hadn't spoken. "Considering it's his first offense, he might not have to do hard time. I got a conviction on a cocaine dealing charge a few years ago. The perpetrator was sentenced to ten years, and he only did ten months. Anything is possible."

"No chance of you refusing to press charges on the murder rap, for Becky's sake?" Granddad asked solemnly.

"I don't have the option," Rourke replied. "And you know it."

"I see." Granddad tugged absently at the sheet, frowning. "I see."

"If he turns state's evidence against his cohorts, it will go easier on him," he added. "And if we can connect them with the Dennis boy's death, they'll do some hard time."

"What about Becky, if he does that?" Granddad asked worriedly. "People mean enough to wire a man's car with a bomb might not stop at hurting a woman."

"I realize that," Rourke said. His dark eyes didn't blink. "They'll have to go through me to get to Becky. They won't hurt her. I guarantee they won't."

Becky glowed. He sounded very fierce and protective, and she lowered her eyes shyly when he glanced her way.

Granddad had noticed that attitude, too. He pursed his lips and smiled, but he didn't let Rourke see him.

"Has Clay decided to do that?" Granddad asked.

"Not yet," Becky said.

"Been to see him lately?"

She hadn't wanted to have to answer that question, but she had no choice now. They were all looking at her.

"They've moved a man into the cell with Clay," she said slowly. "He's in for attempted rape. He...well, he didn't actually say anything, but he looked at me in a way that made my skin crawl. I didn't go back. I know Clay understood why. He didn't like it, either."

"Why didn't you tell me?" Rourke demanded. His blood ran hot through his veins, thinking about Becky in that kind of situation. That was one problem he could solve, and quickly, with one telephone call.

"How could I tell you?" Becky demanded hotly. "We haven't spoken in weeks!"

"We've been speaking for two days," he reminded her, just as hotly.

"You didn't ask," she said haughtily.

He glared at her. "Well, it won't happen again. I'll have him moved out of Clay's cell and we'll both go to see him."

"Clay won't like that."

"Why?"

"He doesn't like you," she said, frowning. "Surely you knew that? You turned him in, for heaven's sake!"

Mack went pale and started to speak, but Rourke silenced him with a scowl.

"Maybe you're right," he said. "You can go to see him alone." He knew Clay was doing what he was told, not letting Becky know that he had already been to see him and had gotten Davis to represent him. He was keeping secrets, but he wanted her in the dark until he was sure of her feelings. Gratitude was a poor substitute for love. The bad part was that she still blamed him for Clay's arrest. That was a cross he'd have to bear forever, because he couldn't tell her that Mack had turned his brother in. He wasn't going to let Mack suffer for it.

"I didn't know about his cell mate," Rourke continued. "They must really be hurting for space. There have been a spate of drug arrests lately. Jails all over midtown and the metro areas are bulging. They're even turning some petty criminals loose so they can keep the hard-core ones inside, in one county. We may have to do that in the not-too-distant future. The crowding is dangerous."

"Why are there so many people in jail? Is crime increasing?"

"No. In fact, some crimes have actually decreased, including murder and rape. But we have overcrowded courts. Plenty of those people in jail are there waiting to be tried, like Clay. Sometimes their cases are called and one key witness can't be found, or he's forgotten the date, or he's sick. The perpetrator goes back to jail then and the case has to be calendared again. You'd be amazed how many cases have to be continued or held over because the defense attorney or the public defender has something come up and can't appear." He shrugged. "It's a problem everywhere. Nobody's got a solution, except to build more prisons."

"And that costs money," Granddad interrupted, letting them know that he'd been listening. "Which hits the taxpayer right in the pocketbook."

"True," Rourke agreed. "But if you want a place to put the criminals, you have to pay to keep them in it. You pay for their upkeep. So do I. The alternative is to turn them all loose and hire somebody to protect your life and property. Not a very attractive prospect, is it?"

Granddad shook his head. "Ought to have public executions," he said. "Somebody goes out and butchers half a dozen people and everybody says pity the poor criminal. How about the poor victim?"

"Well," Rourke said, "the criminal justice system in this country isn't perfect, but it's the best in the world. While we're blaming liberals, we can blame some special interest groups, too, who lobby to take the teeth out of laws like the Rico Statute, which allows us to confiscate illegal drug money and other ill-gotten gains."

"Amen," Granddad said heartily. "These days it seems like dirty politics is the rule, instead of the exception. Every day you hear of some other politician who's done something unethical. Nobody cares about honor these days!"

"People do," Rourke argued. "But they're apathetic about it. Otherwise, why do only about a third of the people go to the polls to vote?"

"Beats me," Granddad said. "I always voted. Becky does, too."

"So do I," Rourke said. "But until the silent majority starts getting really involved, nothing will change very much."

Becky was beaming. Granddad was almost his old self again. Rourke had tricked him into fighting back to life.

The nurse came in to check Granddad's vital signs and gasped audibly when she saw him sitting up in bed with color in his cheeks. She didn't ask any questions, but she was smiling when she left the room.

Rourke herded Mack and Becky out of the room a few minutes later, with a promise to Granddad that he'd be back with Becky to bring him home Monday morning.

"How are we going to manage that?" Becky wanted to know. "I have to go to work."

"So do I," he said carelessly, digging in his pocket for his keys as they reached the car. "I'll get off for an hour. So will you."

"But there won't be anybody at the house to look after him," she groaned.

"Sure there will." Mack grinned. "I can give him his medicine and talk to him. Then I won't have to stay with Mrs. Addington. She's real nice, but Granddad's my buddy."

She hesitated. "I don't know..."

"Mack's almost eleven," Rourke reminded her when they were in the car driving back toward the farm. "He's smart and he can keep his head. He has your telephone number at work. I'll give him mine, too. He'll do fine, so stop worrying. Okay?"

She gave in. It was just too much work, and she was feeling incredibly tired. She leaned her head back against the seat and closed her eyes. "Okay," she murmured drowsily.

She was asleep when they got home. Rourke put a finger to his lips, gave Mack the key to unlock the door after he'd fished it out of her purse, and gently lifted her out of the car.

She woke up just as he was taking off her shoes in her own room.

"I went to sleep," she murmured drowsily.

"You've had a long day," he said gently. "And you tire easily. Now you just rest, little one."

"What about Mack?"

"He's gone over to visit his friend John. I said it was all right. Was it?" he added.

"Yes. John's mother said it was all right any time."

"You're just worn out from overwork. A paper route," he muttered, glaring at her from his superior height.

"Well, it was all I could get that would fit in with my regular job," she said defensively.

His dark eyes went from her wan, freckled face to her slender body and back up again, seeing the gauntness in her cheeks, the dark circles under her eyes. "I shouldn't have stayed away so long," he said, his deep voice pleasant in the stillness of the room. "But relationships are difficult for me, even on good days. I've spent most of my adult life alone. It made me angry that you were more concerned about Clay than you were about me, especially when it was me he was accused of trying to murder." He stuck his hands in his pockets. "Maybe putting your family first is natural. I don't have any family, so I don't really know. But I shouldn't have allowed that resentment to make me desert you at a time when you needed someone."

"I didn't help by saying I was sorry the bomb didn't work," she said softly, searching his hard face. "I didn't mean it. It hurt me that you spied on Clay to have him arrested. I guess that was the most damaging thing of all."

His teeth ground together. It was the biggest stumbling block to their future together, and he couldn't do a thing about it—not without incriminating Mack. He looked away.

"I'm not perfect, honey," he said tersely. "I never claimed to be."

She nodded. She lay back against the pillows with a tired sigh. "Thank you for what you did for Granddad," she said softly. "But we can manage, now."

"I'm glad to hear it. But you're not managing without me," he said stubbornly. He moved closer to the bed and stared down at her. "You don't want me around. I understand that. But you need someone, and unless you can pull a man out of your pillowcase, you're stuck with me. You can't carry all this alone."

"I've been doing it alone for years," she protested hotly.

"You haven't been pregnant for years," he shot back.

"Rourke!" she began angrily.

He sat down on the bed and leaned over her, his dark eyes cutting into her hostile hazel ones. "I've never met anyone half as stubborn as you are," he said under his breath. His eyes fell to her soft mouth. "Or as sweet. I'm lonely, Becky—so lonely."

He knew how to turn the knife, she thought miserably as she felt his smoky breath mingle with hers. He brushed back the long strands of disheveled honey-brown hair from her face and bent to kiss her eyelids. Her heartbeat began to speed up and her breathing changed suddenly as his lips moved from her eyes to her cheeks and then, inevitably, down to her parted lips.

"Do you remember how it felt that night?" he breathed into her open mouth, hearing the whimper that came out of her throat as he whispered the explicit, arousing words. "Yes, you do, don't you? You remember how we clung to each other on the floor, burning so hot that we didn't mind the discomfort, blind and deaf to everything except the sweet, sharp pleasure of our bodies joining in that anguished rhythm."

His hands slid down her throat and found her breasts, swollen under her top. She stiffened as his fingers circled them, burning up with the fever he was kindling.

"You bit me," he whispered, lifting his head so that he could search her misty eyes. "And at the last, I remember being glad my windows were closed, so the neighbors wouldn't hear you when you began to cry out under me."

"Stop," she whispered huskily. "You mustn't!"

"Hush," he ground out against her lips. His hands went under the top to unfasten her bra. He moved it away and then she felt his cool fingers against her hot skin, soothing the ache he'd created.

"Oh, please," she said in a hoarse whisper. Her hands helped him, gathering the top under her chin as she arched, to let him look at her, to invite his mouth. "Please, Rourke, this isn't fair!"

He cupped her gently, nuzzling the taut mauve peak with his nose and then his lips before he took it into his hot mouth with a slow, sweet suction that made her body clench with delight. She stopped protesting and her eyes closed.

His free hand slid to her jeans and found the top button unfastened. He smiled against her breast as he moved the zipper down so that his lean fingers could lie flat and possessive over the soft swell of his child.

"Can you feel the baby yet?" he whispered, lifting his mouth so that it was poised over hers.

"Not really," she said unsteadily. "It's too soon for him to move."

"He's tiny," he said, searching her eyes. "I saw a picture in one of the books. At two months, he'd fit into my hand, but he'd be perfectly formed."

Her blood surged at the look on his face, at the soft, deep words. "You've had women," she said slowly.

"A few," he said quietly. "Never like you, that night. I was barely able to get my clothes off in time. That's why you're pregnant. I lost control completely."

"I did, too," she said. "It felt so sweet when you started to touch me. Nobody ever had, like that. My skin was so hot it burned, and I wanted yours against it."

His mouth crushed down onto hers while his hand worked to get his shirt pulled up. He lifted her in a gentle arch so that her breasts met and flattened against his cool, hair-roughened skin. She shivered. Her body wanted him instantly. It was that simple, that profound.

"What if Mack comes in?" she gasped when he lifted his head again.

He saw the desire in her eyes, the need. His own was fierce. "I'll lock the door, in case he comes back." He did, and came back to her, stripping off his shirt on the way. Everything else followed it, until he was nude and blatantly aroused.

She didn't have the will to protest. Her body was already taut with desire. It knew his intimately and wanted it, demanded it. It had been such a long time. He was the father of her child, and she loved him. She lay very still under his hands while he undressed her. But when his mouth pressed down hungrily on her stomach, she cried out.

His body slid onto the cool coverlet beside her, dark

against her paleness. His eyes glittered even as he smiled at her undisguised eagerness.

"God, I've gone crazy remembering," he breathed. He looked down at her breasts, touched them reverently while she watched his hand, breathing unsteadily at the erotic sight.

He bent and kissed her breasts slowly, enjoying their softness. His body eased down, so that he was hard against her hips, and his powerful legs eased between hers in a lazy rhythm that belied the faint tremor in his body.

She felt him touch her intimately, probe and draw back, both hands beside her head on the coverlet while his body fenced gently with hers and he laughed deep in his throat at the way she reacted.

He teased her with his body while his mouth toyed and tormented hers in the hot silence of the room. And all the while she watched him with her heart shaking her breasts, her body shivering with the need he was escalating to urgency.

"Do you want me?" he whispered wickedly, advancing and withdrawing his hips, watching her body arch in a desperate seeking motion.

"Yes," she moaned, gasping. "Please, Rourke, please!"

"Not yet," he breathed, brushing his mouth over hers. "You don't want it enough."

"Yes...I do!"

He bit her lower lip and his movements became more sensual, more provocative. The faint rhythmic probing caused her to shudder and pull at his arms.

"No, you don't," he whispered. He kissed her roughly and abruptly rolled over on his back. His arousal was so blatant that she couldn't drag her eyes away from it. "If you want me, you'll have to take me," he taunted softly, his eyes so sensual and dark that they made her tingle all over.

She didn't know how to, but her body was on fire. She needed him desperately. With more enthusiasm than skill, she straddled his hips and, blushing, tried to join her body to his. He smiled with pure arrogance at her efforts and finally took pity on her. "Like this, little one," he whispered, lifting and guiding her.

She gasped out loud when his invasion met with no resistance, and he smiled hotly.

"Now," he breathed, grimacing as the pleasure shot through him. "Move on me, like this."

He taught her, welded her to him with steely fingers on her thighs, watched her with fierce possession. He'd never liked this position with other women, but it was madly exciting with Becky. He liked the shy fascination in her eyes, the way she blushed when he lifted her and made her watch. Most of all, he liked the exciting little noises that jerked out of her when the pleasure began to take her.

"You aren't quite strong enough for this," he whispered when her muscles gave out. He turned her so that she lay beside him, one lean hand gathering her hips so that he could control them.

"Now, look at me," he whispered.

She opened her misty eyes and looked into his as he moved against her, inside her, with a slow, steady rhythm that was audible when their damp bodies touched. "Feel me."

"Oh!" she cried out, shuddering, at the first sharp twinge of pleasure.

His lean hand slid down, pulling her hips roughly to his. "Harder," he whispered huskily. "I want you so close that we'll have to be pulled apart. That's it! Yes!" He ground his teeth together and his other hand joined the first, his fingers biting into her soft thighs as he moved rhythmically, faster and faster, his eyes still blazing into hers, his breath jerking out.

She heard the springs under them, his tormented heartbeat, his breathing, but her attention was focused on the hot tension building in her lower spine and beginning to radiate outward at a fantastic rate. She clung to his muscular arms, moving with him as the pleasure built, weeping a little at the intensity.

"Look at me," he said roughly. "I want to see your eyes when you feel it."

She tried, but the spasms came suddenly and sharply, and after one shocked gasp, her eyes closed while she spun around in a hot maze of anguished fulfillment.

"Becky." He groaned harshly. His breath caught and then he cried out, his hands contracting on her thighs as he shuddered fiercely against her in ecstasy.

It seemed a long time before he released his painful grip on her, but he didn't let go. His arms enveloped her gently and he cradled her, his body still intimately locked with hers while they struggled to breathe.

"We...shouldn't have," she whispered miserably, a little ashamed of her weakness.

"We made a baby together," he said softly. His mouth brushed her cheek, her neck. "You belong to me."

"Rourke..."

He rolled her over on her back, his powerful body between her legs, his arms catching his weight. He held her eyes and began to move, very slowly. Her arousal was instant and ardent, and she gave in without a protest.

This time was slower and sweeter, and the explosions were as tender as the kisses they exchanged. His mouth held hers captive as the shudders rippled through their locked bodies simultaneously in fulfillment.

"So tender," he whispered against her lips. "You and I never do this the same way twice. Each time is new and beautiful and utterly satisfying."

She hid her face in his damp throat, clinging to him. Her body sagged with weary pleasure. "You seduced me."

"Seduction is selfish. This wasn't. My intentions are purely honorable. I've done everything I can think of to get you to marry me and give my child a name, but you won't. I want you. And you wanted me."

She couldn't deny that, but it didn't make her feel any better about her easy capitulation.

She pushed experimentally at his shoulders and he lifted his head.

"It's all right," he whispered. "You can't get pregnant when you already are."

She hit his chest. "You beast!"

"I'm not a beast. I'm a normal man with normal appetites, and I can't live like a eunuch. My God, do you have any idea how beautiful you look when your body achieves satisfaction?" he asked softly, holding her shocked eyes. "Your skin glows. Your eyes go black except for a tiny band of pale green. Your lips swell and part, and you look like a siren. I lose it when I watch you," he breathed huskily. "Looking at you pushes me over the edge."

She averted her face, her cheeks red.

"You won't watch me, will you?" he murmured dryly. "Does it embarrass you, to look at me when I'm totally at the mercy of my body?"

"Yes," she confessed.

"You'll get used to me. This is a deeply personal thing, Becky. There are no rules, no requirements, except pleasure. The sharing is the most important part of it."

"It's just...sex," she moaned.

He tilted her face back to his. "Don't ever say that again. Sex is a commodity. You and I don't have sex, we make love. Don't cheapen it with cold labels just because you find it embarrassing to go to bed with me."

"I don't like casual interludes!"

"It isn't an interlude, or casual. You're carrying my child. And sooner or later, you're going to marry me," he added.

"No, I'm not!" she raged. "You don't love me! You just want me."

He stared down at her angrily. She was blind as a bat and naive as a child. Why couldn't she see it?

"Think what you like," he said curtly. He lifted himself, amused at the expression on her face when he separated them, at the way she averted her eyes.

He got up and dressed while she pulled her own clothes back on and tried not to look at him.

He pulled her up from the bed and framed her face in his hands, his body lean and strong and warm against hers while he looked at her solemnly.

"You belong to me in every way there is," he said quietly. "I'm not going away, and I'm not giving up. You might as well get used to having me around. Mack and Granddad need me, and so do you."

"They don't like you," she muttered.

"Mack does. Your grandfather will come around." His hands slid to her hips. "Becky, you've got my baby in your body," he whispered, shocking her. "If you could just manage to trust me, a little bit, we could have a good life together."

She lowered her face to his chest. "I trusted you once," she said miserably. "You betrayed all of us."

He couldn't answer that. He straightened. "I did my job," he replied. "My job has nothing to do with you and me and the baby."

She bit her lip. "All right. I'll think about what you said. But I don't want this to happen again, please," she whispered, her eyes glancing toward the bed.

He tilted her chin up and searched her mutinous eyes. "I can't promise you that. I want you too badly. What we did in that bed is as natural as breathing," he said. "Desire isn't the black plague. You and I are going to be intimate for a long, long time, and we have a child to raise. I'm offering you a commitment, for life. If you don't like making love out of wedlock, marry me, then."

"My family…" she began miserably.

"You have to decide whether I come first or they do," he said firmly. "Let me know when you work it out. Meanwhile, I'd better get home. Will you be all right alone?"

She nodded. "Mack won't be gone very long."

He looked down at her quietly. "You think I'm being cruel, forcing you to choose, but there's a reason. You'll understand one day."

She didn't reply. He let his eyes run down to her stomach and then he turned away and left the room.

She didn't see him out. She had a lot to think about. He was going to make her choose between her family and him, and she didn't know how in the world she was going to do it—especially after today.

She spent Sunday going to church, visiting Granddad, and worrying. By the next morning, she was a nervous wreck.

CHAPTER NINETEEN

Rourke dragged out of bed early Monday morning, and when he thought about all he had to do, he almost climbed right back in again. His consolation was that Granddad was almost surely going to get better now, which would take one more burden off Becky's shoulders. It felt rather nice to have someone to look after, he thought absently. Uncle Sanderson had been self-sufficient and independent right up until the sudden heart attack that had killed him instantly. Rourke had never been responsible for anyone except himself. Now he had Becky and the child to think about. Because of them, he had Clay and Granddad and Mack, as well. He smiled as he remembered Mack's antics in the car, Granddad's sudden display of temper, and Clay's belated friendliness. It didn't feel bad at all to have a family, even if he was its unexpected acting head and half of it hated him.

Then he thought about what he and Becky had done in her bed Saturday, and his body went hot all over. It was magic with her. He wanted her completely, achingly. If only he could make her understand that she was entitled to her own life—that it wasn't wrong to put her happiness first.

If having to choose between him and her family was the only way to open her eyes, it would have to do. She had enough pressure, but the baby was growing by the day. He had to get her to a minister, and soon.

He got through his most important tasks early in the morning at work, and arranged to get Clay a new cell mate. Interfering in the way the county sheriff's department ran the jail wasn't something he usually did, but these were special circumstances. He explained the problem to the sheriff, an acquaintance of many years, who immediately solved it.

"How do you feel about people who pass bad checks?" he asked Becky as they drove to the nursing home to get Granddad. He'd picked her up at her office, grinning when Maggie gave him a curious but amused look.

"Well, I don't think I know any people who pass bad checks," she said. She was wearing a green print dress that made her look younger, and while the gauntness was still there, it was less evident this morning. "But they probably do it out of desperation, don't they?"

He chuckled and lifted his cigar to his lips. "They do it out of greed," he said. He glanced at her. "But they make better cell mates than rapists. I've just have one moved in with your brother. You can go and see him whenever you like."

"The bad check passer, or my brother?" she asked with the first glimmer of humor in her voice that he'd noticed recently.

"Either or both," he replied. He glanced at her and smiled. "Feeling better?"

"Yes," she confessed. She let her eyes meet his shyly, and then she averted them to the window as vivid memories of two days before washed over her. His ardor seemed to grow, and she couldn't deny him. She hoped he didn't think less of her for her inability to say no, but she was too uncertain of herself to ask him. "You gave my grandfather a reason to live. I think he meant to lie in that bed and die."

"I got that idea myself. He'll have a lot more fun sparring with me, when he gets back on his feet." He glanced at Becky and grinned. "He's got a mission in life now—to save you from my evil clutches."

"He's a little late, isn't he?" she muttered. "Especially after Saturday."

"Saturday was magic," he said huskily, his hands tightening on the steering wheel. "I dreamed about it all night long."

"You didn't give me a chance to say no," she said tightly, not looking at him.

"It wasn't deliberate, Becky," he replied quietly. "Once I started, I couldn't stop."

Her lower lip trembled. Neither could she, but she wasn't admitting it. It seemed indecent to want someone that badly, especially in her condition. "Well, you might have waited until I agreed to marry you, at least," she muttered.

"I may be too old by then." He raised an eyebrow. "Go ahead. Lacerate my conscience. Everybody picks on the poor district attorney."

"Well, I'm justified!" she exclaimed. "You got me in trouble!"

"I got you pregnant, which is another thing entirely. Considering that I did it on the first try, I feel pretty smug about the whole thing."

She felt her cheeks grow hot. She'd never discussed things like this with anyone, and she was pregnant out of wedlock, not to mention having given into him with shaming ease, which she found embarrassing. And here was the cause of it all, bragging about his prowess!

"I have never...!" she began hotly.

"Oh, yes, you have," he murmured dryly. "Four times, already."

She went scarlet and gave up trying to fence with him verbally. No wonder he was such a good district attorney. She wrapped her hands around her pocketbook and ground her teeth together. Arguing with him got her nowhere. She'd try ignoring him altogether and see how that worked.

It didn't. He turned on the radio and began to hum along with a popular country and western song.

"Have you thought about names?" he asked suddenly as they turned into the nursing home parking lot. "I like the sound of Todd, for a boy, and Gwen for a girl."

"It's my baby," she said stubbornly. "I get to name it."

"Half of it is your baby," he replied as he pulled into a parking space and cut off the engine. "You get to name half of it."

"Rourke," she said.

He put a long forefinger over her lips, stilling the words. His dark eyes looked straight into her hazel ones in the sheltered closeness of the car, bringing back the sweetest memories of how it felt to kiss him.

"Of all the things two people do together, I think having a child is the most poignant," he said gently. "I want to share every step of it with you, from morning sickness to labor." His hand slid to her cheek and stroked it with a light, caressing pressure while he searched her eyes. "I've never had anyone of my own," he said slowly. "Don't shut me out, Becky."

She wanted to give in. She wanted to throw her arms around him and tell him that she'd do anything he wanted her to, but there had been too much deception already, and too many lies. She didn't trust him. He wanted the baby, but that didn't mean he loved her. She couldn't really see him taking on her whole family just to be a parent, either. The first glow of fatherhood had enveloped him, but that might wear off. Worse, there was always the danger of a miscarriage this early in her pregnancy. She couldn't take the chance of letting him too close right now, until she was sure of his motives. And love was the one word he'd never mentioned to her, not even during their greatest intimacy, like yesterday. Men could desire without loving, couldn't they?

She lowered her eyes to his tie. "All right. I won't shut you out. But I won't let you take me over, either, Rourke."

"Fair enough," he said solemnly. "Now, let's go and get your grandfather. I hope you remembered the rope and chains," he added mischievously as he helped her out of the car. "I wouldn't give five cents for my chances of getting him in the car without restraints."

"No? I would," she murmured, walking alongside him toward the nursing home entrance. "He respects people he can't push around."

He glanced down at her warmly, liking the way she looked walking beside him. He felt a thrill of pure possession. She was his woman, with his child growing inside her. It was enough to make a man strut.

Becky noticed the way women's eyes went to him when

they were walking down the spotless hall toward Granddad's room. He was a handsome man—all dark sensuality and wicked spirit. He towered over her and made her feel small and feminine, and she liked the way his gray suit hugged the powerful lines of his body, emphasizing its fierce masculinity. He was a strong man, and not just physically. She allowed herself one sweet second to wonder if her child would be a boy, and if he would look like his father.

Granddad was waiting impatiently in his chair. Dr. Miller had already released him. Once Becky signed the papers, he could get out of here and straighten out the mess Rourke Kilpatrick had made of his family.

"It's about time," he raged at her, and then glared at Rourke as he came in with her. "You, again?" he muttered.

"I'm glad to see you, too," Rourke said, unperturbed. He grinned. "Becky signed you out before we came down here. If you're ready, I'll have the nurse bring the wheelchair."

"I hate being beholden to you," Granddad fumed minutes later, sitting rigidly in the front seat of Rourke's car while Becky—and Mack, who'd been picked up at Mrs. Addington's house on the way home—sprawled in the back seat.

"Oh, I can imagine," Rourke said with an aplomb that made Becky want to giggle.

"And I hate those damned cigars you smoke," he added.

"So do I," Rourke said, taking another puff as he wound through the open country and down the road that led to the farm.

Granddad glared at him. He tried to think of something else to complain about, but it was getting harder to come up with things. He sighed and looked out the window. "Nice car," he muttered.

"I like it," Rourke replied. "It has advantages over the Mercedes-Benz, because it's newer. But I miss my dog."

"Mean, low-down thing, to kill a man's dog," Granddad said reluctantly.

"Yes."

"How's MacTavish?" Becky asked gently.

He glanced over the back seat at her. "He's fine. He misses going on picnics and out to the parks, but he's adjusting."

She averted her eyes to the farmhouse in the distance.

"You need something done about that roof," Rourke remarked as he parked in front of the house. "Those shingles over the porch will come off in the first strong wind."

"I can't climb up there," the old man said with ravaged pride.

"I can," Rourke told him. "I'll take care of it. We can't have Becky pelted with falling shingles, in her condition."

Granddad reached for the door handle, looking uncomfortable. "Shameful, letting her get in such a condition unmarried," he said under his breath.

"I quite agree. You might use your influence to convince her that I'm excellent husband and father material," he replied, and Mack did giggle this time.

"You ought to marry him, if he's willing," Granddad told her when they were all out of the car. "Having a baby and no husband is scandalous."

"Besides, he likes trains and basketball," Mack said.

Becky glared at her relatives. "You both hated him only last month," she reminded them.

"I didn't say I liked him, did I?" Granddad asked impatiently. "I just said you should marry him."

"I like him." Mack shrugged.

"Thanks, Mack," Rourke said, clapping a big hand on the boy's shoulder. "It's nice to have friends."

Later, he felt as if he needed more than just one. Becky was polite and grateful for what he'd done, but she was suddenly as remote as the moon in every other way. He might have pushed too hard, he decided. Seducing her again seemed to have put more distance between them than ever. He should have remembered her bristly pride. He'd probably shattered it by making her succumb to him so easily. Apparently she felt even guiltier because she couldn't say no to him. He was almost sure that she loved him, but until she admitted it and he could make her understand what he felt, they were at a stalemate.

He went to see Clay, mostly to see who his new cell mate was. The bad check passer was only a little older than Clay, and not belligerent or rude. Becky would manage with this one, he decided.

"How's it going?" he asked Clay, after he'd had him moved into an interrogation room so that they had a little privacy.

"Slow," Clay said. "Is it always so slow?"

Rourke lit his cigar and nodded. "Welcome to the criminal justice system."

"I wish I'd had the good sense to keep my nose clean," Clay muttered. "This is the pits. How's Becky? She hasn't come back, and I figured it was because of the creep they put in the cell with me, but they moved him this morning and put this new guy in. Is she okay? How about Granddad and Mack?"

Rourke leaned back precariously in his chair and propped his long legs over the desk. "You have been kept in the dark, haven't you?" he murmured dryly. He blew out a cloud of smoke. "Granddad is home. He pitched a fit when he found out Becky was pregnant, and he's decided not to die because she won't marry me. He thinks babies should be born to married people."

Clay stared at Rourke blankly. "Granddad is at home because Becky is pregnant?"

Rourke flicked an ash into the dirty glass ashtray. "That's right."

"My sister is going to have a baby?!" he said, saucer-eyed.

"Yes," Rourke said, then frowned thoughtfully. "Maybe more than one. I think there may have been twins in my family a few generations back. I'll have to ask Becky if she knows of any in hers."

Clay's eyebrows began to lever upward. "It's your baby?"

He glowered at Clay. "What kind of girl do you think your sister is? Of course it's my baby."

"But Becky doesn't do that sort of thing," Clay said, trying to make the older man understand that she couldn't be having a child. "She doesn't even go out with men, and she goes to church on Sundays, and she gets all excited and mad when people talk about abortion and living together."

"Yes, I know," Rourke replied.

"She doesn't go around getting pregnant when she's not married!" Clay burst out.

Rourke grinned at him and stuck the cigar in his teeth. "Yes, she does."

"Well, what are you going to do about it?" he demanded.

"I've given that some serious thought," Rourke told him. "And considering how stubborn she is, I've decided that the only way I'm going to get her in front of a minister is to arrange the wedding, invite the guests, and carry her bodily down the aisle. It won't be easy. Handcuffs might be overdoing it a little, and I suppose people would notice if I gagged her," he added thoughtfully.

Clay's face broke into a helpless grin. He still couldn't quite believe it. He was going to be an uncle. "How did Granddad take the news?" he asked.

"He got up out of his bed in the nursing home and demanded to be taken back to the farm so that he could save Becky from me. Then, when he found out she was pregnant, he demanded to be taken back to the farm so that he could make her marry me."

"She doesn't want to?"

Rourke shook his head. "I don't really blame her. She thinks I set her up so that I could spy on you. I did, actually, but she grew on me." He smiled wistfully. "The baby is one big bonus. It was like Christmas, when I knew for sure."

Clay sighed. He'd never have figured Kilpatrick for the paternal sort, but nobody could accuse him of being a womanizer. If he'd only wanted Becky for a casual interlude, he certainly wouldn't be enthusiastic about her pregnancy, or keen on marrying her. He studied Kilpatrick for a minute, while another worry began to play on his mind.

"Mr. Davis talked to me about turning state's evidence," he told Rourke. "I wouldn't mind for myself. But what about Becky and Granddad and Mack?"

"Your grandfather said the same thing," Rourke replied.

His dark eyes narrowed thoughtfully. "I won't make any promises, but there may be another way. I'll talk to Davis. The fact that you were willing may go a long way. If we could talk your friends into confessing that they railroaded you, we might even get you off with a suspended sentence."

"Which is more than I'd deserve," Clay said. He'd had a lot of time to think, cold sober, and the past few months seemed like a nightmare. He still couldn't believe he'd been so thoughtless and cruel. "If I have to do the time, it will be all right, Mr. Kilpatrick," he said in a subdued tone. "I guess taking your licks is part of being a man, isn't it?"

Rourke smiled. "Yes. It's part of being a man."

He didn't tell Becky about the conversation he'd had with Clay, or what he was planning to do about the Harris boys. The less she knew, the safer she would be. The Harrises were probably already convinced that Clay was going to spill the beans, and that was why they'd volunteered to testify against him. He had one ace left up his sleeve, and he was going to play it.

It took Granddad the better part of a week to regain his strength, but he ate like a horse and cursed Rourke for sport. Rourke came and went as his free time allowed, ignoring Becky's cool politeness and Granddad's restrained antagonism. He patched the shingles on the roof Saturday afternoon. He'd shown up in old, faded jeans and a stained white cotton sweatshirt and sneakers, carrying a toolbox.

Mack had stayed outside at the foot of the ladder to fetch and carry as needed, talking enthusiastically about basketball, a passion that Rourke shared.

Becky had tried not to notice that he was there, despite

her frantic heartbeat and the furious excitement having him around engendered. She put her hair in pigtails, wishing she looked less frumpy in her long print skirt with the waistband unfastened and a floppy oversized shirt with "Beam Me Up, Scotty" and a drawing of the USS *Enterprise* on the front. She was barefoot, too, her usual condition around the house.

Rourke came down an hour later, just after the banging and hammering and cursing stopped. He had a cut on one brawny wrist, which he held out to Becky as naturally as if they'd been married twenty years and he was used to having her patch up his cuts.

"I've got some antiseptic and Band-Aids in the kitchen," she said gently.

"Remember to kiss it and make it better, Becky!" Mack called after them as he sat down beside Granddad to watch an old western movie on TV.

Becky went to get the first aid things out of the kitchen cabinet. Rourke unobtrusively locked the kitchen door before he joined her at the sink. "Mack made a good suggestion," he murmured dryly while Becky cleaned the cut and applied an antibiotic ointment through the thick hairs on his dark skin.

"You don't need kissing better," she murmured. "Does it hurt?"

"No. District attorneys are tough. Predators, you know." He leaned down. "Do you know why sharks don't eat lawyers?"

She glanced up warily. "No. Why?"

"Professional courtesy."

She laughed in spite of herself, and her face brightened.

Her freckles stood out on her nose, and her hazel eyes were big and soft and radiant.

He framed her face in his hands and bent, drawing his open mouth over hers in a teasing travesty of a kiss that aroused her at once.

She gasped, shocked at the force of what she felt from such a light caress.

He searched her eyes. His own narrowed and darkened as they fell back to her parted lips. He did it again, and again, and again, feeling her body tauten as he moved his hands to her hips and pulled her against him. He made a sound deep in his throat, and all at once his mouth settled on hers and hardened insistently.

She couldn't even make a pretense of holding anything back. Her dreams had been feverish and explicit only the night before, and the memory of how sweetly they'd made love was all too fresh in her mind. Her body knew the pleasure he could give it. It wouldn't let her fight.

The smoky state of his hard mouth was heaven, the possessive ferocity of his arms ecstasy.

He moved her backwards until she came up against the cool, rough wall, and his hands flattened against it beside her head while his body levered down over hers in blatant intimacy.

She gasped, which only gave him deeper access to her mouth. His tongue stabbed into it, deep and hard, and her short fingernails dug into his back as the fever began to kindle in her body.

It wasn't until she felt his hands under her skirt that she opened her eyes. His own were almost black, his face rigid, his arousal stark and demanding against her belly.

"Here?" she gasped under her breath.

His eyes glittered. "Here. Now." Holding her eyes, he stripped the briefs down her slender legs, then his lips brushed behind the briefs in a caress so sensual that she gasped.

He worked his way back up her legs blatantly lifting the skirt and blouse up under her chin so that his mouth had free access to her heated skin. He took her hard nipples into his lips and tormented them, his arm half supporting her sagging weight. There was a metallic sound and his mouth lifted and he positioned her gently and readjusted his weight so that his legs were between hers.

He held her shocked, misty eyes and pushed, impaling her.

"Rourke!" she groaned achingly, shivering.

"Hold on," he breathed huskily, repositioning his hands on either side of her as he began to move. "It's going to be hot and quick, and you're going to want to scream. But don't. They'll hear you."

His mouth bent to hers. He ignored the incredulous protest. Of course it was insane, but his body had him on the rack, and she was nothing if not welcoming.

"We can't," she whispered as he began a sharp rhythm against her. But even as she said the words, her hips arched up to his to help him. Her mouth opened in a soundless cry. She saw his face harden, felt him becoming part of her body, felt the rhythm become tormented pleasure.

Above her, his teeth clenched. "God," he breathed jerkily. "God, Becky, I can't stop!" his face contorted. He groaned helplessly, his body out of control now, mindlessly lifting into hers, his eyes closing as he fought to suck air into his lungs.

"Feel how bad it is for me!" he ground out, pausing for an instant so that she was completely possessed, his eyes staring tormentedly into hers. "Make it stop hurting, Becky," he whispered into her mouth. "Make me whole."

Becky watched him, shocked by what was happening, delighting in his fierce pleasure even as her own body sought desperately to satisfy him.

"Is it good?" she whispered huskily.

"Ecstasy," he managed. His eyes opened into hers. He was shuddering. "Touch me," he whispered under his breath.

It amazed her that she could, and so hungrily, giving in to his demands with frantic eagerness. He caught his breath when he felt her shy hands. He covered them with his, teaching her how.

The pleasure was digging into her like hurting hands now, and she was as wild as he was. His breath was audible, tormented, as he moved down against her roughly, sharply, his eyes never leaving hers.

"Watch," he managed just as the first shudder hit him.

This time she didn't look away. His face registered the anguished pleasure her rapt gaze gave him, his eyes black and steady on hers. He began to tremble and she watched his face contort, feeling her stomach tauten as the sharp pleasure echoed in her body.

His breathing was audible, like his heartbeat. He pushed down against her suddenly, desperately, and a hoarse cry escaped his mouth as his throat arched and his teeth ground together in anguished completion. Incredibly, watching him triggered her own, so that the same silvery pleasure washed over her like fire, even as he convulsed above her in blind completion. Seconds later, his heavy body collapsed on hers and ground her into the wall. She opened her eyes, looking up at him with shocked awe.

Her heartbeat shook her. She swallowed, astounded at what they'd done, and where they'd done it. Her wide hazel eyes met his with disbelief.

Neither of them was breathing normally or steadily, and she could hear and feel his heartbeat on her bare breasts. She stared up at his damp hair dazedly.

"Now you know," he said with shaken humor. "It's possible to do it standing up when you're too desperate to get to a place where you can do it lying down."

"It's nothing to joke about," she said miserably, feeling unsettled by her ready accommodation.

He touched her cheek gently. "I wasn't joking. I want you so much that it doesn't matter where or when, which is why I couldn't give you the promise you wanted. You can't stop what happens any more than I can," he added quietly. "It's a fever, burning so hot and high that ice couldn't quench it."

"It's wrong," she whispered.

"Why? Because we're not married?" He bent and brushed his lips over her heavy eyelids. "That isn't my fault. I want to marry you. You're the one who won't cooperate."

"I guess I seduced you?" she asked half angrily.

He lifted an eyebrow and looked down. She flushed furiously. He moved back then and she blushed even more, quickly straightening her clothes while he did the same.

"What a blessing that you're already pregnant," he murmured, watching her frantic movements, enjoying the radiance in her face. "We don't have to worry about getting you that way."

She gave him a killing glare. "You have to stop doing this!"

"I'm doing my best," he said heavily. "Can I help it if you're so damned sexy that I can't get within ten feet of you without getting aroused?"

That was a hard question to answer. In her condition, it wasn't exactly an insult to be thought of as sexy, and she had to admit that he tried to get her to marry him almost constantly. His motivation was her one big hang-up. He wouldn't tell her what his feelings really were, and she couldn't marry him until she knew. *Men,* she thought furiously.

"What an expression," he murmured, smiling with pleasant fatigue as he pulled his shirt down and bent to kiss her nose.

"In the kitchen, standing up, with the door unlocked," she began in a strained voice.

"They were so wound up in that movie that they didn't know or care what was happening in here," he whispered. "But just to reassure you..."

He moved away from her and put a finger to his lips as he gently turned the key to unlock the door.

"You locked it!" she exclaimed, almost sinking to the floor with relief.

"Of course I locked it," he said, rejoining her. He traced her swollen mouth with his forefinger. "I'm not kinky. Not that kinky, at least," he added gently. "Did I hurt you?"

"No. But you shouldn't..." she began uneasily.

"If you don't like being made love to in unusual places, marry me and we'll do it like normal couples, in bed at night." He moved back. "I want you. I can't turn it on and off."

"It's just sex!" she burst out.

He shook his dark head, very slowly. "It's deep, and rich, and lasting. I hate being away from you at all, especially with my child inside you."

He could say things that made her feet melt. She stared at him helplessly. "I can't just walk out on Granddad and Mack," she whispered. "Even if I could leave Clay to his fate. Don't you understand? Granddad looked after all of us when Mama died and Dad left. Mack was as much like my child as my brother. I've done for them and looked after them and loved them all my adult life. They're my family."

He moved closer, framing her face in his lean, warm hands. "So am I," he whispered. "The baby and I are your family, too."

Her eyes looked wounded as they met his. He was putting her in an impossible position. Couldn't he see that?

"I can't choose," she whispered. She looked down at his chest. "I wish I could make you understand that it isn't a matter of choice. You don't just jettison people when they get in the way of things you want to do. Isn't that half of what's wrong with society today? Everybody wants his or her own pleasure first, and everything that gets in the way is expendable. I can't feel like that."

He frowned as he studied her face. "Are you telling me that I'm expendable, Becky?" he asked softly.

"Rourke, if I put Granddad in a nursing home and Mack in a foster home, how am I going to live with the guilt?" She lowered her eyes. "That being the case, you don't have to feel, well, obligated to do things for us."

He let his eyes slide over her body and back up again. Even though he was satisfied, the sight of her could still arouse him. He didn't like the feeling of being out of control, but he was never any other way with her lately. Making love to her was only going to increase her guilt and fortify her suspicion that all he wanted was sex. If only he knew what she really felt.

His doubts made him irritable. "You're carrying my child. I have a responsibility to him, if not to you, for seducing you into pregnancy. I'll do what I can to make conditions livable around here," he said, his eyes sliding with patent disapproval around the rough walls. "I owe the child that much."

"Becky, how about lunch?!" Granddad called suddenly from the living room.

She felt sick all over. "I have to fix something to eat," she mumbled.

"Becky! How about lunch?" Granddad yelled again.

"How about it?" she yelled back at him, driven to anger by her own raging emotions.

"What are you doing in there?!" the old voice raged.

Becky moved away from Rourke and refused to look at him. Men were the absolute pits and she was certain that she didn't love him anymore. "I'm undressing Mr. Kilpatrick and preparing him for the oven!" she shouted. "What do you think I'm doing?"

"I don't want roasted district attorney for lunch," Mack interrupted, peeking around the kitchen door. "Could I have a hot dog instead?"

Becky threw up her hands. "Yes, you can have a hot dog."

Rourke stared at her rigid back with faint remorse. He suddenly realized that he hadn't even had breakfast. Perhaps she might be willing to suspend hostilities long enough to feed him. "May I have one, too?" he asked.

She gave him a killing stare. "Only if I get to pick where I put it when it's cooked," she said icily.

He pretended not to hear her. He sat down at the table and lit a cigar. "I like mine just barely boiled, and with lots of mustard and catsup and relish. I like chili or slaw on it."

"I don't have chili and I'm not making slaw," she said curtly, slamming a pot under the faucet to fill with water.

"We have chili left over from last night in the refrigerator," Mack pointed out.

Becky didn't say a word. She fixed hot dogs and heated up chili, still simmering from her confrontation with Rourke. Her headlong response was her worst problem. He sat there with that damned arrogant look in his eyes and she knew he was remembering it, too. He was almost purring with satisfaction.

Well, she wasn't giving up Mack and Granddad, so he could just be arrogant all alone. She'd be better off without him anyway, she told herself. If only she'd never gone to work for the law firm in the first place, she might never have met him!

"What were you doing in here?" Granddad demanded when Becky called him to the table.

"Guess," Rourke murmured with a sensual glance at Becky.

She blushed scarlet and couldn't look at anybody. How could he embarrass her like this? Of course, it was only later that she realized nobody would believe what they'd done. He'd only given the impression that they'd been kissing.

Rourke insisted on helping with the cleaning up. Then he

produced two tickets for an Atlanta Hawks basketball exhibition game that night.

"Atlanta's air force!" Mack exclaimed, using the nickname that the Hawks' promotional spots on TV had given it. He went wild. "You've got to let me go!" he told Becky, grabbing her arms. "You've got to! I'll die if you don't let me go!"

"Do you want your brother's death on your conscience?" Rourke asked her.

She shook her head. "God forbid. All right, you can go."

"I didn't say so," Granddad muttered darkly.

Mack went and took Granddad by the arms. "You've got to let me go!" he repeated. "I'll die if you don't let me go!" He glanced at Rourke without a trace of remorse. "B-ball is my life," he explained.

"Go on, for heaven's sake." The old man gave in as quickly as Becky had.

"I have to go home and change. I'll be back for you about six," he told Mack.

"I'll be ready!" Mack said enthusiastically.

"Thank you for fixing the roof," Granddad said without looking at him.

"My pleasure. Thanks for the hot dogs," he told Becky. "You'll make some lucky man a good wife."

"Not you, of course," she said curtly, still stinging from the argument they'd had and his refusal to understand how badly she was needed here.

His eyebrows levered up. "I didn't say you'd make me a good wife," he reminded her. "I know you don't want to marry me. Don't worry about it—I'll never ask you again."

Becky averted her eyes, vaguely aware of Granddad's hard stare.

"It's your child," Granddad said sharply. "It won't have your name."

"Becky knows that," Rourke said. "If that's how she wants it, who am I to argue? Poor little kid's going to have hell in school, though. I did."

"Why?" Granddad asked.

"I'm illegitimate," he told the old man, without a hint of emotion in his face. "My father, I'm told, didn't believe in marriage."

"Idiot," Granddad said, glancing up at him and then down again. "A child should have a name."

Becky shifted uncomfortably. They were making her feel terrible. But it was Rourke's fault, dammit! He was the one who was forcing her to make impossible choices. She turned away. "I'll make sure Mack has something to wear."

Rourke watched her go with quiet, speculative eyes. He wished he hadn't backed her into that particular corner. He'd only made things worse.

He actually had no problem with taking on her family, but he hadn't told her that. He'd made her think that he was going to take her away from them and leave them to sink or swim on their own.

He hadn't realized how it would sound to her when he put it into words. What he'd meant was that he wanted to be loved. He wanted her to care so much for him that everyone else on earth would be second in her affections. But she hadn't understood, and now he'd created an even worse problem.

Besides that, making her give in to him physically was compounding the complications. His temper had gotten away from him and he'd as much as told her that his interest in her was mainly sexual, so seducing her coming and going wasn't going to help matters. He'd have to get his body under control, along with his tongue, or they'd never get together.

He packed up his toolbox and left to get ready for the game. It didn't escape his notice that Becky didn't see him off, or that she avoided him for the rest of the evening. He and Mack came home late, to be told by Granddad that she'd gone to bed with a headache. Rourke had one of his own, but he'd created it for himself. He couldn't blame it on Becky or her family.

CHAPTER TWENTY

Becky went through the motions of working, but her heart wasn't in it. She felt as if she'd taken a wrong step somewhere along the way and everything had changed because of it.

Rourke was still around. He'd arranged for a retired man to take over care of the livestock and the plowing. The same man, a soft-spoken apartment dweller who missed the land, was going to plant the fall garden and maintain it. Rourke had sent a carpenter to put the front porch and the screens to rights, and he'd insisted on buying a basketball goal and net for Mack. He'd put it up over the ramshackle garage, and now Mack did nothing but play with his NBA regulation basketball and sing Kilpatrick's praises.

Granddad grew spryer by the day. He was up and around now, and there was a spring to his step. He'd gone with Becky to see Clay, who was still awaiting trial. His case had been called two weeks past, but J. Davis had been out of town on an emergency and it had to be continued.

That suited Rourke very well. He had used the extra time to good advantage.

He'd gone to see Frank Kilmer, an old friend of his uncle's and a former public defender who had some of the oddest acquaintances any officer of the court ever assembled. There was a rumor—unproven, of course—that his gardener had once been a hit man for the big boys up north.

"Nice of you to come and see me, boy," he chuckled, walking around his estate with Rourke. "But from the look of your face, I think I can be forgiven for asking if this is purely a social call. You don't usually look so preoccupied when you come to visit."

Rourke turned to the older man, the wind catching his dark hair and lifting strands of it. "I need some advice."

"Not to do something outside the law, God forbid?" the bent, silver-haired old gentleman asked with his stock horrified expression.

"God forbid."

He grinned. "What is it?"

"I want to make the local organized crime element give up two of its more expendable colleagues. They set up a friend of mine. Unless I can get them to admit it, he stands to do some hard time."

Kilmer nodded, scowling. "The Cullen boy."

Rourke's eyebrows arched. "Am I wearing a sign?"

"I always know what's going on." He glanced sideways at Rourke and grinned wickedly. "I know about the baby, too, but I'll pretend not to if it will embarrass you."

"My God."

"What you want isn't all that difficult. All you have to do

is find a politician with ties to them and put him in a compromising situation."

"I'm an officer of the court," he reminded the old man.

"I didn't say you had to create the compromising situation. And," Kilmer added with a sharp laugh. "I know just the politician for you. He's a compulsive gambler. He has a standing Saturday night game, and he's running for reelection. He also has ties to the gentlemen to whom the Harris boys owe their souls." He glanced up at the taller man. "Will that do?"

"That," Rourke replied with a smile, "will do nicely. Thank you."

"Thanks are not necessary. You can invite me to the christening. I've always had the urge to become a godfather."

"You shady character. You'd have my son or daughter sitting on the knees of hit men and playing tag with numbers runners!"

"I would not," he returned, offended. "My God, I have nothing to do with the numbers racket."

BECKY INVITED MAGGIE HOME with her for supper one Friday night, grateful for the older woman's moral support through the long ordeal. Maggie accepted, and there was nothing critical in her brief appraisal of the house when she arrived.

Granddad didn't even open his mouth when he discovered that the Maggie his granddaughter had talked about for so long was black. He smiled at her naturally and behaved like a perfect gentleman. Becky hoped her shock didn't show.

"Are you going to get married before this baby is born, or not?" Maggie asked later, when they were sitting on the front porch swing.

"He wanted me to choose between my family and him," Becky said miserably. "How could I?"

Maggie whistled. "Rough choice."

"Yes, it was. Impossible. I can't put Mack in a home."

The older woman wrapped her long, elegant fingers around the chain that supported the swing. "Doesn't he like Mack?" she asked.

"Of course he does. He took him to a Hawks exhibition game, and he's always bringing him something for his train set." Becky stopped dead. Why, Rourke was crazy about the boy. He was even fond of Granddad. It was he who'd made the old man want to live again.

"I think you might have gotten hold of the wrong end of the stick, my friend," Maggie said gently. "Wanting to come first doesn't have a lot to do with kicking your family out of the house. Kilpatrick doesn't have anyone of his own. That makes it hard for him to understand dependents and family loyalty. He may not know that love grows the more you spread it around, or that you can love plenty of people and never run out of the stuff."

"Oh, no," Becky said slowly. "No, it couldn't be that simple. He said there was no future for us as long as I put my people ahead of him."

"He's right. Listen, honey, I had no family of my own when I married Jack. I was jealous of every minute he spent with his parents and his sister and brother. I did everything I could to keep him away from them. Eventually it broke up my marriage, because I gave him an impossible choice. Don't do that to Kilpatrick. Make him part of your family. Then make him understand that you can love him and still have room left for them."

"If it's not too late," Becky said miserably. "Oh, Maggie, I've ruined everything!"

"No, you haven't. A man has to care a lot before he'll take on a burden like yours."

"That's what Clay said," she recalled.

"And doesn't it look as if Kilpatrick has done exactly that?" she added, smiling. "Look around. He's fixed up the house, taken responsibility for the bills, got Clay that dandy attorney..."

"What?"

Maggie's eyebrows arched in the light from the window. "You knew, didn't you? I had lunch with one of the girls who works part-time in the district attorney's office. She told me it was the talk of the courthouse at the time."

"He got Mr. Davis to represent Clay?" Becky gasped.

"Yes. Quite a trick, considering that Lincoln Davis was using Clay and Kilpatrick's involvement with you to get himself elected. But Kilpatrick talked him into it. He paid your grandfather's hospital bill, to boot. Does that sound like a man who doesn't care about you?"

"But, he never told me!" she wailed. "He never said a word!"

"The man wants love, not gratitude. Are you blind?"

"I thought he only wanted sex," she said.

Maggie laughed. "They all want sex, honey," she murmured dryly. "But if he'd only wanted that, why would he keep coming around when you turned up pregnant?"

"I don't know." Becky put her head in her hands. "I don't know anything anymore."

"There are none so blind as those who will not...well,

what's this? Do you have friends that I don't know about?" Maggie murmured, watching as a coal-black Lincoln Continental pulled into the front yard and stopped.

Becky frowned. "I don't know anybody in that income bracket," she said.

The door opened and a tall, well-dressed man got out. He was built like a wrestler, with thick, curly hair and a broad face. He came up the steps, spared Maggie a quick but appreciative glance, and turned to Becky.

"Miss Cullen?" he asked politely. "I'm J. Lincoln Davis, your brother's attorney."

"Mr. Davis!" Becky got up and hugged him.

He chuckled a little self-consciously, and his dark skin looked very much as if it flushed. "I wasn't sure if I'd be welcome..."

"What a silly remark," Becky said, "when you've done so much for Clay. There's nothing we wouldn't do for you, and of course you're welcome." She took his hand and tugged. "Come inside and meet the rest of the family. Maggie?"

"Right behind you," Maggie murmured. She got up, noticing without conceit that Lincoln Davis seemed to find her as interesting as she found him.

Granddad looked up from the television and his eyebrows arched. His visitor was black. He was wearing a very expensive tan suit, a silk tie and leather shoes. Granddad was impressed. He could only think of one black man who would come here without an invitation and, remembering Rourke's words, he decided that a little gracious hospitality wouldn't go amiss, despite his old prejudices.

He got to his feet. "Mr. Davis, isn't it?" he asked formally, and stuck out his hand.

Davis shook the old man's hand. "Mr. Cullen," he replied. "It's a pleasure to meet you. Clay speaks highly of your integrity and honor."

Granger Cullen blushed. "Won't you have a chair, Mr. Davis?" he invited. "Have mine."

Davis sat down, crossing his long legs. "I'm sorry to barge in at this late hour, but I've been out of town. There are some new developments in Clay's case, so I thought I'd talk them over with you while I had a few minutes."

"I should leave," Maggie began.

"You should not," Becky said firmly. She glanced at Davis. "Maggie is my friend. I don't mind if she hears what you have to say. And can I say how proud we are that you're representing Clay?"

"All you like," he murmured dryly. "I felt I owed it to you after some of the things I said that were misquoted." He studied her quietly, his eyes going sharply to the faint bulge under her tent dress and back up again. "May I just ask, when the hell is Kilpatrick going to do the honorable thing and marry you?"

Granger Cullen laughed out loud. "He's trying," he informed the other man. "But Becky won't say yes."

"Why not?" Lincoln asked her. "He's crazy about you!"

"That isn't what he said," Becky replied primly. She folded her hands in her lap. "What about Clay?" she asked evasively.

"Oh. Clay. Well, the trial comes up week after next. As you know, we're pleading not guilty to one count of possession of a schedule two drug—cocaine; one count of possession for the purpose of resale; and one count of possession for the purpose of distribution. Each of those counts carries a ten-year sentence, at least, with or without an additional fine. Then we come to the aggravated assault charge—the attempt on Kilpatrick's life. If convicted, he could go ten years on that charge as well."

"Is aggravated assault a capital crime?" Becky asked miserably.

"No. Only murder. He's being accused of attempting it. If he'd been charged with a capital crime, bail wouldn't have been allowed under Georgia law."

"I see," Becky said miserably and tried not to cry. "Nobody told me what the penalty could be if he's convicted. I was thinking of a few years."

"God, I'm sorry!" Davis said fervently. "I thought you knew all this!"

"Clay didn't tell me," Becky said solemnly. "Neither did Rourke."

"I suppose they were trying to spare you," Davis said, "but it was in all the papers and on television."

"We didn't read about it or listen to it," Becky explained. "We thought it would be better for Mack if he didn't have to be exposed to so much bad publicity, so we protected him from it. I had no idea."

"Better to face it," Granddad said, his voice quiet in the still room. "What are Clay's chances?"

"We've moved to suppress certain evidence, and I'll try a few other legal maneuvers if that one doesn't work. Their case isn't as airtight as they want us to think, and we've got Francine Harris. She's a cousin of Son and Bubba, and she's willing to testify for Clay."

"Will her relatives let her?" Becky asked.

"Good question. We don't know. In fact, she hasn't been to see Clay in a week and nobody's seen her around town," Davis replied. He leaned forward. "I want to put you on the witness stand," he told Becky. "Your character and reputation for honesty are well known. It might give Clay a better chance if we can show the jury that his family isn't connected with this sort of thing."

"That could backfire," Granddad said. "My son was involved in some shady deals before he went to Alabama to live. If they dig that up, it could hurt Clay's case."

"You haven't heard from your son lately?" Davis asked, frowning.

"Not in two years," Granddad said sadly. "He's had no use for us."

"Did he ever serve time?" Davis asked.

"No. There wasn't enough evidence to convict."

"Then there's no problem," the younger man said. He leaned forward with his hands on his knees. "Listen, we've got something on the back burner. I'm not at liberty to tell you what it is, but I've tipped the police to something that may give us a fighting chance in court." He didn't dare bring Kilpatrick's name into it. His participation in breaking the Harris ring could have serious repercussions. It wasn't unethical or illegal, exactly, but the press could make something nasty of it. "The problem is going to be if it works. A cornered animal is dangerous, and the Harrises have a lot more to lose than Clay does. I want you to let Kilpatrick hire a bodyguard for you."

"A bodyguard!" Becky gasped.

He nodded. "He and I think it's necessary. We have just

the man, too. He works for an old friend of Kilpatrick's uncle. He's sort of...a gardener," Davis said hesitantly. He looked around at their faces. No. He couldn't bring himself to mention those stupid rumors. "He's fit and tough, though, and he won't let anything happen to you. Will you do it?"

"I can pay for him," Becky said stubbornly.

"Kilpatrick can pay for him. It was his idea," Davis said.

"Hush, Becky," Maggie said gently. "There's a time to give in, and this is it."

"Good advice," Davis said, smiling at Maggie.

She smiled back. "Thank you, Counselor."

"You work for the same firm as Becky, don't you?" Davis asked conversationally.

She nodded. "I've been there a long time."

"I thought I recognized you. You married Jack Barnes."

"I divorced Jack Barnes years ago," she murmured.

Davis's eyes twinkled. "Did you?" He leaned forward. "How do you feel about reptiles?"

Oh, Maggie, Becky prayed silently, *don't tell him about your pet snake.* She hated seeing her friend go dateless because of her pet preference.

But Maggie couldn't read her mind. She stared at Davis. "Well," she hesitated, "I'm not too keen on lizards, but I'm crazy about snakes. I've got this baby python..."

"Will you have dinner with me tomorrow night?!" Davis asked with evident delight.

"I said I like snakes," she emphasized. "I keep one, right in my own apartment."

"She does," Becky said, shivering. "I don't even like to go in there."

"I have a fifteen-foot python named Henry," Davis said. "I've had him since he was a baby. We could talk about her petology."

Maggie beamed. "We could?!"

"Indeed we could. Are you ready to go? I could drive you home."

"I brought my own car," Maggie said hesitantly.

"I'll have it picked up." He stood up. "I'll be in touch with you as soon as we get any news about the Harrises. Meanwhile, Turk will be here first thing in the morning. He's nice. Feed him a sandwich once in a while and he'll die for you. Okay?"

"Okay," Becky said reluctantly. "Is Rourke going to come with him?" she asked helplessly.

Davis studied her and smiled to himself. "He might. Take care of yourself. Sorry to steal your dinner guest, but a lady who likes snakes is too rare to pass up."

"I quite understand," Becky laughed. She shook his hand. "Thank you, Mr. Davis."

"My pleasure."

Granger Cullen got to his feet and extended his own hand. "You ever wrestle?" he asked Davis. "You're sure built for it."

"I played football for the University of Georgia," Davis grinned. "But that was some years ago. Law is less strenuous and more fun."

"Thanks for what you're doing for my grandson," the old man said.

He searched the wrinkled old eyes, and he didn't smile. "My grandfather went to prison for a crime he didn't commit. He served thirty years before they discovered their mistake—all because he couldn't afford a good attorney. He's why I went into law. I make good money, but I never forget my motivation. Poor people deserve the same chance rich people have. Clay's pretty much a victim in all this, despite his original motives for doing it. I think he's innocent of the charges, and I'm going to prove it."

"If you ever get in trouble, you can count on me," the old man said, and meant it.

Davis shook the other man's hand firmly. "That works both ways."

He smiled at Becky and took Maggie's arm. "Now, about snakes..."

"Thanks for dinner, honey," Maggie told Becky as she was half led out the door. "I'll see you Monday!"

"Okay. 'Bye." Becky laughed.

Mack wandered back into the living room, having just spent half an hour on the phone with his friend John. "Who was that in the Lincoln?" he asked with interest.

"Clay's attorney," Becky told him.

He frowned thoughtfully. "Maybe I'll go into law for a profession," he said. "After my basketball career is over, of course."

Becky grinned and hugged him. Despite the worry, things were looking up a little bit.

ROURKE SHOWED UP early the next morning with a heavyset man who resembled a human basset hound in the face. He had sagging jowls and eyes that betrayed no emotion at all, with heavy eyelids. He was big-boned and a little sluggish, and Becky wondered how in the world he was going to protect any of them, but she smiled and tried to make him welcome.

"This is Turk," Rourke said, introducing him. "He works for a friend of mine, and he's handy around the house, as well as being one of the best bodyguards in the business."

"Pleased to meet you, ma'am," the big man said genially. He smiled, but it fell flat.

"We appreciate your help, Turk," Becky said. "Have you had lunch?"

"Mr. Kilpatrick bought me a hamburger," he replied. "I like hamburgers. Do you have a garden?"

"Well, a small one," she said. "It's grown up pretty badly. It's out back."

"Do you have a tiller?"

"No, I'm sorry," she faltered.

"A hoe?"

"Yes, in the barn."

"Thank you, ma'am."

He went out the back door while Becky stared after him. She looked up at Rourke.

"Are you sure he's a bodyguard?" she asked.

"I'm sure." He studied her quietly. "Has Davis been out here?"

"Last night," she said. "What's going on? Do you know?"

"Haven't a clue," he lied with a straight face. "How's Granddad?"

"He's fine," she replied. "He's taking a nap. Mack's over at John's. Is it all right for him to do that, with what's going on?"

"As long as Turk walks him home. Call and tell him."

"Okay." She did, as Rourke settled himself in an easy chair

with his cigar and an ashtray. He looked tired, she thought, and gray hairs were evident in his thick, dark hair. She wondered if he worried about her, and thought that he probably did. After all, she was carrying his child.

She hung up after Mack agreed to wait for the bodyguard and went to sit on the sofa across from Rourke's chair.

"Can I make you some coffee?" she asked gently.

He shook his head. "I'm due back in court at one," he said. "Why aren't you at work?"

She studied her faded skirt. "I was too sick to go this morning," she replied. "It doesn't happen often."

He leaned forward. "If you'd marry me, you could come home."

"I know your conditions for marriage and I couldn't meet them," she said stiffly. "Thanks anyway."

He frowned, and then remembered what he'd said to her, about giving up her family. He started to speak, but this really wasn't the time. He shrugged and stood up. "I have to get back," he said.

She stood up, too. Her hazel eyes searched his dark ones. "Rourke, why didn't you tell me that you'd talked Mr. Davis into defending Clay?" she asked. "Or that you'd had a hand in paying Granddad's hospital bill?"

His face closed up. "Who told you?" he asked curtly.

She shook her head. "I won't say, but it wasn't Mr. Davis. Why?" she added softly.

He took a draw from the cigar and turned his head to blow out the smoke. "Let's just say that I had a vested interest in Clay, since I inadvertently sent him to jail. Maybe I felt guilty," he added with a mocking smile. "Leave it at that."

Her heart sank. She'd hoped that he might admit that he cared about her a little. It was a forlorn hope now.

"Well...thank you, anyway," she replied formally.

He tucked a lean hand under her chin and lifted her face to his keen eyes. "I don't want gratitude from you."

"What do you want?" she asked with a harsh laugh. "My body? You've had that."

His thumb moved gently over her soft mouth. "And that's all I wanted? You're very sure?"

She sighed miserably. "You want the baby," she added, lowering her eyes to his broad chest.

"At least you give me credit for that. Yes, I want the baby."

"But not me," she added fearfully.

"Only if you love me," he replied. "And that won't happen, will it?" he asked with bitterness in his deep voice. "Because I'm the man who turned in your brother."

She couldn't deny that. But somehow, even if he was doing his job, it didn't seem in character for Rourke to use information that he obtained by subterfuge. Other men, maybe. But not him. She could only see him using information that he was given.

She searched his dark eyes. "It sounds silly, I guess," she murmured hesitantly. "But it isn't the kind of thing you'd do, is it?"

His face lost its rigidity. He stared down at her hungrily. "Isn't it, little one?" he asked tenderly, and he smiled.

She reached up with a long sigh and put her hands on his lean cheeks. "Sometimes I think I don't really know you at all. Oh, come here!" she whispered, tugging.

He let her pull his face within reach, and spears of white-hot pleasure went through his powerful body as she kissed him with pure, sweet ardor.

"Becky!" he groaned. His arms contracted and he lifted her against him, savoring the rough kiss until his body protested that he couldn't do that any longer without paying for it.

He let her slide down to the floor, laughing huskily at her expression when she felt the raging force of his arousal.

"Say you'll marry me, or so help me, I'll throw you down on the floor and make love to you right here," he threatened gruffly.

"You're kinky, Mr. District Attorney," she murmured. She leaned her head against his chest and closed her eyes, savoring his closeness. He was so good to lean on, and she loved him so much. All the arguments and fighting seemed not to matter at times like this. "But yes, I'll marry you, if you won't make me give up my family entirely. I can get a nurse for Granddad. But Mack..." Her face tautened as she tried to think about putting him in a foster home.

His arms contracted hungrily as he realized what she was willing to give up. "My God...I didn't mean you had to farm them out! If and when your grandfather can manage on his own, we'll find someone to stay with him. But Mack will live with us. You crazy little idiot, I only wanted to know that you loved me!" His mouth found hers, stilling the words.

She reached up to him, tears seeping into their locked mouths from her eyes. "Love you?" she sobbed against his hard lips. "I'd die for you!"

His mouth hardened. He lifted her in his arms and stood holding her in the middle of the room, the cigar smoking, forgotten in his fingers, his mouth devouring hers.

"Becky?" Granddad asked hesitantly from the doorway, his eyes like saucers as he stared at them.

She moved her face toward him, her eyes dazed. "We're getting married," she whispered huskily.

Granddad smiled mischievously. "It's about time," he murmured, grinning. "I hate to interrupt, but do you think you could fix me a sandwich? It's been a long time since breakfast."

"Yes, I can fix you a sandwich," she said, lifting a radiant face to Rourke's. "Want one?"

"I had a hamburger with Turk," he reminded her. He kissed her once more and set her on her feet, moving away with his cigar, even though his eyes devoured her. "There's a banquet next Friday night to honor Judge Kilmer," he said. "You can wear that witchy black dress you bought. The Friday after that, we're getting married."

"Whatever you say, Mr. Kilpatrick," Becky said gently. "But...what about Clay?"

He smiled wolfishly. "Wait and see."

CHAPTER TWENTY-ONE

Davis was never certain exactly how Rourke and his off-duty police cohorts had managed to do it. But he was called down to Rourke's office late the next Thursday night. Sitting around inside it were the Harris boys, their father, the acting D. A. on the Cullen case, Mr. James Garraway, two uniformed police officers, and Rourke.

"I don't think you know Jim, do you, Davis?" Rourke said, introducing him to the much older attorney.

"Your reputation precedes you, Mr. Davis," Garraway grinned. "Nice to meet you. These are the Harris boys and their father," he said, nodding toward them. "They've just confessed to setting your client up on a bogus aggravated assault charge, as well as unfounded violations of the Georgia Controlled Substances Act."

"In other words," Rourke said through a puff of cigar smoke, "Clay walks, on all four charges. As soon as we get the paperwork through, he can go home."

"The confession is on videotape," Garraway said. "I'll have your nolle prosequi on Judge Kilmer's desk first thing in the morning."

"Fortunately, you haven't put yourself out of a job," Rourke said with a smile. "You still get to prosecute these three." He stared at the Harrises with thinly concealed anger. "I'll enjoy standing as a witness for the prosecution, however."

"You won't keep us," the elder Harris said curtly. "We'll be out by morning."

"On bail, undoubtedly," Rourke agreed. "But you've made some stupid mistakes and you won't be excused for them. Once you're on the streets again, you're on your own." He leaned forward. "You'd better remember what we discussed earlier," he added, watching their faces go rigid and pale. "You've put your cronies in a bad spot, and they aren't forgiving people. Being on the outside will give them a dandy chance to get even."

"We can waive bail," Son said dejectedly. "Dammit, Kilpatrick, you had no call to put us in this spot!"

"You had no call to blow up my dog," he returned, ice in his voice. "You'll have years to regret it."

"You promised us a deal," he said, turning to Garraway.

"And you'll get it," the older man promised. "In return for your testimony. If you want to turn state's evidence on your suppliers, I think you'll find we can arrange protective custody through the federal boys. Your pipeline is one of the biggest in the state. We'd love to close it down."

"Protective custody?" the elder Harris asked narrowly.

"That, a new identity, a new start, for all three of you,"

Rourke said. "Think about it. You might not get a better chance."

He moved out into the corridor with Davis, leaving the rest behind. "Don't ask," he told the other man when he opened his mouth. "It's enough that it worked. Call it a calculated risk. And I think Turk can go home now."

"You're going to leave Becky unprotected?" Davis asked, aghast.

"Not quite," he murmured dryly. "In fact, we're getting married tomorrow afternoon. After the banquet tomorrow night, we're going to fly down to Nassau for a two-day honeymoon while a nurse and housekeeper stay with Granddad and Mack—and with Clay, too, I suppose."

"Well, well. Becky and a baby, too." He shook his head. "You're luckier than you deserve, Rourke. Are you going to run for reelection?" he added with an intent stare.

"Wait until tomorrow night and find out," he said. He walked away, grinning.

The Judge Kilmer appreciation banquet was well underway when Rourke, sitting beside a radiant Becky in a new and larger black dress than the one she'd worn before, and sporting a brand-new wedding ring, was invited to the podium.

He looked elegant in dinner jacket and black tie, his skin very dark against the white shirt.

"I suppose you're all waiting for me to announce," he said after he'd made some praising remarks about Judge Kilmer and cracked a few jokes about his own failings in the judge's court. "Well, I am. But it's not the announcement some of you have been anticipating. I've enjoyed my job. I hope I've done it well. But I've learned some very hard lessons over the past few months about the plight of people who are thrown into the judicial system and have to cope without financial backing."

He stuck his hands in his pockets. "Law is only just if it provides equal opportunity in representation to rich and poor alike. Law that favors the wealthy, or that restricts the rights of the poor, is no law. I've been on the winning team for seven years. Now I want to see the courtroom from the other table's vantage point. I'm hanging up my prosecutor's suit to go into private practice, where I hope to specialize in juvenile law."

There were murmurs and some protests, although none came from a beaming J. Lincoln Davis at one of the front tables.

Rourke chuckled. "I'm flattered at the dissent. But let me add that I have a brand-new wife and baby on the way," he said, smiling at Becky. "My priorities are different now, and I have reasons for wanting to spend my nights at home instead of the office."

There was laughter and applause. Rourke winked at Becky, who looked pretty elegant herself in that black dress with her long, honey-brown hair around her shoulders and her cheeks flushed.

"I won't say that it was an easy decision to make. I've enjoyed life in the prosecutor's office. I have a fine staff and good people to work with. But," he added, looking at Becky unsmilingly, "my wife is my whole world. There isn't another human being on the face of the earth whom I love as much. I'm going to be a family man from here on out." He glanced away from Becky's shocked, rapt eyes to his audience. "That being the case, I hope you won't mind if I throw my support to J. Lincoln Davis, who's sitting out there in the front row trying not to look like a cat with a mouthful of feathers!"

Everybody laughed, Davis included. He was sitting with a delightfully pretty Maggie, who was staring at him as if he were the moon.

"I'd also like to publicly thank J. Lincoln Davis," he added, "for his exemplary representation of my brother-in-law. I have it on good authority that he won't be called to do it again."

Davis held up a thumb and nodded. Rourke went on speaking for several minutes, but Becky didn't hear what he said. She was drinking in the fact that he'd publicly confessed his love for her—something he'd never even done privately. She had to fight tears. There were no more barriers. Even the one he thought was left had been removed last night, when a tearful Mack had confessed that he'd given Rourke the information that had led to Clay's arrest. She'd have to tell Rourke that she knew, but not right away. They had other things to talk about.

Clay had come home earlier in the afternoon, looking subdued but happy. Francine had come with him, and Becky thought that she might even learn to like the girl. Clay was talking about getting a job, and helping out at home, and he meant it.

Becky could hardly cope with her own happiness. From such misery, to this. She touched the soft mound of her stomach and stared at Rourke, love making her beautiful. He glanced at her and smiled, and she had to hold on to the table to keep from floating right up to the overhead lights. Life, she thought, was full of surprises. All you had to do was get through the storms. There was always sunshine waiting on the other side.

CHAPTER TWENTY-TWO

Becky always thought secretly that the most boring part of court was the judge's instructions to the jury. They were incomprehensible, they took forever, and with an impatient toddler on one's lap, they tended to become irritating.

She glanced beside her at Todd, who was eight now and very well behaved. He watched his father with awe, because this was the first time he'd been allowed to hear a summation. Really, she thought, it was the first time he'd been mature enough to sit through one. A bright boy, he had the impulsive and impatient nature that Becky shared with Rourke. Not surprising that Todd had inherited those traits. Little Teresa, squirming in her mother's lap, seemed bent on the same course as well.

Next to Todd, Clay and Francine were sitting close together. They had no children yet. They had only been married for two years. Clay was in line for a promotion at the grocery store where he was assistant produce manager, and Francine was almost finished with her beautician's training.

Mack, sitting next to Clay, was half a head taller than his brother. He was in his first year of law school at the University of Georgia, following in his adored brother-in-law's footsteps. Becky was so proud of him that she could have exploded. He and Rourke were very close, which made things so much easier at home.

Granddad was in a nursing home. He was lucid some days, and hardly aware of them others. They all went to see him regularly, and it made the pain of separation bearable. He was too feeble to stay at home without round-the-clock nursing, and the home had been his idea in the beginning. Two of his war buddies were there, and until the past year, he'd enjoyed himself. Now, it was a matter of time. Old seed going into the ground to make way for new, winter taking away the remnants of the old to clear room for the young growth. Life, in other words, in all its fierce beauty and stark routine. All things went to the soil eventually. It was the way of life.

Rourke had explained it to Todd the other night. "We come from seed," he told his son, smiling. "We grow up, blossom, and produce fruit. Then the fruit dries and goes into the ground to make the next crop. The old plant doesn't die so much as it gives itself to the soil to nurture the new plant. Since energy is neither created nor destroyed, only altered, dying is the other face on the coin of life. Nothing to be afraid of, really. After all, my boy, we all pass from this plane into another. It's inevitable, like the rainbow after the storm."

"That sounds nice," Todd had said. "Will Granddad be a rainbow?"

"I expect," Rourke had said solemnly, "that he will be the most splendid rainbow of all."

Looking down at Todd, Becky was grateful for her husband's way with words. The boy's face was without the strain it had held since they had been told that Granddad didn't have much longer. She smiled. It made things easier for her, too. Rourke probably knew it. He was such a sensitive man—he almost read her mind sometimes.

The jury was finally sequestered in the jury room and court was adjourned until a verdict was reached. Rourke picked up his case, shook hands with a grinning J. Lincoln Davis, and joined his family.

"Their godfather wants us over for supper tonight," he said as he kissed her, very gently. "He and Maggie have an announcement to make."

"She's pregnant," Becky whispered into his ear. She laughed at his expression. "Incredible, isn't it? She's shocked and delighted and scared to death. But they both want it, so much."

"She'll be all right. Davis will make sure of it," he chuckled. "All right, gang, who's for hamburgers?" he asked the family.

"Cheeseburgers for me," Mack said, almost trampling his brother on his way out. "Look, why didn't you object when Mr. Davis introduced that old deed? I'm sure you could have said..."

"God deliver us from law students," Rourke muttered with a hard glare. "Two months at the university, and you're F. Lee Bailey!"

"Three months," Mack corrected. "And I have a very good professor. Now, about that deed..."

"Francine and I have to rush back to the store," Clay said hurriedly. He squeezed Francine's hand. "Don't we, honey?"

"Oh, yes, of course," Francine stammered. "I'll call you later, Becky!" she added as she was dragged away.

"Craven cowards," Mack muttered, glaring after them. "No stomach for dissertation, huh?"

"We're having dissertation right after the barbecue," Clay called back through a cupped hand at his mouth. "Apple pie!"

"Do you believe this?" Mack threw up his hands as they vanished into the crowd. "My own brother thinks a dissertation is something you have with coffee!"

"Not everyone has your fervor for the law, old son," J. Davis chuckled as he joined them. He clapped Mack on the back. "How's it going?"

"Great! I'm making straight A's, so far!" he said.

"You'd better, after all the time Rourke and I have put in on you," he replied. "I want to talk to you about that Lindsey case," he told Rourke seriously. "We may be able to work something out."

"Not at lunch," Becky wailed, shifting Teresa while Todd roughhoused with Mack.

Davis glanced at the squirming child and chuckled. He held out his arms and Teresa went laughing into them.

"You're spoiling her," Becky accused when he produced a lollipop.

"Be quiet," Rourke said sternly. "Don't offend him until *after* I've got my plea-bargain."

"Oh." Becky clapped a hand over her mouth. "Sorry."

"Let's eat, can't we?" Mack groaned. "I'm starving!"

"When aren't you?" Rourke chuckled. "Okay. Todd, stop practicing karate kicks on your uncle."

"I learned this watching *The Karate Kid*," Todd protested, demonstrating a high kick. "It's great."

"Go and watch *Batman*," Mack advised. "You can learn how to fly."

"Buy me a Batcape and I'll give it my best shot," Todd promised. "Mom, can I have a milk shake with lunch? Why don't we go to a restaurant? I'm tired of hamburgers. Look, isn't that Big Bob Houser, the wrestling champ?" He pointed at a huge man in the distance.

Todd and Mack wre arguing about the identity of the huge man, while J. Lincoln Davis spoke in an odd language to little Teresa as the crowd closed around them on their way into the corridor.

Becky moved to Rourke's side and pressed close into his shoulder. He looked down at her, his dark eyes possessive and full of soft, sweet memories. His gaze dropped to her mouth.

"You can't," she whispered, laughing.

"Yes, I can," he whispered back, bending.

And he did.

* * * *

Look out for Diana Palmer's next novel
Outsider *from M&B in June 2007.*

Turn the page to find out more!

Outsider
by
Diana Palmer

A thrilling story of a man who is larger than life, and twice as exciting...

Colby Lane has retired from his dangerous work as a CIA operative and mercenary in favour of a position as the assistant chief of security for the mammoth Ritter Oil Corporation. A fresh start is all he wants.

But his past is never far behind, and Colby is soon embroiled in a plot to snare a notorious drug trafficker. Matters are complicated still further by the appearance of his ex-wife, Sarina Carrington – whom he cruelly left after just one day of marriage – who seems more involved in the operation than she is letting on.

Not only is Colby's self-control being stretched to the limit by his proximity to the woman who still makes his pulse race, but Sarina also has a daughter whose father is mysteriously absent – or is he?